Antares and the Zodiac

Antares

and the

Zodiac

J&L Wells

Matador
9 Priory Business Park
Kibworth Beauchamp
Leicestershire LE8 0RX, UK
Tel: (+44) 116 279 2299
Fax: (+44) 116 279 2277
Email: books@troubador.co.uk
Web: www.troubador.co.uk/matador

ISBN 978 1780882 949

British Library Cataloguing in Publication Data.
A catalogue record for this book is available from the British Library.

Typeset in Bembo by Troubador Publishing Ltd
Printed and bound in the UK by TJ International, Padstow, Cornwall

Matador is an imprint of Troubador Publishing Ltd

In loving memory of Steven

CHAPTER ONE

A Night They'll Never Forget

"Late again! No doubt he's pigging out as usual! Well, I'm not waiting a minute longer!" Ebony said, her eyes narrowing as she tossed her long black hair over her shoulders.

The hurdy-gurdy music of the fair and the screams of laughter from the rides filled her with excitement. She longed to be a part of the hustle and bustle of the crowd, but as usual, one thing stood in her way – DAZ!

"No patience! That's always been your problem! I'll ring him," Eve said, as she scrolled through the contact list in her phone, before being distracted by a familiar voice.

"'Ang on, me ducks, just had to stop off for something," Daz said, trotting ungainly to where Eve, Oli and a very disgruntled Ebony stood waiting.

"It's obvious where you've been, or stopped off as you so eloquently put it!" Ebony snapped.

Oli, fed up with Ebony's sarcastic quips, gave her a sharp prod in the side.

"Now you've got something real to moan about for once!" he chuckled.

A grin spread across Daz's face, like the cat who'd got the cream, and dried chocolate cracked around the corners of his mouth. Eve often compared Daz to a circus clown, and red-faced, he quickly pulled a crumpled tissue from the pocket of his black leather jacket and removed the residue.

Ebony paced up and down like a bear with a sore head. "Stop thinking about food; by the time we've queued up and been on any decent rides, the firework display will be well and truly over!"

Daz sniffed the air like a hungry dog. "Hmmmm, chips, burgers, yumm!"

1

"Well, I much prefer candyfloss and toffee apples; I've always had a sweet tooth!" Eve said, and linked arms with Daz as they strolled towards the waltzers.

"He doesn't need any encouragement, Eve!" Ebony grunted. "If he has anything else to eat he certainly won't be sitting next to me on any rides!"

Standing in the queue, Ebony shivered. "If you were any kind of gentleman, Oli, the least you would do is offer me your jacket!"

Annoyed, Oli continued to talk to Daz, and Ebony stormed out of the queue dragging Eve with her.

"Well what do you expect, dressed in a skimpy top and short skirt? At this time of year as well, I have to add! It's the 5th of November, NOT THE 5th OF JUNE!" Eve said, huddled up in her knee-length black duffel coat.

"At least I don't look like a freak! What the hell do you call them?!" Ebony said, pointing at the small amount of leg that peered out from beneath the coat's hemline dragging slightly on the floor.

"BLUE PYJAMA BOTTOMS! AND? We're not all prima donnas at the age of sixteen! If you don't like them you don't have to look, do you?" Eve turned to Daz for backup, but he had disappeared. Where was he? And Oli for that matter?

"They're bored of your constant whinging, Ebony! They've gone on the ride without us now!"

Ebony frowned. Although she couldn't bring herself to admit she was in the wrong, she realised that if it hadn't been for her having to make a point they'd all have gone on the ride together. She just stood quietly and sulked.

"There you are!" Eve bounded over to Oli and Daz as they exited the waltzers.

Daz's face was a peculiar shade of green, and he swayed from side to side.

"Feeling a bit seasick, methinks, me duck. That chocolate might not have been a good idea after all."

"The only way you learn, Daz, is the hard way," Oli smiled, as he buttoned up his grey fleecy jacket against the bitter wind.

"Think a burger might settle the old stomach, though. What do you say, Oli? Eb and Eve can wait for us, eh, we'll only be a jiff."

Daz and Oli fought their way through the crowd in search of a burger van.

"EBONY! Look, no queue!" Eve shouted, hurrying back to the waltzers and expecting Ebony to follow.

"Sure you're tall enough?!" Ebony joked, scrutinising Eve's small frame.

Ebony's mood was still unfavourable and she had a face like thunder.

"Have it your way!" Eve said. "You're nothing but a spoilt baby!"

She had the whole car to herself, and she spun round and round, the flashing lights and colours all merging into one. She squealed with excitement. The ride operator took an instant liking to her pretty pixie-like face and spun her faster and faster. She pulled her blonde tousled hair loose, and the wind took it as she held tightly onto the bar, head back. She felt totally at ease and free.

Finally, the ride came to a halt. Eve jumped off and raced over to Ebony, whose arms were folded tightly across her body in an attempt to keep warm.

"Look, look!" Eve pulled up her sleeve and revealed the word Dave, the ride operator's name, and a phone number scribbled on her forearm.

"As if I care!" Ebony turned her back on her friend and didn't seem interested in the slightest.

"Be a loner then! Best thing you can do is go home!" Eve said, growing tired of her attitude. "I'm going to find Daz and Oli, and make a proper night of it with people who want to have fun!"

Ebony stood open-mouthed as she watched Eve walk towards the food vans, where Oli and Daz were standing. Daz put a black and white striped woolly hat on, pulling it down sharply over his blonde spiked hair. Eve couldn't help but smile to herself. With his round moon-like face, black jacket and now the addition of a hat, he resembled a large cockroach.

"Oh you do make me laugh, Daz!" she smiled, as he presented her with a rather unsightly toffee apple. "EEWWW! It's got fluff on it!"

"Bit of fluff won't hurt ya, duck, adds to the taste. It's bin in me pocket by me hat." Daz reached up to his hat, which felt sticky to the touch.

"Is that Ebony calling us?" Oli half turned to see an exasperated Ebony waving her arms, trying desperately to get their attention.

"I say we ignore her; she's rarely got a good word to say for herself," Eve said, hoping that if they ignored her for long enough she'd get fed up and go home. "Let her stew for a couple of minutes."

Their conversation was interrupted as the bonfire had just been lit and large rockets shot out in all directions, decorating the night sky with their vivid gold and silver patterns. Roman candles crackled and the rockets banged overhead. Daz rested his arms on Eve's shoulders as they watched the display. They'd completely forgotten about Ebony, her voice well and truly drowned out by the pandemonium.

"Maybe this will cheer Ebony up," Oli said, pulling a pink rabbit from behind his back. It had floppy pink and white ears with a life-like face, and a felt carrot in its paws. "Won it on the coconut shy while Daz queued up for the food."

Daz felt rather outdone, but went on to say, "Well, I did buy you a toffee apple, Eve."

"I'm not fussed, Daz, it's the thought that counts; thank you." She planted a sticky toffee-apple kiss on his cheek.

"Better go give Ebony this rabbit. Feel a bit daft carrying a pink bunny around with me," Oli said.

As they walked back over to Ebony, they saw that her face was now a light shade of purple, and it was clear she couldn't wait to get something off her chest. A long string of words exploded, which were all jumbled together and made no sense whatsoever. Oli thrust the rabbit into her hands.

"Take a breath, ducky, the world's not going to come to an end!" Daz sniggered.

Ebony gazed down at the fluffy rabbit and held it tightly to her chest. "Aww, it's lovely, Oli, thank you."

Oli's chocolate button eyes softened, and he blushed when she smiled. She had an unobvious beauty about her that made him go weak at the knees.

"I've been trying to tell you something! Explain this…" Ebony pointed to where the waltzers had been only moments before.

Now in place of the ride stood a bizarre antique gypsy caravan covered with the most captivating engraving; a burnt sienna red overlaid with embossed gold patterns.

"Where did that come from?" Oli rubbed his eyes, not quite believing what he was seeing. "Surely the waltzers can't have been moved that quickly."

Baffled, the four looked at each other hoping for an answer.

"It's beautiful!" Ebony exclaimed, totally in awe of its elegance and external beauty. She had always loved the niceties of life.

"Yeah, it's nice, but so what? It's just an old gypsy caravan. We're here for the rides, and that bungee ball's got our names written all over it," Eve said. She was completely uninterested and had something much more exciting in mind.

"WAIT! This is no ordinary gypsy caravan!" Ebony ran her fingers over the indentations carved so eloquently. The patterns transformed before her eyes, and now resembled peculiar animals: bulls with long horns, goats, crabs with giant claws... She was completely captivated by the unexplained carvings, and shuddered with excitement. "Look at these! Just look!" she shouted, curiosity etched all over her face.

But the others were far too busy, and talked about which ride they intended to go on next, unable to see what Ebony saw.

"Come on, Eb, this is so boring, duck!" Daz said, and he and Oli grabbed an arm each in an attempt to move a rather stubborn Ebony.

All of them were fed up with her time wasting, and they turned towards the rides; suddenly, a creaking noise made them turn back round. The door of the caravan now stood wide open, and a tall haggard woman, dressed in a deep ocean-blue silk gown, stood awkwardly on the top step. Her eyes seemed to look straight through them. Inquisitively, they took a couple of steps closer, and in doing so were able to make out her dark lined complexion and black wiry hair, which fell in an unkempt fashion around her waist. Her appearance was that of a typical gypsy traveller, but why did they all feel so uneasy?

"Ha, it's you in fifty years' time, Eb!" Daz sniggered. It was nice for him to get his own back for once, as it was usually him who received all the sarcastic remarks and jibes.

"Shut it!" Ebony's emerald eyes looked daggers at him.

The figure's long twisted fingers beckoned them towards her and she stepped backwards, retreating inside the caravan.

"I'd love my fortune told, then I promise I'll go on all the rides," Ebony pleaded, but deep down she had already made her mind up. She held onto the rickety banister and stepped cautiously up the worn metal stairs. The heels of her inappropriate shoes made a loud clanging noise as she approached the doorway.

Oli stepped back. "It's not really my bag, all this fortune malarkey."

"Me neither, duck! Not into it to be honest," Daz agreed.

"Well, you know how stubborn she is, and we can't really leave her. We haven't got to take part, we can just watch; it shouldn't take long," Eve said, and proceeded to climb the steps, followed by the despondent lads.

Upon entering the caravan, the scent of joss sticks and aromatherapy oils filled the air. The room was dimly lit, with tiny oil lamps scattered around the walls with varying coloured silk materials draped over them, giving the effect of a multifaceted rainbow around the room. The soft furnishings were colour coordinated, identical to the caravan's outer shell. Burnt sienna cushions embroidered with a rich golden thread were scattered over the floor like pouffes, and obscure tapestries hung from the walls; the room had a somewhat mystical aura.

The gypsy had been well and truly overlooked as they took in their surroundings. It was only when she cleared her throat that their attention was once more drawn towards her. She sat behind a small oak table, with deep knots buried deep within its wooden legs, which fell in various directions and gave it a bowed appearance. A husky voice commanded them to sit, and without thought of questioning the order, they obeyed.

Eve sank into one of the plush pouffes, which moulded to her body like memory foam. Ebony followed suit, while Daz and Oli knelt down awkwardly on the cold wooden floor behind them. Out of sight, out of mind, or so they thought.

"Welcome, travellers."

"Stupid woman," Daz whispered in Oli's ear. "We ain't travellin' nowhere."

"How dare you speak over me!" the gypsy hissed.

Daz took a large gulp. "She's got the ears of a flamin' bat."

"Come here, boy; it's obvious you have much to say!" The gypsy kicked a small stool towards Daz. "Sit, boy!"

For once, Daz managed to keep his mouth shut.

"Your name, to start with." Her almost black eyes gawked at him across the table.

"Daz."

"DAZ? What sort of name is that? A stupid name for a stupid boy!" She reached under the table and revealed a crystal ball and a pack of cards.

"I'm not standing for that!" Oli said, quick to defend his friend. Jumping to his feet, he said, "Come on, Daz, we're out of here!"

"SIT DOWN!" Her crow's feet aligned and an evil expression became fixed like a mask to her face. A voice came from her direction, but her lips were taut and her mouth tightly closed. Her facial features alone were too much for Oli, and he sank to the floor like a naughty child who had been scolded, his tail well and truly between his legs.

"The name's Heter." She began to spell it out. "It won't be a name you forget in a hurry," she sneered. "Now, let me see…" She gazed into her crystal ball and her eyes rolled into the back of her head. "All your stars have aligned, and with this will come dire consequences… I see broken houses… No, that's not right, broken doors… No, that's not it either…"

"We don't have to pay for this rubbish, do we?" Daz blurted out, unable to keep his mouth shut any longer.

Heter refocused and snarled. "Put your hands on the table, ALL OF YOU!"

They knelt in a semicircle around the table and placed their hands palms up on its surface. They couldn't put into words the gypsy's expression, which looked like it had been chiselled into the very pores of her skin and appeared to pulsate. Her irises contracted and their colour drained away, making her eyes turn completely white.

"This can't be! How is it possible? How are you standing here in front of me?" Heter barked. Her spider-like fingers reached for a deck of cards, which she skilfully shuffled, asking each of them in turn to pick one.

"LADIES FIRST!" Ebony pushed her hand towards the gypsy and snatched at the pack to make sure she had first pick.

The gypsy grabbed her wrist and pulled her close, so close that Ebony could smell the hag's foul-smelling breath; her whole body released a pungent stench, so strong that it made Ebony wretch.

"Your beauty and curiosity may do you no favours in the future, my lovely!"

Ebony tore her arm from the gypsy's tight grasp, which still had the reddish indentations caused by the talon-like fingers. Eve chose a card sheepishly, followed by Oli and finally Daz, the joker of the pack. They each placed their cards face down on the table and waited.

"Let me see then…"

"After three, me ducks," Daz said, trying to get things moving. "One, two, three…"

Four death cards stared up at them from the table. A wicked grin crossed Heter's face.

"You see, there is only ever one death card in the pack, the card being number thirteen… I've been waiting a long time for you, all of you, and today is the day your journey begins!" she cackled shrilly, her egg-white eyes reverting to a deadpan black.

"I've had enough of this! She's barking mad!" An enraged Oli stormed out of the caravan, and the others blindly followed. "Next time you come across a gypsy caravan, I suggest you walk in the opposite direction!" he panted, bent double as his breath slowly returned.

As they headed for the bungee ball, Ebony turned for a final look at the caravan, but it was nowhere to be seen. In its place, the waltzers stood and the long queues waited as the cars continued to spin to the repetitive music. She'd caused enough agro for one day, so she decided that it would be best if what she had just discovered stayed undiscovered; although she momentarily questioned her own sanity.

The queue for the bungee ball had reduced dramatically while they had been in the gypsy caravan. Two immense iron stanchions, with rotating neon lights, stood parallel to each other. A long elastic cord hung between them, holding a large yellow ball dead centre and awaiting its next victim.

"Come on, darling." The ride operator gave Ebony a cheeky wink and showed them to their seats. They sat in two rows facing each other, and he fastened them in securely.

"Eh, mister, fancy looking after my bunny?" Ebony flung it at the unsuspecting operator.

His unshaven face and whisky-tinged breath were the last things they remembered before being catapulted into the night sky. Their screams drowned out the music below as they were lifted high above the shimmering lights, and they buzzed as the adrenalin kicked in. They spun round and rocked at great speed backwards and forwards, and could see for miles.

"I FEEL SICK!" Daz closed his eyes and hoped the ride would soon be over. "Think I've got vertigo!"

Eve reassuringly held his hand in hers while tears streamed down her cheeks. The gravitational force distorted their faces as they were pinned back in their seats.

Instead of slowing, the ride gathered speed and started to spin uncontrollably; higher and higher they went, until the ground below was no longer visible. They were going so fast now that they were beginning to lose consciousness. The ball shook violently; the yellow bars were visible one minute and gone the next, like a cruel hologram that found great pleasure in the art of deception. The thick rubbery black harnesses disintegrated into small dust particles, which were whisked up and resembled mini tornados that revolved around their heads. Then a sudden jolt and the ball stopped dead, almost as if it had been welded to the spot.

"That was some ride!" Oli shouted; he loved the rush. "Let's go again."

Their eyes finally adapted to their surroundings and they realised that it was anything but over. Where was the ball? Their seats? The fair? They saw that they were inside a murky translucent cell floating high up in no particular direction. Bright stars peered down at them, eerily close, almost within touching distance and quite happy to lend their light to the four lost souls.

"This is no ride!" Oli said, cautiously trying to stand, but the height of the strange object prevented him and forced him to stoop. He tripped over his own feet as he rushed to push his way through its thick outer membrane.

"This is surreal, almost like an outer body experience," Eve said as she followed Oli's lead.

"Think we've died and gone to blumin' heaven, Eb" Daz said, and as he jumped up he tumbled clumsily before gambolling his way through the cold congealed substance.

Ebony had no intention of staying in the unexplained mass on her own, and she struggled to her feet. This caused her stiletto heels to sink into the jellified matter and so she decided to remove them, and tiptoed gracefully to meet her friends on the other side.

Finally, they were on the outside looking in at this strange organism, which seemed to have its own life force, contracting and expanding.

"It's breathing!" Oli gasped, as he meticulously inspected the unknown entity.

Deep blue and red veins bulged out around its outer rim.

"YUK! It looks like a massive eyeball!" Daz always had to go a step too far, and he prodded it with his index figure as hard as he could.

It emitted an unearthly scream at such a high decibel that they had no option but to press their hands firmly against their ears to block out the horrendous sound and ease the pain. Just as they felt that their eardrums were about to perforate, the noise dispersed momentarily. The organism continued to pulsate uncontrollably, and expanded beyond its capacity…

"It's gonna blow!!!" A quick-thinking Oli immediately covered his face with his arms and Eve buried her head in Daz's chest, while Ebony guarded her precious image and used Oli as a human shield.

An immense explosion ejected them up into nothingness; an

outer sphere. Luckily for them, the gravitational force pulled them back like a magnet.

Daz spat out a mouthful of nauseating acidic liquid.

"You killed it, Daz! You've just murdered our only ticket home!" Ebony cried as she knelt down by the outer wall, which now lay deflated like a giant jellyfish. Droplets of liquid trickled out and made a small sticky puddle around their feet.

"I can see the fair! We're still on the bungee ball!" Ebony peeked into the punctured outer skin.

A past reflection had them imprisoned, or was it now a memory they sought so badly?

"We're on the moon!" Daz chuckled. A bewildered expression crossed his face. "They'll be calling me Daz 'Armstrong' in no time, just you wait!"

"This is no laughing matter, Daz, we're on no moon! Look down and tell me what you see!" Oli said.

As Daz looked around, he couldn't make head or tail of where they were or why. He could see nothing, just a dark void, as if an unexplainable black hole had swallowed them up. The stars that had once illuminated the sky had dwindled, and even after their eyes had adjusted, they could barely make out each other's silhouette.

"It's a sign! We must be dead!" Daz squealed.

A vibrant brightness emerged from the darkness. It seemed quite a distance away, but it was so intense and its rays gave out a fluorescent light as they waded through the unnerving abyss.

"Is that one of your many fashion accessories?" Eve asked, tugging at the random objects that stuck out of a small pocket on Ebony's denim skirt.

"Get off, you freak!" Ebony snapped, as she turned and gave Eve's roving hand a sharp slap. "Don't you think I'd know if I had anything in my pocket?"

"What do you call these then?" Eve held up the four death cards they had chosen earlier. "Somehow, I didn't think you'd have seen these as keepsakes!" With disgust written all over her face, she flung the cards at Ebony.

"But … but, I…!" Ebony stuttered and began to plead her

innocence; however, she was interrupted before she could finish her sentence.

"See? Told you, ducks, we're dead! That's what that bright light is… It's waiting to take us to the pearly gates to meet our maker!"

"For goodness sake, Daz, shut up! There has to be a logical explanation for this; things like this only happen in films!" Oli said, moving closer.

The light hung like a torch and glided restlessly in a circular motion, but where had it come from? It had no obvious beginning or end, it just was. The area of effervescent light was wide enough for any of them to stand in at one time.

"Well, guys, if we are dead …which we're not, and this is the light to heaven … which it isn't, I should be the first to suss it out!" An obviously nervous Oli edged his way into the light's core. Its immense power gave him tiny electric shocks all over, and a singed smell filled his nostrils. "ARGGHHH!"

"Oli! Come back! COME BACK!" Ebony cried hysterically. Tears rolled down her olive cheeks and her emerald green eyes shone. A combination of her dark features and jet-black hair enhanced her beauty, which came to life like a purring Egyptian cat. "Daz, why did you let him go?" she sobbed. "It's all your fault! We've lost him! If you hadn't been late tonight, none of this would have happened!"

Daz and Eve didn't think her stupidity warranted an answer, and just grabbed her hands. The light had grown and was now shaped like a funnel; it radiated an unpleasant heat, but there was no going back. The three friends tiptoed into it and then they too were gone.

CHAPTER TWO

Through the Gate into the Unknown

Their bodies travelled at the speed of light, and before they had time to draw breath they found themselves lying in a heap, buried in a thick pea soup like mist. Winded from the pull, a strange g-force made it impossible for them to speak. Their faces were pale, all colour having drained away, and their constricted pupils slowly began to dilate. Eve pulled herself up apprehensively; whatever lay beneath her had a texture similar to candyfloss. She rubbed her cold clammy hands together and looked down at Daz and Ebony, who were still in a state of shock.

"OLIVER!!! Where are you?" Eve scoured the vicinity; a teal stratosphere overwhelmed her as murky cloud formations hung suspended and lingered aimlessly.

"Over here!" A dishevelled Oli poked his head out of the mist and shrugged his shoulders despondently. "Some kind of nightmare, this is!"

"What's that, duckies?" Daz said as he reappeared.

A colossal unidentified flying object hovered only inches above them.

"It's got so many sides to it; reminds me of something!" he said, scratching his head deep in thought. "I've got it! It's a Rubik's cube! That's what it is! Never managed to conquer one, mind!"

"It's beautiful! Look, an amethyst! Pearl! A ruby!!!" Ebony was almost hypnotised by the many faceted gemstones encrusted in each face of the charismatic formation.

Very slowly it began to move, steering itself in a clockwise direction and resembling a planet in orbit. Its golden casing sparkled like a large star.

"It's a hexagon! I'd know that shape anywhere… A Rubik's cube? Daz … REALLY! Should be common sense at our age!"

Ebony said, making another dig at Daz's less than average IQ.

"Well, he may not have a lot of common sense, but your general knowledge isn't much better," Oli chortled. "If you stopped ridiculing everybody else and took the time to count each side, you'd see it's got twice as many sides as a hexagon... It's a dodecahedron and has twelve faces, not six."

"Yeah, whatever! Don't care what the stupid thing's called anyway!" An immediate frown took hold of Ebony's face. She couldn't stand anyone getting one up on her, especially Oli.

A ghostly figure, a kind of menacing apparition, suddenly emerged through the walls of the dodecahedron and the shape came to an abrupt halt.

"Get back in your bottle, genie! That's after you grant me a couple of wishes of course, duck!" Daz was in stitches; he licked his lips, and it was obvious to the others what his wish would be.

"Shhhhh, Daz, just this once. Don't think for one minute that's a genie." Eve placed her hand firmly over his mouth, muffling his laughter.

The gangly figure stood proud, its outstretched arms missing the normal pink hue of a healthy human. Instead, its face was ashen, and the cracks on its chafed, dehydrated arms were almost crying out for fluid.

"It's the grim reaper," Ebony said, and she shuddered.

She stared at the featureless face shrouded by a heavily set grey shawl wrapped untidily around its shrunken head and shoulders. The unattractive sack cloth material then continued to fall in big pleats and swaddle the rest of its being. A charcoal smoke drifted out of the bottom, but there was no sign of any feet.

Oli found himself eating his words, for what possible explanation could there be for this? Even he started to wonder if Daz was right and this was the start of their journey into the afterlife.

The figure ascended to the top of the dodecahedron and visited four of the twelve faces, removing a large gem from each. It aborted its mission and descended until it landed only a hair's breadth away from the unsuspecting four. It reached down and placed a gem in each of their hands. On contact, it was hard to distinguish between the ice-cold gem and the creature's corpse-like flesh. A quiet voice grew and seemed to thunder from the very depths; the echo it released bounced like a ping-pong ball from each and every wall of the dodecahedron, then back into their awaiting ears.

"Twelve signs of the zodiac, twelve gates, one key; it's for you to figure out."

They felt an awful tremor beneath them, like an earthquake, yet they stood on nothing concrete. Stone pillars fought their way up through the mist below, like seedlings pushing their way closer to the sunlight. The pillars housed twelve large silver gates, all of which stood proud around them in a 2D replica of the dodecahedron.

"Ea'are, gates of heaven, told ya so, ducks," Daz said, as a shiver ran down his spine; he was determined to get his questions answered. He turned to confront the entity, but it was too late, for what had been seconds earlier had evaporated into the humid air. The grey hessian cloak was all that remained, spread on the floor like a discarded blanket. Everything around them snowballed out of reality and the gems fell into insignificance.

Ebony glanced at the emerald in her palm and placed it in her skirt pocket.

"Why go through a gate if there is nothing on the other side?" Oli said, gazing through the empty void that lay beyond. "I'm out of ideas. Maybe we best stay put?"

"I'm not hanging around 'ere forever! If heaven's waiting, I'm 'a going!"

"I agree with you, Daz," Eve said, inspecting all twelve gates; "that's the one for me."

"We've all come this far and that's the way it's going to stay. There's not room for four of us to pass through the gate together, so I suggest you and Daz go through first, and me and Ebony will follow right behind."

They stood in pairs before the gate; the not knowing was hard to deal with. The last thought in Eve's mind were the words the apparition had spoken so clearly, yet they made no sense to her whatsoever.

Eve and Daz stepped anxiously through a blinding mist and

entered a completely different dimension, but before they had time to fully embrace it, they spun round to check that Oli and Ebony were safe. That first glance put their minds at rest, but why was distress written all over Oli's face and how come Ebony's lips were moving but they couldn't hear a word she said? Were they lost in a double-sided mirror? Trapped in two very different time zones? This realisation had a formidable impact on Eve.

"Daz, it's … how can that be…?"

"I know, duck, we need to go back!" He pulled her through the gate, but to their horror they realised that they may as well have been walking around in circles.

"We're back where we blumin' started!" Daz watched as the mist that had trapped Oli and Ebony vanished along with the gate, like a porthole closing behind them.

Now four became two, and there was no going back. Eve sank to the floor and rested her head in her hands in total disbelief.

"I'm still holding this stupid gem! It's red, so my guess is it's a ruby." The tip of the stone had dug sharply into her cheek. "What good this'll do me is anybody's guess!" She shoved it angrily into the deep pocket of her duffel coat, which already contained random coins, old tissues and the half-eaten toffee apple.

"I got a pearl," Daz said, opening his hand for Eve's approval before slipping it into his pocket.

Eve's mind wandered and she scanned their newfangled environment. Dark terracotta blended with bright scarlet to create a rich two-toned sky and a perfect sunset. The ground was parched and the air putrid, like that of an old incinerator which had smouldered for eternity.

"Smells like ash," Eve said, bending down and picking up the dry flakes, which slipped gently between her petite fingers. "It is ash, Daz!" It was surprisingly deep and rested unevenly on the top of her beige fleecy boots.

Daz gathered some handfuls and threw it at her; it fell like confetti and rested messily in her shoulder-length hair.

"Oh, Daz, you can't help yourself, can you?" She smirked as she shook her head, freeing her blonde locks from their grey camouflage.

With every step they sank deeper, making their progress very tiring. Grey images were sketched on the horizon; unfathomable pictures too faraway to make out. A cloud of smoke drifted and partially concealed the sky's radiance. As they got closer, the images took on the shape of unattractive, unorthodox mud huts scattered awkwardly around a dormant volcano. Daz couldn't resist and shuffled even closer, poking his index finger into the mushy exterior.

"Eww, it's vile, like papier mâché!" He wiped the residue from his hands.

"This place must be inhabited," Eve said, as she admired the misshapen windows with their little sills set back in a skew-whiff fashion, and an obscure iron door that had a slight tilt to it and hinges on either side.

"Whoever lives 'ere, Eve, with a door like that methinks they must be ambidextrous! Ha, and people think I'm stupid!"

They only just managed to jump out of the way before the heavy iron door opened like a miniature drawbridge.

"It's a blumin' knight, Eve! RUN!"

A figure emerged in the doorway and they stopped dead in their tracks.

"Before I introduce myself, what brings you two here to my abode, whatever you are?"

"Well, I'm Daz and this is Eve. If you've got all night, me duck, I'll start at the beginning…"

"You do realise you're talking to a goat, A GOAT WEARING CLOTHES!?" Eve said in amazement.

How he had got them on was beyond their imagination, but nevertheless, he wore a thick red knitted woolly jumper that had seen better days – more dropped stitches than not – and bottle-green dungarees that were rather worn at the knees and turned up at the bottom to reveal two small hooves.

"A goat?! Well I never! I'm a Ram, and don't you go forgetting it! This is Aries, the first sign of the zodiac! What star signs are you, for that matter? I've never come across anything quite like you before. Suppose I'd better invite you in, you've got some explaining to do." As the Ram led them inside, he took hold of a heavy iron chain from the floor and pulled the door up until it was tightly sealed.

"How cute!" Eve said, her eyes wandering as she admired the quaintest room she had ever seen. The walls were concave, slate grey with hairline cracks. A lopsided table with three legs and four rickety chairs stood in a kitchen through a door at the far end of the room. The main wall had been skilfully bevelled out and housed an inglenook fireplace. A reddish-brown urn balanced precariously on a three-legged structure, the contents of which bubbled profusely.

"What stinks in 'ere?!" Daz exclaimed, pulling the collar of his jacket up to cover his face.

"Don't know, but whatever it is my contact lenses don't think much of it either," Eve replied. Her eyes were streaming, but she tried her best not to rub them.

"It's home-made broth, my speciality. Keeps a few going round here, I'll have you know. My culinary expertise is second to none. Main ingredient being the ripest red onions, which I handpicked today, and if you take a gander in my little pantry, just over there," he pointed, "you'll find my second most important ingredient."

Daz pulled open the sliding door and they both peered inside. It was rather dark, but the aroma of concentrated onion juice was as strong as it was in the main living area. Long green stems hung from the ceiling untidily from long pieces of string.

"Bet you can't guess what they are?" the Ram shouted over. "Your time's up! They're my prize leeks, and if you look on the shelf to your left, the little wicker baskets are filled with garlic cloves. I chop these up very finely and then marinade them overnight in juice from the honeysuckle plant, which binds it all together. Now you see, that's how it's done. Why don't you take the weight off your feet?"

He pulled up a chair and waited for Daz and Eve to be seated.

"How rude of me, I haven't even introduced myself. The name's little Gee, hence the size." He chuckled. "My friends call me Gee for short."

His head was a light sandy brown, while the remainder of his scraggy coat was a much deeper conker brown. Between his chocolate button eyes lay a random white smudge, and ornate black horns protruded from each side of his head. He was the strangest little two-tone animal they had ever seen, but he purveyed a very regal energy.

Daz's mouth watered. "Okay, me duck, that broth smells good enough to eat."

"Told you once, I'm not a goat, and I'm definitely not a flipping duck!" Gee's dark eyes squinted angrily in Daz's direction.

"Okay, okay, keep ya hair on!"

Eve chuckled to herself. "Fancy saying that to a goat," she whispered in Daz's ear. "You certainly have a way with words."

Putting his foot in it came naturally to Daz, although it wasn't really the done thing to offend your host. A shrill siren interrupted their introductions.

"You're all of a twitch, Gee; what's the matter?" Eve asked, slightly puzzled.

"You don't understand! We are being summoned. Can't you hear the siren?" he said abruptly, becoming even more agitated. "No time to explain! Follow me!" He quickly took the urn off the fire and sipped some of his home-made broth from a silver ladle he'd taken from the top drawer of a wooden dresser in his L-shaped kitchenette.

"Darn it!" Daz rubbed his tummy. "That would have gone down a treat," he sighed.

"Less talking, more action!" Gee pulled the chairs hastily from beneath them, and a shocked Daz and Eve shot to their feet. Gee grabbed the metal chain and lowered the door until it lay in a horizontal position, quite a feat for an animal with hooves, and small ones at that. He wasted no time, and bowed his head before hurriedly butting them through the doorway.

The air changed, and the climate had grown hot and oppressive. Both Eve and Daz fought for their breath. Stifled by the smoke and ash that spewed skywards from the volcano, red-hot molten lava spat high into the atmosphere. Volcanic bombs erupted, emitting luminous balls of fire that fell to the earth and caused large craters.

"Stay close!" Gee shouted, reverting to running on all fours.

"That's easier said than done!" Eve gasped, as she rubbed her smoke-filled eyes.

"Where's he gone?" Daz wheezed.

Luckily, Gee's red jumper kept him just about visible, and they watched as he zigzagged to avoid the bombardment of fiery missiles. They followed his footsteps as best they could. Ram became rams as they appeared from every direction, emerging from a sprinkling of mud huts between which they manoeuvred blindly. They closed in until they reached the base of the volcano, where they came to a sudden halt and stood in a large huddle.

"We're being squashed, me duck!" Daz said as he pushed his elbows out, struggling to gain an extra few inches of room.

"Yeah, like sardines," Eve replied, as she stood on her tiptoes and fought to see what was going on.

Gee stood in complete silence. An outer sphere, an unearthly twilight, engulfed the entire volcano. When the sea of rams began to move, Daz and Eve were cajoled along so that they were all heading slowly in one direction. There was no going back now.

Eve reached up and tapped Gee on the shoulder. "Where are we going?"

"We've been summoned. Shhhhh!"

"Summoned for what? We've got a gate to find, so we can go home." Eve placed her hands on her hips indignantly.

"Kanika's grand banquet, and then to work... Anyway, how do you know about the gate?" Gee's ears pricked up in curiosity. "How did you get here, for that matter? We never get visitors from the other signs, not in this domain." The questions rolled off his tongue.

"We came through a gate not far from here, so presumably we need to go back through the same one to find our way home. We don't belong here like you do," Eve tried to explain, with a solemn expression on her face.

"One problem there, ducky, the gate disappeared behind us," Daz reminded her.

They were hit with the realisation of the un-reality in which they found themselves, and both felt extremely homesick.

"That's impossible. The only gate in Aries lies in a diamond maze and is situated in Kanika's hidden playroom. This can only be found deep in the core of the volcano and is kept under lock and key for the chosen few. So this fictitious gate you speak of must be a figment of your imagination!" Gee laughed.

"Well, we didn't just appear out of thin air, me duck." Daz looked up. "Been meaning to ask ya, Gee, how come ya sun's red?" he asked, pointing to the large red ball high in the sky.

"Sun? That's no sun!" Gee looked up and shrugged his shoulders. "That, my boy, is Aries' ruling planet, Mars."

"Mars is a planet, Daz, it doesn't radiate heat. My guess is that it's their moon," Eve said, offering him a more logical explanation.

"You're wrong, me duck," Daz said as he removed his jacket and tied it loosely around his waist, exposing a bright red and white striped T-shirt. "I'm boiling, so it must be some kinda sun!"

"Oh, my dear boy, look around you. We're standing in front of a multitude of fireballs! If you look up, you'll see the canons they're being fired from." Gee shook his head. "You're not exactly the sharpest horn in the flock, are you?"

"Yeah, me duck, I see them. Thought the volcano was erupting."

"Well, we wouldn't be standing here if that was the case," Gee grinned.

An immense sound reverberated through the vicinity, encompassing the whole flock. Eve almost jumped out of her skin; she'd never heard anything quite like it before. Daz was also visibly shaken. None of the rams appeared to move a muscle, and just stood resolute like programmed robots. A fissure halfway up the volcanic wall spread downwards causing a large division from top to bottom, like a giant zip being undone.

"Abracadabra or what?" Daz chuckled, as he waved an imaginary magic wand in the air.

Even at a time like this Eve couldn't help but love his quirky sense of humour.

A sturdy-looking Ram dressed in medieval attire marched out of the dark opening. An animal in clothing was funny enough, but one in full body armour was even more bizarre. Daz found it very hard to keep a straight face, but as they stood in the middle of the crowd of oddly clothed rams, vastly outnumbered, for once he managed to keep a stiff upper lip.

Pushed and shoved by the congregating rams, they edged ever

closer to the open cavity, which resembled a large mouth as it waited to engulf them. On entry, the unnerving darkness lasted only momentarily, as incandescent beams of light shot backwards and forwards like miniature boomerangs.

"They come quite sharp!" Daz said, rubbing his head as one ricocheted away. He gave the next attacker a good hard crack and the little light dropped to the floor like a stone.

"PACK IT IN! Look … you've killed him!" Gee growled, and he bent down and picked up the flickering ember in his hooves.

"Him? Him? Killed a light? Are you mad?" Eve shouted, as she ducked the flying onslaught.

"No, look here," Gee said, passing the faded light to Daz, who held it gently in the palm of his hand.

"It's just a lantern, isn't it, duck?"

"Take a closer look, boy!" Gee looked glum.

Daz prodded the faded ember that lay lifeless, and as he turned it over he was shocked to see that it had a head, legs, rounded body and the tiniest little wings imaginable.

"What is it, Gee?" Eve bent down to take a look for herself.

"Not what it *is* … what it *was*," Gee said, shaking his head as he glanced at the lifeless creature, whose light was about to go out for the last time. "It was a firefly, boy. You've made enough of a spectacle of all of us." Gee turned around, scared that the affray would attract the guards; under no circumstances did he want them to intervene.

The queue of rams just ahead of them seemed to dwindle as they dispersed through a large wooden door. With a quick glance over his shoulder, Daz noticed the rams pouring into the volcano thick and fast.

"It's like being in an underground cave," Eve whispered to Daz.

It was cold and dank, and a few fireflies flitted back and forth. Droplets of ice-cold water dripped in abundance from the stalactites that hung like large fingers pointing down from above. Stalagmites protruded from the ground like important monuments, their sheer size dominating the area and giving it a claustrophobic feel. A damp musky liquor-like substance oozed from within the walls.

"Gettin' rather chilly in 'ere," Daz complained, untying his jacket from around his waist and hurriedly putting it back on. His left hand still gripped the half dead firefly, and he felt real sympathy for the little creature. He placed him gently in the opposite pocket to the one he had placed the pearl earlier.

The dapple-grey Ram that they had previously encountered heavily laden with a thick metal body suit now stood before them, his stance rigid. Poker-faced, he scowled at the scores of waiting rams. The overbearing armour coat appeared to weigh him down, and the only contrast were the bright red feathers that protruded from his shell-shaped head guard. He gave his orders and left the work to his little minions, who began to organise the rams into single file.

"We must stay together; under no circumstances should you let anyone separate us. Due to our size we are insignificant in comparison with a lot of the other rams who are head and shoulders above us, so keep quiet, keep your head down and go with the flow," Gee instructed, feeling quite important as he gave his knowledgeable pep talk.

"Eww, look Eve, what's that?" Daz couldn't help himself as he pointed at the guard. "He's got something hanging out of his nose… Dirty little…"

"Shush, what have I just told you? It's a gold ring, Daz; all the guards wear them as a symbol of their authority," Gee whispered, as he did his best to keep them all inconspicuous.

"Eve, it's a bogey!!" Daz shouted, ignoring the Ram. His voice echoed around the chamber, and he went from insignificant to feeling all eyes upon him, as they burnt into the back of his neck.

A deep voice penetrated the silence and the principle Ram's demeanour changed. His nostrils quivered as smoke billowed out in an overriding fury. He charged through the silent flock and positioned himself in front of Daz, sniffed the air and paused momentarily.

"You don't smell like a Ram! Or look like one for that matter!" He was obviously not impressed by this unwelcome trespasser.

"Manners, Achcauhtli, manners!" Gee said, puffing out his chest and nearly bursting the frayed stitches on his over-worn red jumper in the process. "For your information he is a Ram, but a different strain! A new breed! His coat has been shorn and his horns docked!"

"Look at its size! Is it a pigmy?" Achcauhtli snorted.

"NO, IT'S NOT! And nor am I!" Eve shouted, as she pushed past Gee and stood next to Daz, like they were two soldiers on parade.

"Two of them! I do hope they're not catching!" the ram coughed, as he took a closer look at Eve. "What's a water nymph doing down here? A very unattractive one, I must add."

"I beg your pardon!" Eve frowned. "A water what?"

A quick-thinking Gee had more than one trick up his sleeve. "Yes, she's a water nymph that's lost her way! And that," he said, pointing to Daz, "is a hogget! You know, an adolescent! He has plenty of growing time left in him!"

"Well, hoggets should be seen and not heard; has he lost his way also? Make sure the nymph is returned to the bathing quarters!" His cold charcoal eyes focused on Daz's face. "Maybe you could be of some use after all…" the guard said as he stood deep in thought. "A fool like you could have his uses… I'll be catching up with you later, hogget," and without another word, he turned and walked away.

Like convicts on death row, Daz and Eve nervously awaited their fate. They passed through the open doorway and soon left the roomy chamber behind them. The damp porous walls closed in as they proceeded down a much narrower, arched corridor. Fireflies hung only inches above their heads, giving out just enough light for them to follow the procession of rams.

"Look, Eve," Daz said, pointing at the floor to his right, where a small train track lay parallel.

"What on earth's a train track doing in a volcano?" Eves eyes followed it as it disappeared round a sharp bend.

"It's the transportation for our iron and diamonds, and us of course. How else do you think we make our way round this monstrosity?" Gee explained.

The small track was like a miniature prototype of the railways Eve and Daz had seen back home. The tarnished iron and rusted bolts had seen more than a few journeys.

Eve couldn't help smiling to herself; rams dressed in brightly coloured jumpers that walked on two legs was like something out of a dream.

"Come on, you two," Gee said.

Eve and Daz were not so quick on their feet as Gee, both busy taking in their bizarre surroundings.

"Got a train to catch. It won't wait, you know, I'm telling you, it won't wait." Gee tapped his hoof on the floor impatiently.

Startled back to reality, Eve and Daz trotted along behind until they finally reached the peculiar station. The fireflies congregated in large clusters, their previous insignificant light becoming an irregular luminosity, which replenished the dim setting. The station soon overshadowed their first impressions of the dusty tunnels and rusty old track. The uneven rutted floor littered with rough shale had been revamped into horizontal wooden slates that lay in unison, their bevelled edges fitting together snugly, any distorted knots and visible flaws a sanded perfection. There were no detectable blemishes, and each panel's natural beauty was enhanced by a transparent veneer.

"I wasn't expecting this, Gee," Eve said, blown away by the sheer intricacy and attention to detail.

"It's incredible what a goat can do when he puts his mind to it, ain't it, ducky?"

Gee threw a brusque glance at Daz. "R A M does not spell goat! I don't expect to have to tell you again." But as usual, Gee's words went straight over Daz's head.

Two harsh bristle brooms glided between the rams' legs, attached to two rather busy guards as they swept with gusto at the unwanted intruders. Rough shale debris and ash residue were then released over the platform edge and came to rest somewhere between the sleepers. Eve picked up on the sense of pride between the two, even though it was a relentless task they had taken upon themselves. A narrow platform stretched out in front of them.

"Right, don't move either of you … back in a jiff; just got to check which carriage we're to board," Gee said, and with that he disappeared into the bodies of chattering rams as they fidgeted in apprehension of the oncoming train.

Two sheds like kiosks were set in a spacious carved-out aperture, the first of which had a rustic red roof that sloped down at an angle and met a mahogany base with an open counter. A smartly dressed ram in a navy blue uniform and peaked cap stood inside. He proceeded to hand out miniature scrolls of paper, which he stamped twice and ripped in half, and then handed a counterpart to each ram as they waited in turn. Eve, who always had an eye for detail, couldn't help but notice the quaint whistle tied around his neck with a long cord that seemed to resemble something between string and a thin twine.

"Must be the tickets, duck," Daz said.

Eve watched in disbelief. "Well, you can't board without one now, can you?" she chuckled.

"He's taking his time, isn't he?" Daz groaned.

"Have a bit of patience, he's only just gone!" she laughed. "Have you seen those queues?"

"I certainly can't see Gee," Daz moaned, as he jumped up and down trying to catch a glimpse of their little friend amidst the camouflage of the oversized rams.

"Think I'll just have a gander over there, ducky." Daz's words merged into one, and when Eve suddenly realised what he was up to it was too late, and she hadn't time to stop him.

He headed in the direction of a ramshackle bridge that crossed over to the opposite side of the track. In Eve's opinion, its dilapidated form didn't look too safe, or even sturdy enough to hold Daz's body weight. It turned out to be more durable than she first thought, though, as he reached the other side no worse for wear. With his charismatic charm it didn't take him long to coax Eve to join him.

"Gee won't be amused when he comes back now, will he?"

"Chill, ducky, train ain't even in yet, and lookin' at that queue he'll be there for a blumin' age." His eyes once again wandered, this time towards a crystallised glass statue with ornate golden horns and an unobvious red undertone to its prevalent eyes.

"Looks important from where I'm standin', duck…" Daz said, as he touched its smooth, cold exterior and ran his fingers over its many facets.

Eve elbowed his arm abruptly. "Look with your eyes; you don't want to break anything now, do you? Could be of great value for all we know." Eve jumped as a high-pitched screech came from the track. She looked behind while Daz, in his own little world, continued with his exploration.

The little train rattled into the station, but it looked nothing like the trains Eve remembered. Although it had mirror-like, highly polished iron with ornate diamond castings moulded onto its exterior, the carriages were no more than glorified open mining carts. Its interior was furnished with plush silken materials, and plumped-up cylindrical bolsters were arranged throughout for extra comfort.

"Daz, the train! Best find Gee, don't you think? He's the one with the tickets after all."

"Hmm," was his only response, and that just a half-hearted mumble.

Four thickset rams stood in pairs face-to-face in an odd contraption that would normally have been the train's engine. Manually operated handcars propelled the countless carriages by way of a pivoted sea-saw arm, with its alternating push-down pull-up movements.

"I could have sworn that was Gee. Come on, Daz, or we'll both be for it!" Eve tugged at his arm, but Daz's concentration was elsewhere and he lost his balance.

"Now look what you've made me do!" An awkward-looking Daz stood with the statue's eye resting in the palm of his hand, and an empty socket gawked at Eve.

"Give it here! Quickly, I'll stick it back in." But whatever angle she tried, it just didn't seem to fit. "No, that's not it … nor that." She cursed after trying for the umpteenth time.

"I thought I told you pair to stay put!" Gee's tone was somewhat agitated, as he bounded across the bridge on all fours. "We're in the ninth carriage along, that's if we make it," he shouted, breathless. "Beginning to think you two had done a runner."

Eve secretively popped the diamond into her coat pocket and hoped beyond hope that Gee was too distracted with all the comings and goings to notice.

"Think we've seen enough for now," she grinned. "Don't you agree, Daz?"

He blushed. They heard Gee's hooves go clip-clop as he rushed back across the bridge. They quickly turned to follow ... but what a shock they got!

CHAPTER THREE

A Change of Scenery

"What on earth happened?" The colour drained from Eve's face as her eyes were drawn to the bridge. The wooden joists were like charred timber skeletons; it was now a feeble structure beyond repair, and barely passable.

"We'll have to feel our way across; this could give at any time," Eve said.

Step by step, the two precariously made their way back to the platform. Daz sniffed the air and caught the essence of burned firewood, as a peppery smoke wafted between the withered slats.

"A catastrophe of this magnitude, and we've both managed to miss it..." Eve said.

The entire station had been ripped apart. Intense anticipation, like a touch paper that waited for a second strike as it quietly smouldered and revealed its devastating aftermath. Gee had now boarded and was seated comfortably in his carriage, waving his hooves in the air. Daz and Eve hadn't a clue what had happened or why, and were surprised that the ram seemed so unfazed by the visible carnage.

"Hurry up, Daz, the train's moving off. Gee needs to fill us in on a few things ... big time!"

They jumped in and sat alongside him.

"Who put the fire out, ducky?"

"What fire? You must have hit your head when you crossed that bridge." A very confused Gee shook his head and sat back relaxed, completely at ease.

The rams that accompanied them on their journey had acquired a bad case of mange, their frazzled hair hanging unkempt. Like partially shorn sheep with an uncanny difference, their drab charcoal coats held a deep burning smell of death that oozed from within.

"Where are all the attractive rams hiding?" Eve asked.

"Ha-ha, these unsightly things look more like chargrilled burgers you'd find on a barbeque!" Daz shuffled in his seat, afraid the charred remains would rub off on his clothes.

The smell of burned flesh fastened itself tightly inside Eve's nostrils. The silken fabrics and bolsters lay in tatters, like an ashen jumble sale for those down on their luck. Eve jumped to her feet and shook Gee in complete exasperation.

"Are you blind, or just stupid? This isn't a station, Gee, it's a crematorium, the only difference being that everything's been burned alive!"

"That's quite enough of that. Now sit down, you hysterical child! You're hallucinating; that's the only explanation for your irrational behaviour."

"Well that makes two of us, me duck … so maybe it's you who's seeing things."

Eve couldn't get over the fact that Daz and Gee were untouched by this tragic event that had taken place. How was it possible for Gee to see things as they had been, not as they were now? Painful cries echoed and ricocheted off the walls like homesick boomerangs, while Gee heard only cheers and frivolity as the rams' excitement increased for the imminent banquet.

"I must be going mad!" Eve's eyes were everywhere, and each time she scanned the carriages, the images that confronted her grew more grotesque.

"That makes two of us then, me duck," Daz said.

They had travelled through some kind of unrealistic reality, and were unable to distinguish which one their journey fell into.

The carriage's momentum seemed to slow, and they made a rickety arrival at their destination. This was a much roomier station, and it was a pity they couldn't have seen it in its former glory.

"It's the end of the line," Gee said as he got to his feet.

"I've been thinking that for quite a while," Eve sighed, as the train slowed to a halt.

"Come on, this is the good part, guys!" Gee, visibly excited, leapt onto the platform.

Daz and Eve were a trifle more lethargic after what they had witnessed, and although Gee changed to a slow trot, they still lagged behind, unable to make sense of these ghastly visions they walked between.

"Look, they're falling apart in front of us!" Eve gasped as she watched the rams' frames smouldering.

"Look like blumin' snakes, shedding layer by layer," Daz said, watching as piece by piece their skin disintegrated into dust particles. Their remains were strewn over the floor, a coating of cinders.

Gee disappeared through two rather disfigured pillars.

"Well, have you ever seen anything like this before? I'd say it was a true work of art myself, our very own Roman baths!" he said.

Eve, close on his tail, took a gander for herself. "Work of art? Are you serious?" she snorted in disappointment, as an incinerated veil loomed.

They stepped into a spacious room with archways at both ends. Its focal feature was a high decked pool that filled the majority of the space, leaving only a small outer perimeter where sectioned-off changing and seating areas lay between the facing arches.

Gee's red woolly jumper took on the appearance of a straitjacket as his hooves thrashed around in an attempt to remove it, while his horns moved in the opposite direction and did everything possible to stop him, poking their way through the ragged holes his pullover had acquired over time. It was a light-hearted moment of distraction that both Daz and Eve needed.

Gee suddenly took a flying leap into a gloopy mess that resembled rice pudding with a charred skin; his face was a picture.

"This milk does wonders for the skin … face mask and moisturiser all in one!" he said.

Eve screwed her nose up in disgust. "Think we'll give it a miss thanks, Gee. We'll just have a wander round."

Many of the rams lounged around in pairs, chatting between themselves on stone benches. Cindered togas were draped around their blistered bodies, and in every direction disfigured faces emerged. Yet when they looked back, there wasn't even a blemish or a hair out of place on Gee, or themselves for that matter.

"There's more of us, Daz; look …we're not the first." Eve paused. "Erm…"

"Well, me duck, I have to agree with you. They certainly look foreign to Aries."

Eve and Daz noticed a group of what they thought were human females. They lay back in an elegant pose, their bodies extended like mermaids as they stretched their shapely legs along the pool's edge. Their taut skin made for expressionless faces, and puce pink tinges scarred their mottled complexions giving them a two-tone appearance. Irregular tufts of scorched hair protruded sporadically from misshapen withered scalps, and a white film lay dormant in their eyes, a visionless matt glaze.

"Looks like they've been to hell and back," Eve said, feeling quite sorry for the unsightly figures. "It's like an invisible inferno has engulfed the volcano and all its inhabitants… Maybe there's something we can do to help them?"

"Or maybe, me duck, that's the way they're supposed to be. We're not all blessed with good looks ya know. Seems like they're havin' a good time from where I'm standin'." Daz looked at Eve and then down at himself, just to double check. "We both look fine … don't we? And so does Gee."

They weaved between the arches, where grooming sessions were taking place. A monumental mirror played back its captured images as it hung down over the room's occupancy.

"One thing for certain, duck, I ain't lookin' in that. Seeing it first hand is good enough … certainly don't need a double take on this one."

"Well, that's your prerogative," Eve replied. Like any other young girl, to pass a mirror without a quick glance was a near impossibility. Her expression was indescribable as she turned her head from the mirror to the room and back again.

"I thought Eb was the vain one, ducky."

Eve's sudden pallor and deathly silence unnerved Daz, who quickly returned to her side.

"Just look…" were the only words she could muster.

Their faces were a replica of disbelief, for what they saw defied any kind of logic. The room's charred configuration was hidden from the mirrors reflection, as if behind a masked veil; one room, two very different perceptions. In the mirror Eve and Daz didn't even exist, two reflection-less beings, yet their eyes were drawn to it and they marvelled at what it purveyed. Gee's description of the Roman baths came back to them and now it made sense. Polished iron walls and embossed carvings lined the domed ceiling, and multicoloured marble-chipped terrazzo flooring graced the surrounding walkway. The oval pool emitted a translucent steam, and warm and cool air intermingled above its creamy milk-like substance that glistened so invitingly.

Eve's eyes shot to the archway through which they had entered. "Daz, it's Gee."

"Ha, so it is, duck, and we're with him."

They both watched as Gee proceeded to remove his red jumper and launched into the pool. Daz watched himself as he removed his leather jacket, and took a running jump and belly flopped in after him, while Eve sat on the side and just dipped her feet, striking up conversations with nearby rams. There was no sign of the vast burnout and disfigurements; instead, everything looked just as it should. Beautifully groomed rams and Adonis-like water maidens in ivory gowns, with soft crushed taffeta that fell off the shoulders. They sat with ornate earthenware pitchers and poured rich milk over the coats of the bathing rams. Eve watched herself stand, walk to the other side of the grand bath and join them. They saw themselves in the same room, yet in two very different dimensions. How was it possible that a reflection was not actually a reflection at all?

"What can I be doing for you two?" a strange voice asked, momentarily pulling them back to reality.

There was no need to turn round, as his image was there for them to see, as perfect as the background the mirror pictured him in. He was a smallish ram of stocky appearance, his sandy-brown coat interrupted only briefly by a white mark that resembled a three-quarter-length sock that sat snugly on his left foreleg.

"Name's Echo… Pleased to meet you." He held his hoof out, a polite and formal greeting for Arien newcomers.

"How rude of me," Eve said, turning to return his greeting before reeling in disbelief. "DAZ, wake me up, I can't do this any longer!" Tears of exasperation burnt the back of her eyes.

Echo, as he called himself, now carried extra baggage as an unrecognisable burnt image manifested itself. Eve turned back for reassurance, but good or bad, image or not, the mirror like a clouded sepia cloak hid its secrets well.

"Life's been cruel to you," Daz giggled as he shook Echo's singed hoof.

"I must say, compliments aren't your strong point… Look, my immaculate reflection say's it all," he said as he admired himself in the mirror, but neither Daz nor Eve had any idea what it was he could see…

"I've been looking everywhere for you," Gee said, bounding over.

"I wouldn't mind the name of that aftershave, me duck," Daz commented, as his nose picked up the appealing scent.

Gee, like an atomiser on legs, emitted perfumed waves into the air.

"Eau de cologne, I'll have you know," he grinned.

"Well, you do look a handsome chappy," Eve said, admiring his makeover.

They could almost see their faces in the sheen of his coat, and there was no knot or imperfection anywhere. Echo felt slightly put out.

"Beats the reception I got. Can't see why for the life of me… I'm just as handsome." He sniffed. "Well, the mirror never lies."

"Well this one has done on more than one occasion," Eve said, as her and Daz's eyes bounced between each other and then back to the mirror, with its curtain-drawn camouflage.

"The fête's about to start, we need to dress. Eve, follow the water nymphs; you too will look that beautiful."

Eve's face dropped as Gee nudged her in their direction.

"When you're all done, wait outside the changing room," he added.

Eve stamped her feet like a petulant child and slowly made her way over to the blemished cronies, before following them through the shuttered saloon doors. Gee and Echo assisted Daz through the neighbouring archway.

"Just the hogget I was looking for. Got the perfect outfit for you, my little friend."

"Recognise ya voice, but the name slips me memory," Daz said, thrown into confusion since they all looked exactly the same.

"Achcauhtli, we met earlier; call me Archie."

Archie flicked through the freestanding wardrobe's ensemble.

"I didn't recognise ya, ducky, the burnt look you wear don't do any of you rams any favours ya know."

"Does your humour come naturally, or are you rehearsed?"

"Do you always talk in riddles, Archie?"

"GOT IT! The perfect outfit." Archie removed a frazzled two-tone jumpsuit, 'cap' and 'bells', and pointed booties.

Daz didn't look too impressed. "Is it fancy dress; am I to be the clown?"

"No to both, you're to be Kanika's main entertainer at his banquet. The title into which you fall is jester, the fool. If he favours you, you'll be his complementary guest on the top table and will sample some of Aries' finest cuisine."

"If acting a fool and wearing a clown outfit equals food, then I'm already dressed."

"Good on ya, hogget, I'll be seeing you later. Back to work for me." Archie bid them all farewell.

Daz smiled. His stomach had had several conversations with him of late, and the delicious food Archie had tempted him with had his taste buds turning somersaults.

"So, do you think I'll pass as a guard?" Gee asked, presenting himself in a polished iron-plated suit of armour. He wore a metal helmet with a moveable visor that he had pulled down firmly over his face, although the slats allowed him reasonably good vision.

"Look, just like Archie, me duck. Except his armour was a tad black, even looked rusty in parts."

"Stop talking nonsense, boy, looked just the same as mine… Don't usually find these lying about, feel quite grand. Mind you, Kanika won't be too happy if he finds out I'm impersonating one of his rams, especially one with hierarchy status… They're above us, you see, and they take direct orders from Kanika. With their responsibilities, the best pickings always come their way. Think I better make the most of this." He lifted his visor. "Just one little thing I think you should remember – don't address me as Gee in front of Kanika or any of his guards, or I'll be for it."

Daz had had to squeeze his oversized waist into a pair of skin-tight breeches. He wore a red-flecked and parched-charcoal coloured outfit, with a matching poncho-style dress pulled over his head and secured tightly around his waist with a chunky cord. Pointed burnt-out booties and a three-way pointed hat, not forgetting the bells, completed his quirky outfit.

"Well, how do I look?" Daz asked, as he paraded up and down the changing room.

"Okay, you two, enough of the fashion show," Echo said. "The fête will be up and running by now. Tell you what, you pair take your time." Echo looked at Daz and Gee, who were obviously in no hurry. "See you at the banquet; I'll have your places set next to mine. Might be able to introduce you to Ebo, my twin... I hope so anyway..." With that he left the changing room.

"Come on, you two!" Eve yelled, as Echo and a multitude of rams passed her on their way to the fête. She thought Daz and Gee had had more than enough time to get themselves suited and booted.

"Think I'll slip this on, take it everywhere with me," Daz said, picking his crumpled jacket off the floor and draping it over his shoulders.

Eve waited in the doorway in an off-white dress made of paper-thin material with rustic patches and an odd tear along its seams. Her wavy hair was coiled into a bun that rested messily on top of her head.

Gee checked that the coast was clear before he spoke. "Looks like we're all ready then."

"Why are you dressed as a guard?" Eve asked curiously.

"Well, I can assure you I haven't got a promotion, it just happened to be lying around with the other outfits. By the way, Eve, already told Daz, but don't go calling me Gee while we're dressed in this attire; let's just say I'm incognito."

Eve looked at Daz with his jacket strewn over his shoulders. "Knew I'd forgotten something," she said, and dashed back to the changing area to return donning her knee-length black duffel coat. "That hides a multitude of sins," she laughed, as she looked at her burnt ragged gown.

"What do you mean? You look beautiful," Gee stuttered, his helmet hiding his momentary embarrassment.

"Ya wearin' a helmet or a blindfold, me duck?" Daz joked.

"For your information, it's a visor, and I've got twenty-twenty vision."

"Think ya need to take ya twenty-twenty vision to an opticians, don't ya agree, Eve?"

"Least I'm not a man in ladies' clothing, tights and a dress," she laughed. "You do look a picture."

Gee's patience was wearing thin. "If we don't get a move on we'll miss the fête and the banquet, and all your dressing up will be of no consequence."

They left the washroom and bathing quarters behind them, and veered off towards another winding corridor that hugged the drab and burnt-out volcanic walls. They fell upon a large open-top room; its immense circular structure housed a smaller identical room within it, and was graced with pillared archways. The outer room contained the celebratory fête the rams had all been raving about.

"This is the very top of the volcano, you know," Gee informed Daz and Eve. "We haven't long before the banquet commences. I have to look like a guard, keep order, so best keep myself to myself. I'll see you later," he said, and began to circulate.

Rams flocked around the many stalls, their wooden skeletons as bare and unappealing as the trinkets they held within them. Eve and Daz found it hard to show much interest in the burnt-fest. Distorted and therefore tuneless instruments played around the room, and Daz pointed out a quartet of flautists, while Eve watched an odd ram whose bow glided elegantly over its fiddle-awaiting strings. It was just a shame it wasn't music to her or Daz's ears as it screeched out its inharmonious composition.

"We can't just walk around in circles!" Eve moaned, growing bored of the invisible sea of flames that had caused such unsightly devastation.

It should have been a joyous event with its duels, dancing, talented musicians and various stalls with their bountiful wares. Alas, all of this was hidden to Eve and Daz because of the shadows of the aftermath. Yet no one else seemed to notice, and Aries was carrying on as if nothing had happened. Eve was seriously starting to question her own sanity.

"My feet are aching," she said, hobbling over to the nearest stall and leaning against its wooden stanchion.

"Well ya should 'av left ya boots on, duck. Walking barefoot won't help, ya know."

"Those water nymphs … as Gee called them … all walked barefoot," Eve explained.

She noticed a couple of very interesting-looking antique hand mirrors, not nearly as damaged as the jewellery boxes and candleholders set around them. She lifted the nearest one by its cold metal handle; it had its own scars to bear in the form of a large hairline crack.

"Do I dare to peek?" Eve's eyes lit up. Something drew her towards the reflections she was yet to see, but as she lifted it to her face, a smile didn't greet her from the other side.

The room had seen a complete transformation, but before she had time to take it in, she saw herself dancing with Daz, who had settled into his role as jester perfectly and was prancing around and acting the fool. Shocked by her radiant reflection, she called to him.

"Look here a minute! Things are getting even crazier." As she spoke, the doors to the central room opened and two guards positioned themselves on either side. The crowds round the stalls began to disperse as the rams formed a long queue outside.

"Look, I'm sure that's Echo…" Daz waved.

Eve had completely forgotten about the mirror and its reflection, and followed Daz to join Echo at the end of the line.

"Just a few odds and ends to take back to my home," Echo said, opening a small hessian bag to reveal a couple of charred tapestries rolled up neatly at the bottom, together with two good-sized earthenware pots to serve his culinary delights and a tapered candle.

"Can see you've been busy," Eve said, trying to look enthusiastic as she saw Echo's face light up as he rummaged through his little bag to show off his well thought out souvenirs; to Daz and Eve, it just looked like a load of old tat.

"There more stalls in 'ere or what?" Daz stood tall as he tried to see above the rams' heads.

"Don't be daft, it's the banquet room," Echo licked his lips. "Wait till you see the food, it's a feast to be savoured."

"Hmm, I can only imagine. If it's anything like the rest of Aries, we've got a lot to look forward to!" Eve said.

Echo didn't pick up on Eve's slightly sarcastic remark and continued. "These festivities make me very proud to be an Arien. Many other star signs would love to pay us a visit, but Kanika's very picky about who he lets in, as you'll know only too well being a pretty water nymph. You're very pleasing to the eye. Kanika has such a soft spot for elegant dancing." Giving Daz the once-over, he said, "Didn't realise until Archie said… Now it's obvious why you're so ugly. Hoggets don't get their well-defined looks until they mature. Adolescents are never seen, and are kept with the females deep in the volcano until they're old enough to fend and work for themselves. Then their elders help build houses for them on the outside. So with that in mind, what are you doing here? Where's your nanny?"

"I'm starvin', duck! Explain the whys and wherefores later after we've eaten; can't think on an empty stomach ya know." How they'd got here, the gate and how they were going to get home was all too much for Daz to get his head around, and it didn't really concern Echo anyway. While everyone thought Eve was a water nymph and he a hogget they'd got nothing to fear, and that was how he intended it to stay.

They had their first glimpse of the room.

"You won't get much grander than this," Echo said, shuddering with excitement.

Neither Daz nor Eve could understand how he could find beauty in this burnt-out shell, which lacked any of the niceties he exuded. At the far end was a semicircular top table, with two adjoining tables at each end that ran the full length of the room. With a blackened mahogany finish, they were encrusted with the dishevelled remains of crocheted table coverings and doilies. Candelabras were situated equidistantly along the tabletops, their beauty concealed by waxen remains that had cooled into statue-like appendages and misshapen teardrops. Tarnished silver dinner plates lay at each place, and serving dishes and salt cellars stood periodically.

The rams quickly seated themselves, while Echo walked up and down the nearest table.

"Won't be long, just looking for our place names." Echo was true to his word, and he soon came across the upright cards on which each of their names was printed. Frayed and a little worse for wear, they were only just about legible.

"I told you we'd be seated together."

Eve and Daz took their seats.

"Wonder where Gee's got to," Eve said as she looked around.

A handful of round tables were scattered randomly around the room's outer perimeter where the guards had already been seated, but as yet, no sign of Gee.

Everyone in the room fell silent, all except Daz of course.

"They serving food in this restaurant, ducky?" he said impatiently, waiting to be handed a menu.

"Shhhhh, hogget. It's etiquette for a short silence as we welcome our guest of honour and his twelve disciples. You're about to meet Kanika." Echo sat back in his seat as thirteen rams entered through a side door to a fanfare of trumpets.

"Which one's Kanika?" Eve whispered in Echo's ear.

"The clothing gives it away; do you really need to ask?"

But to Eve and Daz, they all looked the same in their dehydrated clothing toasted to a crisp. Each ram rose, stood and clapped as the thirteen took their seats. The water nymphs took on the role of waitresses and poured ale from fluted jugs into heavy-bottomed goblets.

"A toast to my predecessor," the ram at the head of the table said, as he stood and raised his glass. "To Kanika, and my predecessor," he toasted, and the others followed suit.

"To Kanika!" Their cries echoed around the room.

His disciples composed themselves as they awaited his decision. Kanika walked towards the empty floor space in the entertainment area between the tables and turned to face the twelve that remained. He counted along the row of rams until he reached number four...

"Lyndon, your time has come. My soul needs to live on. You are my host, the chosen one to continue my reign and Ariens' prosperity. Join me."

"What's happening?" Eve asked, tugging at Echo's sleeve.

"Keep watching; everything will soon become clear."

"Hope they hurry up, I'm starvin'!" Daz moaned, nursing his rumbling stomach.

Lyndon knelt before Kanika, who had lowered his head. A water nymph who had previously served them ale walked over and removed a tainted pendant very carefully from around his neck, placing it over Lyndon's head.

"Now you need to concentrate. Look into my eyes, and do not for any reason break your concentration." Kanika took a step closer and his eyes locked with Lyndon's.

"Shhhhh, Daz…" Echo murmured.

"Don't blame me, ducky, it's me stomach 'aving its own one-way conversation."

Flames ignited in Kanika's eyes, and white florescent rods passed through and burned into Lyndon's subconscious. The old host possessed by Kanika crumpled into a heap, his frame weakened and debilitated. Then he rose in the form of Lyndon, strong and triumphant, having successfully entered his new host. He returned to his seat, and a cheer broke out around the room.

"Maybe I'll get my brother back now," Echo said, feeling a rush of emotion as he looked at Ebo's lifeless body.

A ram in immaculate iron-plated body armour walked towards the head table. Eve and Daz just smiled at each other as Gee made his debut entrance. Why was he the only ram whose clothing looked so immaculate? Whatever disaster they'd befallen, what was the key to their imperviousness?

"Take him to the playroom," Kanika ordered, "his work here is done. May his retirement be a happy one." He toasted Ebo, "For the time you have given me," and took a big swig from his goblet. "And to the longevity of my new host…" He sent Gee to his bedchamber for the pass key to the playroom. "Take him with you," he ordered, and Gee threw Ebo's limp body over his shoulder and exited the banquet hall.

"I'm still not exactly au fait with the goings-on around here," Eve said, as she tried to cling onto some resemblance to the reality she had left behind.

"I didn't even get to say goodbye. The only way I'll ever see my brother again is if Kanika happens to pick me to sit at his table, and then in time become a host for him to dwell in. I just have to live in hope. You see, before this, my brother and I have never been separated. Seeing him tonight has brought back just how much I miss him."

"I'm sure we'll find him in the playroom."

"If only it was that simple, Eve. It's only for Kanika's past hosts. They have served him well and so get the chance to live out the rest of their lives in a playroom that's said to be constructed to Kanika's exact specifications. They have the best food and living quarters, and also the chance to find a mate to continue our race." Echo paused as a water nymph leant over and placed an oval plate between them containing slices of warm bread.

"Just smell that … freshly baked bread." The aroma was just too much of a temptation for Echo, who tucked in.

Daz screwed his face up in disgust. "Looks like burnt toast from where I'm sittin'! And that smell you talk of is chokin'! It hasn't been baked, it's been cremated!"

"Well, Daz, you don't know a good thing when you see it. I'll have yours if you don't want it… Won't see perfectly good food go to waste!"

"Make that mine as well … I've suddenly lost my appetite, too!" Eve pushed the plate towards Echo.

"Well at least it's only the appetiser; you might find the entrée more pleasing," he said, after removing the last few crumbs from his plate.

"What is Kanika, and why does he need a host? Is he some kind of spirit?"

"He's the origin of the star sign Aries. He was forced to work in the volcanic mines alone after a catastrophic eruption and only he and a couple of females survived; they bred, and Aries escaped extinction. As time went on, his offspring helped design the bathing quarters and banquet hall which you've now seen, and also many more hidden rooms for his own purposes. Few of these have ever been entered, as the yews are quarantined in separate chambers. They, too, had everything they could desire in life, and were frequently visited by rams of Kanika's choice. Kanika also wanted somewhere for his children…" Echo paused. "He was a kindly ram, you know. Deep in the volcano's core an immense playroom was erected. The young rams and hoggets had an enviable childhood, with living and food quarters built for their pleasure. They hardly ever surfaced, as they had everything they needed down there. He visited them on a regular basis, and as they reached adulthood he decided which ones he would send into the outside world as workers, whose houses would then be built in readiness, or those he'd keep close and would therefore stay in the proximity of the volcano and become his guards."

"Okay, but that's only half the story. How can he jump from one body to another? Does he posses spiritual powers?" Eve watched as the water nymphs ladled a thick kind of stew into the serving bowls that sat along the table.

"Now we're talking!" Echo rubbed his hooves together as smaller soup bowls were laid down in front of them.

Daz frowned. "Looks almost as appetising as the toast!" he said, looking at the black curdled mass in which coagulated vegetables floated aimlessly in an oily film.

"Don't know about a spoon, ducky, methinks I'd 'av better luck with a fishing rod! Would have got meself a prize catch lookin' at the size of the suckers in there!"

Echo gave Daz a somewhat sharp glance. "I don't know, these days you hoggets have no respect." He ladled a third spoonful into his bowl. "Looks like you two will be going hungry then." He sighed at the sight of Eve and Daz's empty dishes. "Now where was I? Oh yes, I remember. Story has it that during one of Kanika's visits to the playroom, when he was looking to extend it even further, he fell upon a huge diamond wedged into one of the rock faces. He summoned a workforce of rams who began major excavation work. They were said to have discovered a crystalline carbon mass, the only natural element since the playroom was all ram made, a maze of infinite facets. Kanika's curiosity was unfortunately his downfall, and it took him many failed attempts to reach the maze's core. An unexplained fire burnt with ruby red flames that came from nowhere. A distraction or perhaps camouflage from a wrought-iron gate was positioned behind it. The flames grew fiercer, a warning perhaps... Then a silent explosion ripped through the playroom, killing all in its path, including Kanika's children. This was to be Kanika's torment, as the gate should never have been discovered. From then on he was cursed and his body was instantly cremated, yet his soul was granted eternal life, enabling him to watch his loved ones grow old and then perish. Rumour has it that his children play in the maze till this very day... But like I said, it's only a rumour. Although the playroom has been rebuilt on Kanika's orders with all its former beauty restored, his conscience has never allowed him to step back inside."

"That's awful. Why didn't he just seal it up, instead of digging up the past?" Eve asked.

"I suppose in Kanika's mind it was his only way of keeping his children alive, and the maze has never caused any problems since. So he found a way to body hop and was able to use any ram of his choice without causing them irreparable damage."

"But why? Why does his spirit possess others?"

"He just wants to live a normal life again and be granted the kindness of death at the end of it... Unfortunately for Kanika, he's hit upon a major problem, as each and every host rejects him after only a short while and so his hunt to find his perfect match continues. The playroom is now a way of him thanking his previous host, giving them the pleasure he so wanted for his own offspring. He carries endless pain behind those eyes, and each banquet he calls is a new search."

Eve looked at Daz's empty chair. "Now where's he gone? I knew I shouldn't have taken my eyes off him!"

"You won't have to look far," Echo sniggered.

Daz stood in the middle of the banquet hall trying to entertain Kanika and the other members of the top table by doing what he did best ... acting the fool.

"Maybe they think he's the real court jester. Let's just hope they like him," Echo said, knowing how much Kanika enjoyed his entertainment.

"Bet ya all rammed, ay?" Daz said, followed by a loud burp.

The room fell silent, but then Kanika began to chuckle.

"Carry on, boy, you're a breath of fresh air."

That was all the encouragement Daz needed, and his jokes then got progressively worse. He attempted some not so immaculate break-dancing moves and spun on his back like a disorientated crab, splitting his breeches in the process.

"Nearly lost me crown jewels," he tittered, and the whole room was in stitches.

Echo clapped. "He's working the crowd like an old pro! He certainly fits the bill as the jester."

"Ha, yeah, think you mean the fool," Eve said, rolling her eyes, but the louder he got, the more everyone seemed to love him.

"He's made more than a good impression on Kanika," Echo said, as he watched a guard add a chair to the main table. Daz was now an honourable member, one of the select few. "It's time for Kanika to pick his next disciple to fill Lyndon's seat." Echo held his glass for a top-up as the water nymphs walked round with their pitchers.

"How's it done?" Eve asked, finding the banquet fascinating.

The many questions Eve put to him made Echo feel quite important for a change. "It's an elimination process, and it's all done in his mind. It could be any one of us. He looks deep into our souls… Shhhhh, he's looking our way."

Kanika's eyes glowed, and their white light reached out and stopped at every seated ram, eventually coming to rest three seats away from Echo.

"Looks like it's Mackie's turn," Echo whispered. "Guess I won't be seeing Ebo for quite a while." He shrugged.

An excited Mackie trotted behind Kanika, buzzing with excitement as he took Lyndon's place on the top table. The banquet drew to a close, but not before Kanika's final toast.

"Can you once again raise your glasses … to Mackie, our new twelfth member."

Eve lifted her glass into the air. "To Mackie!" she cried.

A small section of the goblet remained undamaged, and a reflection jumped out at her. Crimson flames flared and vicious tongues of fire lapped at the walls, their individual sparks intertwined; a network blockade formed across the exits. The room was in anarchy, and Eve could almost smell the flesh as it smouldered. She felt dizzy with the high-pitched screams in her head as she watched the poor rams as they were slowly burnt alive. She saw Kanika standing in the flames, and his eyes burned into hers. Shocked, she dropped the goblet.

"What's wrong, Eve? You're shaking."

Speechless, Eve stared across the room, and just like in the goblet's reflection, Kanika's eyes met her own, their expression dark and unfeeling.

She gasped and briefly lost consciousness.

"Eve, wake up!" Echo shouted.

She opened her eyes and could hear the sound of Echo's voice, but the room was an empty burnt-out shell. *Was this the past being re-enacted in my mind*, she asked herself, *or were those events yet to come?* She felt a strong connection to something, but didn't know what, and had no idea why…

CHAPTER FOUR

Breaking the Rules

"Well, looks like I got meself a permanent job; Kanika loves me!" Daz said, as he trotted back to the table with Kanika following behind.

Eve had just about pulled herself together, and Echo was finishing off the last dregs of his ale.

Kanika addressed Echo. "I'll let it go this time, but when a water nymph enters Aries she must dine with those of her own kind. Can you escort…" He looked down at her name card. "…escort Eve to the bathing chambers? As for Daz," he smiled, "I think the entertainment quarters will be very comfortable and meet all your needs. Echo, can I trust you to carry out my wishes?"

Echo was only too pleased to oblige. "Yes, Kanika, right away, Kanika." He led Eve and Daz into the hallway, where the fête had taken place earlier. All the stalls had been cleared and a few guards swept the littered floors, which were now almost pristine.

"I think I'll take over from here," Gee said, stepping out from behind one of the pillars.

"Well, I've had me orders… Eve to the bathing chambers and Daz to the entertainment quarters."

"They belong in neither!" Gee snapped.

"Well, that's the rightful place for hoggets and water nymphs."

"But, Echo, they're neither. Don't know what they are or how they came to be in Aries. They just turned up on my doorstep."

"That's impossible, Gee. You know it's prohibited for water nymphs or hoggets to leave the confines of the volcano."

"How did you get here then?"

Eve shrugged. "That's what we've been asking ourselves. We're a very long way from home; let's just say it all started off at a fair… If only we could turn back the clock."

47

"Well, the gate's the only way out of Aries, although I can't promise it'll take you where you want to go," Gee said.

"That's a risk we're prepared to take," Eve replied, suddenly feeling very homesick.

"And Kanika handed the way out right into my hooves... Mind you, did take a while for me to find his bedchamber... Got lost, and fell across the females on the way..." Gee smiled. "Think I'll pay them an extended visit next time."

"Kanika will be furious! When he takes his wrath out on somebody, it'll be me at the front of the queue. I'm not having it! I'm going to find him and tell him about your scheming; at least it will let me off the hook." Echo shuffled away uncomfortably.

"Hold it right there!" Gee snarled. "Have you forgotten something, or should I say someone? Your brother Ebo, he spoke very fondly of you when I escorted him to the playroom and said how much he misses you. You could see him you know; come with us... Forget about Kanika, his thoughts weren't of either of you when he selected Ebo as his host, so think of yourself now. Maybe we can all get through the gate – word has it that Cancer is an ideal star sign in which to take refuge."

Echo weighed up the pros and cons. "It's not an easy choice for me. Aries has always been my home, but on the other hand, Ebo's always been my brother. If I do come with you I know there is no going back. I'd be branded a traitor and thrown in the dungeon to rot."

"The choice is yours, but if you don't come along, at least give us time to get through to the playroom before you tell Kanika of our plans. You see, there's only one key, so once inside I can lock the door and nobody can bother us..." Gee said smugly.

Echo butted in. "You've got it all planned out I see, but there's one major important factor you seem to have forgotten ... the key to the gate, which Kanika wears around his neck at all times."

"Well, Daz, did you do as I asked? Did you manage to come up trumps?"

"You mean the pendant, Gee? Yeah, got it, ducky. He was so pleased with the show I put on that he gave me a hug, and I snapped the clasp and with a quick slip of the fingers it was off, with Kanika none the wiser." Daz chuckled. "I'd 'av made a blumin' good pickpocket."

"In that case, why are we waiting? Got everything we need," Echo said, his mind made up. His thoughts were now of his reunion with his brother, and it was a risk he was prepared to take.

"Good on ya, Echo!" Gee said, giving him a friendly pat on the back. "Knew you'd do the right thing, just needed a bit of persuasion, ay?"

The corridors seemed endless, with rooms leading off to other rooms and no apparent structure. Although Gee had been there quite recently, he was still as confused as ever. The dim lighting was an added hindrance, as each walkway they turned into looked the same as the last.

"Think we're going in blumin' circles, ducky," Daz said.

"No, I'm sure that's the yews' quarters. Fancy a peek, Echo, see what you're missing?" Gee laughed.

"Thanks, but no thanks," Echo replied. Luckily for him, the door stood ajar and so he managed a sneaky peek as he walked past. *A couple of real beauties in there*, he thought to himself.

"Missing out big time," he thought aloud.

"Now, now, Echo, mind back on the job please," Gee said as he walked towards a large oak door. "This is it." He looked round to check that no one had followed them.

"Hurry up and open the door before we're seen," a nervous Echo instructed, worried they'd be caught.

Gee proceeded to insert the key into the cumbersome lock and turned it clockwise. A double click was heard and the door released itself. Gee opened it just wide enough for them to slip through and closed it as carefully as he could behind them.

"This is as far as I took Ebo," Gee said, as he locked the door.

They stood in a small confined room, with a black hole in the centre.

"Call this a playroom?" Daz said, looking very disappointed.

"No," Gee said, balancing precariously over the edge of the hole, "the playroom's down there!"

"From where I'm standing it looks like a vertical drop! How do you suppose we get down?" Eve asked as she knelt down. "Come look at this, Gee."

Gee knelt beside her. "You're right about it being vertical. Kanika had some amazing ideas, and he's built a vertical slide; that's our way down to the playroom." He smiled. "I'll get stuck dressed like this. Give us a hand, Daz, this armour is so uncomfortable!"

"Ha! You look like an oversized tin can," Daz said as he pulled off his helmet.

Between them, they managed to remove his metal body armour.

"Here, Daz, think you might be needing these… Slipped your clothes inside my metal tunic earlier, as I didn't think you'd want to be dressed as a jester permanently."

"Thanks, ducky. Now, no peeking, Eve, know ya eager to see my six-pack."

"You mean your boobs!" Eve chuckled as she turned away.

"I haven't got boobs, they're underdeveloped pecs." Daz looked down and patted his chest before pulling on his stripy jumper, and Eve helped him with his jacket.

"The back of the door, hanging up…" Eve pointed to an array of hessian mats hanging from a sturdy metal hook. "That's more like it," she said. "Now we can all make it safely to the playroom." She unhooked four, kept one for herself and passed the others to Daz, Gee and Echo.

"Ladies first," Gee winked.

Eve hesitated, rather apprehensive of the daunting black hole. "Erm … well…"

"It's no good standing lookin' at it, ducky."

Still Eve didn't venture any nearer.

"Well, in that case, I'll take on the role of lady," and with that, Daz jumped on his hessian mat and disappeared. His squeals of excitement soon faded into the distance.

"Okay, Eve, you next."

She positioned her mat over the edge and pushed herself off. The slide seemed to go on forever, and the sheer drop took her breath away. When she felt she couldn't take it any longer, the slide's vertical drop curved and levelled out, before she came to an abrupt halt.

"Daz?" she cried. As she called his name, she was pulled to her feet and dragged through a congregation of bodies.

Yet again, it was a room of epic destruction and ashen décor. A voice shook her from the grim images and said, "This is for you; wear it at all times." A dark figure pushed a black mask onto her face. "Now turn around," it ordered.

Eve felt the mask being pulled tight around the back of her head and secured.

"Take a look at yourself and join in our masquerade," the voice said, and the dark figure turned and vanished into the crowd.

Had she entered a different chamber without knowing? Eve now found herself in a room covered floor to ceiling in reflective mirrors, like the inside of a crystal vase. It was so bright she could hardly focus, and it took a while for her eyes to grow accustomed to its radiance. The mirrors were so overpowering that they almost pulled her in. She stood in the middle of a masquerade ball, and she'd never seen a room on such a grand scale. Yet when she turned away from the reflections, she saw that her surroundings were no more than a four-walled incinerator that reached out for a light that never came, where the charred remains of crippled rams moved around in an ungainly fashion. Trapped in a world of horror, she sought solace in the mirrors. The room was two-tiered, its marble balconies filled with rams and water nymphs in fancy dress; a kaleidoscope of colours swayed in time to the beat of hypnotic music. A concerto of absent musicians, it played only in her mind. The numerous chandeliers with sculptured metal frames hung down from chains, with endless fireflies attached. At the far end stretched a grand staircase, dressed with a plush velvet carpet in deep cerise, and ceiling paintings edged with gold embossed dado rails clung to the walls.

Then Eve honed in on herself and saw that she wore a crushed white taffeta A-line gown that fit her trim figure like a glove. Her butterfly mask with floral patterns embroidered in red and gold silk sat against her pale skin, her reflection like that of a porcelain doll. A matching shawl rested softly on her shoulders. Everything was so beautiful that she almost totally lost herself in the mirror's reflection. Hands stretched out towards her, and she reached out to the mirror's surface; their fingers touched. But the fingers that touched hers were her own, and they pulled her closer until her face pressed firmly against the cold mirror. The reflections took on a physical presence and she felt bodies brush past her as they danced to the heady music that grew out of nowhere. A distorted voice echoed as she watched the agitation grow on her face. She felt the frustration as their eyes met.

What are you trying to tell me? She asked herself.

A familiar reflection … she'd recognise Daz anywhere, even wearing his jester mask. He took her by the hand.

"Eve, come back! What are you doing?"

She felt herself jolted backwards and into the darkness. Daz wrapped his arms around her waist, as he did in their reflection.

"It's a mirror, duck; you can't walk through 'em, ya know."

"It's a masquerade, look, it's beautiful. You're with me?" Eve said. Entranced, she pointed towards their reflections.

"But that's impossible, ducky!" Their reflections turned to face each other and Daz took a bow; Eve responded with a ladylike curtsey, and he took her in his arms.

"It's uncanny! How can we be in two different places at the same time?" Daz said.

They were both thrown back to reality as the mirrors reverted to an undisclosed vortex, as swirling clouds grew into a darkened mist and then nothing at all.

"Our reflections! The beautiful room! It's all gone," Eve sobbed, while Daz just stood open-mouthed.

"So this nightmare we're trapped in is actually a masquerade? Then why can you see it and we can't?" Eve asked Gee.

He and Ebo looked at each other, but couldn't find an answer.

"Think you're delusional! Everything's beautiful, just as it should be," Echo piped up, as he swayed to and fro. "Come on, we've found Ebo. He's over there dancing; he's partnered a water nymph…"

Jealous, Gee said, "He hasn't done bad; she's a bit of alright. A vision dressed in a flowing ivory gown." Her graceful ballerina-type movements were an instant attraction for Gee, whose instinct was to wander.

All Daz and Eve could see was Ebo as a solitary ram marred by ashen remains, his ungainly movements resembling anything but dancing; a sad specimen barely clinging to life.

"He said he'll take us to the playroom," Echo continued.

"Well, we won't need these then," Gee said, removing his mask.

"I'll need a hand with mine," Eve said, as it was much too tight to remove herself.

"Alright, me duck, stand still." When Daz had finally managed to unknot the thick strands of ribbon, it disintegrated and only dusty remains lay in his hands. "Ashes to ashes, dust to dust," he said, as he blew them into the air.

Gee and Echo were dumbfounded by his actions. "That mask was one of a kind, why would you throw it away?"

"Ha, don't you mean blow it away, duck?" Daz had forgotten that they were seeing very different images, he and Eve having completely lost any concept of reality.

Eve looked at Gee. "Why do the mirrors talk to us in a different language?"

"Whatever do you mean?" Gee asked.

"Everything we see, bar you and ourselves … are disfigured embers, unforgiving flames that have bestowed their damage. In our eyes, even Echo is one of its captors."

They followed Ebo's decrepit figure up the unsightly stairway, its singed pile running away in several directions.

Gee's face dropped. "I had the pick of the crop, yet I picked the playroom." He watched the spectrum of colours as the water nymphs' dresses merged. *A perfection that I'll have to put on hold*, he thought, as he reached the top step.

Ebo led the way as they passed through an oak door with deep indentations that looked like scratches.

Daz shook Ebo by the hoof. "If you can show us the gate, we'll be more than happy."

"You have the audacity to go against Kanika's rules and throw Aries' very existence back in his face? The path is anything but easy, but if that's your desire, I will show you. Kanika will not be pleased and he will seek you out; you'll never find a hiding place…

He'll have your scent and he'll come for you; you'll spend the rest of your days looking over your shoulders."

"Maybe not!" Gee interrupted. "Daz, you must keep the pendant; it transforms into a key which will fit every gate you pass through. Lock each and every one behind you, and don't look back."

"But that goes against all astrology, and you will be breaking every rule of the zodiac – the gates must be left open at all times." Ebo shook his head. "Promise me you won't lock the gates… If you can't adhere to this, our journey ends here."

"Okay, me duck, I promise," Daz said, but his eyes met Gee's and said something very different.

They walked down what appeared to be a continuation of the grand staircase, but it was in fact its mirror image. Its ashen wall coverings hung in despair and there was a melancholy feel to a place that should have exuded fun and laughter. Once again, Eve and Daz's perception was tainted. A glorious room destroyed by spontaneous combustion, its fiery destruction having sucked away all its outer beauty. Eve and Daz were no longer fazed by their noxious surroundings and its emaciated occupants. They were greeted by a vast irregular-shaped room, where the walls collided rather than met, each embellished with its own individual mirror, which in turn possessed a very unique personality.

Echo's rationality disappeared and he totally ignored his surroundings, racing ahead in excitement. "Wow, just take a look at that!" he shouted.

A perfectly designed cuboid stood on its axis at the far end of the room, with ten diamond-encrusted faces situated on each side. A slight bloom to its surface had obviously been brought on by the disaster Echo had spoken of earlier.

"It's the only thing that wasn't completely wiped out. As you can see, it's suffered very little damage." Echo walked round the multifarious object in awe. "Rumour has it that the maze lies within, and that somewhere within the maze lies the gate."

"Everything Kanika promised and more is here," Gee said, mesmerised.

The playroom was amazing. This immense uninhabited space

contained its own compendium of games, but what he found even more bizarre was that they all moved freely. The game of chess seemed to be playing against itself as he watched a white knight move two spaces forward and one to the left. Spinning tops hummed and danced, at times almost colliding with one another. Toy soldiers played out their own battle scenes, and music boxes wound from behind played as the beautiful ballerinas pirouetted in their bell-styled tutus, their silken gowns an array of resplendent colours.

Gee, briefly lost in the moment, tried to piece together what he was seeing. Then the mirrors called and his attention wandered.

"Kanika was true to his word! Every word he spoke … it's all true," he said.

"So it is, Gee," Ebo said, as his concentration drifted to Echo.

"You must come and see this!" Echo called. "This cube's an enigma."

"Come on, Gee, it does look rather interesting." Ebo headed over to his brother, followed closely by Gee.

"Eve, Daz, have a look around, play with the games if you so wish," Gee called back.

Daz frowned. "Games? What flippin' games?"

He and Eve stepped between the ashen remains and charred building blocks protruding from the debris. Partial remnants of iron-framed horses had no visible riders, yet they rocked, perhaps in anticipation. The mirrors seemed to shout out, and while Gee, Ebo and Echo were totally absorbed by the cube and its properties, Daz and Eve were drawn in a trance towards the outer wall, whose mirrors seemed to beckon them ever nearer. Once again, Daz and Eve's eyes met a very different picture to the surroundings in which they found themselves. The playroom was a surreal vision, and they could hear shrill laughter as young hoggets played a multitude of games. They saw chalk-drawn hopscotch courses, and watched as each hogget hopped from one numbered square to the next. Another donned a blindfold and played the old game of blind man's bluff, which they remembered well from their childhood. Extra large wooden building blocks were being built in a variety of different shapes, and carved wooden jack-in-the-boxes popped up to show their faces. Two hoggets sat cross-legged and deep in concentration, their eyes scanning sculptured wooden chess pieces either side of the board and contemplating their next move. A beautiful rocking horse with her polished iron frame held an eye-catching glazed finish, while her perfectly groomed chestnut mane was draped over her long neck, complemented by a matching thick glossy tail.

Sat astride her was one of the smaller hoggets, who took the reins and gained quite a momentum. Eve smiled as she watched the little ram rock backwards and forwards, backwards and forwards. She turned to Daz in disbelief as they shared this unexplainable reflection. Upon doing so, she caught sight of the burnt-out rocking horse that stood slightly to the left of the cube. A cold shiver tore through her body as its rapid rocking motion was in perfect time to that of its reflection in the mirror. But no hogget sat astride this horse, and even a slight breeze couldn't have explained its unorthodox movements. She turned back to the mirror and the hogget turned its head to look into her eyes. Its saddened face was awash with tears.

"Help me," it said. "I don't want to play any more."

"What do you mean, ducky?" Daz asked.

Eve covered her face and then looked again. All the hoggets had stopped moving, and the building blocks, spinning tops and games had all come to an abrupt end. The hoggets had lost interest in the toys strewn across the floor and stood upright, supported by their back legs, and then walked towards Eve and Daz. Their eyes were transfixed as they stared into the playroom's burnt-out shell.

"Help us!" they cried, despair oozing from their distorted voices. Were these really Kanika's children trapped in the mirrors, lost souls with no way out?

Eve reached out for them, but all she touched was the cold glass. As her hand made contact, the glass rippled and dispelled a watery secretion. Instantly absorbed, it left no trace, just like the mirror's untraceable reflections; the room once more wore its charcoal complexion.

Meanwhile, Gee, Ebo and Echo were still pondering over the cube.

"Did you see any of that?" Eve cried as she walked towards them.

Echo's concentration was focused on finding an opening through which they could get in, but he was baffled by the cube's complexity.

"The hoggets, the mirrors! It was so sad! They so wanted out."

"What do you mean it's sad?" Gee gazed at the mirrored walls. "Well, can you believe it? See, it's true what they say about the myth; it must be Kanika's offspring, and I'd say a few generations of them from where I'm standing... They're playing next to us with the toys; we can't see them, but the mirrors can ... and the mirrors never lie."

Eve looked around for the second time. "Toys ... in here? Ashen remains of them maybe; this room has been totally burnt out."

"What about those beautiful rocking horses, and the soldiers in the corner? Everything in this playroom, in fact everything in the volcano, is spectacular, utterly breathtaking! There's something definitely wrong with you pair!" Gee sighed.

"Everything was nice until you took us to that train station and..."

"Stop talking in riddles, boy, and help us get this cube open and find the gate."

How sweet that word was to Daz and Eve's ears, who longed to leave Aries and its unexplainable complexities behind them.

Echo ran his hooves over each and every one of the cube's reachable faces, feeling for any indentation or a clue to its opening, but he came up against a brick wall, an invisible seal that had no intention of harbouring any unwanted intruders. Eve and Daz's morale was now at an all time low, as they watched each ram in turn try his hoof at the cube, but to no avail.

"Well, in that case," Echo puffed, after his umpteenth failed attempt, "we really are in a fix. If we can't find the gate, we best get back up to where we came from."

"Don't be daft, duck, we can't walk up a vertical slide, even I've worked that one out."

"The cube definitely opens, so there's definitely a way out of here," Gee insisted. "How do you think the water nymphs gain access to the Roman baths? We're just not looking in the right places!"

"Think we should all take a break and gather our thoughts, then we'll split into two groups, and myself, Ebo and Gee will work on the cube while you…" Echo looked at Eve, "and Daz can search the walls for a hidden door."

"But they're all mirrored!" Eve exclaimed, looking from one to the other.

Gee wracked his brain. "Well, one must be double-sided. Pressure provided to the right place, perhaps that's where the answer lies; an opening, or another stairway. They're just guesses of course, I don't really know, but I've got to be on the right track."

"Okay, just give us some time to try and figure this thing out," Eve piped up.

The rams stopped what they were doing and spoke in unison. "Time? That's all we've got!" This was followed by an awkward silence.

"Come on, Daz, we haven't got time for this. Best start on them mirrors."

But Eve knew it would take an age, even if they discovered an exit at all. There were far too many mirrors, and as they walked to the far end of the room, the rams were barely visible.

"That's right, me duck, let them stew for a while," Daz said, as he prodded the glass's cool exterior. "Eve, it's happening again." He could not only see the multitude of toys and hoggets, but between their younger counterparts the reflection held all the volcano's occupants. Their faces were ghastly, reflecting an inward cry for help, in total contradiction to their outer form which reflected great beauty.

"Eve, I'm hallucinating! Unless I'm mistaken … there's Archie," Daz said.

"I'm sure that's Echo, I remember his reflection in the Roman baths… You saw him too, didn't you? Look, he's got his little socks on."

"Ya know, me duck, I think you're right."

"Look, the ram standing alongside him is identical, even down to the socks."

They both thought the same thing ... EBO!

"Are we losing it completely, Daz? Ebo and Echo are over there ... I can see them..." Eve turned, but she couldn't see either. "There's Gee ... Ebo and Echo must be round the other side of the cube."

The occupants of the mirror were led by Echo, who walked towards Eve and Daz.

"WE HATE YOU, BOTH OF YOU! BREAK THE CYCLE, BEFORE IT'S TOO LATE!" the rams and water nymphs shouted, pounding their hooves and hands against the inside of the mirror.

Daz and Eve could hear their mournful cries, which reached an ear-piercing crescendo.

"What are you trying to tell us?" Eve cried.

"You of all people should know, Eve! It's time to face what it is you've done."

The room began to spin, the voices echoed and the screams grew more desperate. Eve felt the colour drain from her face.

"Eve, Eve, wake up!" Daz bent over her limp body as it lay crumpled on the floor.

"The fire, Daz, it was awful," she wept.

"Yes, it would have been, ducky; those poor hoggets, but that was a long time ago. Now wake up, Eve, you fainted." He cradled her head in his lap. "Think we should keep what we've seen to ourselves; Gee already thinks we're losing it big time! Come on, maybe they've managed to find a way into the cube."

Gee waved his hooves around. "Hurry up, I can't hold this any longer, I can't hold it any longer I say... It opened from the inside, but we only found that out because a couple of water nymphs passed through on the way to our bathing quarters. They often re-home here, you know. We have a lot to offer water nymphs, and word gets round between star signs. On the other hand, the ten other star signs have so far given Aries a miss... Just as well when you think about it; what have we got to offer them?" Gee wheezed. "Enough talking, this is really heavy!"

"It's you that's doing all the talking, me duck," Daz laughed.

He and Eve turned for a last glance at the playroom. This time, only the hoggets resided in the mirrors and directed the water nymphs to the exit. A revolving mirror, just as Gee had imagined, led them out of the playroom. The door sprang back fiercely, and they found themselves inside a singular cube within the cuboid (one of many).

"Not more blumin' mirrors!" Daz groaned.

Gee trotted on ahead. "Just check Ebo and Echo are okay. Now don't you two get lagging too far behind," he said, disappearing into a maze of mirrors.

"No fear of that, me duck. Quicker we find that gate, quicker we're out of here."

The first cube contained a selection of distorted mirrors. Daz howled at his shrunken body, which resembled a large ball with arms and legs, while Eve looked like she'd visited the land of the giants with a large, thin body and shrunken head attached. It lifted the mood between them as they jumped from one to the other, comparing their peculiar reflections.

"Daz, you've got horns!"

"And you've got hooves, me duck!"

But their reflections had been overshadowed by a sudden bombardment of hoggets. Now hosts of the cube, they'd jumped from the playroom mirrors just as Kanika had jumped from ram to ram.

"Get out! Run, and don't look behind!" their voices reverberated, playing over and over again.

An overwhelming terror almost shook the cube.

"We can't go back, not now. I say we find Gee, and let's stick together this time," Eve said, remembering what she had heard many times before, that there was safety in numbers.

The hoggets' resilience was relentless, and their words of warning continued. Their monotonous chants were interrupted by one solitary word: "Catch."

As an automatic response, Daz turned towards the voice. A hogget caught his eye, and then proceeded to throw a red fist-sized ball towards the mirror. The mirror's reflection rippled, and the ball hovered momentarily, bounced and then passed through. Daz grabbed at the air and the ball landed snugly in his hand.

"Drop it, Daz, it's not real!"

"Well, me duck, feel for ya'self, it's as real as you and me." He looked back at the mirror.

"It's too late now; you didn't heed our warning, so you're going to have to play our game," the hoggets laughed.

Daz threw the ball back towards the hogget, and once again it bounced and passed through the mirror's rippled exterior, landing back where it belonged. On the other side, it was gripped tightly between two small hooves.

The cube began to shake violently, and Daz and Eve were thrown from side to side and up and down.

"Hold on, me duck!" Daz shouted, as he wrapped his legs around Eve's waist.

The two proceeded to bounce around like two pillowcases in a tumble dryer. Their somewhat untimely movements changed into a set pattern, one way and then the other. The cuboid was a life-size impersonation of a Rubik's cube, and they were lost in a vast maze of transparent square blocks. Would they ever find Gee? The gate? Home? Was this the reality the hoggets had tried to warn them about?

CHAPTER FIVE

It's All In the Game

They uncoupled their intertwined limbs and stood to regain their bearings. Clear glass walls were their new surroundings, and the cube had taken on a completely different appearance, taking them to an unknown and uncharted variant. Eve looked down at what was now a mirrored floor. She was surprised by the bird's eye view she had of the playroom, which she'd seen in the mirrors previously. There was neither rhyme nor reason for it; it was as if the mirrors showed exactly what they wanted, when they wanted – every game imaginable brought to life by the fun-loving hoggets.

"Why is it we can only see beauty through the mirrors?" Eve asked, as she peered down in wonder.

Once again, the room was a vision of perfection. Stone walls were graced with embroidered tapestries, with Kanika's image sewn into many, and deep cardinal reds were the focal colour, bordered by gold, giving the room a rich, warm feel. The hoggets and a selection of games gave an overriding feeling of love to the room. A long rope knotted at each end was pulled between a chalk-drawn line, and the hoggets scrambled for an end. Dominos were stacked in piles as they waited to grab a passing hogget's attention. Some young hoggets sat in pairs and rolled colourful dice along the polished tiled floor, while others played dressing-up, trying on the fancy clothes the old rams had grown tired of and passed down. The young females wore A-line silken gowns and masks, and the males stood in tight breeches and embossed tunics as they re-enacted their very own masquerade.

"Up there, ducky, it's Gee, Ebo and Echo." Daz looked in three different directions, the glass's transparency allowing him to locate each ram in turn.

Gee was higher up than Ebo and Echo, and their charred coats made it very difficult for Daz to differentiate between them.

"Think we've got some unwelcome visitors, duck. If you can see the same as me, you're not going to like it."

"What do you mean?" Eve asked, almost too scared to look.

"I don't think explanations are necessary."

Eve's jaw dropped as she saw snakes of various sizes draped between the cuboid's many levels. Their flat heads were situated in one singular cube, while their bodies passed between many, held in place by the cube's walls. Ladders were intermingled between the snakes; some were extended just enough to fill three of the cubes from top to bottom, while others stretched as far as their eyes could see and reached the cube's highest point.

Eve didn't know whether to laugh or cry. "This might sound crazy, Daz, but I have a funny feeling we've both been pulled into a three-dimensional game of snakes and ladders."

"Game on then, ducky!"

Eve looked down searching for the base of the ladders, but her vision was completely impaired by the mirrored playroom. She watched as a couple of hoggets threw their dice into the air, playing a game she hadn't seen before. Were the dice left to float in an infinite reflection, for she never saw them land? Their display of numbers was now a guessing game, without result, or so she thought. Deep scratches formed furrows, chiselled out with an invisible hand. Two separate markings appeared simultaneously and took on the shape of the number forty-four. The scratching continued.

"Look, Eve, the number forty-five is to our right."

"Yeah, and the number forty-three's just appeared."

The corresponding numbers popped up above them, each floor identical to the next. A ten-by-ten three-dimensional snakes and ladders board started to take shape before their very eyes, and the very tip of one ladder poked its way through the base of the number forty-one.

"Daz, something's coming up!" Eve watched as the floor partially opened.

An obscure life-size cube pulled its way up through the opening with a pair of odd-looking disjointed arms, followed by what Eve could only describe as its double.

"Well, Daz, you might not believe what you see, but I can assure you it's a pair of dice."

"They've got arms and legs, me duck!"

Each side was numbered one to six, like any standard dice, the difference being that instead of the usual painted dots depicting each number, encrusted diamonds of the highest carat had been used.

"They are the same dice I saw the hoggets throwing in the playroom … just a lot bigger."

"Ha, and arm and legless I guess, ducky."

"Daz, this is surreal!"

"They look damn real to me!"

The two dice wasted no time and hobbled over to cube forty-four to join Daz and Eve and start their game.

"Oh my! This is getting even more uncanny," Eve said, flabbergasted. "The rams have their own set of dice too! We're all playing the same game. At least we're playing it together; it must be mind-blowing for Gee, Ebo and Echo playing in their solitary confinement."

"What do you suppose happens to the losers?" Eve asked. She glanced at the snakes, their flame-shaped tongues moving in and out sporadically and their hypnotic eyes searching for prey.

"Well, let's just hope it isn't us, and that these dice are weighted on our side. If not, duck, the outcome don't look too clever. Talking about these dice, they ain't doing a lot!"

"I've got a funny feeling they're waiting for our command. Don't just stand there pondering, make yourselves useful!" Eve instructed the dice, giving them both a hard slap. "That should get them moving."

Their arms and legs recoiled, and they somersaulted around the floor space. The first to land displayed the number six, and waited accordingly. The second was only just behind, and revealed the number one. They linked arms and proceeded to square fifty-one. A ladder sat waiting.

"That must be our cue, duck."

The walls between each cube were a hologram, and its invisible form had created a passable walkway. They were soon able to join their dice.

"I haven't got a great head for heights," Eve said, as she stared at the rungs of the ladder disappearing into the distance.

The first die had an obvious aptitude for climbing and scaled the rungs with graceful ease. Unfazed, Daz set his foot down on the first rung.

"Feels secure enough to me. Just remember, Eve, don't look down," he warned, and confidently, but not so gracefully, Daz made haste.

"In this case, dice first," Eve chuckled.

The die tapped its foot impatiently, but Eve made no attempt at the climb and so it swung its arm back as far as possible and gave her a hard slap on her behind, making her wonder if it was getting its own back.

"Ouch!" she shouted, as she jumped onto the second rung. The die, hot on her tail, gave her no option but to climb, staying only one step behind her.

They passed diagonally through the three floors of the cube, and finally, the first die pulled itself out, its destination now number sixty-six. Daz shot up right after, but had to wait a while for Eve since her uncertainty meant a much slower climb. When she finally surfaced and looked around, she saw that the immense cube was completely transparent.

"'Bout time, ducky," Daz sniggered. "If we get a move on, it won't be long before we catch Gee up."

Eve looked up and could see Gee as he waited to make his next move. His dice gambolled around, by Eve's judgment two floors up. It was hard to predict exactly due to the cube's transparency and vastness, with images getting lost in their own optical illusion. The mirrors had vanished, so how could she see silhouetted movement in each of its surrounding faces?

"Daz, what do you make of this?" she asked.

They both stared at the glass, watching as silhouettes turned into images of themselves.

"What happening Daz?" Eve cried. "Look, look into the mirrors, I can see the train station... It's sucking us in."

With undulated movements, the glass took on the appearance of liquid, which surged towards them in waves. Daz and Eve soon stood totally submerged in an aqueous fluid, and then they weren't there at all! Cube sixty-six was now unoccupied… But where were they heading and why? The hands of time had suddenly turned back, but why only now could they see the perfect picture of Aries seen by Gee, and every other resident in the volcano? Finally a reality to Eve and Daz rather than just mirrored images. They'd been there before, but unfortunately, it would be a journey they'd have to relive several times before finally uncovering the truth. So their contradictory replay began…

★ A Beautiful Replay ★

"Look with your eyes. Don't want to break anything now do you? Could be of great value for all we know," Eve said, jumping up as the train rattled into the station. "Hurry, Daz, we'll miss it if we don't get a move on."

Daz couldn't bring himself to move away from the crystallised statue, and as Eve tugged at his arm, Daz, in his own little world, lost his balance. "Now look what you've made me do," he shouted. As he gazed down, he saw the statue's eye lying in his hand.

"I've got your tickets; we're in the ninth carriage along, that's if we make it," Gee puffed breathlessly. "Beginning to think you two had done a runner! WHAT HAVE YOU DONE, DAZ?"

"It was an accident, I didn't mean to… It just sorta fell out."

"Well, if your fingers hadn't have been medalling in the first place it wouldn't have just fallen out, now would it?" Gee snapped. "If Kanika finds out about this, we'll all be in trouble! Give it here, boy," and he snatched the diamond from Daz's hand and wedged it back into the statue as best he could. With that he turned and bounded across the bridge on all fours, hurriedly boarding the train.

"Wait for me, Daz!" Eve yelled, but he was already halfway across the bridge. She took one final look at the statue. "Oh no, not again. Daz, you idiot!"

But this time Daz had played no part in its disappearance, as the diamond lay on the floor.

"This is the last call for all boarders; the train will be leaving shortly."

Eve saw a conductor checking the tickets as Daz and the last few rams boarded.

"Wait for me!" Eve swooped the diamond up off the floor. "I'll have to put you back later," she said, as she gazed at its sparkling facets. She thought no more of it and dropped it inside her pocket, before racing across the bridge and breathlessly jumping into the carriage next to Daz and Gee.

"That was a close call," she said, as she puffed up an unused bolster and sprawled out on its plush silken covering.

The carriage's (or mining cart would probably be a more appropriate definition) movements were rather jerky, which was perhaps not surprising as its engine was a manually operated handcar that had to propel the weight of many carriages; this was achieved by four thickset rams. Eve was fascinated by the fact that the rams and a sea-saw handle determined the train's speed. Each cart was full to the brim, with most of the rams dressed in khaki dungarees or trousers and thick knitted jumpers in an array of colours.

"We get off at the next stop. It just gets better from here on!" Gee said, all of a twitch.

"What then, me duck?"

"Our first call is the Roman baths for a wash and brush-up; we have to be dressed in our finery for Kanika's banquet… Look, it's the end of the line."

***

Gee fought with his red woolly jumper, which seemed to have a mind of its own. He ran towards the lush Roman bath in the centre of the room and launched himself into its warm milky depths.

"Well, me duck, I ain't missing out on this!" Daz said, and threw his leather jacket on the floor before taking a running jump. His entrance was a rather harsh belly flop. "Ouch! Have to work on me diving skills," he chuckled. "Come on, Eve, get ya clothes off and have a dip."

"Ha, I think not!" she laughed. "I'll sit this one out." She sat on the side and dangled her feet over the edge.

As she looked around the room, she admired the polished iron walls and the ornate mouldings that graced the domed ceiling between the numerous embellished archways. A mosaic floor was beautifully set into two tiers as it stepped up around the pool. A rich scent of milk exuded from the large bath.

Eve watched Daz and Gee as water maidens in taffeta gowns poured the rich milk from earthenware pitchers over their shoulders.

"This is the life," Daz laughed, as he lay on his back and blew fountains of milk into the moist air. "I could get used to this."

Gee looked up at Eve as she sat alone. "Don't be shy, go say hello… They're water nymphs; very friendly you know, they don't bite."

Eve pulled her feet from the warm milk and sat for a moment, waiting for them to dry. She couldn't help but smile as she watched the rams lounging around on stone benches, with soft cream woollen togas draped around their drying bodies. She wandered to the other side of the immense baths and sat between two of the prettiest little creatures she had ever laid eyes on. Golden ringlets cascaded to their waists as they sat like mermaids in white silken gowns on the bath's outer perimeter. Their fair colouring and smooth complexion on elfin faces purveyed a flawless picture.

"I hope you don't mind me introducing myself like this, the name's Eve. My two companions," she said, pointing to Gee and Daz as they floated between the other bathers, "have deserted me for a while. I have it on good authority that you're water nymphs? I didn't know you existed in Aries, thought it was just a star sign of rams."

The nearest of the two turned to Eve, her china-blue eyes smiling. "Pleased to meet you, the name's Iris. You're right about Aries, it is predominately inhabited by rams. Over time, the word was that Kanika was building these vast Roman baths, and as former Pisceans we thought we'd take our chances. Pisces holds an evil undercurrent in its waters, but our only concern was that Aries is a fire sign; you see, fire holds our greatest fear. But Kanika's kindness and hospitality has won us over, and as word gets out, more of our kind pour in through the gate. We're so happy here …

at last we have found a place we can call home." Iris looked puzzled. "No other star signs venture into Aries as it has nothing to offer them. So what are you?"

"EVE! Come here!" A voice called from the other side of the room.

"Oh, can't explain now, Iris, Daz is calling me. I promise I'll explain later."

"Before you go, I've got the perfect dress," Iris said, looking Eve up and down. "Just your size. If you have time, look for me in the changing quarters." She leant over and gave Eve a soft kiss on the cheek.

At the far end of the room, Daz was admiring his reflection. "My skin, it's glowing. Gee said that the milk works as a face mask and moisturiser all in one... I feel rejuvenated."

Eve looked him up and down. "But you're soaking!"

"Yeah, going to dry off in a jiff. Join Gee and be groomed," he grinned.

"You're not a ram, you know!"

"I know, duck, but a bit of pampering from those little beauties won't hurt," he joked, his attention drawn to the water nymphs like a magnet.

Eve frowned. "Well, I'm okay with a brush ... I don't mind..."

"What can I be doing for you two?" A strange voice cut through the atmosphere, and Eve and Daz turned round to introduce themselves.

A sandy-brown ram, rather on the small side and with a peculiar-looking white sock on his front left leg, stood before them.

"Name's Echo ... pleased to meet you." He held his hoof out, a polite and formal greeting for Arien newcomers.

***

The fête was filled with excitement, and harmonious melodies from flautists to fiddlers all seemed to blend together perfectly.

"Did I tell you how very pretty you look?" Daz complimented.

Eve blushed. "Yes, more than once. Your jester outfit is perfect;

couldn't have picked better myself," Eve replied, thinking his clothing and personality had met their match.

"Think a dance is in order then," he said, and taking her by the hand he spun her towards him.

"You call this dancing?" she laughed.

Daz definitely had two left feet, and he pranced around and acted the fool. But Eve, caught up in the moment, didn't really care, and for the first time in quite a while they both felt happy with life. Eve broke away to admire the many stalls around the room; it was like eye candy for her. Illuminated manuscripts with Arien texts inscribed in gold and silver threads hung from metal hooks for the passing rams to admire. A small table was decorated with cooking utensils and colourful ceramics, glass jars ideal for pickling with thick rubber seals, patterned jugs and earthenware pitchers similar to those she'd seen in the Roman baths.

A shopper's paradise! she thought.

A beautiful water nymph was using a combination of thin wire and precious jewels in a wire-wrapping technique to make some very unusual pieces of jewellery. Eve tried on a pretty charm bracelet and various drop earrings. A thought suddenly popped into her head and she reached into her coat pocket. She pulled out the ruby that the eerie figure had passed her from the dodecahedron and showed it to the water nymph.

"Can you do anything with this?" she asked.

"I've never worked with a precious stone of this enormity before. Let me see what I can do," the water nymph replied, opening a small drawer.

"Daz, over here. Have you still got your pearl?"

"Yeah, it's buried in here somewhere," he said, reaching into his pocket and pulling out some screwed-up tissue and an old phone. "I've got it, Eve," he said, as he felt something hard.

The water nymph presented Eve with a rather cumbersome silver pendant. "I hope this meets your requirements," she said. The large ruby fitted snugly, as if it had always belonged there.

"Well, Daz, will you do me the honour?" Eve asked, and as she turned round he slipped the chain around her neck, fumbling momentarily as he fastened the tiny clasp. It lowered and rested heavily on her chest.

"I was bargaining for an earring, but looking at that I think it might be a little on the large side." Daz smiled politely. "Looks like my pocket will just have to do."

The whole room was picture perfect, with Aries' very own tight-knit community all coming together for Kanika's formal banquet.

★★★

The water nymphs were perfect waitresses and the ale flowed by the jug full. Echo just kept drinking, while Daz and Eve had never tasted anything quite like it before.

"Yuk; that milk tasted better!" Daz said as he sipped at it very slowly.

"Kanika does look grand," Eve said, as she sat down after his introductory toast.

He wore two-toned silken breeches; rich gold blended with a shocking amethyst. These were complemented by a deeper plum waistcoat on which gold embroidered stitches embellished the cuffs and collar, lifting its plainness. Over this lay a matching plush velvet cloak with a lambswool trim. A chunky neck chain from which hung a gold pendant completed his outfit.

"Well, I don't brush up too badly myself," Echo boasted, although his outfit was not quite so grand.

The room was a lustrous monument of which Kanika should have been very proud. Fine mahogany tables were covered with ornamental crochet tablecloths, and candelabras of the finest artistry sat along the centre, while silver dinner plates gleamed up at their guests, enhanced by their matching serving dishes and salt cellars.

"What's happening?" Eve asked, tugging at Echo's sleeve.

"Keep watching; everything will soon become clear."

"Hope they hurry up, I'm starvin'!" Daz nursed his rumbling stomach.

As they all sat back and watched the changing-over ceremony, Kanika took on a new host. The excellent quality of the food lived up to that of the room, and the goddess-like water nymphs placed delicious slices of warm bread between them on decorative oval plates. Echo was the first to tuck in.

Daz's face lit up. "This is amazing, ducky!" His nose soaked up its pleasing aroma as he took his first bite. "Now we're talking!" he mumbled between mouthfuls. "You know, Eve, I could get quite used to this."

"And this is only the appetiser; just you wait for the entrée..." Echo said proudly.

Completely lost in the room's ambience, home became no more than a distant memory for Eve.

★★★

Iris, her face concealed by a black lace mask, danced over to Eve.

"What good is a masquerade without a mask?" she smiled. "This is for you; wear it at all times." She gently placed the mask over Eve's head. "Take a look at yourself and join in... Have fun," and with that she skipped between the dancers, who closed in around her.

When Eve looked again, she had disappeared. Eve now stood in an enchanting two-tiered room, its marble pillars extending between both floors. An orchestra of musicians played heart-warming concertos, the balconies were bursting with celebratory rams and water nymphs in fancy dress, and a kaleidoscope of colours swayed in time to the beat of the hypnotic music. The room was filled floor to ceiling with reflective mirrors, like the inside of a crystal vase. She admired her perfect reflection. Her mask was like a beautiful red admiral, with its fine scarlet and flaxen threads. Her hair was scraped back into a neat bun, and her pallid complexion like that of a porcelain doll stared back at her. She placed her fingers on the mirror and leant her face against it; it was almost too good to be true. She felt herself and her reflection become one.

"Please don't let this end," she said. An anxious look invaded her face as she knew the gate was near.

"Eve, come back. What are you doing?" Daz laughed.

She jolted backwards and Daz wrapped his arms around her tiny waist. They both stood and stared at their reflections. Daz spun Eve round to face him, took a gentlemanly bow, to which Eve responded with a curtsey, and then took her in his arms.

"Like your mask," she sniggered, as she reached up and stroked his face. "You lost the jester's clothes and gained a jester's mask!" She ruffled his hair between her fingers as they spun round and round to the heady music. Enthralled by the fireflies that hung from sculptured chandeliers, Eve admired the grand staircase with it rich cerise floor covering as she was whisked past in Daz's arms, her crushed taffeta gown spinning around her.

"Come on, we've found Ebo," Echo piped up. "He's over there dancing; he's partnered a water nymph." Echo pointed to a beautifully groomed ram dressed in the finest attire; the only visible sign he was related to Echo was his identical white sock.

Gee was quite jealous. "He hasn't done bad for himself; she's a bit of alright."

"I know that vision Ebo's dancing with. It's Iris, we met in the Roman baths," Eve said.

"He said he'd take us to the playroom," Echo continued.

"We won't be needing these any more," Gee said, removing his mask; the others followed suit.

Eve hovered between the dancers until she spotted Iris. "Mind if we borrow Ebo for a while?" she interrupted, but before she had time to finish her sentence the water nymph had already taken up with another handsome ram and was dancing around the room.

"You're a dead spit of your brother," Eve smiled. "I'd never be able to tell you two apart."

Daz shook Ebo by the hoof and Ebo led them up the thick-piled stairway.

"If you can show us the gate, I'll be more than happy," Daz said.

A disheartened Eve followed in silence. Daz looked at the pendant Gee had given him previously, having explained that it was a multiple key for each star sign's gate.

"We've got a key, me duck," Daz explained. "Don't worry, Ebo, we'll lock it behind us."

"But that goes against all astrology and you will be breaking every rule of the zodiac. The gates must be kept open at all times," Ebo said, shaking his head. "Promise me you won't lock the gates… If you can't adhere to this, our journey ends here."

That's stupid, Daz thought to himself. What was the point of having a key if they weren't allowed to use it?

"Okay, me duck, I promise," Daz said, but his eyes met Gee's and said something very different.

They walked down a mirror image of the grand stairway they had just climbed and left the masquerade ball. An immense room lay in front of them, and Echo raced ahead.

"Wow, just take a look at that!" he said, as he dodged between life-size games strewn across the floor. He raced towards a perfectly designed cuboid which stood on its axis at the far end of the room. Ten diamond-encrusted faces were situated on each of its sides.

Gee looked around. "Everything Kanika promised and more is here," he said, mesmerised; the playroom was amazing. What he found even more bizarre was that all the games and toys moved around freely.

Eve and Daz watched a game of chess that was under way, as piece by piece was moved in turn. Spinning tops danced, yet came from nowhere. Eve walked between life-size toy soldiers, as battle scenes took place around her. Daz watched as keys were turned in musical boxes, yet no hand visibly wound them, and ballerinas pirouetted to their soft melodies.

Gee caught a glimpse of the mirrored walls.

"Kanika was true to his word! Every word he spoke… It's all true."

"What do you mean, Gee?" Eve asked.

"Look in the mirrors, tell me what you see."

Both Daz and Eve stopped what they were doing and looked into the mirrored walls. Hoggets were everywhere in the playroom's reflection. Four or five at a time queued up for a turn on the hopscotch courses as they jumped and hopped between the numbered squares. Hoggets sat and built their imaginary houses and castles from large wooden building blocks, and polished iron rocking horses, each with their own rider, rocked to and fro. Daz and Eve looked back to the room, where every game being played and every toy materialised in the room's reflection. These unexplainable happenings explained themselves perfectly through the mirrored images.

"These are Kanika's children; they died in the fire and now their souls are trapped in the mirrors forever … lost souls with no way out."

Ebo was fascinated by the two-way chess game taking place between reality and its mirrored unreality.

A hogget sat astride one of the rocking horses and suddenly looked straight at them.

"I think it can see us," Gee whispered.

The games stopped abruptly and all heads turned towards the visitors.

"I think they can all see us," Eve said, beginning to feel a little uneasy until their faces lit up with excitement.

"Play with us!" they sang.

"If you want to find the gate, we haven't got time for this," Ebo grunted.

"Where are the other hosts? Surely they could play with them," Eve said, looking for any other signs of life.

"You've seen them yourself, they're all at the masquerade ball; and that's where I want to be!" Ebo sighed, thinking about the mysterious water nymph who had taken his fancy earlier. "They make very attractive companions those water nymphs. I do hope no one else has managed to woo her."

"Well, me duck, plenty of other nymphs in the water … many more beauties where she came from," Daz chuckled.

"Is that how you see it?" Eve snapped. "You were happy enough to dance with me!"

Daz looked somewhat puzzled.

"Well, you can't be in that much of a rush to get back to the masquerade ball," Gee said, as he noticed Ebo starting a new chess game.

"White pawn to E4!" Ebo shouted, as he moved two spaces forward.

Each young ram stood and waited for their turn to move,

controlling their own individual chess piece. A small chestnut-brown hogget in the mirror moved the opposing black pawn, which likewise moved on the board Ebo was playing on.

"Black pawn to D5!" the infant yelled.

Eve gazed back at the mirror. "Look, the hoggets have left us a piece each." She ran and positioned herself behind the queen, while Daz stood next to the king and Gee trotted up to the knight.

"White pawn to D5," Ebo laughed, as he took the first piece of the match.

The small chestnut-brown infant stomped over to the corner and sat with his back to everyone.

"Too easy," Ebo laughed. "It'll be checkmate in no time!"

But a rather rounded white hogget had different ideas. "Black queen to D5," he said, and swept Ebo's pawn right from beneath him, and with it wiped the smug smile right off his face.

"You must come and see this!" Echo called. "This cube's an enigma."

"Come on, Gee, it does look rather interesting, more interesting than this game of chess anyway," Ebo said, heading over towards his brother, followed closely by Gee.

The hogget's expression had changed significantly; their game had been cut short due to no fault of their own and their saddened faces were awash with tears.

"We don't want to play any more," they said, and went back to the countless other games the playroom had to offer.

Eve and Daz headed over to Gee, who was waving his hooves around anxiously.

"Hurry up, I can't hold this any longer, I can't hold it any longer I say… Echo had quite a lot of difficulty getting in, but the whole time it opened from the inside."

The door sprang back fiercely and they found themselves in a singular cube inside a cuboid.

"More blumin' mirrors," Daz groaned.

Gee trotted on ahead. "Just check Ebo and Echo are okay. Now don't you two get lagging too far behind."

The cube was a block of mirrored walls, and in every direction they could see their reflections.

"Looked like a blumin' Rubik's cube from the outside," Daz said. He sniggered at their ever-changing images through the concave and convex mirrors.

The maze of mirrors looked solid, but it was deceiving, like a hologram; many of the walls weren't there at all and were just elongated corridors that met as and when. The maze was clever enough to conceal Gee, Ebo and Echo's whereabouts.

"Look, Daz, this place has got ladders," Eve said, as she looked up at rungs which stretched up farther than the eye could see. "I haven't got a great head for heights…" Eve laughed. "With the playroom and its many games, all we're missing in here are the snakes."

CHAPTER SIX

Eve and Daz's Revelation

"I've got this strange feeling, almost like we've gone and come back," Daz said, glancing around cube number sixty-six. The dice had already rolled, and a three and a four lay in wait. The life-size dice linked arms and moved on seven spaces until they resided in cube seventy-three.

Eve frowned. "What are you talking about? We've only just come up the ladder." She looked down at the uppermost rung that poked up towards them.

"Probably me daydreaming, never mind," Daz said, and being Daz he thought no more of it as he and Eve proceeded to cube seventy-three.

There was no ladder in sight, but instead an immense snake's head, its tongue releasing pungent fumes as it flicked backwards and forwards between its lips, which appeared to be locked in anger.

"We're okay, duck, it can't reach us … just get the dice to roll again."

The snake's hypnotic eyes became transfixed on Daz and Eve, and its elongated neck lunged as it executed a strike of the utmost precision. Daz and Eve stood in complete darkness, imprisoned inside this monstrous reptile.

"Eww, Daz, this is disgusting!"

A debilitating thick slimy secretion seemed to ease their passage to the snake's gut, and its strong muscular body constricted and contracted as they were pulled further down into its digestive cavity.

"Well, it doesn't look like we're going to make it out of Aries after all," she sobbed.

"I'm not giving up without a fight, me duck," Daz said, and

began to kick and punch as hard as he could at the snake's innards.

The muscular contractions diminished and they were both in freefall. Without the slightest warning, they found themselves in a knotted heap.

"Who turned the lights back on?" Daz blinked.

Eve sat bolt upright.

"Daz, we're alright, we're not dead at all, we're back in the playroom."

"Took your time, didn't you?" Gee piped up. "We're all waiting for you; can't start without you, you know."

Gee and Ebo stood on a floor-sized chessboard. Gee had taken the place of the white knight, and a charred and disfigured Ebo was the white pawn.

"Where's Echo?" Eve asked.

Gee shrugged. "My guess is he's still somewhere in the cuboid, hopefully lucky enough not to have come into contact with one of them snakes! Anyway, there are only two empty spaces, and they're on our team I'll have you know. I'd say they're waiting … wouldn't you?"

The two positions left unoccupied were the white queen and, most importantly, her king.

"That'll do fine for me, me duck. Always said I'd got royal blood running through me veins," Daz said, as he tore over to his square and stood proudly upon it.

"Well, for your information I'd make a much better looking queen any day," Eve laughed.

But this was no ordinary chess game; all the pieces had come to life and were now playroom toys. Each castle was a differently shaped building block construction; the bishops had become four rather regal skittles; the rocking horses had made their way across the room and taken their positions in the knight's quarters; the opposing queen resembled a matryoshka (better known as a Russian doll), painted ladies with alabaster-white complexions; the king had become a shiny jet-black jack-in-the-box, his head bobbing backwards and forwards, then from side to side, as he kept a careful eye on his loyal subjects; the pawns were all individually crafted into wooden soldiers, their unique facial features carved out with such precision and each with their own unique look; and the young hoggets had come to life and now stood in two groups on either side of the chessboard, depending on which coloured pieces they supported.

"Let the game commence," a small chestnut-brown hogget called out to the young rams and the playing pieces.

"Come on, Ebo, let's kick their butts!" Gee grinned.

"Well, a white pawn always starts, so may as well be me," Ebo said, rubbing his hooves together. "Just hope I remember the rules, it's been quite a while since I played. Very tactical game, you know."

"Come on, Ebo, there's only one way you can go!" Gee laughed.

"Right." Ebo scratched his head. "Just testing, Gee, just testing... White pawn to E4." With that he took two paces forward. "Over to you." Ebo grinned as he looked towards the black pieces and waited in anticipation.

A soldier's voice called out, "Black pawn to D5," and he also proceeded two steps forward.

"White pawn to D5..." Ebo laughed, as he kicked the solider off the board towards his team's awaiting hoggets, who cheered excitedly. "Just too easy, it'll be checkmate in no time!" Ebo grinned like a Cheshire cat.

The opposing queen looked rather smug. "You're not as clever as you think, are you?" she said, as she gave Ebo the evil eye. "Black queen to D5..." She slithered forward. "Coming, ready or not." Her head spun round in an anti-clockwise direction and her top half fell onto the board; then a smaller identical version of her stood inside, and she hopped out and left the board. The queen now lay in two halves on D6.

"That's your cue to enter," Eve said, and she, Daz and Gee watched enthralled as Ebo stepped into the queen's lower half.

"As I said ... black queen to D5." As she shuffled onto D5, the queen's head lifted into the air and slammed down tightly over Ebo. Frantically, she began to turn clockwise as she tightened her grip on her captive.

"Things are hotting up around here," she smiled.

"Daz, what's she wittering on about?" Eve groaned. "This game's getting so confusing."

D5, the square that contained the Russian doll and Ebo, suddenly ignited, consumed by molten flames.

"Do something, Daz, Gee!" Eve looked from one to the other.

They ran closer, but were held back by the immense heat. Eve buried her head in Daz's shoulder; she hadn't got the heart to watch as Ebo was burnt alive. The grasp of the finger-like flames tightened as they preformed their own malevolent cremation. The floor, the walls and the playroom began to spin round and round, faster and faster. Kanika's overwhelming presence took hold as his prominent face danced between the flames. A dark curtain closed around them, its heavy shroud appearing from nowhere; their vision was now lost.

"What is it about the number sixty-six? How did we get back here? Did you see what I saw?" Eve asked Daz.

★★★

"CHECKMATE!" a voice echoed, as a translucent image of a ram materialised, as did a complex room of mirrors, and in each and every reflection lay a gate.

"Eve, I'd know that ram anywhere. Think back to the station, the golden horns and vibrant red eyes; it's Kanika, coming to us as an entity."

"The game ends here," the apparition laughed. "You wanted the gate! Now take your pick. Though I don't think it'll do you much good. But before you take your leave, are you ready to admit what it is you have done?"

"What do you mean?" Eve asked.

"You need to look back deep into your subconscious, both of you. You can't go round in circles forever. You were happy here. You, Daz, in particular could have been my right-hand man; you'd have had the best living quarters, the best food, the best of everything Aries had to offer. As for you, Eve, you'd have been very comfortable living out the rest of your days with the water nymphs. But that wasn't enough for either of you, was it?" Kanika sighed. "I built everything so that my offspring and all Arien subjects could have a fulfilled life of happiness and contentment. I have paid the price for my mistake; well, that's not actually correct, I'm still paying for it. I built the volcano's interior with my own hooves as my children matured and grew, and they helped me. I put on banquets and fêtes, and provided bathing chambers. But I wasn't content, as the more children I brought into Aries, the more I wanted to give them. I worked harder than ever before, and meticulously planned and built a masterpiece... Well, you've seen the playroom for yourselves, where every toy is crafted to my own specification. But with age I lost the ability to breed and grew bored, and my children and my children's children didn't need me any more. Over time, the diamond I excavated grew into an obsession. I found my way in and erected ladders, but it was only by luck that I fell upon the gate and the water nymphs that now grace Aries. My curiosity led to my downfall. The deep scratches in the gate were actually a warning, which could only be read in the mirrors."

"What did they say?" Eve asked sheepishly.

"Go, don't look behind, but if you happen to be a true occupant of Aries, do so at your peril... But I went anyway. Some kind of magnetic force pulled me back, but it was too late; red flames engulfed me and the playroom, killing all of my children. I still hear their screams to this day, and I'm now forced to live as an entity and watch my loved ones die. I live on in search of a host that I can permanently posses, as only then will I be granted absolution."

"How's a host going to grant you absolution?" Eve asked.

"Because then and only then can I live out the rest of my natural born life and die like every other ram. This permanent hell I've suffered so long ... will release my soul."

"Problem solved! We've seen ya children playing in the mirrors. Why don't you go join them, ducky?"

"You call that happy? Ashen corpses, that's all I see, all my guilt will allow me to see... Now, Eve, you of all people should know! It's time to face what it is you've done."

"You're talking in riddles, Kanika! We haven't got time for this; we've got a gate to go through," Eve cried.

"Time? That's all we've got!" Kanika said, fixing his eyes on Eve.

"We just want to go home; please, Kanika!"

"You've already been through the gate once before, and had many other opportunities... Do you care to elaborate, young lady?"

Eve's facial expression changed and her eyes dodged Kanika's glare. "Things are starting to come back to me. It's something to do with that bug, the firefly Daz put into his pocket when we first entered the volcano... We reached cube sixty-six, a mirrored room, and the gate stood dead centre. We just wanted to go home, and this is how I remember it...."

★★★

"Took your time, didn't you?" Gee piped up.

"You certainly have," a tired Echo said, lying in the corner with his head resting softly on his front legs.

Daz climbed up the final rung of the ladder, followed by a trembling Eve.

"Think this is what you've both been looking for. Cube sixty-six; this is the home of what it is you seek," Gee said, crossing the mirrored floor and standing in front of a broad iron gate. "You're free to leave, my friends."

"Where's Ebo? We can't possibly leave without saying goodbye," Eve said, as she looked round for the absent ram.

"There weren't supposed to be any goodbyes, we all intended to leave with you," Echo sighed. "That was before we were faced with those gut-wrenching words." He pointed to some odd-looking symbols in word formation etched around the gate.

"What words, ducky?" Daz asked.

"Look behind you, in the mirrors."

The symbols transformed and took on a legible sentence, which Eve read out. "Go, don't look behind, but if you happen to be a true occupant of Aries, do so at your peril..."

"It's a warning you see, so we're stuck, grounded. It was all too much for Ebo; he's a lot more sensitive than me," Echo sniffed, as he tried to excuse his brother's untimely disappearance. "I'll say goodbyes on his behalf, as well as my own."

"Yeah, but where is he, duck?"

"He went down the ladders; knowing Ebo, he's probably in the middle of a game of chess with the children by now." Echo threw his hoof around Eve's neck and hugged her tightly. "I hope you find what you are looking for. You make for a great water nymph. Put it there, Daz…" He offered Daz his hoof.

"Yeah, let's shake on it, duck," Daz reciprocated.

"There'll never be another jester quite like you," Echo said, giving him a wee wink just before he disappeared down the ladder and from sight.

"I'll be seeing you!" he shouted up.

"Not if we see you first…" Eve laughed.

Daz felt something vibrating and warm against his side. "What the heck?" He delved deep into his pocket. "Ah yes, now I remember," he said, and pulled a rejuvenated bug from his jacket.

"Hello, the name's Shai Nefer, but you can call me Shai. Pleased to meet you." The funny little firefly stretched his wings. "Still feel a bit on the stiff side, and my light's seen better days…"

★★★

Eve took a deep breath. "Well that's all I remember. We left Shai with Gee and went through the gate."

"Maybe I'm finally starting to get somewhere," Kanika said, looking pleased. "Every time we've reached this point, you've never admitted to anything; maybe this is the end of a very long cycle."

"Do you mean a bike, me duck?"

"Not that sort of cycle, silly," Eve said, scratching her head. "What do you mean by every time we reach this point, Kanika?"

"From the word go you have treated Aries with blatant disregard and total disrespect. Where shall I begin? Maybe the beginning… At the train station, even my engraved image wasn't sacred. You stole my eye and never once attempted to put it back."

"That was my fault, me duck, slip of the finger…" Daz said.

"But I did try to put it back … I did…" Eve said, red in the face as she tried to defend her actions.

"No, Eve, Gee did… When it fell out for the second time you just dumped it in your pocket and forgot all about it… But what you didn't know was that it was my eye and I've watched your progression through Aries."

"I don't know where you keep getting this many a time from? We've only been in Aries and its volcano once. I'll prove it…" Eve reached into her pocket. "But that's not possible!" She pulled her hand out in disbelief. Beautiful diamonds with an eye-catching red undertone spilled out between her fingers. "But … but … I don't understand!!!"

"Hopefully, this will finally make you open your eyes. You've been replaying Aries over and over, and now maybe you can see for yourself. Look again," Kanika smiled smugly.

On second glance, however, only one diamond eye lay in Eve's palm. "I'm more confused than ever, Daz; please tell me you know what's going on?"

"Well, me duck, to be honest … NO. Think it's best you keep me out of this one," he said, looking at the floor.

"It was you, the pair of you who destroyed my beautiful Aries! It's all your fault! You need to stop living in denial!" Kanika's voice boomed around the cube.

"Beautiful? Everything and everyone in the volcano is burnt, charred and ugly!" Eve said.

"I should have gotten angry a long while ago if I'd have known it would jolt your memory. Are you telling me you remember and are ready to admit what you've done?"

"Yes, Kanika, I remember, I remember it all," Eve said, her eyes reaching out to Daz. "You know as well … don't you?"

Daz's eyes gave their own answer and he didn't need to say a word.

"We came into Aries and everything was spectacular. It even got to the point where I didn't want to leave; I could have lost myself with Daz in the masquerade ball forever. The delicious cuisine, the hospitality of all your beautiful water nymphs, the playroom, your adorable children; we had fun, and even played chess with them in the mirrors… Oh, but what am I saying?" She put her hand to her mouth. "Now I can see a very different picture. Everything is burnt, the water nymphs are like ashen hags and their corpse-like bodies hang in the Roman baths. Tuneless concertos are played by misshapen instruments, the food is inedible chaff, each course burnt to a cinder, and the rooms are skeletons of their former selves. But somehow, both myself and Daz could see it in its flawless stage, as whichever mirror we chose to look through we saw a perfect picture." Eve tried with every ounce of her mind to piece together this unfathomable jigsaw, yet whichever way she tried, the pieces locked her out.

For the first time, Kanika admired her fortitude. "Go back once more, Eve, this time to the banquet. You sat with goblet in hand for the final toast… Tell me, what did you see?"

Eve thought back. She could see herself with the goblet raised level with her face.

"Mackie!" she cried.

In the goblet's reflection she saw deep crimson flames as they tore around the room and lapped at the walls.

"The fire!" she gasped.

Kanika's eyes met hers, their expression dark and unfeeling.

"Yes, the fire." His voice grew cold. "The whole room was in anarchy. I could smell the flesh as my family burned in front of my eyes, the flames interconnecting and forming blockades at every exit. You left us to burn; you killed us, all of us. Now go back to the gate, Eve, and tell me the truth."

Eve snivelled. It was all getting too much and she broke down, only just managing to compose herself long enough to continue from where she left off…

★★★

"Hello, the name's Shai Nefer, but you can call me Shai. Pleased to meet you." The funny little firefly stretched his wings. "Still feel a bit on the stiff side, and my light's seen better days…."

"I'd forgotten about you to be honest; in fact, I thought I'd killed you," Daz sniggered.

"No, you're my hero. I'm forever in your debt." The little firefly buzzed around his head. "Think I'll have to build myself up gradually," Shai said, as he struggled to stay airborne. After a rather clumsy dive, he headed straight back for the warmth and comfort of Daz's pocket. "See you later," he yawned, and disappeared.

"You can't take him with you, you've seen the warning," Gee said, repeating the words over and over again. "I'll take care of Shai, give him here, might make quite a good companion."

"Daz, we haven't got time for this, can we just go please?" Eve didn't want to leave and found it harder by the second. "Bye, Gee!" She was far too upset for goodbyes and grabbed Daz by the hand.

"EVE, NO! WAIT!" Gee called. But Eve didn't want to hear, and she, Daz and Shai passed through the gate.

★★★

"So are you telling me it was all my fault?" Eve wept.

"Would you like me to fill in the last pieces of the jigsaw?" Kanika asked, to which Eve just nodded. "The very first time you came into Aries you saw it as it was, how it really was, perfect. It had so much to offer you; you left the gate with the addition of Shai after you read the warning. Arien rules were laid down for a reason, but you thought you knew best and took the law into your own hands. The gate's magnetic force pulled you back, with the addition of Gee who tried to help … but not before the volcano was ripped apart by flames, every single ram and water nymph being cremated before my very eyes. You, Daz Shai and Gee floated in an empty vortex between the star signs, and that's the reason you never saw yourselves burnt. When you were transported back, the deadly carnage had drawn to a close, so you went back, back to the start, back to the station where it all began, and relived it over and over again. This time, it was a warped journey that you yourselves created."

"Aries has to take some of the blame, or should I say a lot of the blame. We were almost eaten alive by one of those snakes in your poor excuse of a 3D snakes and ladders game. Instead, we were delivered to the playroom, where a death trap lay in wait in the form of a chess game, and we stood by and watched as Ebo was murdered by the black queen. Aries can't wriggle its way out of that one, now can it?" Eve hissed.

"Silly, silly girl, once again you try to pass the blame. Haven't you done that enough? One time too many, I'd say... You go through the volcano over and over in your mind to try to come to terms with and reach an understanding of what it was that happened, yet each time all you do is fabricate the truth with these farfetched ideas of yours..." Kanika sneered. "Snakes and ladders games with murderous chess pieces. One thing you can't escape from, however, is what you have done. The snakes and ladders are simply another figment of your imagination, and as for Ebo, he died in the fire along with all of the rams and water nymphs. It's about time you faced reality."

Within an instant, Eve and Daz were surrounded by the repugnant odour of burnt flesh. Their eyes shifted, only to be met by singed tormented beings. The burnt occupants closed in around them as they stood in the middle of an ashen wall of death; the worst thing was that some of them looked all too familiar: Archie, Iris, Ebo and Echo stood in a decomposed state.

"I'm sorry!" Daz cried. "Please forgive us!"

It was the first time Eve had ever seen Daz shed a tear.

"We hate you! Both of you! Now run, don't look behind!" the rams shouted, and their dishevelled hooves and the water nymphs' charred arms reached out towards them.

"We're so sorry!" Eve screamed, as her and Daz cowered in fear.

Kanika stood back and watched. "Ashes to ashes..." he screeched.

★★★

"Get up, both of you!" Gee's voice echoed.

In almighty relief, they lifted their heads.

"Gee, where are we?" Eve asked.

They stood in the remainder of a burnt-out cube, its identity still visible.

"Where do you think you are? Cube sixty-six. We never moved," Gee replied.

"Kanika ... Ebo, Echo!" Daz looked round. "Where are they?"

"In the mirrors of course, that's where you've put them ... all of them."

88

"So where have we been then, me duck?"

It suddenly all fell into place and everything made sense.

"We've been in the mirrors with them; it was all part of the gate's curse, and only now have we finally broken the chain," Eve replied.

Kanika appeared to them through a mirrored reflection. "Now and only now have you admitted your guilt, and this has allowed the mirrors to release your minds. You see, you were not able to return to reality until you could face your demons head-on."

"So where have we been then?" Daz asked.

"Apart from the first volcano encounter? You have resided in this empty room the whole time. Your minds were lost in the mirrors, so you've replayed the events over and over in your minds. That's why you only really had one diamond eye in your pocket."

Eve smiled. "Why sixty-six?" The question had to be asked.

"Well, six and six added together amounts to the number of star signs. It's closely related to the tarot, the number twelve being the hangman... Give anyone enough rope and they'll hang themselves." A wry smile formed on Kanika's face. He turned, as did the reflection, and he, his children, the rams and the water nymphs all played together happily back in the playroom. The day would never come when Kanika would find his true host, but it really didn't matter any more. His soul had been granted a pardon, and all his children and family were there, waiting with open arms. At last, Kanika had found inner peace.

Eve smiled at the masquerade ball and thought how she had loved her time there, especially her dance with Daz.

"We've set them free," she whispered.

"One thing still bugs me, ducky; if we replayed everything over and over in our minds, why didn't we see the volcano in its former glory? Why was it burnt, disfigured?"

"I think it's because no matter how many times we went over what happened, however much we tried to dress it up, our minds wouldn't let us run from the reality of what we'd done, and that's one thing we could never change."

"Maybe this is our cue to go," Daz said, and he and Eve looked round for the last time at cube sixty-six, both agreeing they'd spent more than enough time there.

"Gee, are you coming?" Eve asked.

"I'm afraid this is one I'll have to sit out," Gee replied, sitting alone in the burnt-out room, trapped between the gate and the much happier reflection held in the mirror; he had taken the place of Kanika.

"Have you still got the pendant?" She asked with a wink.

"Yeah, safe and sound, me duck," Daz replied, patting his pocket.

"Must say, Gee, I am pleased to be going now. We were only a heartbeat away from madness," Eve said.

She looked back into the playroom and saw that the children had chalked a farewell message on a rather sturdy blackboard.

Kanika's voice filled the room. "Something to take with you from Aries!" he called.

Daz glanced at Eve. "Read it then, ducky…"

Every word made so much sense as she recited it out loud.

"Echoing footsteps on dust-covered floors
Marble pillars, how many I just can't be sure
Walls on parade so straight, yet they bend
A network of corridors, seemingly with no end
I rush to the mirrors as the evening sun sets
The faster I walk, the more distant it gets
Faces engraved in beams carved from wood
Once smiled now frowned, so misunderstood
Droplets of moisture travel a wall
On an arduous journey to nowhere at all
As voices start chanting, run, don't look behind
BUT WHERE CAN I RUN WHEN IT'S ALL IN MY MIND?"

She smiled at the playroom's reflection. Ebo and Echo stood on either side of the blackboard and gave them both a friendly wave.

"See you, me ducks."

"Well, Daz, looks like our acceptance saved our sanity."

"Speak for yourself," he winked.

"Bye, Gee!" they called.

Gee was left all alone, cube sixty-six his own solitary confinement, as Aries now lived on only in the mirrors.

"STOP! Aren't you forgetting something?" Gee yelled. "I'm afraid some people just never learn."

Visibility dropped as Daz and Eve found themselves in a swirling mist.

"DAZ! YOU'VE STILL GOT SHAI IN YOUR POCKET!! LOCK THE GATE QUICKLY!" Eve shouted, terrified that Kanika would find a way to pull them back.

"I've got it, me duck!"

"Quickly, Daz!"

He struggled to locate the lock as the mist thickened. "Ah, that's the one, Eve, I've got it!"

Just as Gee had told them, the pendant adapted and fitted the lock perfectly. Daz turned the key and felt it click into place, once, twice, three times. They locked the gate and left Aries behind them for the VERY last time.

CHAPTER SEVEN

Where To Now?

"A bit different from Aries, ay duck?" Daz said, as he perused and drank in the ambience of their new surroundings. He hadn't noticed the tears that streamed down Eve's pallid face.

"I thought this would be it, that we would be home!" Eve broke down; Daz had no idea how to comfort her when she showed this vulnerable side to her nature. "First we lost Oli and Ebony, and as for poor old Gee ... we just left him; good friends we turned out to be." She knelt on the floor distraught and covered her tearstained face with both hands.

"Hang on, ducky, least one good thing came out of Aries," Daz said as he plucked Shai from his pocket.

Eve briefly lifted her head and managed a wry smile. Tears welled up in Shai's eyes too, but these were tears of happiness.

"I'm alive! I'm free!" Shai glowed. With his newfound brightness came a confidence that seemed to exude from him like a ray of sunshine.

Their first glimpse of the sky was a beautiful clear crystal blue that lasted only momentarily before vaporising into a deep marine that housed a shock of luminous stars, many spontaneously shooting out at the most peculiar angles, burnt and branded into the enigmatic night sky. A multitude of rock formations unfolded around them and tiny droplets of water trickled between small crevices, their destination being ornamental pools illuminated by the moon, which lent its silvery brilliance to the water's normally dull complexion.

With a change of heart, Eve took a deep breath. "Strange, but a nice strange I think," she murmured as she returned to her feet.

"I'm not so sure," Daz said, shaking his head; something in the air gave off an unpleasant vibe.

Shai didn't utter a word; he didn't need to, as the broad smile across his face said it all.

"You've got the key in your pocket," Eve said, her spirit returning briefly, "so I say we all go back through the gate and lock it behind us. We've got eleven more to go through, and we've all had enough adventures for one lifetime."

"What gate, duck?" Daz looked around. "Gates and us just don't go!" he sighed.

"That's the problem, Daz, they just do go, walkies in our case!" Eve's mood once more became deflated.

"Well something's amiss," Shai buzzed, and landed gently on Eve's shoulder. "When star signs pass through other star signs' gates, the gates remain so they can leave at any time. Whatever reason you're here, something or somebody has no intention of making this easy for you, either of you."

"Well, if the gate ain't gunna come to us, there's no point hangin' round 'ere for too long. Our only option is to find the gate for ourselves." This was the most sensible thing that Daz had had to say for himself so far.

All this excitement proved too much for Shai, who dived deep into the safety of Eve's hood.

They walked at a snail's pace to begin with, but this soon quickened due to their ever-growing curiosity. The barren rock land soon transformed into a hive of energy-filled hustle and bustle, home to the strangest little creatures Daz and Eve had ever laid eyes on.

"'Ello, what we got 'ere then?" a voice chirped.

"Hum … what we got here then?" Eve retorted, looking up and down at the little fella.

"I'm Wilton!" he answered abruptly.

"Ay up, duck, you're a Wilton?!" Daz sniggered, finding the little chap quite amusing.

"No, I'm a Goylin! My name's Wilton, silly!"

"Nice to meet you, Goylin, I'm Daz."

"I'm WILTON! Not Goylin! Told you once!!!"

"Here we go again, Daz; you've got a track record of offending folk," Eve joked.

"Oh, by the way," a little voice sprung out of nowhere, "what's a Goylin?" Shai flitted around them.

"OH MY!!! A BUG!!! IT'S A BUG!!! KILL IT!!!" Wilton tried his hardest to swat the little firefly.

"Don't kill him, duck! It's a Shai … I mean it's Shai; he's our friend." Daz plucked him from the air and placed him back into his pocket. "Think it's best you stay out of sight!"

Wilton started to do a funny little jig, hopping from one foot to the other and rotating in an anti-clockwise direction. "With all this confusion I think I'll stop, rewind and start again," he chuckled. "You're now in the star sign of Cancer, I'll have you know."

Daz scratched his head, rather bemused. "Well, I know my star signs, me duck, and you don't look much like a crab to me."

Wilton stamped his feet in utter frustration. "Don't you listen? I've told you before! Twice before to be precise. I'm a Goylin, name's Wilton! Listen up, this is important…"

Wilton stood about three feet in height, had blemished skin with a ruddy complexion, and his oval topaz eyes were overshadowed by a bulbous nose that protruded way too far. But the thing that stood out most to Eve and Daz was his one solitary tooth that showed when he smiled.

Daz elbowed Eve in the side and whispered, "Best not give him a bite of your toffee apple."

His oversized ears were like elongated petals that poked out from either side of an oddly shaped hat made of slimy green seaweed. The small amount of hair he had was wispy thin and hung limply around his cherub-like face. His clothes were also tailored from seaweed, and he wore a leaf-shaped skirt tied up with a dirty old rope that hung around his waist.

"He must be Scottish, Eve, he's wearing a kilt," Daz said seriously.

"I'd like to see what clan he comes from then," Eve replied, trying her best to keep a straight face.

Wilton continued to waffle on obliviously. They couldn't decide what material his boots were made from, but eventually agreed that the colour was a mid-brown. As for his tail, it would have looked more at home attached to a lion; it appeared to have no purpose and was thrown aimlessly over his shoulder so as not to drag on the floor.

"…That's everything you need to know. If you keep heading in the same direction you'll find the gate. Leave straight away, there's nothing for you here." Wilton was unaware that they hadn't heard a word he'd said, preferring to ridicule his appearance and be none the wiser about anything to do with Cancer.

"What's that?" Daz's eyes fixated on what was going on around him. "It's time Daz had some fun. You see, I'm not going anywhere yet! The gate can wait!" With that he disappeared into the little village.

Wilton shook his head in dismay. "Didn't he listen to anything? He'll get into no end of trouble you know."

Eve hadn't planned to stop in Cancer a minute longer than she had to, but Daz's unplanned disappearance put a different spin on things.

An agitated Wilton paced up and down. "We need to get him back, and quick!" he stressed. "It's not safe for folk like you to stay around here."

"What do you mean, folk like us?" Eve asked, quite offended by Wilton's choice of words.

"That's a question I hope I never have to answer," Wilton replied, and headed towards the unconventional village, with a disgruntled Eve lagging behind.

"Get out here, Shai, you're missing out! This is awesome, ducky!"

Shai didn't wait to be asked twice and circled around Daz's head before nestling on the top of his woolly hat to get a better view. A salty liquor lingered in the air, which tasted bitter as he rubbed his tongue over his top lip. Goylins and other peculiar folk scurried here, there and everywhere. Daz couldn't believe his eyes as they bobbed in and out of immensely oversized ornamental shells set back on narrow pebbled walkways, each identical to the next; except one. A narrow, slightly arched structure widened to resemble an elegant fan, with varied colours gracing its many indentations. On entry, Daz would have had to take on a crouched position, but at its highest point his five-foot-six-inch frame would have been able to stand inside comfortably, with a good four or five inches to spare.

"It's a lion's paw, Shai! That it is, ducky!"

"Have you totally lost your marbles? Can't you see it's a shell?"

The words were taken out of his mouth as a half-man-half-horse bent double squeezed its way slowly through the shell's narrow opening, standing at over six feet directly in front of them.

"Hey, Shai!" Daz called. "Perhaps it's a circus, some sort of freak show?!"

"Hmmm, you're the first Sagittarian I've been fortunate enough to see that hasn't got an ass!" the queer character replied, leaning over and placing a monocle over his eye to get a better look at Daz.

"Ay up, duck, no need to swear, we're all friends here ya know!"

"It's not a swear word, you idiot, it's his flippin' anatomy, take a closer look! His ass is his bottom half!" Shai tutted. "With a brain like yours, I'm your better half!"

"I'm Clement, from Sagittarius, the same star sign as you by the looks of it. Pleased to meet you."

"Well I'm Daz, me duck, and I'm a human; the star sign's Earth," Daz chuckled.

"That's no star sign, it's one of the elements," a puzzled Clement said; he didn't really know what to make of Daz at all.

"By the way, I'm Shai, I'm from Aries, and my star sign depends on which gate I happen to fly through."

"You're obviously not from this star sign, and you're not a crab, and definitely not a Goylin, so what you 'ere for, me duck?"

"I'm from Sagittarius; just visiting, and now I've got what I came for I'm going back through the gate."

Daz's neck ached as he had to constantly look up to make eye contact with Clement, whose chestnut-brown hair fell like a mane and flowed in large waves that caressed his waistline. A bronzed muscular torso was preceded by a horse's body that matched his hair perfectly.

"You'da been one hell of a catch where I come from," Daz said, almost jealous of Clement's immaculate physique.

Clement smiled, but he wasn't really on the same wavelength as Daz; not many people were really!

"What did you come for then?" Shai asked.

Clement didn't answer and instead tipped his head back and shook his shoulders firmly; and then the most marvellous pair of wings concertinaed out. Variegated swan-like feathers that criss-crossed and interwove were sheer perfection in motion.

"I've earned them! Sagittarian hierarchy are only allowed this privilege, and when I go back I'm with the elite of my kind." Clement bent his left knee and gave a regal bow, quick to show his newly gained importance.

A quizzical expression came over Daz's face. "Shai's got wings coz he's a fly. You've got wings coz you're some kind of unicorn. If I went in there and got a pair of me own, wonder what that would make me?"

"A fat boy trying to be a bug!" Shai cackled.

"Well, duck, I always imagined meself flying. Think I'll just pop in and give it a go."

"The potions you're allowed are only ones that relate to you and your origin," Clement explained, rising gracefully into the air. "Just a warning!" he shouted down. "Only use the shops that look the same as the one I've just left. Don't let temptation blind you; if you do it's a hard mistake, and one you'll have to pay the price for... See you, maybe in another star sign..." He gave a friendly wink, turned and disappeared from sight.

"Come on then, Daz, what are you waiting for? Gotta be some goodies inside for us to try out."

Daz's priority had changed, and he was totally engrossed in what he saw. "It's a mother of pearl," he said, walking blindly towards it. "It's uncanny, Shai, I know all the names of these shells," Daz boasted, as he showed off his newly acquired knowledge. He was mesmerised by this particular shell, but had no idea why.

"Remember Clement's warning? You can look, but we mustn't go inside!" Shai reminded him, but Daz's head was firmly in the clouds.

A compendium of different star signs and Goylins scurried past him, but all headed in the opposite direction to the grand mother of pearl except for Shai and Daz.

"Look, a bull, Daz, must be a Taurean, love to know what he was after… Over there, a Piscean!" Shai pointed. "Pufferfish, my favourite; not very often you see a fish out of water, is it?" But Shai's tomfoolery was by the by as the shell's hypnotic properties drew Daz closer, like the invisible pull of a magnet.

A spellbinding crystalline outer shell made it quite irresistible, its mirror-like pastels of pink, blue and different shades of silver enchanting to the eye. Daz didn't stop to consider Shai, and just shuffled clumsily through a misshapen opening into an open-plan area. He stood still briefly.

"Shai, it's like an old curiosity shop," he said.

Every wall was taken up by a multitude of different items, a combination of palm-sized screws and grey bonnet shells filling each and every one.

"Very pretty, but no chance of me getting me wings 'ere," Daz said.

Daz looked rather disappointed. They hadn't noticed the counter on entry, as it blended in so well and curved all around the shell's inner wall. Empty crab shells with their claws as legs made ideal little stools that stood neatly around the counter.

"Think it's a bar, me duck." Daz tried one of the stools out for size. "Hum, surprises me how comfy these shells are," he said as he took the weight off his feet. "I could murder a drink and some pork scratchings." He looked over the counter's surface for a bell to ring to attract the bar tender's attention, but unfortunately there wasn't one.

"Well, Shai, think we're harbouring a lost cause 'ere. Clement had the right idea. I suggest we go and pay that lion's paw a wee visit. Gunna take sumat worthwhile out of this star sign with me if it's the last thing I do, duck." Daz got up and walked back towards the opening, the mother of pearl all of a sudden having lost its appeal.

A melodic, rather high-pitched voice called out, "Can I help you?"

They turned to be greeted by an oddly coloured crustacean.

"What the heck's that?" Shai muttered.

"Well, duck, considering we're in Cancer I'm guessing it's

some kind of crab. Much larger than the ones I'm used to at home, though," Daz added.

Mammoth in size, it appeared from nowhere and stood behind the counter, its shell and claws a rusty orange enhanced by a dappled grey symmetrical pattern. Its eyes were like expensive rubies, neither one looking in the same direction at any one time.

"What star sign are you then? Seen sumat similar." The crab tapped the counter as it tried to gather its thoughts. "No! Can't put my claw on it."

"Star sign? I'm no star sign!" Daz paused for a moment and took a deep breath. "I've got it on good authority from Clement, who I'll have you know is a Sagittarian..."

"That's it, took the words right out of my mouth! You're a Sagittarian, I knew I'd seen your sort before."

"Without the ass though," Daz chuckled. "In fact, I'm an element. You see, I'm from Earth ... that's what Clement told me anyway, erm, well..." Daz was talking complete nonsense, having become totally tongue-tied and even managing to confuse himself in the process.

"Don't forget little old me! The name's Shai, but I'm definitely no star sign and have lived my whole life in Aries."

"Who said that?" The crab's eyes circled round the room until it finally located Shai.

"A snack ... yum..." The crab's large pincers ended up in knots as they snapped uncontrollably in different directions. Its misjudgment was all that prevented Shai from becoming an entrée, its eyes and claws totally out of sync with each other.

"Shai, whatever you do stay out of sight!" Daz grabbed him and held him firmly in the palm of his hand.

"Good job you're here now and not in Aries with that volcano erupting and all. Anyway, now you've put your pet away I think we'll get down to business, my friend. The name's Mesi, welcome to Illecebra; if you've got the notion I've got the potion, whatever your heart so desires."

"The volcano?" Daz gulped. *I do hope Gee's okay*, he thought to himself. With his short attention span, Daz's thoughts soon veered off in a different direction. "First on my list, Mister, is definitely wings; I want to fly like Shai." Daz ran round and round, his arms outstretched, making odd noises as he tried to imitate a plane in flight.

"It's Miss not Mister. Here, males are the weaker sex. As for your wish, only crabs and Goylins can benefit from my potions. But..." she went on as she leant over the counter to whisper in Daz's ear, "...there's always ways to get around these little problems and I think I may have just the one for you and that little bug of yours. You see, I can always turn you into Goylins."

Shai wriggled out of Daz's tight grip. "'Ang on a sec, Clement had wings and he didn't have to turn into some odd-looking goblin."

"Goylins you mean! They have very different attributes to your average everyday goblin. Don't you see? As soon as you've used the potions you want, I have an antidote that will turn you back to your former selves. Then you can go on your way."

"Why was Clement allowed to take his wings with him?" Shai asked, still not convinced, though he felt a little braver and flew and landed on the counter; maybe a tad too close for comfort as Mesi's claws were in striking distance, but he was determined to get his point across.

"This was a potion well earned, a special reservation. That's why he was able to take them through the gate. But nothing comes without a price tag, you should know that by now; nothing in life is free." Mesi turned her back on them, stretched up to the top shelf and removed two small shells. She then placed them on the counter in front of Daz and Shai. "I haven't got time for time wasters; you've got two choices, drink up or get out of my shop!"

"If you turn into a Goylin, Shai, at least you won't end up becoming someone's crab sandwich! Remember, if we're not happy we can always change back," Daz said, becoming more and more impatient. He hoped Shai felt the same gut-wrenching excitement he did.

Daz's persuasiveness had started to rub off on Shai, especially at the thought of ending up on someone's dinner plate.

"Okay, okay, but still think there's something fishy about all of this ... like how come Wilton is still a Goylin..."

"For a bug, I'll have you know, you're getting very annoying! I think I've answered enough of your questions." Mesi shook her head, her patience now wearing extremely thin. "But if you really must know, a lot of star signs are happier as Goylins living in Cancer than they would be returning to their own star signs. It's their choice, so everything you see here is above board, but if you don't believe me then buzz off, little bug, I've got bigger fish to fry." Mesi flicked her pincer across the counter, which sent the little firefly into the air and out of the way; just long enough for Daz to lift the snail-shaped shell to his lips and drink the bitter substance inside.

"Yuk, that was disgusting; don't smell too nice either!" A foul fishy aroma travelled up his nostrils.

A disorientated Shai made a crash landing on Daz's shoulder.

"Well, Shai," Daz said, "looks like we're going to have to do it the hard way with you. You'll thank me in the long run, you'll see, duckie." He placed Shai in the palm of his hand, picked up the grey bonnet shell and poured exactly three drops to cover him from head to toe. A few minutes went by and nothing happened.

"I thought we were gunna turn into Goylins, duck?"

"Patience, my dears."

The words had barely left Mesi's mouth when the transformation started to occur. Daz's skin began to bubble and foam, like he was on fire. Burning pains shot through his body that were so bad he fell to the floor. Enveloped like a chrysalis, he rolled around until totally exhausted.

Mesi looked down at him. "You make one hell of an ugly Goylin!" She bent over and lent him a claw, and Daz pulled himself back up to his feet, his bulbous nose now only just above the counter.

"…Hmm, Mesi, I must have lost about three feet!"

"You've gained half of that on ya nose, haven't ya!" Shai chuckled as he sat on the counter and kicked his legs backwards and forwards.

"You're a Goylin too, Shai! It's worked … I've never known pain like that before!" Daz said, obviously still in shock.

"Pain? What pain?" Shai jumped to the floor and admired his

and Daz's new physiques. "Bit of a problem, Mesi … haven't seen many naked Goylins around here, and Daz can fit both of us in what he's wearing." His old clothes hung off him like a big sack. "Think we'll need a new wardrobe."

"Forget about the wardrobe," Daz said. "Think my potion was a blumin' dud'en; that was agony, me duck! Think you flies must have a much higher pain threshold."

Mesi briefly disappeared and then returned with two brand new seaweed outfits and spanking new boots.

"We're Wilton parts two and three now," Daz chuckled as they dressed. "Bit cold round ya bits, ain't it, duck?"

"Never mind ya bits, I'm quite happy being a three-foot Goylin. Beats being a three-inch fly any day!" Shai grinned.

Daz sighed as he felt the leathery skin on his face. "Bet I'm well ugly now!"

"You weren't exactly good looking before," Mesi muttered under her breath.

"Now I've done this, it's 'bout time I had me wings, Mesi!" Daz said; he couldn't wait to fly.

"I'm sorry, guess something must have slipped my mind. You see, potions will only give you wishes relevant to your star sign."

"We don't have wings on Earth, Mesi."

"Exactly my point. What do you have on Earth that brings you pleasure?"

Daz scratched his head. "It's a hard one is this, me duck…" But somehow the answer suddenly seemed to be on the tip of his tongue. "FOOD! That's it! What say we share a twelve-inch pizza, Shai? They're super yummy!"

Shai looked dumbstruck. "What's pizza? My diet consists of pollen and plant parts, but I'll try anything once."

Mesi moved from shelf to shelf, eyeing up her vast range of shells. "Think I've found just the one. Just one thing, before you can enjoy any of my potions there is something you must do for me." Mesi handed them two empty shells.

"You don't want urine samples do ya, ducky?" Daz spluttered.

"No, no, don't be daft. How should I put it? For want of better words you could call it a keepsake, a deposit if you like," Mesi replied. "Just blow hard inside them," she urged, and tapped impatiently on the counter.

"We may as well seal the deal, no time to waste." Daz's stomach rumbled uncontrollably and he couldn't wait any longer.

They both blew as hard as they could into the palm-sized shells. Mesi then took each one and placed them under the counter out of sight. "Think this belongs to you," she said, handing Daz a fan-shaped shell similar to the lion's paw only smaller. "Drink 2.5 cubitors each, no more no less." She passed Daz a small measuring cylinder, and between them they poured it out the best they could; then both took a large gulp.

"Yuk!" Daz shuddered.

The bitterness grabbed the back of his throat as he struggled to swallow the foul-tasting liquid. Then, to their delight, two steaming hot pizzas appeared in front of them on the counter. Daz's mouth watered. "Now that's a wish and a half … I could kiss you, Mesi!"

Mesi lifted her pincers to shield her face from Daz's advances. "YUK! A kiss off a Goylin? Don't think so somehow."

"So that's a pizza?" Shai poked at it. "Err, what are those ghastly things sticking up?" He wobbled them between his fingers.

"Fish heads!!! That's vile!! I asked for a pizza not a fish pie!" Daz barked, more than a little disappointed.

"You're in Cancer now; everything is fish or shellfish, you should know that. Like it or lump it, that's what you've got," Mesi growled sarcastically.

Daz wasn't going to let a good pizza go to waste, so he picked the nasty little suckers out and wolfed down each slice, hardly taking the time to chew.

"Buuuuuuuuuuuuuurrrrrrrrrrrpppppppppp! Wasn't at all bad," he said, his burp and words merging together.

Shai just picked at his, finding the whole thing very unappetising. He might have been a Goylin, but his taste buds were still very much those of a firefly.

"Waste not want not," Daz said. He dug into pizza number two and polished that off as well.

"Now, Mesi, for our main wish, give us a potion that'll send me home, back to Earth; and Shai, of course."

Mesi crawled out from behind the counter and handed Daz his old clothes.

"Well, my little Goylins, a word in your shell – that's one wish you'll never be granted. You took my potion out of pure greed, and although you were quite happy to become Goylins so you could have your every wish and dream fulfilled, this has now turned full circle and it's the greed that has you." She ushered them towards the opening they had come in by and pushed them out. "GO … shop till you drop, to your hearts' content, and get used to your new home. I can assure you, you will never, ever leave Cancer."

"'Ang on, duck, what about the antidote you promised us?"

"Don't always believe what you see or hear, not in Antares, not in the zodiac," Mesi said. She gave them a smug smile, turned and disappeared back into her quaint little shop.

"I'm not having that! A promise is a promise where I come from!" Daz shouted, took Shai by the hand and marched back in.

But the shop was now just a derelict shell; no shelves, no counter and no Mesi.

Shai looked troubled. "Think we best find Eve before we get into any more trouble!" he said, and they ran blindly outside.

"I don't see them anywhere, Wilton!" Eve popped her head inside yet another shop in the busy village.

Wilton frowned. "If they'd listened to me earlier they wouldn't even have contemplated shopping, especially on their own."

Eve and Wilton walked the length and breadth of the village several times over, yet still Daz or Shai were nowhere to be seen.

"Alright, duck!"

A familiar voice chirped up from the crowd. Eve turned and looked around.

"Daz, is that you?"

But all she could see were Goylins and a selection of different star signs. Something tugged on her coat, and she looked down and saw a Goylin she'd never met before.

"Eve, it's me! Daz!"

"And me Shai!" Now two Goylins stared up at her.

"Don't lie to me! Daz is a human and Shai a firefly, away with you!" Eve had never heard so much nonsense.

"Well no longer, me duck, we are now both bona fide Goylins."

Those two little words were all it took to stop Eve dead in her tracks, as no one but Daz referred to someone as 'me duck'. Her face dropped.

"Well, Eve, they had the chance, they could have listened; I only gave out good advice. Due to their ignorance they are now trapped in Cancer forever like me!" Wilton frowned as he glared at the two new Goylins. "You see, I wasn't always a Goylin. I came from Sagittarius to claim my wings, but the fool that I was I also didn't listen and went in the one shop I was told not to. Tricked by a crab, I changed into a Goylin … and you know the rest, I'm still here. All you had to do was find the gate, but your curiosity got the better of you. Goylins can't pass through, and now you're neither one thing nor another, just Cancer's joke."

"But, but, Mesi, she promised us an antidote! We went back into the shop but it was empty," Daz dithered. "This seaweed's so cold!" He couldn't help but fidget in his new clothing.

"Well, you're holding your jacket, aren't you? Might be too long, but just drape it round your shoulders, it's better than nothing," Eve suggested. "And as for you, Shai, there's a T-shirt going spare."

Daz handed it to Shai, who struggled to pull it over his enlarged head.

"Mesi's got to be around here somewhere! Come on, Shai, let's go find her!" Daz said.

"Good luck with that one, Daz; if it were that easy all us Goylins would be doing it. We don't stay here by choice, you know. We're treated as vermin; it has its perks at times, but before you find out what it's really like it's too late! If it looks too good to be true, it usually is. You, like me, will have to learn the hard way." Wilton gave a loud sigh. "Oh well, at least you can pass through the gate, Eve. Come, I'll walk you there, it's not safe for a Merussk like you."

"A WHAT! What do you mean it's not safe?" Eve's face looked anything but impressed.

"It means un-changeling. You're vulnerable here, believe me; go while you still can. I'll try and help your friends, but there are no guarantees." Wilton took the lead, but felt that Eve, Daz and Shai hadn't taken him seriously.

Wilton stood still for a minute. "It's around here somewhere, this is where they all come and go."

"Well I can't see no gate, me duck." Daz squinted. "Think I might need to borrow your contact lenses, Eve. Us Goylins don't seem to have the sharpest of eyesights."

"Yeah, I've got the eyesight of a bat now. When I was a firefly my eyes were second to none."

"It's there! Over there, as large as life!" Eve ran towards it. "Get the key ready, Daz, to lock it when we get through to the other side."

"It's not that easy for our kind," Wilton piped up. "The reason we can't see it is because it doesn't exist for our sort, so we can't pass through what's not there."

"Well I can see it for all of us!" Eve grabbed Daz's little hand. "I'll get us through." She took no notice of Wilton's over-exaggerated hysteria.

"Okay, you do that!" Wilton snapped. "I'll wait here for you shall I? Coz I assure you, Daz and Shai will be back! Don't you think I've tried myself? Been there, got the T-shirt (seaweed though it may be)."

The three joined hands and stepped into the gate's opening, but no matter how many ways or from different directions they tried to enter, just as Wilton had told them, only Eve could pass through.

"Now do you believe me?" Wilton called after them. "Go, Eve, quickly. I'll look after your friends; I'll take them back to my home."

Momentarily, Eve disappeared and Wilton gave a sigh of relief, but this was to be short-lived, as she had no intention of going anywhere without Daz.

"We came here together and by hook or by crook we're going to leave together! I only had a quick glimpse, but what I saw was probably worse than it is here."

"Stupid, ignorant girl, don't you understand you've just sealed your own fate? 'Spose I better take you home then." Wilton looked anything but pleased, but he couldn't see another option. "Eve, there is something I must tell you; not here though, too many earwiggers about for my liking."

The three sauntered along, none feeling very much like talking. They passed back through the little village with its queer shops and folk, after which they found themselves in a much more open and rocky terrain, where a number of large shells were situated in no particular order. Daz's voice broke the silence.

"Hey look, it's a black murex, a turban, a Nautilus, and oh, look, a helmet." The names rolled off his tongue. "I'm turning into quite the intellect, but I've no idea where I gained all this information."

Shai grunted. "Pffhht, for all we know, Daz, it's just made-up nonsense!"

"No, Shai, he's right, so right that wherever he came from he must have been a conchologist," Wilton said, taken aback by Daz's impeccable knowledge.

"A conch what!?" Shai looked more confused than ever.

"It's someone who collects shells; now who's the dimwit?" Finally Daz had one up on someone.

"We know the names, Wilton, but what are they? What are they used for?" Eve asked as they walked past.

"What do you think they are? Homes for us Goylins!" He led them up a narrow path to a shell that was the tallest and narrowest of them all.

"It's a unicorn!"

The shell had a coral-coloured complexion that was broken up by its deep ridges, giving it the appearance of a helter-skelter as it spiralled from top to bottom.

"Okay, Daz, you've made your point. Welcome to my home; might not look much from the outside, but it's done me proud." Wilton took a little key from his pocket and popped it in the lock of a frameless door.

"Think we'll fit?" Daz whispered to Eve.

"You're half the size you were," she chuckled. It was she who had to squeeze through the narrow entrance.

It had a deceptively spacey interior, and Daz couldn't help but go round and touch everything in sight. The inside was immaculate, a place for everything and everything in its place. Engraved ornaments carved out of pearl rested on narrow ledges, and the quaintest little vases were filled with a mixture of the most beautiful geraniums and white roses. A tall, shiny metal table stood against a large curved wall, which was masked by a spellbinding mural of a full moon being held up high in the sky by the pincers of a very ornate-looking crab. Multifaceted mother of pearl bowls also lay scattered on various items of furniture, each decorated with one solitary water lily, which lifted them to a completely different dimension. The whole room captivated the three of them, even down to the quirky wooden furniture, all of which Wilton later explained was made out of maple wood. In the middle of the room stood the most elaborate spiral staircase, embellished with a silver trim and enhanced with opal hieroglyphics and maple wood carvings. It was utterly breathtaking.

"See, told ya there were some perks to being a Goylin!" Wilton said, enjoying their admiration. "All our furniture and decor comes from Cancer's most treasured and richest assets, pearl being the most obvious." He went on. "Then there's my table, which happens to be a very sought-after metal; you know, it's the same as the trim on my staircase."

"For what reason would metal be sought after, duck? It's just metal after all."

"As I was saying, Daz, it's not just metal, it's silver! A very special silver that can't be found anywhere else. So now you've seen it, this is my home, a home I'm very proud of." Wilton sat on a wooden stool. "I gather you like what you see, but what do you see?" Wilton continued. "These so-called treasures are just bars, bars that make one very elaborate prison; I suggest you get used to it fast, because this is the path you have chosen."

Shai walked around and admired the flowers. "I can't believe I used to eat these. It's nice having two legs, being tall and feeling important for a change, knowing someone won't swat me against a wall and dispose of me without a second thought. I could actually get quite used to being a Goylin."

"Speak for yourself, duck! I've shrunk, got a tail and am even uglier than I was before!"

"Daz, I'm sure your new looks will grow on you," Eve said, grabbing his tail and giving it a sharp tug, which made him jump. "I think they could even grow on me in time," she laughed as she leant on the banister of the spiral staircase. "Can I have a look upstairs please?" She was dying to see if it held the same beauty.

"Well, you can if you like, but every room you see is a mirror image of the one you're standing in now," Wilton replied.

"What about the bedrooms, duckie?"

"Bedrooms? You'll find no bedrooms here. Us Goylins never sleep, our body clocks are very different; that's why I tried to tell you earlier that you need to be extremely careful. Sleep brings with it great danger, it's a curse in Cancer; that's the reason you needed to go through the gate." Wilton's eyes met Eve's.

"It can't be that hard to stay awake!" she snapped. "I'm not even tired!"

"Oh, but you will be, just give it time," Wilton added smugly.

CHAPTER EIGHT

Search for Mesi

"Take it you both went into the mother of pearl shop then? Of course you did; you wouldn't have been Goylins if you went to any of the others! I fell for it too! Who did you say served you?"

"It was Mesi, Wilton," Shai was quick to answer.

"You can certainly pick them, can't you! Mesi of all Cancerians! Right, I'll go and see if I can get you out of this mess, and Eve … please stay awake! Before I go, make yourself at home, there's food in the Ramous." Wilton left and closed the door behind him.

"How are we supposed to know what a Ramous is?" Eve said; all of a sudden, she seemed to have discovered her appetite.

"Just follow me, duck. It's a shell, and I know them all. I'll find it." Daz ferreted round and it didn't take him long to find it. He was quite surprised by its intricacy, with tiny compartments fitting together like a complex jigsaw, each containing different types of fish, bugs and seaweed. "Clever little chap that Wilton, got his own fridge freezer down 'ere! I say we tuck in," he said, and pulled up three stools for them to sit on.

"These aren't stools, Daz, they're starfish!" Eve said, remaining on her feet. "They don't look very durable, and I'm a lot bigger than you pair. I'd hate to break one, Wilton's been good to us."

Daz tucked in hungrily, but Eve and Shai were anything but tempted by what Wilton's fridge had to offer.

"While I think about it, something's been bothering me for a while," Daz said; bits of chewed-up fish hung out of his mouth as he tried hard to chew with his one solitary tooth.

"Surprise, surprise, the mess we're in! I think there's something bothering all of us!" Eve scolded.

A knock on the door stopped the conversation dead.

"It must be Wilton. Didn't expect him back yet," Shai said, and ran hastily over to open it. But what a surprise he got; it wasn't Wilton at all.

"Hello," a soft voice spoke out. "Heard we've been blessed with new Goylins, so thought the least I could do was pop over and show you the ropes, so to speak."

She was definitely a female Goylin, with much softer features and her wispy hair replaced by a thick black mane that flowed over her shoulders and framed her elfin-like face.

"I'm Kerricia; pleased to meet you. Thought I'd give you a guided tour, maybe even set you up in your new home."

"Well, now I'm getting used to these two legs, may as well put them to use. Come on, Daz, Eve; Wilton will never know," Shai pleaded as he stepped outside to join Kerricia.

"You can count me out!" Eve hissed. "How's it going to look if Wilton comes back and none of us are here? We can't just throw his hospitality back in his face! I'm not going anywhere."

"What about you then, Daz?" Shai asked sheepishly, pushing his luck.

The expression on Daz's face made it obvious to Eve what he wanted to do.

"Just go then! You don't need to stay around here and babysit me. I'll put Wilton in the picture when he gets back," Eve said, and sat down on the floor cross-legged.

"Well, me duck, we'd be daft not to take her up on her offer. We won't be long." Daz gave Eve a cheeky wink. "I'll leave me trousers and trainers in your good care. By the way, lock the door and don't let anyone in."

"Kerricia, please take us back to the village where we can try out more potions, there's so many things I want," Shai said. He felt cheated by his only wish, a pizza that Daz ended up eating anyway.

"Hold it there, Shai!" Daz jumped in quickly. "No more shops, no more anything! We've let Eve and Wilton down enough already."

"The potions can become quite addictive, and to be honest we hardly ever use them; that is, unless it's an absolute emergency," Kerricia explained.

"That's why we changed into Goylins, to use the potions. That's what Mesi told us anyway," Daz insisted, as Kerricia led

111

them away from the shell in the opposite direction to the village where Shai wanted to go so badly.

"The potions encourage greed, and you'll just live for possessions and the highs the potions provide for you. You'll have no purpose or worth; in fact, you'll just be one of them." Kerricia pointed her finger.

"Ay, what's ya point, duck?" Daz struggled to understand.

"My point is what I'm pointing at; you'll become just like them over there!"

"What, shells?" Daz couldn't find any reasoning in what she was saying.

"Yes, shells, empty shells. Is that what you want?"

All of a sudden things became much clearer and Daz and Shai shook their heads; neither wanted to become the empty shell Kerricia spoke of.

"Now you can see why the potions are off limits. We don't have to rely on those manipulating crabs; we have our own towns and villages, we make our own fun, and although trapped in Cancer, we are genuinely happy here. Those who can't settle and want to return to their own star signs are usually the ones who try all the potions, think there's a way out, can't accept this is their life now and end up almost vacant beings."

"What star sign are you, Kerricia?" Shai asked.

"I'm a Piscean; greed got the better of me too. Given the chance I'd have loved to go back. I was homesick in the beginning, but now I'm settled. Cancer's become my home, and in time it will become yours."

She led them into another village, where Goylins were going about their daily lives. Younger Goylins played unusual games, ones that Daz had never seen before. They sang catchy little tunes, their voices high-pitched but sweet nevertheless. It even had its own marketplace, and numerous stalls were scattered around as the Goylins shouted their wares. The fruit and vegetables looked absolutely amazing, their colours much more vibrant than Daz had ever seen at home. The scent of the fruit rose to greet them, and Daz's and Shai's mouths watered. A young Goylin must have noticed, as he bounded over and offered Daz the ripest piece of watermelon he had ever seen. Boy was it good, and as he took a bite all the juice ran down his chin.

"Eeew, Daz, you're dribbling!" Shai said.

"See if you can do any better then, duck!" Daz said, and shoved a large piece into Shai's open mouth.

Shai took a bite and found himself in the same predicament. Kerricia laughed at the funny pair, who were now an unsightly sticky mess.

"Looking at you two I think we'd best head in that direction," she said, pointing towards a couple of small rock pools that lay hidden under Cancer's very own maple trees. At first glance Shai and Daz saw them as rock pools too, but their eyes deceived them. The water channelled off in a number of different directions, like small streams, yet all met at the same point. These widened into vast open lakes and were cleverly divided into leisure areas, where the Goylins spent their spare time. They seemed to be having endless fun as they swung off the maple trees' large branches and jumped into the water to see who could make the biggest splash. Others sat in oval wooden boats and various sized shells – their own makeshift dingies.

"This is the sort of life I could get used to," Shai said, as he lay back on the bank totally relaxed and reached into the cool waters to wash the melon juice from his hands and mouth.

Daz glanced down into the lake and had the first glimpse of his new, not so good-looking face.

"Come on, fancy a dip, Daz?" Shai asked, proceeding to wade in up to his knees. He lifted Daz's T-shirt up and tied it in a knot around his waist.

"No! You can't go into the shell homes wet; we'll come back later if you like," Kerricia shouted, and led a disappointed Daz and Shai away from the market and beautiful lakes.

"There are two plots vacant at the moment. Over to your far right you'll see wentletrap, and opposite a pearl troca," Kerricia pointed out two of the many shell houses in a quaint built-up neighbourhood.

Out of the darkness, little lanterns shone like street lamps that resembled fibre optic Christmas decorations as they lit up the street. They watched as many Goylins returned to relax for a while.

"When will it get light again round here? When we came it was sunny, not a cloud to be seen, the sky a clear blue."

"I'll stop you there, Daz. Cancer hardly ever sees the sun. Our ruling planet is the moon, and daylight to us is just a glimpse; you were fortunate enough to catch it." Kerricia opened the door to the pearl troca.

"Don't like the look of this one, duck! Looks like a common snail shell," Daz said, feeling disheartened. "Can't imagine living in something like this for the rest of me days."

But Daz had to eat his words as, once again, the inside was very spacious. Unfurnished, it had a staircase that ran down the circular walls and it was very much open-plan.

"Both shells are unfurnished; however, whichever one you decide on, your neighbouring Goylins will help you with the interior and assist you with the move," Kerricia explained, heading towards the stairs. "Do you want to go up and have a look?"

"Nah, ducky, no point if Wiltons is anything to go on. It's the same top and bottom anyway."

"Come on then, I'll show you plot number two across the street."

They left the pearl troca behind and headed towards the wentletrap. Its appearance was very different; it lay at an angle in a horizontal position and looked like a decoration you'd normally see on top of a cake, piped in pink icing – it was beautiful.

"Looks more like a blumin' bungalow!" Daz said, as he walked in followed by a not-so-enthusiastic Shai.

It was like nothing he'd ever seen before; everything was the wrong way round or the wrong way up. Stairs spiralled around the walls, but due to the shell lying on its side, climbing them was an absolute impossibility.

"THIS IS THE ONE! Me topsy-turvy home!" Daz exclaimed. He loved it and could hardly contain himself. "This is it, it's the one."

"Are you mad? There's neither rhyme nor reason to this house! I like order not disorder. It's impractical, unworkable and unconventional, for anything that has two legs that is. Maybe if I were to turn into a firefly again I'd reconsider, but no way am I living in this monstrosity!" Shai paused briefly. "Anyway, it's not just up to you, Daz, there's a third party you're forgetting about."

It was a third party they'd both forgotten about for too long.

"Kerricia, we've got to go, ducky! We've left Eve for far too long; we weren't supposed to leave her at all. We'll bring her back with us tomorrow and decide together."

Daz and Shai rushed off. They hurried past the rock pools and through the little village where the market stalls stood, which were now being packed away.

"Ay, Daz? Shai?"

"It couldn't be, could it?" Shai whispered.

But it was. Wilton's dulcet tones rang loudly in their ears, and he trotted towards them looking around for something, or rather someone.

"Kerricia took us house hunting," Shai said sheepishly.

"Yeah, found a couple of beauties, one in particular," Daz said, his excitement overflowing.

"We're undecided, Daz!" Shai snapped. He had no intention of giving up without a fight.

"'Spose Eve is still pottering around, making a final decision for you? Typical woman, ay!" Wilton sniggered, expecting Eve to appear at any moment.

"Err, well, actually, as a matter of fact..." Daz scratched his head awkwardly.

"Get to it, stop wittering, haven't got all day!" Wilton said, growing bored of Daz's indecisiveness.

"It's like this, Wilton; she didn't want you going back to an empty house and thought you'd worry. She didn't want you to think us rude, so she's waiting for us. It's okay though, duck, she locked the door." Daz couldn't understand the sudden change in Wilton's expression.

"You did what? You idiots!" He paused for a second and tried to compose himself. "Well, if any harm has come to her it'll be on your heads. For your sakes, she better be okay!" He turned, pushed past Daz and Shai, and marched angrily in the direction of his house.

Wilton's shell looked like a bombsite. The front door now had a jagged opening and shards of broken shell lay scattered on the floor.

"Eve, Eve!" Wilton called, but there was no reply. "Stay down here, I'll check upstairs." He sprinted up the spiral staircase as fast as his little legs would let him and turned the rooms upside down in his search.

"No luck down here!" Shai bellowed.

Daz, who felt responsible for Eve, didn't quite know what to do with himself. He decided to stay out of the way, as he remembered the old saying out of sight out of mind and hoped this would be the case here.

Wilton leant over the banister. "I think you'd both better get up here, see what it is you've done!"

Daz and Shai rushed up the staircase.

"She's here!" a breathless Shai yelled, before breathing a sigh of relief.

"I knew everything would be okay!" Daz threw his arms around Shai's neck and hugged him tightly.

"Well, if that looks fine to you, you need your head looking at!" Wilton growled, as he stroked her hand.

Daz ambled forward and looked at Eve as she sat slumped in a wicker chair.

"I knew it! I knew if you left her alone she'd nod off! You see, forty winks are all it takes and it's gone!"

"What's gone, Wilton? You're making no sense!" Daz crouched down next to Eve.

"Her soul's gone! They've taken it!" he spluttered. "Feel and see for yourself. Careful mind, she's fragile."

"Eve, fragile? Ha, I think not! She can throw a mean punch if someone rubs her up the wrong way," Daz laughed, shaking her arm abruptly.

An unusual cracking noise took him by surprise, and he pulled the cuff of her coat away from her arm and peered up her sleeve.

"Her arm, it's starting to cave in!" he shrieked.

"Well what do you expect of an empty shell? You see, they crack and break so easily. That's all that's left of Eve now! The crabs can sense sleepers a mile off, that's why they've broken into my home and claimed another full soul. They take it by way of her mouth; a Nerite's shell is placed over her face and the soul is absorbed each time she takes a breath until there's nothing left. By now, she'll be well on her way to the Wheel of Life, where her journey will start to the Underworld." Wilton sighed.

"Seems simple to me," Daz said, appearing to have got his second wind. "If someone takes something that belongs to you, you just simply take it back." He kissed Eve softly on the cheek. "It's such a shame; I like Eve, I like her very much." Daz gently placed his jacket over her. "Sleep tight, Evie," he whispered. "Don't let the bedbugs bite."

"If only it were that easy, Daz," Wilton said, and solemnly ran his fingers over Eve's porcelain face. "You see, nobody ventures into the Underworld, that's the crabs' domain where most souls are absorbed ready for dispatch to the shops."

Shai shuddered. "Are you telling me that we drank someone's soul?"

Wilton clapped his hands. "HOORAY! At last, you're starting to get it! That's why you were able to become Goylins. All the shops but one that is. You only have to give one of your attributes; humour, braveness, quick wittedness, they are just a few of the many you can donate, and after doing so you are free to leave."

"Yeah, you remember, Daz, like Clement; that's what he must have done to get his wings," Shai interrupted.

"But you went in Illecebra, Cancer's homemade trap!" Wilton hissed.

Daz and Shai never seemed to take him seriously.

"Well, I've got all my attributes, and I'm getting even cleverer!" Daz insisted.

Shai shook his head. As time went on Daz became more and more of an embarrassment.

"You both blew into a shell, didn't you? Yeah, thought so!"

"Well, me duck, we've lost nothin then, 'ave we, Wilton?"

"That's where you're wrong," Wilton paused briefly; he felt rather peckish and grabbed a fishy snack from his Ramous before he took up where he had left off.

"The reason you can't change back is because when you blew into the shell, half of your souls were taken too. Why do you think it hurt so much? That's the reason you must live out the rest of your days here as Goylins. The shells now float in limbo, an eternal sea of souls waiting to be plucked from the Underworld where they are added to one of the many potions or absorbed by the waiting crabs. They need one hundred half souls or one full soul to attain their freedom…"

"So our imprisonment buys their freedom?" Shai backed away. The fishy snack had had an adverse effect on Wilton, whose breath smelt so putrid Shai could hardly bare to stay in the same room.

"YES! So now maybe you understand. I tried to find Mesi before your shells were placed on the Wheel of Life, but it was too late, Mesi had already taken them." Wilton paced up and down. "Star signs entering Cancer are warned on arrival, and most take the advice given and leave through the gate instantly. It's only the gullible ones that keep the Goylins in existence here." Wilton lifted up his freestanding oval looking glass.

The uninvited soul snatchers had shattered more than his image, they'd broken his heart, and according to Daz he could expect the next seven years to bring him nothing but bad luck.

"Why do the crabs absorb the souls? And how can a soul's potion turn us into Goylins? I don't understand!" Daz said, totally bewildered by what he had heard. He just couldn't seem to get his head round any of it.

"I've told you once, boy! The souls buy Cancer's freedom; only then can they reside in Paradisum. They live in a euphoric state in their own little slice of heaven. You think our villages are nice, but we just live on the outskirts and get the scraps and leftovers; we're no more than vermin. As for the souls, when we seal the deal by blowing into an empty shell we lose half of everything we are, and all the goodness is absorbed by the crabs, in time giving them all the good qualities they need to be accepted into Paradisum. Again, as I said, they need one hundred part souls or one full soul. The potions we drink are the bad qualities that each star sign possesses. Why do you think we look so ugly? The reason we can't see the gate is because we are only half of our former selves, not true beings, and with no self worth, no purpose, we are … and will always be a Cancerian's joke!"

Wilton opened a little cupboard at the top of the stairs and took out what looked like a witch's broomstick. The mother of pearl vases were smashed and the pieces lay embedded in the wooden floorboards, covered by pretty white lilies that now lay wilted and dying. He took his frustration out with each stroke of the broom until every last fragment and the remains of his tropical plants were in a tidy heap, ready for him to dispose of.

Daz and Shai stood in complete silence, saddened by Wilton's grief. His home and everything he'd known were now in tatters. In more ways than one, the realisation finally kicked in. What had they done? They also ferreted through the wreckage and tried to piece together any furniture and ornaments they could salvage. It felt like they were putting Wilton's life back together for him, but their attention was drawn back to the young lady who sat lifeless.

"Eve's soul … can we get it back, or is it gone forever?" Daz asked, suddenly feeling overwhelmed by guilt.

He knelt beside Eve, loosened her bun and ran his fingers through her wavy blonde hair. "I'm so sorry, ducky." A tear rolled down his cheek. He couldn't believe his friend was no more, just an empty vessel. "Is there nothing we can do?"

"I've only heard of one Goylin ever venturing down the Wheel of Life, but unfortunately for him he was never seen or heard of again! So as you can see, the chances of saving her are very bleak." Wilton took a last look at the remnants of the little shell he'd nurtured and built up over time and started to make his way back down the spiral staircase.

Daz and Shai said their last farewells to Eve before they followed.

"Well, we owe it to her to try. What do you say, Daz?" Shai asked. "We must give it a go; she wouldn't have given up if it was us."

"So we're all decided then! What now?" The pair waited in anticipation for Wilton's forthcoming plan.

"Well, one thing for sure is we can't do it alone, we need someone on the inside. Any Goylin that dares to set foot on the

Wheel of Life and enter the next two stages of the Underworld will immediately be put to death!" Wilton explained. "I'm certainly not going to leave my life hanging in the balance, for you or any other Goylins!"

"What about Mesi? She might help us, duck," Daz suggested, after Wilton's crab mural brought her to mind – the only item that hadn't been destroyed (funny that).

"Hmmmm, doubt it very much, as she was the one that got you into this mess in the first place. Remember, she didn't offer me any help either. When I tried to bargain with Mesi and get your souls back she was having none of it!"

"They say there's strength in numbers, so I say we go back to the shop and give it one last shot," Daz said, trying to pull Wilton away from his mural as he took his frustration out on the painting, which now looked even more abstract after his destructive touch.

Wilton felt he had nothing left to lose, and agreed to help Daz and Shai in their plight to go in search of Mesi. He took one more look around his dishevelled home. Before he walked out, he automatically reached into his pocket for his key.

"Don't s'pose I need to worry about locking up this time," he said sadly.

Wilton knew the area like the back of his hand. All the other shells stood immaculate and untouched, and there was a relaxed air as laughter rose inside them as they walked by on the way to Illecebra. The Goylins had made the best of a bad situation and turned a few empty shells into a happy and buzzing community. The most gloriously tended gardens were fenced off with chain-link gates, and extraordinarily shaped flower beds were graced with aromatic white roses, complemented by the deep shades of germaniums in vivid reds and variegated pinks. Over time they had grown self-sufficient with their well-maintained vegetable patches, where hearty white and Savoy cabbages mixed in with bottle-green curly kale grew in abundance, all set in perfectly dug-out earthen rows, next to which the crispiest-looking lettuces flourished. Other gardens seemed to concentrate more on root vegetables, with a good array of turnips and potatoes. They had their expertise down to a fine art with their quaint spice and herb gardens, with saxifrage, verbena and tarragon being just a few that added taste to their home-grown delights. Their initial greed had turned around and become overwhelming contentment.

Daz and Shai lagged behind as Wilton strode on in front with a pace that seemed to quicken, their eyes everywhere. The realisation of all the hard work that had gone into making the shell houses and beautiful gardens what they were gave them a sense of pride in these self-sufficient little beings.

They had walked for quite a while when Wilton began to complain of aching legs. This didn't seem to faze Daz or Shai, who seemed to enjoy the ambience that the Goylins' life lent them. Their minds wandered from Eve and their unenviable journey ahead to save her. They'd both looked around this vibrant and workable neighbourhood earlier, yet on reflection it was only now that they gained the foresight and knowledge to take it all in. Eventually, they reached the village; it lay quiet, the earlier hubbub having died down a great deal, and just a few Goylins scurried here and there as they headed home. Visiting star signs hurriedly made their way back to the gate. As they approached, Illecebra's beauty entranced Daz as much on his second visit as it had on his first, and butterflies rushed to his stomach.

"Well here goes nothin'," he said, and slipped apprehensively into the shop, followed by Shai and a rather reluctant Wilton.

"You're back again; more potions is it?" Mesi scowled, as she eyed up a suitable potion. "Another one of your special pizzas?" she grinned smugly.

Wilton hadn't got the time or patience for her sarcasm, and he banged his first down hard on the counter. "Now listen here, Mesi, you're the only one we can call on for help!"

"Help Goylins?!" She sidled over to the other side of the shell and tried hard to look preoccupied. "Sorry, can't do, won't do! I'M BUSY! Doing a stock check... Gotta have my shell in order, I'll have you know, unlike some..." She sneaked a look at Wilton to see if he had picked up on her ambiguous meaning. There wasn't a lot that went on around there that Mesi didn't know about!

"I've given you the same answer I gave you earlier, Wilton. See you brought ammunition with you this time!" Her vivid red eyes spun round like Catherine wheels as they darted in opposite directions while doing the best they could to centralise.

"You, crab, owe us big time! You tricked us!" Daz squared up to Mesi.

"Back off, Goylin, I trick no one. You took my potion of your own free will. I owe you nothing. Us crabs want for nothing, and we only take what other star signs allow us to. Now stop wasting my time and get out of my shop!" Mesi airlifted Daz in her sharp pincers and swung him back and forth by the scruff of his neck. "If you don't obey I can always help you on your way!"

"Mesi, we're desperate, there must be something we can do to make it worth your while?" Shai pleaded, thinking he might have more luck than his two comrades.

"Hmm, let me think now…" Mesi pondered. "Is it so important that the girl gets her soul back?"

"How do you know 'bout Eve?" Daz asked faint-heartedly, as his life still hung in the balance.

"What I don't know isn't worth knowing. Maybe there is a deal to be made here. If I agree to help you, you must promise me half of the girl's soul; so like you, she'll have to reside here as a Goylin forever. You see, nothing in Cancer comes for free. I want a soul for myself; this is not an everyday occurrence, and I don't usually gain the souls I collect."

"Don't mean to interrupt you, ducky, but you had both of our souls earlier!" Daz butted in.

"Are you trying to catch me out?" Mesi shook Daz angrily and dropped him to the floor like a sack of potatoes.

He jumped up. "Give them back, they don't belong to you!"

"I couldn't even if I wanted to! They're on the Wheel of Life heading for the sea of souls that reside in limbo. Eve's soul will take a very different course, bypassing limbo and heading straight to the Underworld, so it looks like that's where you need to go. If you make it there alive and manage to free her soul, I'll be there; I will lie in wait until I collect my half and any other stragglers along the way. Let's shake on it then!" She offered her claw to each Goylin in turn. "Quiet now, I need to think. Maybe it's a tall order, but it's the only way you're going to stand any kind of chance.

Darkness is on our side, and tonight of all nights we have a crescent moon, which will help our plight, as we'd definitely be apprehended if the moon was full." The coast was clear, so Mesi beckoned them and disappeared out of the shop. Shai and Daz checked to make sure and then followed behind.

Meanwhile, Wilton was busy pinching a few potions. *Just a little insurance*, he thought to himself, as he stuffed them into his pocket.

It was a long walk, and the floor was rugged and uneven. There were no Goylins in sight, and what looked like a large ghost town stretched out eerily in front of them. The crescent moon resembled an orange segment and gave out small rays of light. Daz turned for one last look as they left the village behind.

"Where are the shops, Mesi? They've all gone!"

"No, not gone, just choose not to be seen." Mesi didn't elaborate further, leaving them all at a loss for words.

The Goylins struggled to keep up, with Mesi's eight legs moving quickly in a zigzag motion.

They passed through what Mesi described as the real Cancer, where streams interlinked to form intricate networks of rock pools of all shapes and sizes. The moon's reflection left a silver sheen that floated on the surface and shifted its light between them. The pathways narrowed and grew steeper, and they had to step from one jagged rock to another as they attempted to balance on the large unstable stepping stones. Finally, they reached level ground and entered the mouth of a cave, which sucked them in. The air was cold and damp, and their voices echoed. The moon was there one minute and gone the next, shrouded as if by a vast cloak and now obsolete.

"I ain't going any further, ducky, can't see owt! It's suicide!" Daz backed off.

"Useless, all of you!" Mesi hissed. "Maybe this will do the trick." She seemed to dislocate one of her front claws and then reached up and unhinged her entire shell, which opened up like a book. Blindly, she ferreted around, obviously in search of something, but the Goylins were far too small to see what she was rummaging for. Then she catapulted an obscure object into the air before closing herself back up again.

"Just watch!" she boasted.

The three looked up and saw an unidentified entity open up in front of them to expose a blinding light, and an illuminous silver orb manifested itself, its transparent light hovering around the cavern.

"Just one of the many tricks I've got up my sleeve," she said, before leading them into the depths of the cave.

"Ha! Think you mean in your shell, don't you, ducky?" Daz sniggered to himself.

The largest rock pool imaginable stretched out before them, and midnight blue in colour it had the appearance of a large inkwell.

"We must move quickly!" Mesi stressed, an agitated tone to her voice. "The three of you need to search around the walls; there's a pulley with a wooden handle. It's quite well hidden, so you may need to move some rocks to find it. When you do locate it, turn it in a clockwise direction."

Through the shadows, the three Goylins felt their way up and over the slippery damp walls, pushing their fingers between the undulating cracks.

"Think I've got something here!" Shai shouted. "Lot bigger than I thought. Give us a hand, Daz, and you, Wilton, don't just stand watching me!" As hard as Shai tried, the handle didn't move an inch.

The three pitched in and the handle began to move downwards in a clockwise direction, soon gathering speed, and as it picked up momentum something floated to the surface.

"You've done it!" Mesi said, as she waded into the water.

"Hey, duck, what the heck are they?" Daz asked, none the wiser.

"I've told you 'bout the oyster farm, haven't I?" Mesi replied.

"Well no, as a matter of fact you haven't!" Shai couldn't believe their size.

"They ain't oysters, they're blumin' boats, duck!"

"They need to be that big to fit you inside," Mesi explained.

"'Ang on now, Mesi, I'm not sharing a shell with one of those slimy little critters!" Wilton shuddered, as he released the handle in disgust.

They gazed down into the murky waters and saw that a thickly woven wooden basket completely filled the immense rock pool. It was used as a makeshift net to catch the oysters, and was the strangest contraption they had ever seen.

Mesi ambled into the basket. "Oi, keep hold of that handle now!" she called over to Daz and Shai.

TOO LATE! A sudden jerk threw her off balance and she hurtled forwards head first into the water. Mesi spluttered and coughed as she re-emerged and tried to regain her stance in a dignified manner.

"I don't know! Three heads and still no common sense!" she growled.

But the three others couldn't speak for laughing and were tempted to let go of the handle once more. However, common sense got the better of them and they held on for dear life, just long enough for Mesi to pick the biggest oyster she could find and juggle it to shore in her oversized pincers.

"I'm glad you guys are amused!" she snapped sarcastically. "But on a more serious note, we need to move this oyster and ourselves out of here as quick as we can. Loose the handle, now!" she ordered. "Climb up onto my shell." Mesi instinctively crouched down and they clambered on. "Hold on tight! I can sense movement underfoot, others are on their way; they'll be here in a matter of seconds!"

On her command, the orb dived into the water and once again they were in total darkness. Mesi felt her way as she climbed out of the cave and waded back through the shallow pools, with the bulky oyster shell clamped firmly in her pincers. She used the hanging foliage from the trees as camouflage as they all disappeared into the night.

CHAPTER NINE

Wheel of Life

"Think that's far enough," Mesi said, stretching as she came to a sudden halt. "My back's killing me!" She lay down, totally exhausted, while the others slid to the ground.

They were concealed under a prominent overhanging rock face, which gave them limited shelter and harboured them from danger, but the harsh stony route was what had caused Mesi's back to jar.

"I know, ducky, an osteopath would do the trick for that back of yours."

"A what?" Mesi looked perplexed. "I think you mean an even path, don't you?"

"Whatever!" Daz laughed. "Well, what next then, ducky?"

"You'll see," Mesi said, and with that she started to use her invaluable pincers like a homemade tin-opener. She cut through the middle section of the oyster shell, which proved a lot tougher than she'd first thought.

"I'll help," Shai insisted, as he ran forward to offer his assistance.

Mesi swung an enormous leg round which sent Shai flying into a nearby rock.

"Eh, no need for that, duck, he was only trying to help," Daz said, banging his fist on Mesi's leg. He turned to Shai. "You okay?"

Shai felt rather woozy, but he stood up, brushed himself down and stormed over to Mesi.

"What's your problem? Crab by name, crabby by nature, that's what I say!" he said, and scrunched his face up and spat his tongue out.

"Hold it, hold it!" Mesi snapped. "That, my dear fella, was for your own good!"

"Hmmm, my own good!" Shai huffed.

126

The oyster had an authentic charm, its burnt-orange outer casing graced with elongated spines projecting from it.

"The shells are razor sharp; one touch and you're mincemeat. Be my guest and find out the hard way!" Mesi grunted, as she continued to prise the shell open and reveal its contents.

"Yuk, that's vile!" Wilton said, immediately turning his nose up. "Pffft, the smell of raw fish is enough to put anybody off! Shut it back up," he pleaded as he began to heave, the aroma proving too much for his weak stomach.

"Yum, it's a delicacy. I could down you in one," Mesi said as she turned to the jellified cream mollusc.

"You don't want to do that now, ducky," Daz said, feeling rather sorry for the oyster. "Anyway, I've heard they're an aphrodisiac; don't be getting any ideas, me duck."

"One, I'm not hungry, and two, these are for the crabs in the Underworld. I thought I should put the record straight."

"So your dish of the day tonight then?" Shai pulled himself back up on Mesi's back and peered inside.

He soon wished he'd kept his opinion to himself as the mollusc released a bitter substance, squirted straight at Shai's face.

"Well, Mesi, we're not going to all fit in that shell with that thing inside, are we?" Wilton said. "And we're not going to eat it, so what's the plan?" He distanced himself from the unsavoury character.

"That thing you're talking about happens to have a name!" a voice emerged from inside the oyster shell. "Name's Hobson. Normally I'd say pleasure to meet you, but I think NOT in your case." The ugly invertebrate hung over the side of the shell aimlessly.

"Shut up, you oversized slug; you look foul, and you smell even worse!" Wilton snorted.

"Goylins like you are better seen and not heard. We need Hobson's help," Mesi croaked.

"Well that's Hobson's choice," Hobson chuckled to himself. "You're big enough … or maybe not … certainly ugly enough to help yourselves! So close me up and put me back in the water where I belong."

"It's your lucky day, you're going to be re-homed." Mesi tried to lever his fat body out of the shell but he wriggled quickly to the other end.

"Oi, I ain't havin' this! It's my home and I don't intend on leaving! I've got nowhere else to go!" Hobson wailed.

"This is where I introduce you to your new flatmate!" Mesi added in a rhetorical manner.

"Yeah, me duck, know Wilton would luv a lodger!"

"Don't think so!" Wilton turned his nose up at the slug-like mollusc. "You're not turning my home into some kind of aquarium for outcasts!"

"I've got just the answer," Mesi said, reopening her shell and pulling yet another potion out.

She tipped a tiny drop on the unsuspecting Hobson, and his slimy exterior turned to a thick frothy yellow matter, which bubbled and fizzed. The mollusc then resembled a dish of lumpy custard, and, in the blink of an eye, turned into a half decent-looking Goylin.

"What have you done to me?! I'm hideous, I'm ugly! A mollusc with arms and legs! My cohorts will call me a freak!" Hobson's arms flapped around in an ungainly fashion and his legs were bowed as if made of rubber.

Mesi grew tired as Hobson struggled to coordinate his new limbs, and grabbed him by the tail. Hobson swung backwards and forwards like a large pendulum before being placed down safely next to Wilton.

"Ugly being past tense!" Wilton said. "You look just like us now."

Hobson dithered, his solitary tooth chattering against his bottom lip. "I had my own heating system in my shell, kept me at just the right temperature."

"Ha look, duck, he's got no clothes on!"

"Here you are, try this on for size," Shai said, as he removed Daz's red striped T-shirt and pulled it over Hobson's head.

"If it wasn't for us, duck, you'd have ended up as supper for some oversized crab! So we've saved you," Daz said, feeling that he'd done his good deed for the day.

"Well at least I'd have gone down with me ship!" Hobson added.

"Ha-ha, that ship's a shell!" Shai chuckled, but Hobson missed the boat and the remark went straight over his head; being a mollusc, his IQ was even worse than Daz's.

"Enough of this time wasting!" Wilton said, and gave Hobson brief directions to his home. "I'm sure you'll find it, it's the one with no door and, well, the word bombsite comes to mind. On the off chance you do get lost, just go to one of the other houses, knock 'em up and tell 'em you're with me; they'll direct you." Wilton gave Hobson a friendly pat on the back. "Suppose I'll get used to your company in time. Just one thing, you'll find a girl upstairs; she's lost her soul. Her name's Eve; please look after her till we get back."

Mesi burst out hysterically, "I'm sorry, I couldn't hold it in any longer!" Tears streamed down her face as she attempted to look over at a very bemused Wilton.

"Well, looks like the joke's on me then? What's so funny, eh?"

"You do realise, Wilton, don't you, that due to the large number of potions Hobson didn't have by choice, you'll soon be sharing your home with a rather large mollusc. He didn't even seal the deal, you know, the deposit and all that."

"He who laughs last laughs the loudest, my dim-witted friend, and Mesi, I'll assure you, I'll have the last laugh this time. You see, I took enough potion from your shop to keep that slimy little critter a Goylin till the end of time."

"You stole my potions!!!"

"Come on, me ducks, we need to get this show on the road," Daz said, interrupting their tête-à-tête before Mesi and Wilton got into a full-blown argument.

One of Mesi's large pincers lifted Shai high up in the air, dangling him over the illusive shell. Daz went into fight or flight mode, but froze to the spot and so was an easy target for Mesi, who picked him up also. They had no need to worry though, as she placed them softly in the bottom of the oyster shell and then turned to find her last victim. After he saw Daz and Shai had come to no harm, Wilton breathed a sigh of relief, feeling quite relaxed as

Mesi approached him. He closed his eyes as he was lifted into the air.

"You thought you were clever taking my potions!" Mesi said, as she swung him backwards and forwards like a large conker.

Wilton's eyes opened wide in fear.

"Not nice being out of control is it?" Mesi said, as she manoeuvred the scared Goylin only inches from her face. "Enjoy your trip!" she shouted, and dropped Wilton from a great height. "Well, I had to get my point across somehow. Now who's had the last laugh?" Mesi closed the shell on Daz, Shai and Wilton – Wilton's behind was not the only thing that had been bruised, his ego also having taken a pasting.

She sealed the two halves together with sap that she'd dug out from a nearby maple tree, but made sure to leave a small gap each side to allow air in for them to breathe. The three sat in total darkness as Mesi picked up the spiny oyster shell in her pincers, clamped both sides and headed towards the Wheel of Life.

She passed many crabs on the way down who had also collected oysters to sustain the insatiable appetites of the crabs in the Underworld. She kept her head down, not wanting to draw attention to herself or her plight. The wheel had a monumental status. Only a third was visible to the naked eye, with the majority of its immense circumference concealed below ground level and residing between limbo and the Underworld. Its varnished wooden frame had a charismatic charm that oozed out of every inch of its delicately constructed framework. It truly was the heart and soul of Cancer, and Mesi stood in reverence to the great shrine of her star sign.

By now, fellow crabs had gathered and also stood waiting for their turn to load themselves and their oysters onto the wheel. Guardian crabs analysed the size, depth and overall look, and judged if the shell was worthy to make the journey to the Underworld. If the given criteria were not met, the shells were still escorted down but only to limbo, where they were tossed into the sea of souls and left to rot for eternity. The wheel had numerous slats that slotted together, and the crabs used these for seats. The vast size of Mesi's oyster shell automatically gave it the thumbs-up.

Her eight legs manoeuvred awkwardly onto the wooden masterpiece that constantly moved, and she had only seconds to get seated and buckled in before she was plummeted into the dark abyss that lay in wait beneath. She held her oyster shell close and felt rather apprehensive, as this was still only the beginning of her journey. She left the Cancer she knew behind as the wheel advanced her into limbo. Her eyesight was poor, yet she managed to pick up the different vibrations and the smell of rotten flesh and death that seeped out of the darkness.

"Cor blimey! Come on, out with it, who's let rip?" Daz asked, as he held his nose in disgust.

"No, we've reached the second stage of Cancer," Wilton explained. "This part of the journey is our passage through limbo, and what you smell is death and decay. Hopefully, we've been given the all-clear to pass to the Underworld."

"How will we know, Wilton?" Shai piped up.

"You'll know sure enough. If our shell's rejected it'll be scrapped and thrown into the sea of souls. It's a great Cancerian privilege for a crab to be granted a pass to the Underworld, and is only bestowed if the oyster she carries passes inspection."

Wilton fidgeted; the shell was most uncomfortable.

"What then, me duck?"

"Well, all I know is, something down there gives them the ability to collect the souls they need to get to Paradisum. The unsuccessful crabs stay on the wheel until it has done its full 360-degree cycle, then they are put back at the bottom of the waiting list until their turn comes round again. Any crabs in breach of the natural order of Cancer are sent to limbo post-haste to await their fate. The crabs only have a short lifespan, so if they don't make it to Paradisum where they are granted immortality, they age, die and are thrown into limbo."

The journey was long and arduous, and by now Mesi's eight legs had tied themselves in knots. She tossed and turned one way, then the other.

"We're moving!" Shai shouted, and jumped for joy. "We must have reached our destination. Can't wait to get out of here!"

Unfortunately, he'd spoken too soon, and the gradient of the

131

shell changed from a horizontal position to an angle of 90 degrees. Everything became topsy-turvy as they gambolled around like ragdolls. Shai and Wilton crash-landed into each other, while Daz did an almighty bellyflop and ended up on top of them both, knocking the wind out of their sails. They now balanced on the shell's natural breaking point, where Mesi had fastidiously stuck it together.

"If this shell opens and we fall out, we're dead men walking! Don't know about you two, but I think we've had enough bad luck for one day," Shai panted, as he recovered and his breathing returned to normal. However, he was forced to eat his words for a second time as things were about to go from bad to worse ... MUCH WORSE!

With not a single warning, icy-cold water suddenly gushed into the oyster shell. Shai, who had a total abhorrence to water, jumped on Daz's shoulder and clung on like a limpet. Still a firefly at heart, water was his deadliest enemy.

"Get off me, you idiot!" Daz screeched, as he blindly threw punches at Shai's head.

"Action's needed at a time like this, not panic and childlike antics!" Wilton said, grabbing Shai's arm and managing to prise him off an unsympathetic Daz.

"Well, me ducks, think we need to plug these holes up somehow," Daz said, and quickly removed his seaweed attire and stuffed the garments into the air holes.

"Before you completely lose your dignity, you do realise because of the speed and direction we're travelling that an air pocket will form at the top of the shell so we'll never drown, not even in your lifetime," Wilton said, and lay back in the water, the high salt density keeping him afloat, while Daz and Shai splashed around, well and truly in panic mode.

A slightly embarrassed Daz recovered his clothes from the holes, quickly re-dressed and prayed that Wilton's well-rehearsed spiel wouldn't leave them up to their necks (or above!) in cold water. But the water level just kept rising, and Daz and Shai started to doubt Wilton's expertise.

Daz thought back to Aries. "At least there are no mirrors," he said, as he began to tread water.

Shai, who'd only just got used to walking on two legs, couldn't quite master the technique of this, and imitated someone climbing a ladder in a last attempt to save his life. This, however, had no effect, and he sank like a brick to the bottom of the shell. Wilton didn't hesitate in diving down to pull a half-conscious Shai up by the scruff of his neck to keep his head above water. When all else appeared to have failed, Wilton's prediction came true. The water stopped as quickly as it had started, and the three bobbed up and down and breathed freely in the airlock Wilton had promised.

Mesi smiled smugly to herself. This was her third time on the wheel and she'd made damn sure she wasn't going to fail again. It had worked in her favour to visit the oyster farm early, as it had given her the best pickings. However, her optimism was short-lived, as there was a sting in the tail. When she reached the Underworld and the mollusc-less shell was opened there'd be hell to pay, and then what would become of her? Maybe limbo was her fate after all. She heard the swishing of the water and felt the waves roll softly around the bottom of her spiny legs. She descended feet first into a foreboding icy chill that moulded to her like a second skin. She dithered uncontrollably as the water ran from her extremities and drained from the oyster shell. The Underworld's mindless shades emerged from nowhere and created shadowy silhouettes, lost forever in perpetual darkness.

Mesi quivered with delight like a child on a Ferris wheel for the first time. *Almost there*, she thought, as she took her first few breaths of fresh air. The three bedraggled stowaways momentarily slipped to the back of her mind as she stood precariously and waited patiently until the guardians of the Underworld gave her the all-clear to disembark.

The shell jerked in a sudden forward motion, and Wilton guessed that Mesi's eight legs now stood firmly in the Underworld.

"Pssst!" A large red eye peered through the air hole. "I'm going to have to leave you here for a short while. I'll do my best to find Eve's soul, but whatever you do, stay put. Under NO circumstances are you to leave this shell." Mesi repeated this command once again to ensure her words had been heard and understood.

A slight bump later, the shell came to rest unevenly on the

ground. The three were relieved that their journey was over and they were safe and sound.

"What's all the hype about this wheel then, Wilton?" Shai asked, peering through the gap in the shell. His eyes were screwed up tight to aid his view, but his oddly shaped face and bulbous nose got in the way.

"Well, me ducks, gonna die of hypothermia if we stop 'ere much longer!" Daz said as he paddled to the shallowest end of the shell.

The angle at which the shell had been placed enabled him to avoid the majority of puddles that ran away to the opposite end and lay in a shallow pool.

"You want to know about the Wheel of Life? Well, here goes. What I'm going to tell you now is to the best of my knowledge. The wheel is erected from the only wood that doesn't represent Cancer; it comes from the yew tree. What we do know is that it symbolises death and the never-ending circle of life. Another unexplainable fact is the number of spokes that span out from the wheel's central axis; you see, there are thirteen of these, which to this day remain foreign to the twelve signs of the zodiac. Although Cancer is a prominent water sign, an explosive fire has burned within its epicentre from the beginning of time, and this acts like a heartbeat, keeping a constant rhythm and maintaining equilibrium."

Daz clapped his hands. "Great story, Wilton, but thinks me gonna 'av a gander and stretch me legs; been cooped up in 'ere for far too long, me duck."

Mesi's makeshift glue had endured dramatic climate change and the overpowering pressures from glacial waters, and this had caused the substance to become tacky and lose its adherence.

"Be out of 'ere in no time!" Daz said, as he began to prise open the shell with his bare hands.

Shai and Wilton soon joined him, but the top of the shell proved heavier than any of them had thought, and it took all their strength to unhinge their heavyweight carry case. The three peered out to check the coast was clear.

"We're on a blumin' mountain of oyster shells just like ours!" Daz exclaimed, his legs suspended over the edge. He proceeded to climb down, using the spiny exterior as hand and foot holds.

Shai and Wilton hurriedly followed, neither wanting to be seen.

They stared in disbelief at what lay ahead. The darkness seemed to reach out and touch them like ghostly fingers, and a smell even worse than death rose and crept its way slowly up their nostrils. Daz's eyes moved to the base of the wheel. His eyes became transfixed on its outer beauty, its numerous carvings and the mirror-like varnish that reflected between the shadows and seemed to dance around them.

Shai glanced above him and rubbed his eyes in disbelief before he realised that what he was seeing was actually real and that his mind wasn't playing tricks on him.

"Look up there, Daz!" he said, nudging him apprehensively.

Daz's focus shifted from the wheel and he also looked up and stood open-mouthed.

"What the heck?" he said, to which Wilton responded in a similar manner.

For a few seconds not a word passed between them and they stood transfixed, before Daz finally broke the silence.

"It's the sea, it's the blumin' sea, me duck. How can I see the sea up there? Are we standing on our heads?" He put his head between his legs, but no, he stood the right way up. "Where is the sky for that matter?"

They all looked down, afraid at what they'd discover next, but to their immense relief they stood on something solid, although it was disguised by a black mist that swept around their feet, and the waves moved along by the tide gave off a silvery essence. They couldn't see very well, but enough.

"It even sounds like the sea!" Shai screeched. His booming voice echoed and bounced from one shell to another, the vibrations of which were catastrophic and resulted in an immediate domino effect. The teetering shells began to tremble and sway like an almighty landslide as they crashed to the floor.

"Runnn!" Daz shouted and grabbed Shai's hand.

The three ran blindly into a vast nothingness.

"Think this really is the Underworld," Wilton shuddered when they'd reached a safe distance. "I don't think there's any way out of this one; there's no going back now! We must have been mad to trust a flippin' crab!"

"We trusted you, Wilton. Why are you so different? In fact, why are you even helping us?" Shai questioned.

"Well firstly, I'M NO CRAB! And secondly…"

BUT SECONDLY WAS NEVER TO COME!

CHAPTER TEN

The Sea and Beyond

Branch-like entities swooped down from nowhere, the elongated spiny limbs of the spider crab catching the threesome totally off guard. A dishevelled Daz, Shai and Wilton were savagely forced apart and covered in a cold, wet coagulated fishy matter; ensnared like a spider's prey, they felt suffocated. Asphyxiated, they were catapulted upwards into the stratosphere, then through shallow waters … the sky that had astounded them previously. Thrown off course, their yo-yo like bodies rotated and spun downwards, where they dangled like three puppets. They came to a sudden halt, but not for long, as they spun once again but this time in reverse; their sap-like imprisonment loosened as they were unravelled at hypersonic speed.

Daz slowly opened his eyes. Sweat oozed from him like water from a tap and he felt sick to the stomach as he lay in the foetal position while he waited for his heart rate to decrease. His whole body lay in a state of shock, but he had to find strength from somewhere to pluck up the courage to do what it was he came for – to rescue Eve and for them both to return home safely. An immense beach stretched out beneath him, with its soft, warm sand eliminated by roughly grated shingle that sank its teeth sharply into his leathery skin. He rolled his aching body over to check Shai and Wilton were still his companions and that he wasn't left in this godforsaken place alone. Wilton lay just out of reach.

"You okay, duck?" Daz asked, but no answer came.

Wilton lay face down and had an uncomfortable pallor to his skin, and both his ears hung limp at the side of his head, like those of a dog that had lost its owner.

"Over here, Daz!" Shai shouted, sitting up. By the looks of it, he'd come off the best by far.

"Well, me duck, in your past form you shoulda bin a cat, not a firefly! Talk about nine lives and landin' firmly on ya feet!" Daz said, checking himself for sores and bruises, and feeling slightly aggrieved that Shai wasn't any worse for wear. He brushed the shingle from his wiry hair.

"Is that stupid old Goylin dead?" Shai said, as he trotted over to Wilton. "Or is he just playing possum?"

"What planet are you on, Shai?" For once, Daz didn't see the funny side.

"Antares, stupid, the same as you!" Shai gave Wilton's tail a long, hard tug. "Up you get, sleeping beauty."

"Well, ducky, there's only one way sleeping beauty will wake up," Daz said, puckering his lips and giving Shai a sexy wink.

"Yuk, if you think I'm kissing that ugly disgusting thing you've got another thing coming! I'd rather kiss Mesi's oversized…"

Wilton began to splutter and gasp for breath, shot up red faced and rubbed his streaming eyes as he struggled to get his breath back.

"'Ang on, me duck, can put me First Aid training to good use! I'm comin'!" Daz waddled over in his usual clumsy manner, grabbed Wilton under the arms, thrust his knee into his back and proceeded to do the Heimlich manoeuvre the best way he knew how.

Shai couldn't quite believe what he was seeing; it looked like some sort of comedy act.

"Well, Daz, if he wasn't dead before he won't be long in getting there the way you're going!"

Wilton's chest began to move freely as he puffed out his first proper breath.

"Get your hands off me, you idiot!" Wilton shouted and tried to shake himself free, but in the process managed to elbow Daz in the stomach.

"Well, it was a toss-up between my hands and Shai's lips, sleeping beauty! You ungrateful blumin'…" but he managed to stop himself before he said something he knew he'd later regret.

"Sorry, Daz, but can you please get your hands off me?!" Wilton wriggled free from Daz's firm grip.

"Ha, don't know me own strength sometimes!" Daz apologised, although he did know his own strength and had thought it time to teach that unappreciative Goylin a wee lesson.

A brusque voice reverberated around them.

"HOW DARE YOU ENTER THE UNDERWORLD? Who gave you permission? You're not crabs! You're not souls! So why are you here?"

The three looked up sheepishly at a large object that unwound itself towards them until its head was level with theirs. Its angry nostrils flared and its eyes burned into their very subconscious.

"Wwhhhhaaaaaat…..?" Daz stammered, as his eyes scanned the unorthodox creature. "You ain't a crab either, me duck." His voice quivered as he plucked up the courage to have his say.

"A crab? I'm not a CRAB!" She was furious, and prodded her spiny appendages into Daz's stomach.

Winded, Daz fell on all fours.

"I'm a guardian!" she continued. "A guardian from the Underworld. A rare and very beautiful spider crab!" Her vastly outstretched legs outweighed her insignificantly small and rounded body. Her outer shell was like a coat of armour, and was somewhere between sage and bottle green in colour, giving it the appearance of an army uniform. She looked anything but feminine, and only the pitch of her voice would have made anyone question her gender.

"You've trespassed in our domain so we've transported you here in our seaweed web to make you pay for your sins," she explained.

She turned, pointed left towards the shallow waters that lapped towards them and then immediately right, where foreign objects in the distance protruded out of the shingle, too far away for Daz, Shai or Wilton to make out.

"Don't question, you'll find out soon enough. Let's just say you're caught between the devil and the deep blue sea!" Without another word, she turned and crawled through the shingle dunes, reeled in her slimy seaweed web, which had netted numerous sea urchins and fish remnants, and dragged it behind her as she waded into the murky waters and disappeared from sight.

"Well, one thing's for sure, the smell of fish is making me

hungry," Daz said, licking his lips. Hunger was never far from his mind.

"We need to save Eve, and get your part soul and Shai's back; if we succeed in doing all that, I need to see you all safely through the gate! Even with this in mind, all you can think of is your stomach!" Wilton said, trying to conjure up a plan of action as he paced up and down along the beach; food was the very last thing on his mind. "Guess it isn't exactly rocket science," Wilton thought aloud, his hand pressed firmly against the side of his face. "None of us can swim…"

"'Ang on, 'ang on, ducky, I'll 'av ya know I've got me ten-metres freestyle," Daz said, and began to imitate the arm and breathing actions.

"You dope! Does the sea look like ten metres to you?" Wilton frowned. "More like ten strokes and you'll drown."

"Well, that disgusting spider crab also pointed to the right, so that must be the right way to go," Shai said, squelching about in his little brown boots that were wet through and very uncomfortable, but the shingle was so sharp that he was unable to walk on bare foot.

The protruding objects grew closer, which left no question in their minds as to what this place really was.

"'Ello, 'ello, 'ello, there's finally more of me! Someone else to talk to … instead of you, Beatrice. I'm no longer Billy no mates!" an oddly dressed Goylin said, as he walked towards them, beaming.

"Well in our case, I say three's company, and four, the fourth one being you, is a crowd. Another Goylin is bad enough, but we don't need one who has lost his marbles hanging onto our tails, so to speak," Wilton said, barging past.

Daz and Shai followed.

"Eh, I say, that's not nice. I'm the first Goylin that's ever ventured down here and survived, I'll have you know. Maybe I can help you if you're willing to help me in return," he said, tugging at Shai's seaweed skirt and nearly managing to pull it off.

"Oi, don't get fresh with me! Buzz off!" Shai said.

"Maybe he's got a point, duck," Daz said.

"NO, NO, NO, NO WAY! If he's right in the head, why is he

140

still here? He'll just keep us trapped in limbo and we'll end up playthings along with his so-called imaginary friend, Beatrice. I think not!" Wilton grumbled sarcastically.

"Quiet, all of you! Can't you even give me the chance to explain? I'm a Taurean, and the name's Walter … thanks for asking! Nice to meet you too!" The deep lines on his face twitched as he tried to fathom the three Goylins. "You see, I'm an Earth sign and don't belong in Cancer; that's why I had to take the risk of coming down here unaided, and from that day I have searched for my part soul. I can't possibly make this sham of a star sign my home; you see, I'm brave to…"

"Well for one thing," Wilton interrupted, folding his arms across his chest, "you came to Cancer of your own free will, and greed made you drink the potion. The crabs, as horrible as we might think they are, aren't doing anything wrong! It's their realm, their existence, and we're the intruders! You're brave to what?" he tutted. "Come down here? No, stupid! You see, there's nothing brave about any of us. The only reason I'm here is to save Eve, as she was the only one who wasn't blinded by greed. To be honest, Daz, if it was just you and Shai I wouldn't have bothered; do you know how much of a risk I'm taking by helping you?" Wilton just wanted to get out of there, leave Walter behind and be on his way.

"Thanks, Wilton, thought we were friends! After all, I did take the time to save your life," Daz said, quite upset by Wilton's insensitive remark.

"No, Daz, there are no friends in Cancer, not now," Wilton replied. "It's dog eat dog, or should I say crab eat Goylin. Now, let's make tracks and find Eve and your souls." Wilton felt it was time he put the record straight.

"You best follow me then. You're going the wrong way, the sea is the place you need. You're heading towards the crab graveyard, and anyone who resides there is past helping."

"I disagree, Walter! My bet's the graveyard!" Wilton hissed.

"I beg to differ. The sea of souls is your only route out of here, and even then there's no guarantee. I've been looking for mine for as long as I dare to remember and still haven't come up trumps. Even if you are successful, you still face the Wheel of Life and the journey back up to safety before you can even contemplate the gate," Walter preached.

Daz turned to Wilton. "Walter's experience wins me over all the way; the sea it is."

Walter smiled smugly to himself. "I know the waters and its tides, when best to sail and when best to stay on dry land. If we work as a team we may reap the rewards and one day be able to return to our true star signs."

A brief silence fell between them as they weighed up all their options and how, as individuals, they would benefit if they allowed Walter to assist them.

Shai's little eyes wandered towards the unnerving cemetery. Porous bones of crabs' skeletal remains lay in different states of decomposition. Rotted pincers lay visible, their size preventing them from total burial, and they looked as if they were desperately trying to claw their way out to regain any remnants of their past lives.

Shai gave Walter the once over. "What's the dress code down here then, Walter?"

"It's always chilly down here in limbo, and that seaweed lets the draft in everywhere … I mean everywhere! But the eco-friendly Goylin I am, I use very minimal resources and have collected a combination of crushed oyster guts and broken shells that I pieced together to make this beautiful mosaic coat." He looked down proudly and admired his homemade creation.

"Not exactly designer gear, ducky, and don't smell too clever either; comes a close second in my opinion," Daz said.

Walter's resourcefulness seemed to give Wilton a change of heart.

"Think my mind's made up; put it there," he said, and reached out his hand. They shook on it. "In your case, four is definitely not a crowd," Wilton smiled, as a bond seemed to grow and the two chatted happily like old friends.

"I've rustled up a mollusc stew; anyone hungry?" Walter offered his hospitality, to which Daz's face immediately lit up.

"No time like the present, me duck."

They all dragged their aching bodies away from the crab graveyard and back towards the sea.

"A few more steps and we'll be home and dry," Walter said, as he dodged the many oyster shells that were strewn around the shore. He waded through the shallow waters and headed towards the Wheel of Life.

"I can't swim, Walter!" Shai cried out.

"You'll be up to your knees in it, not to your neck!" Walter laughed as he led them through the water and towards the wheel's mainstay, which was a large stand that resembled the immense trunk of a tree, and was the central beam that supported the weight of the whole structure. Only the middle section was visible, its two cut-off points being the Underworld and the Cancer they had left behind. A mysterious shadowy veil hung like a curtain between the twilight sheen of the sky and her un-benevolent counterpart which encompassed them both, and an orange-peel light flitted between a midnight Prussian and a cobalt blue, yet all looked as one – no beginning, no end; the sky and the sea an ultimate infinity.

"Welcome to my home," Walter said.

"Home, duck? How can you possibly call this oversized windmill a home?"

A rough hole had been carved out and resembled a rabbit's burrow. Once inside, there was hardly room to move, and all they could see was a wooden ladder. If indeed it was a ladder at all, as it was carved into the actual wall of the mainstay. Funnier still, it didn't just go in one direction.

"Does it matter if we go up or down, duckie?" Daz asked, as he looked up at an opening barely big enough for him to squeeze through. He balanced on the edge of the oddly shaped hole that fell away beneath him, scared that he would fall as they were all virtually in darkness.

"If it's my home you want, I suggest we climb up. If you climb down you'll be in the heart of the Underworld. Follow me," Walter said, and disappeared up into the darkness.

Daz waited for his eyes to readjust, and then leant over and held the ladder's bottom rung firmly in his hand before slowly starting to ascend. The climb was long and arduous, and the muscles in his arms and legs ached beyond belief; with each rung he climbed, his elbows and knees scraped against the rough wooden walls. Just when he thought he couldn't go on any longer, the hole opened up into a much larger misshapen chamber, where Walter was warming his hands over a very inviting fire.

"Chop-chop, come in then, make yourself at home," he called, and Daz climbed out of hole and hobbled over to where he sat.

Another head appeared quicker than Wilton would have liked.

"Do you mind, Shai?! Keep your hands to yourself!"

"Stop moaning, Wilton! If your large rear wasn't going at a snail's pace, my hands wouldn't have pinched it! Oh, Wilton, it would be nice if you saw the funny side of things occasionally," Shai grunted, as they came up virtually on top of each other.

The expression on Wilton's face as he took a seat next to Daz left no one in the slightest doubt as to what sort of mood he was in.

"Eh, Walter, how an earth you got a fire up here?" Shai asked, scratching his head and looking confused.

"How could this have ever come to be anyway? It has no wood, no sticks, NO NOTHING FOR THAT MATTER! What's fuelling it?" Shai asked. His eyes were transfixed; he loved fire, it was in his blood, but everything had a reason and there was a reason for everything, and he wanted to know what it was! "It's not even on the ground! A fire that floats? NOW I'VE SEEN IT ALL!" Shai questioned his own sanity.

"It's the eternal fire that fuels the wheel, and it's the same fire that's going to cook our dinner, so I say we eat, don't you?!" Walter balanced an open oyster shell between two giant crab claws and managed to erect his very own homemade grill, which worked wonders in cooking the mollusc meat.

"It's an à-la-carte prepared delicacy, fresh from the sea I'll have you know," Walter chuckled, as he served it up with the utmost precision.

"Caviar is a delicacy where I come from, ducky, and by the looks of that, forget the à-la-carte; it'd be more at home in a dust cart!" Daz said.

His hunger had now got the better of him, and he took a small mussel shell filled with a generous helping.

"I'm glad Hobson isn't here to see this!" he said, and used the smaller claws handed to him by Walter as a fork for the freshly cooked fish meat, which he shovelled into his mouth as quickly as he could.

"I'll tell you one thing, Hobson wouldn't be here for long 'cause I would have eaten him by now!" Wilton sniggered, as he enjoyed eating his well-cooked cuisine.

"MMMM! That's nice! Just because he was an oyster, who happens to be a Goylin, you'd eat him? SO DOES THAT MEAN BECAUSE I'M A GOYLIN WHO HAPPENED TO BE A FIREFLY YOU'D SWAT ME?!!!!" Shai hissed, as he threw his helping at a taken aback Walter.

"No, we wouldn't swat you, but I think you'd have made a scrumptious appetiser," Walter grumbled, now anything but happy as he wore Shai's uneaten dinner.

He licked his lips and Shai gulped, going very quiet all of a sudden; he had no intention of ending up on anybody's dinner plate.

Shai scavenged through the scraps left in the empty oyster shells but got more than he bargained for when he scooped up a handful of mollusc pulp. He flinched, screamed and threw it on the floor, disgust written all over his face.

"EWWWW, IT'S LOOKING AT ME! How can I possibly eat that? It's got eyes! The critter's staring at me!" He shuddered.

The others howled with laughter.

"Should have eaten with us when you had the chance!" Walter chuckled, as he rubbed his full stomach. He felt rather fat and contented, and was halfway towards getting his own back after Shai's earlier outburst.

"Deceptively spacious, this place of yours," Wilton noted, moseying around.

"Took me long enough to find a safe place I could call home. It was just pot luck. I relentlessly carved out the ladder's rungs piece by piece and literally fell upon this cosy retreat. It's the wheel's epicentre you know; you are actually sitting in the heart of Cancer."

"Not being funny, Walter, and call me simple if you like, but shouldn't we be moving if we're in the middle of the wheel? It doesn't make sense!" Daz said as he tidied up the mussel shells, emptied them of scraps and left them ready to wash.

"It's a mystery to Cancer, but actually it does make sense, and you'd have seen for yourself if only you'd looked properly. It's very easy to look and not really see. It gives the impression of perpetual motion, rotating like the thirteen spokes, but actually it's just your eyes playing tricks on you. This whole section is totally fixed. Think about it; we wouldn't be sitting here having this conversation if it was moving, now would we?"

"But, but…"

"No time for ifs, buts or maybes. We should get down to real business. You want your souls back, as do I! But you see, it's not plain sailing, far from it!" Walter said, and got up without further explanation.

Shortly after, they all stood back in the shallow water and headed towards the shore, where Walter took them to a large shell that he kept hidden.

"This blumin' shingle, keeps getting in me boots!" Daz complained, and sat down, removed them and emptied out their annoying contents.

"Shingle!? That's not shingle, it's crushed shells from the crab graveyard that have rotted here since Cancer began," Walter explained, and started to pull out an oversized crab shell that lay half buried.

"EWWWWW! You're telling me that we're walking on dead crabs? Ha, least I didn't have a mouthful of them," Daz quipped, as he looked in Wilton's direction.

They all seemed to take great pleasure in cheap point scoring, and it had almost become a game.

"NOW, GOYLINS! Come along, this boat's heavy!" Walter said, as he struggled and then waited impatiently for someone to give him a hand.

For once, they all pitched in and worked as a team. They pushed and pulled, and soon they had the shell – or boat, as Walter referred to it – in an upright position. It was obvious that he'd worked hard on the monstrosity, with its two little wooden benches that slotted in either side and sealed with mollusc guts to keep the water out. A mast was erected with a triangular piece of seaweed wrapped around it, which made do as a sail when pulled taut in the wind.

"Your carriage awaits," Walter grinned as he took a large bow.

"Oh, and before I forget…" He bent down and began to dig up the crushed crab-like shingle, and after a few minutes he revealed two slightly arced oars. "We'll definitely be needing these!"

"Looking at 'em, me duck," Daz said, picking one up, "me thinks you'll be rowing around in circles and that'll get you nowhere fast!"

"Well we're getting nowhere fast standing here talking, are we? Help me pull the boat down to the seashore. Best work in twos … what do you say, Wilton, fancy coming with me? We'll try and collect some souls, then bring them back for Daz and Shai to open. But to be honest, it's all down to Lady Luck; it's murder out there! After three and we'll get her in the water…"

They all pushed the eccentric crab shell into the shallow waters, which lapped around it. As it began to float, it did resemble something seaworthy.

"Hurry, hurry, jump in, Wilton, before the tide takes it!" Daz shouted.

Wilton and Walter waded in up to their knees and pulled themselves up into the boat, taking an oar each. They perched on one of the little wooden benches and sat opposite each other, rowing in unison as they set sail.

"Arrrr, bon voyage, me hearties!" Daz shouted, as he and Shai waved them off.

They'd only rowed for a matter of minutes when a group of shapeless apparitions swooped down upon them, their ice-cold breath hovering momentarily and then sinking like the night down the back of Walter's and Wilton's necks. They shivered and immediately broke out in a cold sweat.

"Fear not, Wilton, for this time they are just paying us a visit, paving our way to the Underworld. When the sea drains the last drops of our souls from our bodies, then their work here will be done. You see, they are the kiss of death, the souls that never rest, and they will lie in wait for us like hungry vultures until that time. I've been fortunate until now," Walter explained. "As I've only sailed a handful of times, the danger that lies beneath is too great for a solitary sailor like myself; it's like a bottled nightmare waiting to be unleashed. Maybe we should stay as Goylins and be content with our lot."

His eyes met Wilton's, and somehow they both knew that neither was going to settle for that.

The wind picked up, and Walter got to his feet and began to erect the mast, pulling the seaweed sail as tight as he could. The boat accelerated and now moved at a very brisk pace as they headed further out into the dreary depths. A thick oily film lay between them and the shells that contained the souls, which made it difficult for them to detect their whereabouts. Wilton screwed his eyes up as he tried to focus, but just ended up disheartened and disappointed, not knowing how they were going to find anything in this colossal watery grave. Both pulled their oars backwards and forwards, and Wilton tried to make out his disjointed reflection in the ripples that followed them.

"Over there! They must be the new ones!" Walter shouted. He jumped up and pointed, nearly capsizing the boat, and it was only Wilton's quick thinking as he shifted his weight that managed to rebalance it and put them back on course.

An asymmetric phenomenon protruded way above the water line in the distance. It turned out to be a very odd-looking hillock, and as they ventured nearer it appeared to more closely resemble an old derelict scrapyard. Wilton rocked the boat in anger, his face red with rage.

"You brought me all this way to see some atrocious-looking monument?!" Furious, he clenched his fists.

"Calm down, you fool!" Walter demanded. He lowered the sail, which in turn allowed them to drift ahead at a much slower pace. "They're Cancer's new souls and this is their dumping ground. They mount up gradually, then one by one the sea takes them; the oldest first, followed by the most decrepit. This makes way for a resting ground for the new unspoilt souls; like the wheel, it's a never-ending cycle. So to be honest, Wilton, the chances of me finding mine is very bleak, but all I have left is hope. You see, once the sea takes them they are lost forever, irretrievable. That's why in your case we must act quickly, as time is of the essence."

"Well, there's no time like the present. We've got to think this through though; it's like a game, and if we make a wrong move we'll lose the lot ... checkmate, and the game will end before it's even begun! How could we even contemplate explaining that to

Daz and Shai?" Wilton remarked as he remained seated, head in his hands and deep in thought.

The air seemed to become ice-cold, like knives that endeavoured to invade their windswept bodies. Wilton shivered and rubbed his arms as he tried to create warmth. Walter's mosaic coat shielded him slightly from the elements, and he stood and pondered their next move. He looked skywards and prayed for some kind of absolution and help from Taurus, but unfortunately this would never come, as their destiny was in their own hands.

"The only way is up, and somehow we've got to get to the top. If we try pulling one of those shells from the bottom or middle, the whole lot's going to tumble into the sea and take us with it!" Walter said as he felt the boat ground itself.

"Well, you can count me out," Wilton said. "Climbing and me don't exactly go hand in hand. It took me all my time to climb that horrendous ladder of yours, and even then I was so slow. Shai had to give me a shove just to get me moving! I think the word for it is vertigo, but as far as I'm concerned it's a no go!" He wouldn't budge on the matter, and sat and turned his back on Walter, who stepped gingerly out of the boat. The shells beneath his feet bobbed up and down, making them feel like stepping stones.

"Don't just sit there sulking! Make yourself useful, why don't you?" Walter snapped. He had now grown tired of Wilton's temper tantrums. "Drop the anchor! The boat isn't going to stay there! The tide's strong and you'll be washed back out to sea!"

For once Wilton didn't argue, and he picked up a large reel of seaweed and attached it to a hermit crab shell; he could see this had obviously been used as ballast and noticed it was filled to the top with shingle. He wasted no time and hurled it over the side of the boat, then sat patiently and watched as Walter started to climb.

Initially, Walter found his climb up the shells not too difficult. With the mixture of sea, shingle and barnacles, the parasitic invaders had adhered the shells and embedded them tightly together. In no time at all, Walter had reached halfway and felt undaunted by the remaining climb that lay ahead. He felt cocksure of himself, BUT NOT FOR LONG!!!

CHAPTER ELEVEN

A Fly in the Ointment

A gargantuan sinister black form flew like a streamline dagger from the onyx waters below. It collided with Walter's head and nearly knocked him off his shell-like appendage, with only the very tips of his fingers managing to save the wee Goylin. He summoned up all his strength as he buried his feet in the empty crevices and slowly managed to restabilise himself. One of the capacious flying objects was more than enough for Wilton to cope with, but now their sculptured bodies began to dart towards him thick and fast. An empty protruding conch shell was his only way out, and was positioned so that he was easily able to slip inside. This was a rarity, as the majority of them were only big enough to fit in the palm of his hand; the ones that contained a soul, that is! Some just caught up in the wrong place at the wrong time, but this conch shell just happened to be in the right place at the right time.

"It can't be! Surely not!" he said to himself. "They are just a myth!"

But the Black Rock fish, or devilfish as they were known in Cancer, were very much alive and kicking, and certainly no myth. They were just shy of Wilton's meagre three feet, flat and heavily set, the only visible features the tiny orange ring around the edge of their eyes, which broke the severity of their matt-black scaled bodies. Thundering echoes reverberated as they flapped their mammoth raven fins and fantails.

Walter was somewhat amazed by how they'd homed in on the very shell where he had taken refuge, and was shocked by their ferocity.

"Are you there, Walter?" a faint voice rose up from the depths, only just heard by a very shaken Walter.

This took the heat off Walter, as the devilfish redirected their attention to the lone sailor below. They lurched over the unsuspecting boat, their large fangs glistening in the few shards of light the sky gave them. The fish seemed to have constant reinforcements, as they grew not only in number but also in size. The bombardment ricocheted Wilton from one side of the boat to the other, which had also taken quite a pounding. An extra large punishing jolt lifted the boat and tipped it on its side. Wilton wrapped his arms as tightly as he could around one bench and crossed his legs over the other. He lay as still as he possibly could, a breath hardly passing his lips; he prayed and hoped the fish would get bored and leave him be. The boat now being on its side provided an opportunity for Wilton, but he knew he would have to move quickly. With every bit of strength his body could muster, he reached up to the rickety boat's starboard side and pulled with all his might. The boat turned completely over, half rested on the water, while the other half counterbalanced itself on the uneven shells where the boat had previously grounded. Now completely covered, it offered Wilton a safe haven.

Walter used this distraction to his advantage and pulled himself quickly out of the conch shell before proceeding forwards. He used very small movements, as he didn't want to draw attention to himself. After each manoeuvre he curled himself up in a ball and used his coat as a very clever camouflage. Tranquillity fell and the fish, becoming increasingly disinterested, circled the boat one final time before disappearing into the undulating waves. Equilibrium re-established itself once again.

Walter wasn't going to take any chances though, and very slowly, with no fast or jerky movements, he continued his climb until it became unsafe to go any further.

"AAAAGGGGRRRHHH!" he shouted, as the small shell handholds came away as he grabbed them and plummeted into the murky waters.

"Watch it, Walter!" Wilton shouted, receiving a few unwanted blows to the head as he tried to return the boat once more to its upright position.

Still rather on edge, he kept his wits about him, and was in no hurry to see any of those ghastly fish again. His vision became blurred from the sea's salty liquor, and little grains of sand stuck to his lips, burning them and giving him a strong desire to lick them off, which left a foul fishy taste in his mouth.

"Look out below!" Walter warned, as he started to drop the unsuspecting shells that contained the souls down to Wilton in the hope that he would catch them, as he didn't want to lose any more than he had to into the sea. Any one of these could have been one of their souls, and then it would all have been over. He put his faith in Wilton and prayed he would not let him down.

Meanwhile, Wilton struggled with his newfound double vision and tried hard to decipher between those that were real and those that were not. His red bloodshot eyes streamed, and the more he tried to focus the worse they became. The slippery shells he was able to catch only slid like butter between his fingers, and although not ideal, it did manage to break their fall. A healthy number lay intact, scattered on the floor of the boat.

"No more! NO MORE, or I'll capsize again!" he shouted.

Walter took the hint, descended and joined Wilton in the boat.

"That was a close call, we nearly ended up as fish food!" Walter said, letting out a sigh of relief.

They retrieved their anchor and headed back inland, where Daz and Shai waited.

Meanwhile, cold and tired, Daz and Shai huddled together on the shore, hoping their friends wouldn't be too long and that they had come to no harm.

"I'm starving!" Shai moaned, as his stomach made the most peculiar noises.

"Well, duckie, you should have eaten when you had the chance, instead of playing with your food like a big kid!" Daz said.

The air temperature suddenly dropped dramatically and every breath was now visible. The sound of turbulent waves crashed on the shore, drowning out the two very cold Goylins, whose teeth were chattering uncontrollably.

"Look, duck, I'm sure that's our boat!" Daz exclaimed.

Both immediately jumped to their feet and waved their arms excitedly in the air; the light was so little that they thought the boat might pass them by.

"OVER HERE!" they shouted, and made as much noise as they possibly could to get Walter and Wilton's attention.

Sure enough, in no time at all the little boat was once again on dry land.

"This is where you two come in!" Walter said, as he tossed a shell in Daz's direction.

"Okay, Mr Know-it-all, how do we get the souls then?" Daz asked. He shook and examined one of the snail-shaped shells. "Don't 'av to eat it, do I?"

Shai's eyes immediately lit up. "I'll go first in that case."

"Haven't got all day, got to make as many trips as we can under the cover of darkness," Walter said, shovelling the shells hastily off the boat. "They're your babies now, go figure it out yourselves. Give us a push, Shai, time's a wasting!"

The little boat disappeared into the night, and all that was left was the swishing sound made by the oars, which soon faded into the distance.

The two Goylins started at the huge pile of shells, with no idea what they should do with them.

"Well, me duck, as far as I know, if you stick a shell to your ear you'll hear the sea, so maybe with a bit of luck, instead of the sea it'll give us step-by-step instructions!" Daz said. He was in his own little world and began to press the shells one at a time firmly against his ear.

"This is stupid! The souls aren't going to talk to you, you know!" Shai said, and without hesitation he seized the first shell he came across and, much to Daz's astonishment, began to viciously pound it over and over again against a jagged rock until it shattered and the soul dispersed into the ground below. In doing so, it dispelled a straw-like liquid substance that forged out of a channel in the shingle and then trickled inland like a miniature stream.

"What have you done? That's someone's soul! What if it's one of ours, duckie?!"

"How are we supposed to know if it's one of ours or not? Walter didn't exactly spell it out for us, did he?" Shai said. He picked up more shells and broke each one in turn until only a handful remained.

"We're still Goylins!" Daz pointed out. "This is like finding a needle in a haystack! We've got no chance!" He sulked, and his eyes followed the liquid as it drained away.

"Well, Daz, last two and then we've got to do it all again when the next shipment comes!" Shai said. "Go on then, guess you'd better take your pick."

Daz pointed to the most vibrant looking of the two; its smooth, shiny exterior had something about it. Not quite as heavy handed as Shai, he tapped gently on the rock, creating a hairline crack from one end of the shell to the other. He instinctively dug his nails into the crevice and managed to prise it open. It now lay in two halves in the palm of his hands and a strange-coloured smoke that gave off a foul-smelling pungent aroma puffed up explosively into his face.

"THAT'S VILE!!" he shouted, and wafted the black veil in Shai's direction.

Shai's nose automatically twitched up and down as he sniffed the air, but for the life of him he couldn't understand what all the fuss was about, as the only fragrance that filled his nostrils was the salty essence brought in by the breeze on the tide.

"ERRRHHHGGG, Shai, help!" Daz pleaded, as the black cloud began to adhere itself to his face like sticky tar, before spreading like a parasite and swamping his entire body. With the loss of his sight and balance, he slumped to the floor.

Shai watched on, completely helpless; had some evil soul possessed Daz?

"Stay calm! I'll do the best I can!" Shai said.

He heard the words come from his own mouth, but actions spoke louder than words and the actions he needed to take next bewildered him. Shai, who found anything out of the ordinary hard to deal with, now found himself very much outside his comfort zone. Before he had time to act, the most peculiar transformation took place and the gooey tar-like substance took on the appearance of a translucent mist, which enveloped him in a deathly shroud. The life seemed be sucked out of it, and momentarily it hung in the air like an oversized parachute. The suction proved too much for the indescribable grey mist, and it disappeared back into its shell like a genie returning to its bottle. The shell snapped together, with no outward sign that it had ever been divided.

Shai's eyes now resembled large dinner plates.

"Daz, yaaaaa faaaace!" he stammered.

Daz's mind raced, and he thought perhaps he was burnt or disfigured beyond recognition. He lifted his right hand to his cheek, stopping just inches away; maybe this was the kind of reality he hadn't been prepared to accept. As his eyes focused on Shai, he wondered why, at a time like this, he had a grin the size of a cucumber that stretched from ear to ear. What possible reason had he to jump up and down like an over-worked Jack in the box? Cautiously, Daz softly pressed his thumb and finger over his forehead, cheeks and down to the tip of his chin. His skin didn't have that tough leathery feel he'd grown accustomed to. He pinched his nose, which felt less than half the size it had been only moments before. Was he even uglier now? Why was Shai laughing at him?

"Will you put me out of my misery? I can't stand it any longer, duck!"

"Just look at your arms, your legs, then you'll see!"

Daz gazed down at his hands; they were human hands, and his arms human arms. He didn't have to look any further to know that it was back, his soul had been released. He may not have been the best-looking mortal, but just being mortal again was enough for him. He jumped up and swung Shai round and round until they ended up on the floor, and just sat and hugged each other.

"My turn!" Shai said, as he pulled himself free. He mimicked Daz's grand opening, but this turned out to be more like a damp squib.

The shell broke almost symmetrically.

"Looking good so far!" Shai said, quivering with excitement. All of his senses were heightened, like that of a fly, but his bubble was soon to burst.

The smoke arrived promptly and Shai took a deep breath, closed his eyes and opened his arms as if to embrace his transformation; but alas, it was never to be.

"I'm still a Goylin!!" Shai said, as he tossed the shell over his shoulder and watched as the cloud disappeared.

"Better than being a firefly, isn't it, duck?"

"Be nice to have the choice!" he huffed.

"Well, your second chance has just arrived!" Daz said, as he turned and saw Walter drop anchor.

The boat was once again bursting with shells of varying shapes and sizes.

"You won't believe what we've got here! Well, I'll give you a clue, Shai me old boy; you won't go hungry tonight, that is unless you decide to have another one of those hissy fits you're famous for!" Wilton said as he reached into the boat.

With Walter's help, he managed to lift a dark obscure object proudly above his head.

"What the devil's that, ducky?"

"Didn't take much guessing on your part; it's exactly that, a devilfish. Luckily, we got it before it got us!" Wilton said, and tossed the oversized produce towards Shai.

"Well, if this so-called fish is the devil … then Satan here I come!" Daz said, rubbing his stomach as his mouth began to water.

"I see you're back to your old ugly self again!" Wilton sniggered, as he looked Daz up and down.

"WHO, MOI? This handsome figure of a man? You've definitely got problems with your eyesight!"

"And you with your belly! It's not supposed to hang off you like a spare tyre!" Wilton chuntered on while unloading the second batch of shells safely onto the beach.

"You're only jealous, Wilton; it's not every day you'll come across a six-pack like this!" Daz said, pulling his stomach in. He hoped his dignity would stay intact and that the seaweed skirt he loved so much wouldn't end up being worn around his ankles.

"Being the chef here, and as the saying goes 'too many chefs spoil the broth', I think I'll go and prepare a cordon bleu masterpiece," Walter said, and off he trudged through the shallow waters towards the wheel, with the fish wedged under his arm. "Happy soul hunting," he shouted over his shoulder, as he disappeared from view.

This left Shai, Daz and Wilton with a mammoth task ahead of them.

"Let's crack on then, me ducks, dinner awaits! Don't know about you two, but I'm starving; I could eat a horse right about now!"

"As a former Sataterian, I suggest you choose your words carefully," Wilton said, as he apprehensively cracked open the first shell on a nearby rock.

A taupe brown mist exploded in the air and just as quickly disappeared.

"Well that obviously isn't any of ours; hope it finds its way to its rightful owner."

Then something stopped Wilton dead in his tracks.

"We'll be all day at this rate!" Shai said, as he hastily snatched another shell from the pile and pummelled it ruthlessly against the serrated edge of the shingle.

"HOLD IT RIGHT THERE!" Wilton gasped, as he saw yet more liquid pour from the newly broken shell. "Another wasted soul; well done, Shai," he sighed, as it trickled away and joined a miniature stream that had made its own pathway, an undercurrent pushing it in one definite direction.

Instinctively, their curiosity forced them to follow it. It reached out and pushed the shingle aside as its strong flow intensified and its current picked up pace. Entranced, they continued to pursue its course blindly; then nothing, total evaporation into the underlying shingle.

A tuneless echo pirouetted, its unearthly sound relentlessly ricocheting its unmelodious tones into the Crepitus environment. Eerie acoustics bounced between fragmented crustaceans as they were enticed into the graveyard's unreality.

"How come we're made to feel so welcome at this gathering of the dead?" Shai shuddered.

"Maybe we're guests, ducky. Bet they crack a few jokes around 'ere," Daz said, and then jumped, an untimely movement as something stirred behind him.

A partially decomposed crab claw regenerated itself and dragged its perished innards towards a decayed shell, to which it attached itself. Little by little, all the claws and pincers followed suit until they became complete crabs as their ungainly limbs reconnected. The air was contaminated with putrid guts, and they attempted to stand on their rusty limbs.

The three were dumbstruck, and from their ashen complexions it seemed their hearts had missed more than just a few beats.

Wilton shook his head. "It's not safe here any more! Shai, you went blindly ahead and smashed the shells, and now the lost souls have no way of ever finding peace; lost for eternity. You gave them all the ingredients necessary to get the better of us; you've triggered a supernatural phenomenon, a rebirth, and now limbo lives and breathes. No time for questions, we must get out of this godforsaken garden of death while we still have time. Cancer's future is doomed!"

"Where to?" Shai half turned.

"To the wheel!" Wilton yelled. "RUN!"

The crabs manifested themselves before their very eyes, becoming a rigid wall, an army of reincarnated crabs. There was a raucous screeching sound as their appendages snapped back into place, and once rebalanced, the repugnant creatures shuffled along. Shai didn't need to be told twice, and as for Daz, he was already halfway along the beach. The crabs refocused and began to sense the direction in which the three were headed, the vibration of their footsteps an easy give away.

"I can't run any faster!" Shai complained. His legs were more of a disability, always moving in the opposite direction to the one he wanted them to. "I'd give absolutely anything for my wings right now," he panted, as he splashed about in the shallow waters.

"You can slow down, me duck, they'll never catch us. Looks like a bit of oil wouldn't go amiss!" Daz laughed.

Shai turned and saw the army of crabs a safe distance behind, their movements mechanical and cumbersome.

"Wilton, come back, we need you now more than ever!" Daz cried.

But it was too late for Wilton. He'd approached the wheel at an angle and completely misjudged the mainstay so that his tail had become tangled in one of the thirteen spokes. He now hung upside down and swung like an acrobatic fruit bat, tiresomely grappling his way up by prising his fingers between the wooden slats just far enough to be able to support his weight.

"Don't worry about me, I'll go and check on Eve. With all this commotion down here, I don't know what I'm going find." His voice faded out as the wheel lifted him out of sight and away from limbo.

"I say we worry about Wilton's detour later," Daz said as he entered the mainstay and hurriedly began to climb up, Shai close on his heels.

"Now let's see those eight-legged mutants catch us up. Oww! Watch my fingers, you're going the wrong way!" Daz cried out.

Walter's familiar voice drifted down, a welcome sound to Daz and Shai's ears.

"Wish someone would make their mind up where we're going; first it's up, then it's down. These legs of mine are finding it hard to keep up with my brain."

"Well, ducky, that's sumat flies don't 'av much of, brains, ain't that so, Walter?" Daz laughed.

"Guess I'll never know now, will I?" Shai said, as he tried to climb faster. He didn't want Daz's big size tens anywhere near his delicate fingers. "For all I know my soul lives on in one of those ghastly half lives we've left roaming around out there!"

The climb down was even further than Shai or Daz had anticipated.

"When we get down to the Underworld we'll be part of it! Feel like I'm ageing by the blumin' second," Daz wheezed.

They had hardly any room to move and the very little air there was circulated poorly. By the time they reached the bottom, they were gasping for breath. Walter, on the other hand, took it in his stride as he'd had plenty of practice.

"Now, Daz, you might need to breathe in; watch and see how it's done," Walter said as he lay flat on his stomach, which took up most of the space in the small crevice. He slithered like a snake through the cramped opening.

"Okay, I'm through," a supple Shai said, as he shimmied through with ease.

"Okay, Daz!" they called.

Daz lay on his back, bent his knees and used his feet to propel himself along head first. He needed more than a deep breath – a shoehorn would have worked better in pushing his so-called six-pack through a space his body was never meant to fit in.

"I'm halfway there, me duck," Daz said as his head appeared. "If I was still a Goylin I'd 'av been through in a jiffy."

"Got the cork, just need the bottle now!" Shai chuckled.

He and Walter wrapped their hands firmly round Daz's head and gave it an almighty tug.

"He's not moving!" Shai cried.

Poor Daz was stuck fast. "At a time like this a knob of butter would 'av come in useful," he laughed as he tried to wriggle free, but to no avail.

"I'm going to have a wee gander; something round here might come in handy," Shai said, and wandered off.

Within a few moments he returned with his hands full of a slimy wet solution. He cupped his palms so as not to let any drip between his fingers and daubed it around the edge of the hole that encased Daz's oversized frame.

"Don't need a sealant, idiot!"

"No, you've got the wrong idea there; it's an alternative to that knob of butter you were harping on about. Push hard with your feet and I guarantee you'll slide through."

They took hold of Daz's neck for a second time, and with a combination of their brute force and Daz's timely footwork he shot out like a bullet from a gun. The three lay in a heap.

"Who put the lights out?" Daz looked up. "Oh yeah, I remember, we're back in this topsy-turvy hellhole. That putrefying smell of fish is back…" He couldn't understand why Shai and Walter were finding what he was saying so comical.

"It's you, stupid, you smell of fish; well you stink actually… what do you think I used to get you out of that tight situation? Mollusc guts!" Shai sniggered.

"I've kept my part of the bargain, but I'm afraid from now on you're on your own," Walter said. "This is as far as I go, the Underworld is out of limits. Got a certain devilfish to fry anyway. See you around, and good luck."

Walter slid back into the wheel's mainstay, leaving Daz and Shai sitting cold, alone and very much in the dark.

"Best track that oyster shell down before Mesi comes back for us. I got the oyster guts from over there, if my memory serves me correctly," Shai said, but due to the poor lighting he had to go mainly on instinct.

They were stalked by the shadows that grew continually longer, determined by the tidal flow above.

"There they are, Daz! What did I tell ya?" Shai said, and he scurried over as fast as his little legs would carry him.

The subsidence caused by the mountain of oysters left them unsure of their shell's whereabouts.

"Shouldn't be too hard to find, ours is the only one that was opened. There's a small mound still standing over there; if I climb to the top, I might just be able to spot it," Shai said.

"If you had X-ray vision or if you were still a firefly maybe you'd have a chance, ducky."

"Give us a leg up, Daz!" Shai grabbed onto one the shell's spines and paused. "Hang on... Something somewhere doesn't quite add up. I'm sure Mesi said these were razor sharp, and thinking back, we climbed down them before, didn't we, Daz? Why would Mesi say that, why would she lie to us?"

"MAYBE IT'S BECAUSE I WANTED YOU TO STAY PUT!" Mesi said, reappearing. "Not go on your travels, moseying around in the Underworld. You see, you're mine, you belong to me now." Mesi looked around for Goylin number three. "Where's he hiding? He won't get far, I'll smell him out; he owes me!" she said, referring to the absence of Wilton, the lucky escapee.

"Devilfish 'ad him, ducky!" said a quick-thinking Daz, trying to put Mesi off the scent.

Mesi refocused. "I see you've got your soul back... Not for long though, young man; Sagittarian or whatever star sign you were."

"Well, ducky, you brought us here to find Eve and return her soul."

"Eve's soul awaits you; join me," Mesi said, crouching down.

"How can we trust you now?" Shai snapped.

"It isn't only me you have to place your trust in!" Mesi cackled, her bloodshot eyes glowing in the darkness.

Daz and Shai stepped away from her menacing aura and backed into a posse of burley soldier crabs.

"Keep ya claws to yaself, ducky!"

Their azure-blue outer shells glowed like a nightlight, and their hinged claws tightened around Daz's and Shai's waists. These ferocious, ill-tempered crabs differed greatly to Mesi, who was a scavenger and, flatter to the floor, found it easy tearing fish and washed-up seaweed apart with her unique pincers.

"Onwards, soldiers, to the gambling den!" she ordered.

They marched in unison, headed by Mesi. Shai and Daz dragged along behind, unwilling captors through purgatory's wretchedness.

Long walkways led to dark chasms, oily puddles and quagmires until they were frogmarched through the orifice of a dank cavern.

"Red or black? Bets are on!" Mesi called out.

Kerosene lamps hung in strange little alcoves. Total damnation adorned spherical stained-glass windows, signifying the moon, their ruling planet. A collage of colours, where tormented shades met, sapphires, a tinge of deep blue intermingled with slate grey and vivid Persian reds; an everlasting memorial to the crab hierarchy and an undying tribute to Cancer.

"It's a blumin' casino, ducky!" Daz gasped as he tried to wriggle free, but the solider crabs' grip only tightened.

Half-moon tables were assembled, with dried maple leaves pressed together and laid over each with the utmost precision; the green foliage was Cancer's imitation of the green felt of a typical casino table. The room was alive, buzzing with energy as croupiers dealt their cards. Each crab was eager to take her winnings, but there were no chips as such, no money, they played for souls; these were their only rewards, their fast-track ticket to Paradisum.

"Mesi, what they playing?" Daz asked.

"Craps..." Mesi mumbled. "The card games are just light entertainment before we get down to real business."

"CRABS? No, duck, not who's playing, what they playing?"

"Are you deaf or just dumb? They're playing craps!" Mesi turned and gave him a one-eyed glance.

"Why didn't you say that in the first place?"

The room's grand centrepiece was of the same ilk, its solitary full-moon table taken up by a polished silver roulette wheel. Mesi positioned herself behind this, and with a snap of her pincers the crabs divided and left a walkway between them. Two immense wicker baskets, one with two large straps and padlocked securely, the other just an open basket, were pushed from behind by two long-legged spider crabs, who positioned them on either side of Mesi. She turned to face a restrained Daz.

"I know how important it is to you to save Eve by returning her soul safely back to her, but unfortunately for Eve, I'm her soul's new rightful owner. I wanted you to witness my passage to Paradisum, and I also wanted to make sure I witnessed your life being drained from your body while you sleep, and see one of my fellow Cancerians benefit…" She gave a quick glance at Shai. "Not forgetting you of course, another full soul; well, that makes three. Won't I be the popular crab down here!" she smirked.

"You'll never have my full soul, I'm a Goylin!" Shai said. "Mine was lost on the beach in limbo." Shai was sure he'd got one over on Mesi and her scheming ways.

"To the table!" Mesi demanded.

The two spider crabs marched Daz and Shai over to the immense roulette table, where they were forcibly sat on top. The crabs took two steps back and rejoined their regiment. Another spider crab pulled herself up beside Daz and Shai and began to weave her thick sticky seaweed web around them. In a matter of seconds they sat in a dome-shaped cocoon, and this time there was no way out!

CHAPTER TWELVE

Lady Luck

"Just to put the icing on the cake, I thought you might like to say hello to Eve," Mesi said, as she unlocked the padlock on the wicker basket, pulled the lid back and took something from the top. "Think this is what you've come for."

She placed a Nautilus shell on the table next to them. The ear-shaped shell was white with small red markings, its centre a luminous screen that concealed Eve's soul.

"Here's your precious friend!" she added.

"Whatever you do, duck, don't let me go to sleep! I can't live out the rest of me days inside a blumin' crab!" A tear welled up in Daz's eye, but he was quick to wipe it away before Shai had time to notice.

A handful of hairy crabs with spiny follicles covering their sandy claws and outer shells were half the size of Mesi. Lower-class worker crabs played host as they waited on the tables with Cancer's delicacies: oyster shells held high in their pincers, containing a selection of aperitifs and appetisers. Watermelon milkshakes, decorated with diced strawberries and mango, placed on sharp spikes for a classy effect. Freshly squeezed oranges and lemons, and a touch of soda made for one very refreshing citrus punch. Maraschino cherries were used as fruit floaters, poured into mother of pearl shells that resembled large fruit bowls. Daz's and Shai's mouths watered, the air perfumed with the fruit cocktails' irresistible aroma. The hairy crabs sidled in and out of the players with sushi parcels, a combination of mollusc meat, cucumber and avocados wrapped in Saccharina Japonica (a rich leafy seaweed with an aromatic flavour that tantalised the large crustaceans' palates.) A selection of fresh salads were laid out in pretty clamshells, and as their friendly conversations echoed, they drank, ate and made merry.

Mesi passed two of the most succulent strawberries through the sticky web.

"Think maybe we should call this your last supper," she said, the wisecrack proving too good for her to withhold.

"You know what you can do with your strawberries, last supper or not!" Shai said. "Here, Daz, you've never been one to refuse food..." He watched as Daz chewed and dribbled over the luscious fruits.

"Attention, please; can I have thirteen crabs to the table? This is the game of all games, two full souls going today," Mesi said, pointing over to Daz and Shai. "The usual minimum bets of two half souls will be increased to forty for these two games only. Then normal play will resume."

The room went quiet momentarily; no crab wanted to lose that many hard-earned half souls. It was a big ask and the stakes were high, but for the lucky winners the prize would be life-changing. All the new crabs that had gained passage to the Underworld had to be content with the card tables. On initial entry to the Underworld they were given only five sand dollars, equivalent to five half souls – Cancer's chips to play with. Sand dollars were dried-out sea urchins collected from limbo, collected by the spider crabs and brought down with the souls. The flat, round palm-sized objects, white in colour, were perfect chips for the Cancerians' casino. These were their only wagers until they managed to earn more on the roulette wheel. If they gambled, lost and had none remaining, they had to return to Cancer until they could produce another worthy oyster shell. One by one, the seasoned gamblers started to make their way to the table, until thirteen stood around the edge. They opened their shells and removed the required forty sand dollars.

"No odds or evens, this game you just pick a number from zero to twelve, starting with the crab who has the most souls," Mesi explained the rules. "Place ya bets!" she instructed, and watched as all thirteen numbers on the table were covered. She placed a large pearl on zero in the unconventional thirteen-numbered roulette wheel and flicked it hard with her pincer.

Daz and Shai watched as it spun round.

"Well, old chap, was nice knowing ya…" Shai said, breaking the tension between them as he shook Daz by the hand. "Looks like Cancer's our destiny after all. Could have been worse though, ay…"

Daz chuckled. *How could things possibly have gotten any worse?* He thought.

"Number four! It's mine, I've won!" A velvet-blue sentinel crab lunged her claw through the webby cocoon and grabbed at Shai. "My lucky mascot!" she grinned at the ugly little Goylin. "My ticket to Paradisum!" She kissed him firmly on the lips.

"Hold on, hold on! He stays on the table, securely held in the web. When he sleeps, only then do you receive your full soul," Mesi said. She reached across and clutched at the Goylin with her right pincer, but her clumsiness caused her actions to backfire and her claw brushed the Nautilus shell containing Eve's soul, which crashed to the floor and shattered into tiny pieces. A translucent mist dispersed into the air and then was gone.

"EVE!!!! Mesi, what have you done?!" Daz's frustration took over as he became overwhelmed by an insatiable anger.

Mesi managed to retrieve Shai and placed him back next to Daz.

"Sorry, folks, that's bets off for now… Due to the unfortunate breakage, the second full soul goes straight to me. Normal bets will resume shortly."

"Hang on a second, Mesi, rules are rules, they can't be broken on your say so!" a burnt-orange pebble crab confronted her.

"Yes, too right! There's twelve of us now. Join us and put your souls where your mouth is!" a luminous lime-green seaweed crab grunted, fish debris hanging from the hooked hairs on her spiny body and legs. "The odds aren't great, twelve to one, but it's a fair wager – you can't just take what isn't yours. The same rules apply to us all."

The room was in uproar, but all this was drowned out as Daz shook in anger and tears streamed down his mottled red face. Though Shai tried to calm him, its intensity just seemed to grow. Suddenly the room was all of a tremble, and water seeped in through cracks in the cave's external walls. The ceiling of the casino started to distort and buckle, and porous rocks crumbled. Jagged fragments fell around the cave as water cascaded down. True to form, the hairy crabs turned on their backs, curled their legs up and played dead as they tried to appear inconspicuous to the oncoming danger. The great army of soldier crabs burrowed through the cave floor, corkscrewing down out of harm's way. The other species had no strategy whatsoever, and just scurried around in panic mode as the water level rose significantly.

"All out!" Mesi screeched. "Every crab for herself."

A sudden stampede caused even more chaos. The card tables crushed and concertinaed under the heavy rock fall. Spider crabs, their spiny limbs shattered and dismembered, were totally immobilised, legs tightly embedded in a mass of debris and rubble. The smaller hairy crabs that had played dead as a form of camouflage were now very much dead, compressed and fossilised, their imprints pulverised into the ground.

"Oi, Daz, Shai…"

But they didn't dare look, as soaking wet and curled up into a ball they tried to avoid serious injury.

"Oi!" Walter shouted, as he climbed his way out of the wicker basket containing the sand dollars, over half of which were now submerged as the sea gushed down from limbo to claim their souls. He jumped onto the table next to them. "It's me, Walter!"

He dodged a flying rock and held onto the seaweed cocoon for fear of being washed away. He clawed at the small existing hole through which the sentinel crab had pulled Shai, but this was no mean feat, as with every strand he tore off it just as quickly regenerated and sealed the hole around its captives.

"Oi, guys, it's me … Walter. I'm fighting a losing battle here, give us a hand your side!"

Remnants of small tables now floated like makeshift boats, and the freshly prepared banquet was strewn like litter across the water's surface. Although the crabs could live happily immersed in water, the concept of a burial involving being trapped in a watery tomb caused utter mayhem. Riotous behaviour began as a rampage of crabs clawed at each other, pushing and shoving as they all clambered to exit the casino at the same time.

"There you are, Wilton, my little escapee!" Mesi said.

That's what she thinks, Walter thought to himself.

Mesi, who had waited craftily behind for their souls, plucked Walter up from the table. She cut through the seaweed matter with her sharp pincers and lifted Daz and Shai before it had time to knit itself back together.

"You're coming with me!" she said, as she dodged the falling rocks and headed towards the crammed opening. As she did so, the crabs poured back into the casino.

An overwhelmed Mesi became part of the brawl as she lost her footing and plunged head first into the icy-cold water. Daz, Shai and Walter were thrown through the air in different directions before limbo's sea engulfed them, its waves surging relentlessly to and fro.

Daz swam to the surface, grabbed at a piece of wood from one of the half-moon card tables and held on tight with both hands. He kicked his legs as hard as he could in an attempt to move through the waterlogged casino in search of Walter and, more importantly, Shai, who couldn't swim a stroke.

"Help!" a little voice bubbled.

Daz saw a Goylin's arm disappear beneath the undercurrent of the crashing waves and manoeuvred himself awkwardly through broken furniture and crabs' corpses. A small hand bobbed up and down, disappeared and resurfaced, just long enough for Daz to take hold and pull a bedraggled Shai's head above water.

"Grab on!" Daz shouted, as he scoured the waters for Walter.

A half-conscious Shai looked up. *I must be delusional,* he thought to himself, as emaciated un-dead crustaceans from limbo poured in, their mechanical limbs thrashing.

They took their revenge on Cancer's up and coming crabs, ripping limbs from their victims, their mutated claws like nutcrackers that tore through crab shells and ground them into coarse shingle, leaving their ashes to float away on the waves. The reincarnated set about their deadly onslaught like machines, their strength unstoppable. The remaining soldier crabs resurfaced, assembled their depleted regiments and did what they did best. They marched into an overpowering bombardment that ripped them apart piece by piece. Woken devilfish attracted by the fresh blood claimed their victims one by one as they circled their prey, creating small whirlpools that left them feeling dizzy and disorientated before their skeletal remains sank to feed the scavengers on the ocean floor.

"Think we best get out of here, duck, before that's us!" Daz said, and he and Shai kicked like they'd never kicked before.

"Oi, wait for me! I'm over here!"

A quick-thinking Walter had used a crab's claw as a lilo, and he lay flat on his stomach and was propelling his hands like paddles, which moved him quickly and quietly through the water to join his two friends.

Shapeless apparitions hovered overhead like vultures. On occasion, they dived down to collect a soul that had lost its way and sucked the remnants of their last breath from limbo's sea.

"Six legs are better than four. Come, Walter, QUICKLY!" Shai shouted, and moved over to make room.

"As I see it, the only way out of here is through the opening we came in by," Shai said.

"But how, Shai? The crabs … can't you see? They're revolting."

"Well, I'll 'av to agree with ya there, Walter. I've thought the same for a long while, ducky…"

"Fighting, you fool!" Walter snapped.

"Enough of the wisecracks. In my opinion, size is to our advantage, and if we're smart, we can manoeuvre this piece of driftwood and weave in and out of the crabs' legs," Shai explained, taking a deep breath. "They've got their own agenda – kill or be killed. This plan isn't foolproof by any means. We could get maimed or killed, caught up in battle, crushed by their fleshy claws, even drowned if we lose our life raft, so to speak. But it's the only option left for us; I'm afraid it really is sink or swim."

The three looked on in silence, their limited options already apparent. They began with a slow simultaneous leg action so as not to make a splash by breaking the water's surface, and then left hand then right in a breaststroke action they made their way cautiously. The waves grew and they had to fight the tide as they zigzagged between the monstrous crab claws.

Meanwhile, a very aggressive red rock crab, black in colour with a salmon-pink trim, was swimming the wrong way. She was used to surfing the waves, but she misjudged her strike and gouged a large piece of skin from Walter's thigh. The ripped flesh hung like a ready meal for the devilfish, and the blood was a tell-tale sign to follow the three friends, who were now sitting prey. The pain was unbearable, and Walter's body started to go into shock; however, he was still compos mentis enough to know that this accident had put all their lives in jeopardy. As they passed from the casino into the chasm, a large fallen rock jutted out just above sea level surrounded by clumps of seaweed.

"I'll act as decoy – I'll swim over to that rock and climb on it best I can. If I've got the strength to pull some of that seaweed out the water, it'll serve me well. I'll wrap it around my leg to stop the bleeding, and when it stops I'll try and catch you up."

"That's suicide!" Shai cried, resting his hand on Walter's shoulder.

"Well, if I stay here we're all dead," Walter replied.

He loosened their float and swam to where the rock lay. Daz and Shai glanced behind them and watched as Walter struggled to pull himself up, dragging his wounded leg behind him. They dodged the falling boulders as they tried to judge the distance between the claws of the diminishing crabs. The main fight took place in the casino, and they were glad to be well out of it!

"I'm okay, lads!" Walter said, giving them the thumbs up.

"That's a relief! He'll be back with us in no time," Shai said. "He can't possibly get lost; there's only one way out! Unless of course his name was Daz," he chuckled. "In that case, there would be a good possibility of that happening."

Daz splashed him. "Shut up and kick."

There was a thundering charge in the air, like a detonator had been released, and the chasm trembled. Their immediate thoughts turned to Walter and they glanced back once more, terror-stricken by what they saw. Part of the chasm had collapsed, and Walter's rock had been crushed and pushed down beneath the waves. Their vision was impaired, as the majority of the kerosene lanterns had been doused or washed away and the sea's black oily complexion resembled an obscure cloak that kept its secrets well hidden.

"We need to go back, ducky…" Daz said, thrashing at the water as he did his best to turn them around.

"No, there's nothing we can do now, he'd have wanted us to go on. Stop splashing, will you? All you'll do is draw attention to us," Shai said. As a realist, he kept a stiff upper lip, but his pent-up emotions screamed to be released. "If he isn't dead now, I'm sure with those devilfish in waiting it won't be long." Shai knew that only such a callous remark would snap Daz out of his self-pity and refocus him.

A deluge of water flushed them from the chasm while they tried helplessly to cling on. The current was stronger than ever one moment, calm the next; a vast expanse of open water surrounded them, and for the first time they could actually see. Daz blinked as the light almost blinded him; limbo's sea, once the Underworld's sky, had now become one. There was no sky any more, just a plain canvas devoid of depth or colour.

"Look what you've done, Daz! All this because of your greed. Well, that's two star signs you've left in anarchy!"

The wheel appeared in a very different light with the destruction of limbo, two thirds of it now almost visible. Its unique design, architectural brilliance, comprised a grand wooden statue that stood strong and firm; a true reflection and the backbone of Cancer. Its constant rotational movement smoothed the crabs' way between Cancer's three tiers; an uninterrupted revolution that fought against an unknowing transition, its flow jarred and rickety with insecure fixings. The water's immense pressure and gravitational force had taken its toll on the wheel's momentum, causing it to look inferior and perform less well than before.

"Looks like a big waterwheel, ducky," Daz said, as he drifted along its outer structure. "Take my hands, Shai, and whatever you do, don't let go!"

Daz timed their boarding well, and he jumped from their makeshift wooden raft and pulled himself and Shai up onto the slatted bench. Shai clung on for dear life; he certainly didn't want another watery encounter.

A green tinge rose on Daz's face. "Blumin' ek, this sea's got a lot to answer for."

"Ups and downs were part of my everyday firefly existence; don't bother me," Shai said, as he happily swayed from side to side, waist deep in the water; he knew they were safe.

They made small jolty movements as they kangarooed up and vacated the Underworld's depleted existence, the onyx sea curling its eerie fingers around their ankles for the very last time.

"Shai, the water, it's moving!" Daz said, leaning forward to get a better view.

"Of course it's moving! Water usually does," Shai replied, but as he spoke something caught his eye; movement below the surface.

Hundreds of crabs approached them like a large blanket, scrambling over each other as they raced towards the wheel, while the dead were dragged along beneath them. A raucous hissing sound was heard as their claws rubbed together and vibrated, while some still fought with the reincarnated corpses. Each one wanted out; the Underworld was doomed.

The few spider crabs that remained used their long legs to their advantage, and stretched up to adhere themselves with seaweed webs to the wheel's outer rim. Soldier crabs stayed to fight, their allegiance to the preservation of the Underworld as the water bubbled profusely above their onslaught. The un-dead tried their hardest to climb on, but the vigorous jolts and unpredictability caused many to be dismembered mid-flight. Their solitary claws hung in disarray and their empty shells spun on their backs. Then the crab of all crabs...

"MESI! Look, she's still alive!" Daz said, and ducked down, hoping she hadn't seen them.

As the largest rough shore crab of all, she had no problem with the waves and used the other crab shells as stepping stones. With giant strides she battled through the masses, dissecting any that crossed her path.

"Think she's seen us?" Daz whispered sheepishly, edging forward in his seat to get a better view.

Her blood-red eyes pierced his soul; Mesi meant business and had no intention of going back to the Underworld empty-handed. She had them trapped and knew it; it was only a matter of time. Like an acrobat she swung her cumbersome claws around one of the thirteen spokes and began to pull herself up.

A variety of crabs of all shapes and sizes clambered up the weakened wheel, and hung like gigantic Orang-utans as they swung in and out of the spokes.

A familiar voice echoed from the mountainous pod of crabs. "My lucky mascot!"

The velvet-blue sentinel crab prised her way through the congregation of bodies. Their previous acquaintance from the casino snatched Shai from his seat and ascended with him held securely in her pincer. Daz watched his companion as he disappeared into the mass exodus. He thought fast and grabbed hold of the leg of a passing spider crab, her sylph-like movements biding him time as he escaped Mesi's clutches. Mesi, however, had a trick up her sleeve, and shimmied up the mainstay like it was a totem pole. Reaching the top, she lay in wait.

The overladen ramshackle wheel's rotational pull impeded it, until virtually at a standstill it inched its way precariously towards Cancer's highest realm. Shai smiled as Daz swung level.

"If we're gunna go down, might as well go together, duck!" Daz said, as he leapt from his host and landed flat on the sentinel's back.

Her eyes, attached to long antennae that extended from her head, made perfect handlebars for Daz, but she kicked her back claws as she tried desperately to dislodge the unwanted parasite.

"Shoo! Go and bug some other soul-searching crustacean; sure they'd love a ticket to Paradisum! This little critter belongs to me … I won him fair and square!"

"That's what you think, duck!" Daz squeezed as hard as he could, and her eyeballs looked fit to burst as they bulged from their sockets.

Blinded, she shook her head vigorously; however, her other senses still managed to pick up the vibrations as they neared solid ground, their journey's end.

"Is one not enough, Na'ila?" Mesi asked, overshadowing the smaller sentinel crab as the wheel approached and she disembarked.

"I've gained your respect, Mesi, you've never addressed me by name before; it is a true honour."

Mesi laughed. "No, fool, you've pinched my soul and I'm taking it back!"

Before Na'ila could explain how Daz came to be in her possession, Mesi went into fight mode and charged over like an enraged rhino. This caught Na'ila off guard, and she stood up on her hinds and puffed out her chest in defence. As an automatic reflex, she dropped Shai and Daz, who rolled over and tried to avoid the warring crabs' legs.

"Quick, Shai, run!" Daz shouted, as he and Shai scrambled to their feet.

Mesi and Na'ila's pincers were like large swords as they duelled. A spider crab passed by and saw the two escapees. "Not so fast, little chaps; if you're hot property enough for Mesi to fight over, then you're staying put."

A projectile string of seaweed shot from her front claw as she lassoed and pulled Daz and Shai towards her, the web securing them firmly to an igneous rock.

"Think positive, duck, least you're not a fly…" Shai looked himself up and down as he wriggled round in the cold gooey web.

"Might as well be!" he said.

The spider crab gave a sarcastic wave as she walked away. The fight was becoming dirty, and Mesi and Na'ila wrapped their claws around each other, locked in a bear hug, neither about to lose ground as they pushed and pulled. The savage fracas started to attract the other crabs, and once off the wheel they swarmed around them. Other small fights broke out, and Daz and Shai were 'sitting ducks' between the un-dead and the living, unsure where they fitted in.

"Well, see you've managed to get yourselves in a right old predicament," a voice said from behind.

"Clement! What you doing here, duck?"

"Try taking a closer look! We might look similar, but he's chestnut brown and I'm fawn, two shades lighter I'll have you know, and three white socks." The Sagittarian lifted his front leg to show off his knee marking. "I know Clement well; in fact I know everyone in Sagittarius."

"Well, if you're not Clement you don't know us, so go away!" Shai snapped.

"Maybe Clement sent him, ducky."

"Stop talking! It's me, Wilton, my soul's been released! I've got the old me back, and those potions worked a treat; got myself a cracking pair of wings!"

More and more crabs fought around them; torn-off shells littered the ground and sharp disjointed pincers twitched as the last signs of life deserted their tarnished remains.

"If you look closer you might get an even nicer surprise," Wilton said as he knelt down before them.

"Great, ducky, you've brought Hobson," Daz said, as he saw him sat proudly astride the grand Sagittarian.

"AND..." Wilton raised his left wing.

"EVE! But you were, you're..." Daz looked as if he had seen a ghost.

"Well, all I remember is Wilton's house, we all looked round, you went to explore... Next thing I remember is waking up with a strange Goylin and some half breed bending over me..." she said.

"I'm not a half breed, I'm a dashing Sagittarian!" Wilton said, quite offended by Eve's detrimental description.

"We need to get out of this mess before Mesi or Na'ila sort out their differences and come back for us. Our souls no longer belong to us," Shai sighed.

"You've caused quite a stir here; don't know how exactly, but nearly all of the Goylins have changed back to their former selves. Cancer is overpopulated with foreign star signs, they're all swarming round the gate," Wilton explained.

"We know, we saw everything."

"Ha, don't you mean part of everything, Shai? The sea fell down, duck..."

"What he means to say is ... limbo's sea poured into the Underworld, and its souls must have smashed in the process. The only Goylins here now are those unfortunate enough to have been gambled away in the casino. You see, the crabs absorbed them," Shai babbled on.

"Thinking about it, where's Walter? Did he get his soul back? He was a nice fella, when we eventually became properly acquainted, that is," Wilton said with a slight grin.

A solemn look crossed Daz's face. "I'm afraid to say that's one soul the sea claimed."

"Whatever are you jabbering on about? None of what you say makes any sense!" Eve hissed, but Daz, Shai and Wilton understood all too well.

"You need to find a way to get us out of here, and fast," Shai said, as he caught a glimpse of Mesi and Na'ila. There was no way of determining where Mesi started and Na'ila ended as they rolled around in clouds of dust, locked in battle.

"We'll never get out of this stuff, it feels like treacle!" Daz complained, and the more he squirmed the more the web bonded to his body like a large sucker.

"Put me down, Wilton, I think I may have just the thing," Hobson said.

He had noticed the dismembered limbs of the crabs, who now lay injured or far worse. Wilton crouched down and Hobson slithered to the floor, dodging the duelling crustaceans. Grabbing hold of the first spiny appendage that came to hand, the little Goylin dragged the defunct pincer over to Daz and Shai.

"Got my own pair of secateurs here," he said.

As he began to attack the marine algae, its defence mechanism kicked in and released a toxic gas. A foul odour of decomposed rotted fish gushed from the pores of its leafy structure.

"Feeling a bit light-headed," Eve said, wrapping her arms around Wilton's toned torso to steady herself.

"Me n'all, ducky, everything's spinning and making me feel so drowsy," Daz yawned.

"Whatever you do, stay awake; I'll have you both out of here in no time!" Hobson assured them. He soon mastered the art of manoeuvring the claw to get the best results. The quickness of his hands didn't allow the seaweed's regrowth. "That should just about do it," he said, and slowly pulled Shai through an unsymmetrical tear.

"Hold onto my feet, Daz; we'll go through together."

Wilton grabbed Hobson around the waist and said, "Bit of horsepower won't go amiss." They escaped their incarceration like caterpillars exiting a chrysalis.

By the look on Mesi's face it was clear that Na'ila had been well and truly obliterated. An unworldly premonition, Eve's only explanation was that of déjà vu as her and Mesi's eyes met for the very first time… A strange kind of telepathy passed between them and no words were needed. This gammy-eyed crustacean ravaged with battle wounds was the soul snatcher that had paid her a visit at Wilton's, the same crab that had put her friends' lives in jeopardy. Her blood boiled and she saw red, her crystal-blue eyes fixated on Mesi in a kind of hypnotic trance.

"You disgusting immoral oversized crabstick!" Eve yelled, as she watched Mesi close in on them.

"Are you addressing moi?" she said, and snapped her pincers aggressively. "Maybe your soul was meant for me after all… Your attitude fits me like a glove, and I'm sure it would only enhance my je ne sais quoi, that special something your friends sadly lack. Fire burns within your soul, girl, and I want it! What Mesi ruler of Cancer wants, Mesi gets!"

"The only way you rule Cancer is in your mind! There's Cancer's heart and soul!" Wilton turned and pointed to the Wheel of Life. "You're just a pointless placebo, a bitter pill that Cancer has had to swallow for far too long!"

Mesi grabbed Wilton around the neck. "I could snap you in half right now if I wished!" Her grasp tightened and the Sagittarian hung limply.

"Let him go, you murderer! Can't you see what you've done? Isn't there enough blood and carnage around here already!" Eve cried as she clung to an unconscious Wilton.

Crabs continued to pour off the wheel in their hundreds as the massacre grew into a violent bloodbath. Maybe something Eve said would have finally opened Mesi's eyes, but unfortunately for her it was too late. Instead of Cancer existing as a whole, a unit working together, it was now crab eat crab, and every species fought its own. If things continued in this way there would soon be complete annihilation and Cancer would lead itself into extinction.

Mesi's heart missed a beat. She hadn't just heard what Eve had to say, she'd actually listened. Much larger than all the other species she intervened, dropped Wilton in mid-flight and waved her pincers as she tried to call a truce. However, her voice could not be heard over the bloodcurdling cries and the thunderous claws clanging together.

"He's dead! GET HIM OFF ME!" Eve's distraught voice cried out to Daz and Shai as she lay trapped under Wilton's heavy loins.

"Got our own smelling salts 'ere, duck," Daz said, grabbing a handful of the pungent seaweed and thrusting it up the Sagittarian's large nostrils.

Wilton gasped for breath... "Oh, not again, I can well do without your abdominal thrusts after the last encounter!" He rose to his feet, a little shakily, his little hooves in spasm.

"Ha, what you doing, duck? You're the first tap-dancing horse I've seen!" Daz joked.

He glanced over at Eve, but she didn't seem to see the funny side. All she wanted was revenge, revenge on Mesi. Pins and needles rushed through her whole body and she shuddered uncontrollably. Palpitations had brought on an irregular heartbeat, and her whole being was racked with pain as she struggled for retribution. Her eyes cemented to the ramshackle wheel, which was now at a complete standstill. The last stragglers from the Underworld filtered in as Mesi spoke of the fire in Eve's heart. As spontaneous combustion engulfed the entire wheel's framework, bright yellow flames roared and crackled up the mainstay. The fighting stopped. The concept of fire in Cancer had never been understood ... until now.

"RUN!" Wilton shouted, and gave Eve a leg up.

She sat astride him once again and he quickly broke into a canter. Daz kept up as best he could while Hobson and Shai lagged behind, their short bowed legs not built for speed. Once they were a safe distance away they collapsed with exhaustion, except Wilton, who thrived on exercise. The ground that surrounded the wheel began to give way, like a rug being pulled from beneath their feet. It began to subside into the Underworld's dark abyss and took with it the dead, the dying and the injured of every single species; it had no conscience. The sea of souls had now become a sea of flames. The odd spider crab hung onto the spokes hoping for absolution, but all ended up as large fireballs as they swung to and fro on their unique webs. They caused a feeding frenzy for the awaiting devilfish below, as the fat from the barbequed crabs dripped into the icy-cold heart of the Underworld.

"Cancer's going down fast, and if we don't find the gate sharpish, then we're going down with it!" Wilton said, as large fissures ripped through the ground's surface around them and mini earthquakes sent unnerving tremors throughout the vicinity.

Greed alone had caused this natural disaster; sound waves echoed in a breathless cry.

"I'd know that voice anywhere … it's Mesi. Leave her to rot in her self-made hell … or should I say hole. If we don't get moving soon we'll be joining her!" Shai said, and started to walk away.

Daz, Hobson and Eve followed. Wilton felt a pang of guilt; it wasn't in his make-up to leave Mesi to die, but on the other hand he believed she would suffer more in the long run if she was kept alive and had to live with her actions.

"You coming, Eve, or not? I certainly can't go on foot. Give me chance to break in these wings of mine."

"No, you're okay, Wilton; think I'll sit this one out," she replied. As far as she was concerned, the further away she was from Mesi the better.

"Things around here are set to get a lot worse. You go on ahead, I'll catch up," Wilton said, as he stretched his graceful feathered wings into the air.

"But…"

"I'll be fine, Eve, go!" Wilton knelt down, kissed her on the forehead and launched into the air like an elegant swan. "This is going to take some getting used to, and as for landing, don't think I'll go there…"

The air current lifted him higher and he attempted to streamline, although not quite as gracefully as he'd hoped.

"Think you need L-plates, me duck!" Daz laughed.

Wilton hovered over the charred and smouldering remains of the wheel, and through the smoke-filled canyon he located Mesi, who hung from the parapet by a solitary claw that latched on like a vice. There was nowhere for Wilton to land, so he swooped down between the scorched timbers and positioned himself carefully, hovering like a large hummingbird.

"Give me your claw, Mesi!" Wilton called.

Her red eyeballs tried to focus as her life hung in the balance. "Please don't let me die!"

"Death's the easy way out, and too good for you. Going to make damn sure you spend an eternity in the hell you've created," Wilton said.

Time wasn't on Mesi's side, and Wilton grabbed her nearest claw in both hands and buffeted about in the winds that surged up from below. It took a while for him to level out, as Mesi's weight hindered their flight and he couldn't keep at a safe height, the large crab only inches above the ground. Wilton gazed down and their eyes met for the last time.

"I think this is as far as we go. Have a good life," he said, and gave one last sarcastic grin before he let go and watched Mesi's robust shell bounce across the barren terrain.

Wilton didn't hang about and went in pursuit of his friends. He spotted numerous star signs along the way, homeward bound and charging towards the gate. He came to rest near a small crowd of Pisceans, Taureans and water nymphs, who were all that remained. Had Daz and Eve gone without even saying goodbye? Wilton joined the end of the queue. Unhappy Goylins watched on, their fate in Cancer sealed. With no way out, they started to return to the shops and nearby houses to pick up the pieces of their ruined lives.

"Ay up, ducky, you still got any of that potion on ya?" Daz said.

"Thought you'd gone and left me... Yeah, got a couple of shells in my pocket," Wilton replied. Although now a Sagittarian, he still sat in his Goylin attire comprising seaweed skirt and two odd-looking boots on his two back hooves.

"'Ow the heck...? You're miles bigger now; 'ow they still fittin' ya, me duck?"

"Ha, you the pot or the kettle? You looked at yourself recently?" Wilton sniggered, looking Daz up and down, who was also dressed in his seaweed garments and boots.

"Well, looks like one size fits all, I guess; think we're stuck with them," Daz grinned.

"What happened to Mesi, then?" Eve couldn't help but ask.

"Let's just say I dropped her off… Hobson, you ugly slug – see Daz's T-shirt still fits you well! That says a lot for your waistline, Daz…!" Wilton removed a shell potion from his pocket and poured a couple of drops onto the mollusc, who fizzed up like a fruit sherbet.

"Eww, that's vile…" Eve said, backing away from the frothing monstrosity.

"Welcome back, Hobson," Shai said, and patted him on the back.

"Let me tell you I'm glad to be back; got quite used to these legs of mine," Hobson said, dusting himself down.

"How is it possible? How did Hobson just change back to his original self, and how come I can't just turn back into a firefly?" Shai asked.

"If you took the potion of your own free will then you would have felt the pain of your actions… Greed hurts, you know…" Wilton said.

The crowd had now diminished and it was Wilton's turn to leave. "Well, nice knowing you all." He offered Daz his hand. "Put it there, friend, I'll miss your quirky sense of humour. As for you, Shai, look after Hobson. I won't be needing my house any more; needs a bit of TLC, but I'm sure in time you'll make it feel like home. As you know, you won't be needing the key … you'll probably need a new front door, though. As for you, Eve, you have a lot of good qualities which I'll take with me." He gave each of them one last hug, handed Hobson his last few potions, gave them a final wave and disappeared through the gate.

"I can't bear goodbyes," Eve said, and without a backward glance she too passed through the gate.

"Don't leave me, Daz, I … I love you, you big oaf; we've been through so much together," Shai said, tears welling up in his eyes as he reached for Daz's hand.

"Love you too, me duck. I'll never forget you, you've been the best … even though really you're just a blumin' firefly, you're also my best friend."

"Here, Daz, this might come in handy," Hobson interrupted

their emotional farewell. He passed Daz a potion and added, "I'll look after Shai for ya, don't worry ... just go."

A heartbroken Daz took one last look behind him, walked through the gate and left Cancer, Hobson and a very distraught Shai behind him forever...

CHAPTER THIRTEEN

It's a Grey Area

"We did everything we could; think we should lock the gate," Eve said. She could see the pain in Daz's eyes having lost his little companion. She held him close and ran her hand through his hair as she tried to reassure him that things from here on in were bound to get better.

"I can't lock it, duck… The key… My jacket! Left it at Wilton's," Daz said, still visibly upset and struggling to get his words out.

Eve unzipped and removed her coat. "Lucky one of us has got a good memory then."

Daz's jacket was tied neatly around her petite waist. She searched about in his pocket.

"Ahh, think this is the one." She pulled out a tarnished iron key. "Here, I'll let you do the honours." Eve pressed it gently into his right hand.

"Just one more look, me duck, eh?" He leant cautiously into the gate's opening.

Cancer was now gone forever, and a swirling grey mist danced around his head. He closed the gate for the last time with a rueful smile. Before he had time to position the key in its lock, he was taken aback as a bright orb shot through the keyhole like a bullet from a gun.

"SHAI! YOU LITTLE BEAUTY! But how? It's not possible, you're a Goylin!" Daz exclaimed, as he plucked him from the air.

Shai folded his little wings and sat as sweet as a nut in the palm of his hand.

"If your memory's firing on all cylinders, then you should remember Wilton's words. You see, it all makes sense now. I never drank that potion, you just tipped it over me; greed never played a part in me becoming a Goylin, that's why I never felt the pain you

183

did. Like Hobson, the potion's effects have simply worn off; my soul was never taken." Shai smiled up at Daz and swung his little rear from side to side, his light flickering from all the excitement.

"Well, duck, there's a plus come out of this for you... Got a spare potion, the amount you need to change into a Goylin; will last little old you an eternity." Daz paused. "So now you can be what you want, when you want." He laughed.

Eve watched on silently. It was so nice for her to see Daz and Shai's very special reunion. She didn't want to spoil the moment, and so pulled the key slowly from a preoccupied Daz's hand and pushed it firmly into the lock, turning it anti-clockwise. She heard a loud click, and the barrel liquidised and reshaped itself. She had to jiggle it about several times before being able to pull it free.

"Daz, Shai, look, this is most peculiar. It's reshaped itself!"

"Don't talk daft, Eve!" Shai said, his little voice just able to make itself heard.

"I tell you, it has; it looked like a ram's horns before, now it's a slanted number sixty-nine..."

"Alright, Eve, done the trick anyway. Don't worry 'bout it, ducky. Ha, maybe one key fits all."

"Bet Mesi's running around trying to pick up the pieces in Cancer," Eve said, but she could only begin to imagine.

"Only one thing for sure; those crabs in Paradisum are still sitting pretty, and there won't be any more joining them in a hurry. I do hope Hobson will be okay in his new home, all alone," Shai said. He felt quite sorry for the funny little mollusc.

"Forget Mesi, forget Hobson. It's 'bout time we found out where the hell we are," Daz said as he slipped his jacket on.

A tired Shai flew straight into Daz's pocket, searching for a bit of comfort and a well-earned rest. He turned down his little light and closed his eyes.

Did their surrounds bode well this time? they wondered.

"Well, Eve, you look first. If you don't like what you see, we're back through that blumin' gate, Mesi or no Mesi."

"Take a look, Daz, we certainly stand out..."

Daz took a quick peep. "As I walk through the valley of the

shadow of death, I will fear no evil…" he gasped. "Anyway, on a lighter note, who turned out the lights?"

"No, you idiot, who rubbed out the colour?" Eve said.

They turned back to the gate once again and saw that their illusive transportation had taken flight, a secret hidden within their newfound star sign. Their next journey had begun.

A sepia canvas opened up before their eyes, and the only thing that coloured their view was themselves. A forest or a jungle? On first glance, Daz and Eve weren't quite sure. Bay trees' thin stems shot up to their left, a mass of thick foliage decorating each tip; rounded in shape, they individually resembled knitted pom-poms. In the large quantities they were grown they looked more like one misshapen scatter cushion. Black walnut trees, their thick knotted trunks stretching up and reaching for their leafy attire. Underdeveloped nuts, small offspring, a picturesque break in the lavish foliage.

"It's beautiful, without the beauty," Eve said, as she walked through the undergrowth astounded by the colourless vegetation.

Daz lagged behind. "Got a nutcracker on ya, Eve? Sure these would go down a treat!" He picked up a few fallen walnuts. "Just tempting me, aren't you, duck?"

Eve couldn't quite believe that Daz had actually talked to a bunch of walnuts.

"Think you lost your marbles as well as your soul in Cancer," she chuckled as she fell upon more floral species.

Exquisite passion flowers graced the leafy ground creating a lush carpet that called out for admiration. The varied shades of grey swayed in the breeze, and like prima donnas they pirouetted and pliéd like seasoned ballerinas. Eve couldn't resist picking one and held the stem gently between her fingers, lifting it until it rested softly on the tip of her nose. She took a deep breath and waited for its perfumed fragrance, but nothing. No scent, no colour, an absence of all niceties as Eve and Daz wandered through the bland and odourless environment.

"Ay up, Eve, think we're witnessing an eclipse," Daz said, looking up at a black sun hanging in the sky.

"That's something you don't see very often, it'll be gone in the blink of an eye," she replied, marvelling at the sight.

"In that case, ducky…" Daz said, reaching into his pocket, turning his phone on and zooming in with his five-megapixel camera. "This is certainly something to show the grandkids."

"After everything we've seen and been through, you take a picture of the sun!"

"An eclipse, Eve, get it right!"

But was it an eclipse? The black moon's shadow never passed and the sun never regained its light; Eve's explanation went unexplained. A mysterious galaxy without rhyme or reason.

"What was that? I'm sure we're being watched," Eve said. She nudged Daz as a thick laurel bush rustled, yet there was no breeze. Whether it was something in the air or purely down to instinct, she grabbed Daz's hand and they started to run.

"Daz, there's something's after us, I can hear it breathing."

"Yes, it's panting!"

The sound of twigs snapping and fracturing rang out through the undergrowth. Daz took a quick glimpse behind.

"Eve, run faster; don't think ya gonna like what I've just seen."

Eve hadn't got time to answer as the ground suddenly fell away beneath them and both landed feet first in a soft, dark odourless substance that resembled oil.

"Daz, I'm drowning!" Eve screamed, as her hands flayed helplessly in the air.

The more they struggled and tried to claw their way out, the deeper they sank, and soon they were entombed up to their necks.

Daz's legs shot backwards then forwards, like he was riding a bike, but he didn't get very far.

"Eve, stay still, our movements are sucking us further down," Daz instructed. He stood rigid, not moving a muscle. "It's getting warm down 'ere, ducky…"

Eve gazed up. Shards of light glistened through a large gaping hole in the woven twigs and branches through which they had fallen. With a newfound brightness, the eclipse having passed, an unrecognisable silhouette blended with the sunlight as an insipid presence peered down upon them.

"Wonder what star sign this is? We're like trapped animals!" Eve glanced up for a second time. "It's gone…"

"What you on 'bout, duck?" Daz asked. He noticed deep inscriptions etched in the walls around them. "Eve, look…" He struggled to make out the unorthodox words that were virtually illegible.

The morning dew starts to fall
On a nowhere journey
Down a nowhere wall
Like an endless mist
There's no way through
You're a nowhere man
There's no place for you
You travel down that one-way street
There's no one there for you to meet
You look to the sky
But the sun sinks low
You're a nowhere man
With no place to go

"Shai, you okay down there?" Daz asked.

But the little firefly didn't, or wasn't able to, answer.

Eve's teeth chattered. "I'm so cold, Daz! We're going to die down here!" she sobbed, as the sun's rays faded and were masked by long shadows.

Then there was total darkness and a deathly silence, broken only by the sound of their shallow breathing.

"Daz, it hurts! Get it off! Get it off!" Eve cried. It felt like leeches were slithering over her entire body, anonymously piercing her delicate skin and savagely sucking the life from within her.

"I can't get it off, Eve, it's got me too!" Daz splashed around, but the consistency of the pulpy colourless liquid began to congeal, harden and finally set; they were mummified in their own ready-made tombs.

"It's caving in on us, we're going to be buried alive!" Eve tried to wriggle free as the neatly laid branches that hid their entrapment caved in around their heads.

"Maybe I can be of some assistance!" An unidentifiable being leapt down to join them, its big feet barely missed Daz's head. The impact of its landing caused large cracks to rip through the tacky compacted matter.

"Hiya! Name's Kendrick, been watching you."

"You, you … whatever you are, you put us down here?" Eve saw red. "Leave us be! If we're going to die, least let us die with some dignity. You've tortured us enough!"

"Well, if you really want me to go away I can do that too! But actually I've come to help get you out." The dark figure crouched down. "Sit tight. This might feel a bit uncomfortable, but I'll soon have you out!"

He poked and prodded a long cylindrical object into the densely compressed goo. Vibrations pulsated throughout their incarcerated bodies as he chipped away at the tough surface. It soon ruptured and loosened its hold on Daz and Eve.

"Give me your hand! We haven't got much time; the sun will soon be up."

All they could see was the whites of his eyes.

"Ladies first," he said, and his bony fingers reached down between the deep cracks that had crumbled away and held Eve's wrist firmly. He then began to pull her up inch by inch, until finally she broke free. "Don't thank me yet. Climb up the engravings carved into the wall; they are deep, well deep enough for your hands and feet." He placed his mouth around the cylindrical object and blew. An aluminous white powder dispersed and seeped into the writings, a neon glow transforming the darkened pit.

Daz and Eve's eyes adjusted to the new light.

Eve glanced down at her long A-line medieval-style dress. *I'd have been better off in my pyjamas,* she thought to herself. She reached down and picked the material up from the floor to just above her knee, then cautiously began to ascend.

"Thanks, ducky!" Daz said, as he too was rescued by Kendrick, and they began the climb.

Kendrick's expertise showed as he moved with skilled precision, obviously learnt over time. Daz's arms ached and he struggled to pull his body weight, juggling between handholds. When he eventually surfaced, he collapsed breathless at Kendrick's feet.

An ashen man stood in a coarse grass skirt, ruched and beaded round the middle, hugging his scrawny waist. A leathery animal skin hung around his torso like a woollen afghan waistcoat. Moccasins in the same material fitted snugly on each foot and were tied securely around his ankles.

"Pleased to meet you both," he said.

Kendrick's broad nostrils twitched as he sniffed the air with an animal-like instinct. A long matted shroud stood proud around the wide bone structure of his prominent facial features. His almond-shaped eyes protruded like those of a cat, yet the opportunist and cunning traits gave way to an expressionless glare, a dull film, a glazed appearance; his whole being lacked lustre.

"Daz, to friends; pleased to meet you, me duck. Won't drop in or pay a visit to one of those underground holes again in a hurry."

"Those underground holes, as you so call them, are lions' traps," Kendrick said, and sniffed the air again. "Can't be too careful."

"Too careful? What do you mean?" Eve felt a sudden shiver shoot up her spine. "You're giving me the heebie-jeebies."

"What do you expect? You are in the star sign of Leo."

"Thought me eyes were playing tricks on me back there! Isn't an everyday occurrence to find a lion chasin' ya," Daz said, having flashbacks as he spoke.

"You're going to have many encounters with the king of the jungle; it's not safe out here, think you both better come with me. Change is in the air, the sun is on the rise, and if we're not careful the lions' feeding frenzy will be upon us." Kendrick gazed up at the black sun, its outer perimeter a burnt gold as its immense heat began to scorch away its inner darkness.

"Why does Leo lack colour, and why is everything grey, white or insipid? And you Kendrick, you look ill," Eve asked.

"Well, young lady…"

"The name's Eve actually."

"Well, Eve…" Kendrick continued, "the substance you were unfortunate enough to fall into was wax, a wax that has many hidden properties. Here in Leo it is as much a predator as the lions themselves. The sun's warmth melts it until it's in a dissolved

189

state, and that's when it has the ability to suck on its prey and drain every ounce of its personality, life force and very being from within. On reappearance of the black sun, the wax cools and over time solidifies; that's when it stores its well-earned provisions, as with each of its victims it gains strength. But think on, Eve, before you criticise my pallid appearance; you should take a look at your own."

Eve peered down, on first glance not at all worried by what she saw; but she had forgotten the fact that her gown was white. It was not until the slashed sleeves revealed her bare arms that she saw their usual pink tinge had transformed into an anaemic pallor, a lifeless grey.

"Daz, look, look at me!" She gazed at him for reassurance, but he too blended in perfectly with their background. The vibrant colours they knew and loved had been totally wiped out, snatched away from them.

The cylindrical object Kendrick held was actually a tribal spear, and he pointed it in the direction of the vastly overgrown vegetation. Laurel hedges grew in abundance, yet he headed straight towards the middle and momentarily rooted around. He eventually managed to locate a tiny wooden branch, which he used as a lever. With a final look behind him to ensure they weren't being watched or followed, he pulled it down sharply. Its frontage was lowered like a drawbridge, and the branches knitted together and were tied securely with a wax-treated durable rope. A perfect camouflage that, as yet, the lions hadn't managed to uncover.

"Daz, Eve, hurry, there are eyes everywhere! You just never know who's watching."

Quick to obey, they stepped through the leafy opening and helped Kendrick replace his home-made trestle of interwoven leaves and branches. Deep fields of colourless lavender lay beyond a grey scentless mass, which led Daz, Eve and Kendrick to the underground tunnels hidden and protected by the blanket of flora and fauna. A grey earthen shaft opened up between the lavender's foliage and they faced a steep decline.

"One black hole is enough for one day," Eve said, feeling inclined to run in the opposite direction.

Kendrick could feel the warmth of the sun's inner sphere as its crimson flare lit the sky.

"I can't stay out in the sunlight. You have two choices: join me, or take your chances, but I must warn you, the jungle has many hidden dangers." Kendrick stood in the tunnel's mouth, which was slightly shaded. "Well, Daz, Eve, the decision's yours, but I'm afraid I've got to go."

"Okay, me duck, think you've made me mind up. What do ya reckon, Shai?" It was only now after everything that had happened that he remembered the little firefly buried deep in his jacket. "SHAI?" A panic-stricken Daz checked his pocket and detected quiet snores. "Bless him. After Aries and Cancer, he's out for the count."

"Yeah, good job he's asleep. Where we've been, I'm surprised the little bug didn't suffocate. Could do with a kip myself. Have you got anywhere we can rest down here?" Eve's eyelids began to droop; she felt like they'd been awake for an eternity.

"You can rest all you like if you follow me."

That was all the persuasion Eve and Daz needed, and they dragged their tired bodies after Kendrick.

"Do anything for a comfy bed," Eve yawned; Shai's narcolepsy had started to rub off on her.

Bright fluted candles were interspersed around the walls, their white flames waltzing in sequence. Freestanding tribal artefacts made authentic statements. Sundried animal skins were stretched taught and bound together over bamboo canes, hand moulded into ornate hide shields. Next to these were metal-tipped spears fastened together in bevelled niches; an alpha male display of the tribe's antique hunting gear.

"Where are you taking us?" Eve asked, intimidated by the unorthodox decorations. The lack of air and claustrophobic tunnels were making her feel even more drowsy.

"Be patient, Eve, not much longer." Kendrick turned a sharp corner.

Daz and Eve were astounded by what they saw next. An inhabited underground village lay before them, with a number of dome-shaped huts sitting snugly in separate circular communities.

Common grasses had been meticulously thatched together and connected to moulded bay tree frames to make a sturdy beehive construction where the natives resided.

Kendrick led them through several of the quirkily built villages and finally stopped before a straw-woven door embellished by a satanic mask.

"Welcome to my home!" he said.

"Eww! What on earth is that hideous face?" Eve gasped.

"It's a mask, Eve," Daz explained. "We settle for door knockers back home."

"No, Daz," Kendrick corrected, "it's actually a skull of one of our dead ancestors. These are the watchmen who deter evil spirits. When a great warrior dies the skull is embalmed and the soul within watches over us. We reshape the face with a parched material, daub it in black wax and then enhance this with our own personal inscriptions. Its long dreadlocks lend it a lion's strength, and with its eyes permanently closed the senses alone ward off evil spirits. It is a curse to look the dead straight in the eyes."

Kendrick untied a small rope securing his door.

"Come on then, you'll love it inside," he said.

A cosy curvaceous space housed two palm tree hammocks, with a tripod made from bark assembled at each end and a fabricated mattress designed from its leafy foliage.

"Found my bed, duck!" Daz said, and took a running jump. "This is the life." He curled his legs up into the foetal position and closed his eyes; it wasn't long before he was snoring away happily.

Kendrick sat cross-legged on a circular pampas grass rug.

"Join me, Eve," he said.

He picked up two large pieces of walnut bark and placed them a short distance apart, then inserted smaller branches between them. Finally, he added some small twigs and dried grasses in a criss-cross pattern on top.

"Now for the magic, white magic that is."

He unscrewed the metal tip from the sheath of his spear and placed the opposite end between his lips. As he blew a steady continuous breath, a white powder dispersed into the air which surrounded the wooden structure. The dehydrated twigs and grasses kindled and the flames lapped between the thicker branches like elongated tongues, expelling a fierce white blaze.

"Now I'm down here, can I have a magic wand too?" Eve asked. She leaned into the warmth but felt nothing – the flames were cold. "A fire with no heat? Kendrick, what on earth's going on?"

"Yes, Eve, I think maybe it's time I offered you an explanation."

Kendrick opened a small ottoman and presented her with an earthenware bowl. He placed a larger pot on top of the smouldering embers and then went out to fetch two small sacks and a wooden pitcher. He emptied the sacks one at a time into the pot – one contained crushed walnuts, the other diced sunflower seeds – and to this he added some clear honey, which he poured slowly from the pitcher into the mix and stirred vigorously with a wooden ladle.

"Where did you concoct this recipe?" Eve asked as her appetite dwindled.

"It's an Ashman family recipe; porridge with a twist," he replied, as he continued to stir his home-made concoction. "Pass me your bowl." Kendrick spooned out the congealed porridge, which had the consistency of treacle.

Eve tipped the bowl to her mouth; the porridge was surprisingly hot.

"Cold fire, hot porridge? One and one here seems to make three," she said.

"The lions have taken everything from us; they are the devils that roam Leo and they seek our hidden dwellings. The large cats lie in wait, and if they ever root us out our species will be devoured to extinction. The majority of our senses have been wiped out, colour totally banished. Colour brought only war. One lion practised the art of black magic and he was the one who brought this colourless shadow that now hangs over Leo. Our ruling planet, the sun, is the only colour and energy it can't manipulate." Kendrick slurped down some lumpy porridge before continuing. "All the lions are white, while myself and the Ashman tribe, whom you are yet to meet, are a shade off black. Yin and yang, complete opposites. Our paths are ordained not to cross and an un-harmonious segregation has forced us underground where we skulk in the undergrowth during sunlight hours. We are granted a slight reprieve when the black sun visits; that's our time. We become the predators, while the lions retreat and hide."

The hammock creaked as Daz rolled over.

"Wakey-wakey, sleepyhead," Eve chuckled.

"Five more minutes, duck." He stretched his arms into the air as he squinted at Eve. "Is that breakfast? Hmm, don't mind if I do…" A sluggish Daz plodded over. "Cor, this seaweed's gotta lot to answer for, it's really itching me…"

Kendrick interrupted Daz's preening session. "Here you go, Daz." He passed Daz a steaming bowl of porridge before jumping to his feet. "Got just the thing for you…" He rummaged through his ottoman. "Now you're here, you may as well join the tribe. Give us your jacket, and that lettuce leaf you're attempting to wear."

"It's a seaweed skirt, me duck," Daz dribbled, as thick lumps of porridge ran down his chin.

"Try this on for size. Always have a spare – one to wash, one to wear, that's my motto. We'll be identical."

Daz squeezed into the grass skirt. "Don't think I should have had that porridge. My waistline and this skirt aren't exactly seeing eye to eye."

The lion skin waistcoat was a slightly better fit, and certainly a lot warmer than his previous attire.

"You can keep ya slippers to yaself, Kendrick. I'm more than happy in me brown boots; 'bout the only good thing that came from Cancer." Daz looked down. "Well, this ain't gunna keep the cold out, don't even fasten up!" He pulled the waistcoat tighter. "Nah, this ain't gunna do, pass us me leathers back, Kendrick."

"Our tribal celebrations are about to take place; these occur when the sun sits over our sacred grounds. Come, you will enjoy this."

"Don't mean to be rude," Eve said, "and we're very grateful for your kind hospitality, but no thanks. Celebrations are the last thing on our mind at the moment, we just want to find the gate and go home."

"Speak for yaself, Eve, I love a party," Daz said. "Let's go boogie. We can find the gate after, ducky."

"I thought you'd have known better after Cancer!"

"That was Cancer, this is Leo! Hang loose, Eve, chill, let's go 'ave some fun!"

Kendrick scratched his head. "That's got me thinking. Hang on one moment, both of you; who are you, and what are you? How did you get here?"

"We came from the star sign Cancer. We passed through Cancer's gate and found ourselves here. We aren't star signs, we're humans from Earth. We need to find Leo's gate; hopefully this time it'll lead us home, otherwise it's three down, nine of the twelve star signs to go."

Kendrick ushered the pair towards his door. "Well, this is your home now. As far as I know Leo has no gate, and nobody ever enters or leaves. You are a true mystery, my friends, but now you are here I suggest you get used to our ways."

"You can think whatever you want! I know there's a gate here somewhere, and I'm going to find it!" Eve sulked, dragging her feet as Kendrick and Daz walked merrily on in front, deep in conversation.

In the centre of the huts – the tribe's living quarters – they stood around a circle of thick congealed wax. Tribesmen identical to Kendrick poured out of their homes and began to sit cross-legged around its outer edge.

"Look, Kendrick, they've got bongo drums!" Daz exclaimed, as he watched two of the Ashmen make preparations inside the circle.

These were dressed slightly differently and wore lion fur in an apron design, and from the knee down hung perfectly groomed manes that brushed the tops of their feet.

"These are our entertainers," Kendrick explained. "Their dancing and the repetitive drumbeats convert the sun's light and energy from gold to black. Only then can our celebrations move to higher ground, where we become kings of the jungle. The lions slink away and retreat into hiding. Then we hunt out the pride, and celebrate through sacrificial rituals."

"Sounds great, ducky!"

"Come, Daz, Eve, let me introduce you to a few of my fellow tribesmen."

"You go, Daz, I'm not in the mood for celebrating." Eve didn't intend to join in the frivolity, and feeling deflated she leant against one of the huts.

"'Ere, Eve, 'ave me jacket then, don't want to be inappropriately dressed." Daz screwed it up into a ball and chucked it at her.

She watched as he disappeared into the growing number of Ashmen. *Great*, she thought to herself.

The melodious beat of the drums began, followed by loud whistles, screams and dancers jumping up and down. Their bodies revolved in rhythmical snake-like movements and they punched ornate stabbing spears into the air in a mirrored sequence; then nothing…

Oh no! Eve thought as the tribal festivities came to an abrupt halt. *What's he done this time?*

Her view was disturbed by the tribal onlookers as they banged their feet rhythmically on the floor, their rigid bodies moving slowly back and forth as melodic chants filled the air. Eve felt intimidated by the whole experience, and the native war dance gave her a particularly eerie sense of unrest. She swayed from side to side trying to see between the sea of heads. The dancers stood in a circle and faced out towards the chanting crowd. They unscrewed the base of their spears in unison and placed the end in their mouths – Eve remembered Kendrick had done something similar when they were trapped in the lions' pit. Their heads jerked back and looked disjointed. Although her view was still impaired, she then witnessed a cloud of black powder being dispelled high into the air.

"Wow, Kendrick, that's ace, ducky!"

"Quiet, Daz, just watch; you haven't seen anything yet, my friend."

The black powder hung momentarily in the air, before each and every particle was drawn like a magnet towards the waxen circle. In an instant the wax burst into the most unnatural flames Daz had ever seen.

"Black fire, ducky?"

"Everything in Leo is black and white, thought you'd have gathered that by now after your transformation," Kendrick explained.

"Well, duck, I've seen a gold sun, so I just thought the flames would be the same."

"Keep watching, this might surprise you. Look." He pointed upwards.

Daz noticed irregular-shaped holes chiselled out of the earth above them.

"Who climbed up there, duck, and how did they manage it?"

"They didn't, these were hand dug from above ground. Our ancestors spent many black suns surveying the positional rays, each point being marked with boiling wax. These influential elders were learned astrologers... Just watch, it'll all become clear."

The chanting grew louder. Shards of golden sunlight filtered through the antiquated openings, down towards the sepia-coloured congregated natives. Each sunbeam seemed programmed to hit a certain point, and Daz watched as the rays chased one another and hit their preordained targets.

"THAT'S MAGIC!" he shouted. The hypnotic golden light reflected in Daz's eyes and bounced back, penetrating the deathly black flames. Clouds of black smoke engulfed the circle's circumference as it began to disperse, briefly revealing an incandescent white light that transformed into a rich golden glow.

Kendrick laughed to himself. "You'll soon come to realise that fire won't burn you here. You see, Daz, we control almost all colour with our black magic."

"In that case, why is everything grey?"

"That, I'm afraid, is something we made a pact on. It's an Ashman secret, and as you aren't an Ashman my lips are sealed."

The tribal music and dancing spilled out amongst the flames. Ashmen, with the addition of Daz, jumped and cavorted through the heatless blaze. Eve's obscured view had prevented her from witnessing the unexplainable phenomenon, so cold and bored, she sat wrapped in Daz's leather jacket.

"What's all this commotion?" Shai asked. He stretched, then straightened his little wings and flew into Eve's hand.

"Looks like they got you too, poor lil' fly." Eve glanced down at his colourless rounded body.

"Who's got me?"

"You're grey like me, they've taken your colour too!"

Shai looked puzzled. "You don't look any different."

Eve had totally forgotten. "Flies can only see in black and white anyway."

"For your information, Eve, although I'm known as a firefly, I'm actually a member of the beetle family. Due to the limited colour visible to me it wouldn't make a lot of difference what colour you were. Who's taken all the colour anyway? And where are we for that matter?"

"We're in the star sign of Leo; it's the lions who've taken the colour. Daz has done his usual disappearing act, and we've got no idea where the gate is."

"In that case, I think you'll need a hand. It's time I changed my image."

"One drop or two?" Eve joked as she pulled the grey bonnet from Daz's pocket. She placed Shai on the floor. "Don't want you turning here; I'll look like a ventriloquist with my dummy." She tilted the shell and two of the drops dripped down Shai's back.

"As if by magic, a Goylin appeared," Shai laughed, as he readjusted his seaweed attire.

"Now I'm up to size, I think we best find Daz before he gets himself and us in to any more trouble; he's making quite a habit of that!"

Shai took Eve's hand in his and they slowly forced their way through the Ashmen, who were putting everything into their festive occasion.

"Now we're talking!" Like a moth drawn to the light, Shai pulled Eve hurriedly towards the heightening flames that danced around in the cool air. "This is my kind of party." A wee smile spread over his face.

Eve stopped Shai in his tracks. "Don't forget, you're a Goylin now."

"I know, but fire's in my blood."

Eve noticed the malevolent looks the Ashmen had given Shai

on passing. "It's your tail, Shai, it's attracting unwanted attention."

"Well, where do you suggest I put it…?" Shai asked, giving her a cheeky grin.

"Oh be quiet, go tie a knot in it!" she chuckled as she removed Daz's jacket. "Think this should do the trick."

Daz's leather jacket hung past Shai's bony knees and concealed his unfavourable appendage.

"Look, Eve, there he is," Shai said.

They couldn't miss him gallivanting through the flames. Daz's tribal dance was perfect for him as it required no skill, no graceful movement, and boy, did he excel at it, although a herding buffalo would have offered more finesse than his untimely and clumsy footwork.

"If all these savages can walk through the flames unhurt, then I'm damn sure we can."

"Daz must think he's back in Aries. Told him he shouldn't have left those clothes behind," Eve said nervously, as she closed her eyes and walked blindly into the roaring inferno.

Shai followed, but couldn't help but stop for a moment and bathe in its glory. He longed for that warm inner body glow and felt cheated by its heatless energy.

"Pssst, Daz, over here!" Eve called, but her dulcet tones went unheard, drowned out by the tribal chanting.

Eve and Shai watched on as Daz sat while the entertainers knelt around him. They played on the drums, this time with their fingers, in a regular soothing beat that seemed to create calmness, and a change of mood fell over the entire tribe.

"Here, Daz," Kendrick said as he walked over to the fire and dipped his fingers into the melted waxen base. "You're one of us now, my friend." He placed his four fingers on either side of Daz's face and dragged them in a sweeping motion from his cheeks towards his jawbone. The markings glowed white like florescent lighting, then faded and sank deep into his skin, like scratches delivered from the claws of a great white lion. Kendrick reached for his spear. "Do you trust me, brother?" He looked deep into Daz's eyes.

"KENDRICK, STOP IT! YOU'RE SCARING ME!" Eve had seen quite enough and she lunged forward.

Shai, taken by surprise, just stood and looked on.

"Restrain them!" Kendrick shouted, and beckoned two Ashmen to his side. "The ritual's only in its second stage, there's one more to complete… I must finish what I've started. It's Daz's wish to become one of us." He was not pleased by Eve's untimely interruption. "I've told you once, restrain the intruders!"

Eve and Shai had nowhere to go, and their arms were grabbed and forcibly held up behind their backs. Kendrick began to chant, and continued with the third and final stage. He unscrewed the base of his spear and held it up to Daz's face.

"Do you trust me, brother?" he asked Daz for the second time.

Daz nodded. "Yes, Kendrick, I trust you."

Kendrick blew into the spear's shaft and once again a white powder was discharged. The dry substance enveloped Daz's head and clung to the deep scratches etched into his cheeks. The fresh abrasions healed instantly as the powder compacted itself into the superficial layers of his skin. His face appeared to have been invaded by thousands of tiny insects as the top layer literally began to crawl. His rounded face became more angular, and prominent cheekbones were pushed up and an emphasised jawbone protruded, while his small button nose broadened above large flattened nostrils. His small insignificant eyes became enlarged and now resembled two almonds.

"Kendrick, what have you done? Give us Daz back!" Eve pleaded, but her cries went unheeded.

The volume and intensity of the chanting grew, and a fellow tribesman handed something to Kendrick.

"Today you have taken the form of an Ashman," Kendrick said, as he held a lion tooth pendant high in the air, muttered a few native words, kissed the pendant and placed it over Daz's head, where it sat proudly on his bare chest.

The Ashmen rejoiced for the addition of their newly joined member. Short sharp drumbeats accompanied the natives, who divided into two long lines outside the fire ring.

"What's happening, Kendrick?" Daz asked.

"No time for questions, come with me."

They joined one of the lines. Shai and Eve, still restrained, were frogmarched over. The atmosphere suddenly lost its party feel as an apprehensive aura fell over the tribesmen. A grand white lion headed in their direction, on which sat a very distinguished Ashman.

"That's Ashman, our chief, the founder of our tribe; we worship him like a god. He must be obeyed," Kendrick explained. "Only he can tame the large beasts. His black magic has enabled us to partially control the sun, and four out of the five senses. Hearing is the only one he hasn't mastered yet. With each sacrifice we grow in strength, each eclipse lengthens and soon the sun will lose its light forever and Ashman will have total domination of Leo. Then the tables will turn and the lions will be forced to hide away underground like we have to now."

The great white cat stepped through the flames, and the golden glow flickered and the light ebbed, reinventing itself into a swarthy black like a raven's wings hovering over the waxen circle.

"My children, the black sun will soon be upon us, and then we'll take our celebrations to a higher level."

A toneless dirge resonated as Ashman preached a sermon in a foreign tongue to the tribal inhabitants. His dreadlocks of interwoven twigs and walnuts were bandaged tightly in palm leaves that stood proud from his head like a mane.

"What's that on his face, ducky?"

"A yin-yang symbol," Kendrick replied, admiring the black and white compressed waxen image on his left cheek. "This symbolises the workings of Leo, the two energies that at present fight against each other. It shows how the two opposites interact. We are the yin, black, passive and cold, but growing in strength. The lions are yang, white, bright and hot-headed, yet their strength weakens with every black sun. When we have complete control, yin-yang will no longer exist and the only symbol will be yin, and the black sun will become our ruling planet."

"Unless me eyes are deceiving me, Kendrick … it looks like it's movin'."

"No, brother, your eyes do not play tricks on you. At present the continual movement is caused by the two opposing energies working together… This will only be short-lived; our black solstice will reign for infinity."

Ashman's charcoal eyes perused his worshipers, stopping when they reached Shai.

"What is that? Some kind of half breed?" he asked as he slid off the lion's back. "Wait there, Cleon!" he commanded, as he approached the two captors. "Remove your cloak."

Shai immediately dropped the jacket that Eve had draped over his shoulders.

"Who's sent you? Are you in league with the Devil?" Ashman asked. Then he saw it hanging limply between Shai's legs. "It's got a tail! A lion's tail! This isn't your domain, is it?!"

"It's not mine either!" Eve piped up as she struggled for freedom. "For the last time, get your filthy hands off me!"

"AND A FEMALE! We've been cursed!" he roared. "KILL THEM BOTH! Then bring me that tail!"

"Daz, help us!" Eve looked over at an expressionless face. The crystalline lenses of his eyes were clouded and distant, and no acknowledgement came on his part; they were like strangers meeting for the first time.

Kendrick stepped forward cautiously. "My leader, my god, may I offer you a suggestion?" He threw himself to the floor before Ashman and kissed his feet.

"Talk, brother," Ashman commanded.

"Our ancestral offerings are nigh and ritual pickings will be needed, so I say that rather than risk our brothers we should send these two intruders, if they're not ripped apart by the lions." Kendrick looked over sarcastically in Daz's direction. "Their return is guaranteed."

Ashman smiled. "Your prudence will be rewarded. Take them, prepare them; and hurry, the sun waits for no one." He straightened his fur robe and mingled with his fellow tribesmen.

The deafening drum rolls pounded through Eve's head as the festivities continued.

"Come," Kendrick said, as he led Shai and Eve back to his hut. Once inside, he hurriedly closed the door behind them. "Where did you find your pet?"

"His name's Shai, he's a Goylin! Think it's you who should be doing the explaining not me! We trusted you, and now you've turned Daz into a brainless savage," Eve snapped.

"I agree on the second point, but definitely have to question the first," Shai chuckled.

"Oh, a pet that talks!"

"I'm no pet, I'm a firefly… Well, sort of."

Kendrick thought he was as much of an airhead as Daz. But where Shai was concerned, there were no flies on him!

"Silly girl, can't you see I'm only trying to help you? But you've put me in an impossible situation. I needed to speak to you and Daz together."

"You had plenty of time to talk to us earlier!"

"It isn't as simple as that, Eve, ears are everywhere, listening. Have you seen how thin my walls are? You can hear the wind blow through them. I tried to get you together in the celebrations, but you wouldn't come. I couldn't afford to force you and risk you making a scene … the drums alone would have drowned out our conversation, and the tribe, otherwise occupied, would have been none the wiser."

"Okay, so what if I buy that … you had no possible reason to turn Daz into an Ashman!"

"We don't have foreign star signs in Leo … ever."

"We're not star signs, we're humans… Well, I am," Eve said as she looked at Shai.

"Whatever you are and wherever you came from is irrelevant now. I needed you and Daz to blend in with the tribe, stay inconspicuous, and turning you into Ashmen was the only way I knew how. But don't fret, Eve; you see, the magic I use is white, and white magic is short-lived. You wouldn't have had to live with the full effects and its hidden curse; you would have been able to go to the higher ground and live under both suns while you searched for your so-called gate."

"But Daz didn't even look at me… He looked through me like I wasn't even there." Eve said, quite hurt by Daz's ignorance.

"He only did what he was told, what I instructed him to do, and now he lives in harmony, no questions asked. My brothers would have thought Daz's transformation was just another ritual, their low IQs don't lend themselves to reasoning." Kendrick paused to gather his thoughts. "You must collect all these ingredients for Ashman's black sun offerings, for the ritual of all rituals. That has never been successfully achieved, as one ingredient is simply irretrievable. I haven't got time to go into the finer details; if we're much longer Ashman will start to get suspicious. I need to get you out of here and on your way. Cleon will accompany you and fill you in... Come now." Kendrick hurried them out of the hut and back into the midst of the celebrations, which had gathered pace since Ashman's arrival.

"Who's Cleon?" Eve panted.

Kendrick's focus was on other things, however, so her question went unanswered.

"There's the tunnel you must leave by. I'll just go and round Cleon up."

"Wait … the jacket, it's got my potion in, Eve," Shai said. "I left it on the floor; it's over there somewhere…" he pointed.

Eve couldn't see anything through the multitude of dancers.

"And the key... Shai, you need to start using that head of yours. One jester is enough to contend with." She laughed as her thoughts turned to Daz.

"Okay, but we must be quick," Kendrick said as he took a tight hold of Eve and Shai's wrists. "Bear with me, this is just for show." He led them through the crowd.

"What if the shell's broken, Eve? I left it on the floor," Shai stuttered.

"I wouldn't worry too much, pet, no Ashman will go anywhere near that jacket of yours. We're very superstitious, I'll have you know. They'd probably think it's cursed. Let's find it, and hurry up," Kendrick said as he dragged them along.

They waded through the gyrating bodies. "Look, there it is, just where you left it!" Eve squeaked.

Kendrick loosened his grip on Shai's arm momentarily, just long enough for him to run over and pick it up.

"I'm not losing this again!" Shai said as he pulled his arms through the sleeves.

Eve chuckled. "Looks more like a maxi coat on you than a jacket."

Shai flapped his arms in the air, his hands only just reaching the elbows.

Eve turned the cuffs over and folded them back until the tips of his little fingers appeared. "There you go, Shai, that looks better." Then she stopped so abruptly that she almost pulled Kendrick's arm out of its socket. "DAZ!? Look, Shai, it's Daz ... isn't it?" She watched as he shimmied and gyrated his hips, dancing with none other than Ashman himself. She looked at Kendrick. "What was that word you used for Daz? Inconspicuous I believe, wasn't it?"

But Daz was anything but inconspicuous, and seemed to be finding great pleasure in partying and hogging the limelight.

"Leave Daz to me, I'll sort him out later," Kendrick said as he guided them away from the crowd towards the large white lion on which the Ashman had arrived.

"Please, Kendrick, don't let him get into any more trouble; tell him where we've gone and why. He'll just have to be patient." But from where Eve sat Daz looked very much at home as a new member of the Ashman tribe.

"Good luck, my friends, you'll need it..." Kendrick said and took Eve's hand in his. "Be very careful, and I hope you find what you are seeking. If you do, go, don't even look back."

Eve smiled at the well-meaning Kendrick, but she had no intention of going anywhere without Daz, annoying as he was.

The regal beast bowed his head, his large elongated cat's eyes weighing up Eve and Shai.

"They're friends of mine, Cleon, look after them." Kendrick stroked his broad nose. Cleon sank to his knees and Kendrick cupped his hands. "Here you are, think you might need a leg up."

Eve went first and nervously straddled the mighty beast. Shai had trouble getting his leg over and ended up sitting side-saddle in front of her. She used Cleon's mane as reins, her arms acting as a harness for a very unstable Shai.

"I'll be seeing you both ... or not," Kendrick winked, watching as they re-entered the underground tunnel and headed for the mainland.

CHAPTER FOURTEEN

Cleon and the Search

The tunnel led off in many directions, but they took the same path they had come down.

"There's only one way in and out of this hellhole, but I'm very happy to be walking in this direction."

"A talking lion!" Eve gasped. "I've just about seen it all now!" Even though Kendrick's words stuck in her head, that Cleon would 'fill them in', it came as a big shock to her to actually hear words from this amazing specimen.

"You can't be serious, Eve, have you forgotten Gee? In fact all the Rams talked in Aries. Not forgetting Cancer for that matter, even the molluscs talked there!" Shai shook his head. "So, Cleon, where are you taking us?"

"My pride for starters, where you'll be safe."

"Well we weren't safe before up there; we were hunted down, by one of your kind! Then ended up in a trap! How do we know we're not going to become supper for your pride?" Eve began to question why she had ever trusted Kendrick or Cleon. Had Kendrick sent them both to their death? Did Kendrick want Daz for himself, and was this a sure way of getting rid of them?

Cleon grunted as he pushed the drawbridge, which opened out into lush jungle surroundings, quickly resealing and camouflaging the whereabouts of the Ashman tribe's cohabitation.

"Actually, you weren't being hunted at all. You see it was me, I was looking out for you. I took a great risk and left the safety of my pride and our underground lair during a black sun, but in doing so we both got caught out, you trapped and me captured. Other star signs don't visit Leo, and I was intrigued by both your forms. Thought maybe you'd been sent here to overthrow Ashman and return order to Leo."

"We're here visiting and that's not of our own doing. We just want to find the gate and leave," Eve explained.

"There was a gate here once, and star signs entered and left as and when they pleased, but Ashman put a stop to that. Things started to change – first the climate. The temperature plummeted, only occasionally giving way to our sun and its true heat, and the black sun became our enemy; it took away our ability to feel pain from heat or cold. The beautiful fragrances we awoke to from the jungle's once aromatic species were lost in an instant. Last of all was colour, but this was a gradual process – from vibrant shades to pastels … and now the black colourless canvas you see yourselves in, when that went so did the gate."

"But, but, but Kendrick said…" Eve stuttered.

"Kendrick lied! All the Ashmen do is lie, and take from us! They have taken everything we are. Rest now, take this time to reflect and review your previous thoughts. I can well imagine what Kendrick has been telling you, but there again … brainwashing is what the Ashmen do best."

Eve and Shai spent the rest of the journey in silence, confused as they mulled over Cleon's words. The vegetation underfoot grew sparse and coarse-grained granite rocks littered their path, with shallow caves jutting out and interrupting the dry shrubbery. Cleon bounded between the rocks, his tail swinging back and forth, whipping Eve sporadically in the face.

"Meet my pride…" Cleon said proudly. "Welcome to Panthera Leo. Make yourself at home… I wouldn't advise any sudden movements." He laughed.

Eve's face was a picture as Cleon rolled over on the dusty ground and she and Shai were thrown to the floor like rag dolls. Dusty and disorientated, they got to their feet. The atmosphere was surprisingly calm. The sloth-like lions looked comatose, their heads resting heavily on their large front paws and eyes tight shut. Two lionesses seemed to be enjoying their play-fighting antics, their docile snarls and grunts muffled, almost whispered; far from the ferocious creatures Shai and Eve had been led to believe they were, they didn't even acknowledge their arrival.

"Are you hungry?" Cleon looked up through the mouth of the

cave. The black sun had returned like a dark cloud over Leo. He signalled to his pride, and they all rose and retreated to the back of the cave where they cowered from the outside world.

"Sunflower seeds or walnuts I'm afraid, that's all we've got on our menu again tonight." Cleon pointed to two piles stacked up next to each other.

"Thought you were carnivores," Eve said as she tucked into the latter of the two.

"We are by choice, but that too has been taken from us. The other forms of wildlife weren't as resilient as us. The climate change was too much and they were driven to extinction, hence our change in diet."

Eve looked Cleon up and down. "Well you're not exactly a fat cat, are you?" She noticed his protruding ribs and chiselled jawline.

"Not much fun being a vegetarian, is it?" Shai said as he chomped loudly on a mouthful of sunflower seeds.

"I didn't think lions had black spots," Eve said as she noticed strange unsymmetrical splodges on the underside of Cleon's legs that worked their way up to his chest and groin.

"They're puncture wounds, not markings," Cleon began to explain, as the tribal drums and spine-chilling chants grew nearer. "They've moved their tribal ceremony. This is when our numbers fall; they seek out the stragglers and then … I'm afraid we don't know. Presumably they are used by the Ashmen for sacrifices." He shook his head and his long mane puffed out around his face. "Ashman's black magic and tribal voodoo rituals have ultimate control over Leo. Those puncture wounds you noticed are the consequences of our disobedience. We're the marked ones, our time is short. They appear randomly on our fore and hind legs, then make their way up to our groin and eventually our heart … then it's sayonara, farewell."

"That's awful, Cleon! I can't believe Kendrick would be involved in such depravity."

"Well believe it, young lady."

"Name's Eve, Cleon … and this is Shai. Think it's about time we introduced ourselves properly."

"We can't do much now while the sun is black so you may as

well get some rest and save your energy. Trust me, you're going to need it." Cleon lay beside Eve and Shai, who used his thick coat as a cushion and soon fell into a peaceful sleep.

Cleon was the first to wake and he stretched his large paws. "Up you get, the sun is on the change again. Think it's time I told you the ingredients you require for the ritual."

Eve and Shai slowly began to get themselves together.

"You'll be pleased to know we've got two out of the five items you need. We have a constant stock, as we too try to collect these in the hope that when we are successful it'll be the key for the Ashmen to leave us alone." Cleon took them to where a granite rock stood with its centre chiselled out, which was used as the lions' storage unit.

"Very clever," Eve grinned, as Cleon handed her six chilli peppers accompanied by something that resembled grey confetti.

"Crushed marigolds, before you ask. Keep these with you at all times." Cleon walked to the cave mouth. "Just checking," he said as he looked up towards the sun. "Come!"

"Where am I going to put these?" Eve looked down at her hands. "I'll drop them knowing me."

Shai opened his pocket. "They should be safe in here."

Eve carefully placed them inside. The other males of the pride bar one followed suit and hurried out of the cave.

"They not joining us?" Eve asked as she followed Cleon.

"No, the females are the only certainty we have of our race continuing, and we also keep our cubs well hidden. The strongest male stays behind to guard them at all times." Cleon instinctively crouched down and Eve pulled herself up on his mane.

"Don't forget little old me!" Shai shouted up. "Give us a hand!" He stood on his tiptoes, but Eve was only just able to reach him. He awkwardly clambered his way up.

Cleon checked they were both safely on his back before continuing. "Right then, our first stop is Aquert, our sacred grounds where no Ashman would ever dare venture." He stepped briskly through the sunflowers; with individual expressions painted on their pallid grey faces they looked almost as if they had eyes that watched as they passed by. Poppies of different shades pushed their way up to greet them.

"They used to be beautiful once. Ablaze with colour … summer golden yellows and coquelicot reds. Such a waste, such a shame." Cleon sniffed as he continued to walk.

Sprigs of different herbs favoured the sun's warmth. Tall motherwort overshadowed the delicately sown saffron with its dainty oriental flowers. A patchwork quilt of colours that had been masked by an uninviting grey veil.

"How much longer, Cleon? This is time we could be spending looking for the gate."

"Patience, Eve, not much longer now."

The flowers slowly diminished, giving way to long wispy grasses. The terrain became broken and knotted as large overgrown roots crossed their path. Misshapen granite rocks appeared and led into more underground caverns.

"Are we visiting one of the other prides?" Shai asked out of curiosity.

"No, sorry, there's no time for visiting. Our prides don't live here anyway, no animal lives here. This is where we, the big cats, come to die."

A mass of rocks, caves and overgrown roots made up the new surroundings that beckoned them, with eerie sounds, best described as the tapping or ticking that one might hear in an old building or the dead of night.

"What is that?" Eve shuddered. She wrapped her arms around Shai and clung tightly to Cleon's mane for reassurance.

"Have you brought us here to die?" Shai asked. He didn't like the look of this place one bit.

"No," Cleon laughed. "This is the only place you'll get a lion's skull, a dead one that is. Somewhere buried in these caves."

"What could we possibly do with a lion's skull?" Eve questioned.

"Not you, but Ashman. It's the vessel needed for him to mix the ingredients for his rituals and black magic. This is sacred ground we now walk on."

"Those caves don't look too inviting to me… How you going to get a skull, Cleon?" Shai asked.

"Ha, no, Shai, not me! That's your job, I'm just the chauffer."

He lowered his front legs, making it easier for Eve and Shai to dismount.

"I'll wait here, but be on your guard. I've never entered these caves before, so I've no idea what dangers may befall you."

"It's just in your head, Cleon, it's only a cave. A few bones don't scare me!" Shai said. He thought back to the crab graveyard in Cancer and suddenly didn't feel quite so brave or optimistic.

"Sooner we get going the better… Back in a tick, Cleon!" Eve said as she strode ahead, while an unconfident Shai walked gingerly behind. She popped her head into the cavern's narrow opening, which was deceptively spacious. "Looks okay from where I'm standing. Nothing for you to worry about, Shai. Come on." She held out her hand and they walked in together.

The jagged rocks had a crystalline sheen and sharp-edged shale covered the floor. Water dripped from the ceiling and trickled down the walls, leaving small onyx pools that shimmered as a stream of sunlight pierced through the crusted apex high above them.

"Think I'll dodge these," Shai said as he tiptoed between the pools. "If I never see water again it'll be too soon."

Eve was intrigued by the bewitching ambience, while Shai felt hemmed in and overcome by the sinister aura he sensed all around him. "I don't like this one bit, Eve!"

"Stop being such a baby," she chuckled.

"You wouldn't be saying that if you'd seen the graveyard in limbo!"

Eve cast her eyes over a multitude of decomposed skulls strewn in undiscovered recesses and lying on top of one another like misshapen building blocks.

"Hurry up then, Eve, grab one!" Shai turned, ready to head back, but he was stopped dead in his tracks by the sound of tiny feet as they scurried nearby, followed by the familiar sound of slow melodious ticking, like a clock trying to keep time, rising out of nowhere to an ear-splitting crescendo.

"Shai, let's get out of here!" Eve screamed.

But the ground was alive with hordes of infuriated death-watch beetles that swarmed like guards as they kept watch over their territory. Shai and Eve were now pinned against the cave wall, surrounded by these armour-plated horrors. Like thousands of tiny beacons, their startling luminous eyes burnt through the dismal atmosphere with ominous deathly stares.

"Get me out of here! I don't do bugs!" Eve cried.

"I beg your pardon! I'm a fine one to talk to!" Shai snapped.

Eve stepped forwards and trod on one, but the death-watch beetle's tough exterior was undamaged.

Their eyes changed direction and bounced off the walls like laser beams, creating a very picturesque light show. Each in turn headed towards the lion skulls, and tapped their impenetrable heads on the ground as a form of communication.

"Looks like they're going!" Eve gasped.

"We must have scared them," Shai said, feeling a sense of accomplishment.

"Cleon will wonder where we've got to. I should be able to grab a skull in a sec, I'll just wait till they've cleared off."

Shai watched as the beetles began to mutate and crawl inside a decayed skull. "What are they doing, Eve?" The empty vessel bulged with thousands of leathery bodies and protruding legs.

"I don't know, Shai! On second thoughts I think we'll leave the skull and get out of here. Can always find a substitute," she joked.

"Don't look at me!"

Their mutating bodies began to gel together as they underwent some kind of metamorphosis. The skull broadened and regained all the facial features of a healthy lion. Eve and Shai watched in horror as the overspill of beetles re-formed into its strong sleek body, the finish of its coat like luxurious velvet; a jet-black beauty.

No words were needed, Eve and Shai just made a run for it. Their feet echoed, and Shai didn't even notice the puddles he ran through.

"CLEON! HELP!"

Cleon lay stretched out in the long grass, the sun warming his body, totally relaxed and stress free. That was soon to change. Eve's face glowered as she thundered towards him, Shai totally out of breath and lagging behind. Cleon jumped to his feet, bounded towards Eve, butted her over his head and onto his back. Then he saw it, the ace up the Ashman's sleeve; his black magic had even trespassed their final resting place with his unsavoury use of the death-watch beetle and his superiority of the black sun had now progressed to the mutated black lion of death.

Cleon sprinted towards Shai, grabbed him by his mouth and headed for the safety of the long grass and trees.

"FASTER, CLEON! It's catching up with us!" Eve yelled.

A black windswept mane uncovered malicious beastly eyes with a hypnotic stare that focused on its prey. Eve dug her fingers sharply into Cleon's back.

"Can't hold on much longer!" she gasped.

Meanwhile, Shai dangled like a piece of meat between the dagger-like fangs, while the gigantic maneater only gained pace, extending his razor-sharp claws and swiping at Cleon's rump. Shai was catapulted up into the air and Eve was hurled backwards into a nearby laurel bush as the barbarian went in for the kill. Cleon dodged its sharp talons and leapt into the thickening pampas grass; as he did so, his feet cleared Aquert, the sacred ground. The great black force seemed to move in slow motion, and its flesh peeled and hung loose as fragments started to disintegrate. Each piece of skin transmuted back into scores of the unsightly death-watch beetles, which fell to the floor like conkers from a tree. Protected by their armour, they scurried back in the direction of the cave, ticking and tapping as they went. The skull's inhabitants didn't intend on their trappings being poached, and fused their shells together. They tucked their multi-segmented legs tightly into their bodies, making their torsos become ideal wheels as they gambolled over and over, propelling the lion's skull back towards its resting place.

"I'll be taking that, thank you," Eve said. It gave her great satisfaction to lift the brittle bone structure from the annoying inauspicious insects.

Cleon lay exhausted, large abrasions on his side and black blood dried and matted in his fur.

"It's okay, Eve, don't worry, it's only a surface wound," he said as he licked his injuries like a domestic cat.

"Shai! Where's Shai?" Eve looked around.

"Spat him in that direction I think. To be honest, the shock of that fiend's claws… I nearly swallowed the ugly little fella."

"He's not ugly, he's a Goylin … they all look like that," Eve said as she continued to look around.

"They're all ugly then!" Cleon sniggered.

Eve noticed movement from the dense shrubbery and ran over. As she began to part the foliage she saw a concussed Shai hanging upside down like a long-eared bat. His leather jacket spread across the branches would have made perfectly good wings.

"You look quite at home there, Shai; tempted to leave you. You'd make a handsome bat!" Eve said as she helped to untangle and reposition him.

Back on his feet, Shai snapped, "You're so funny, Eve, sorry for not laughing!" His face looked ready to explode, as he'd been upside down so long that all the blood had rushed to his peculiar-shaped head; even the tips of his ears throbbed.

"The sun isn't going to be with us much longer and soon the Ashmen will be amongst us. We need to find shelter," Cleon said as he dragged his injured body to its feet.

"Yes, it'll also give me time to dress your wounds," Eve said, patting him tenderly on the side of his head.

"We'll have to bed down with another pride, we'll never reach mine in time." Cleon led them through the tall canopy of trees until they stopped at what looked like a large rabbit hole. "In you go, quickly!" He looked up. Golden sunbeams filtered through mosaic-like perforations as speckled shadows danced between the leaves and beautified the underbrush.

"We fell into one of those once before," Eve said; she didn't look too impressed.

"Don't worry, Eve, this one isn't Ashman-made."

"Well that's a relief, Cleon," she said wearily as she stepped inside.

Shai held onto her shoulders, not wanting to lose his balance. The steep gradient soon levelled out. Cleon waited for the signal and then arranged woody perennials with thick stems and branches to conceal their whereabouts.

"How you doing, Cleon? Looks like you're still disobeying the

Ashmen," a large white male said as he passed; he couldn't help noticing the growing number of puncture wounds that pierced Cleon's ailing body.

"Don't mock the afflicted, Deakin, your time will come; you can't hide forever."

"Only one of my pride ever leaves here for supplies, whatever the sun. Be my guest, all of you." Deakin's glance turned to Eve and Shai. "Strange-looking lions, I have to say. But any friends of Cleon will be readily offered a safe haven here."

A lioness beckoned him from the shadows.

"My lady awaits," he said, and plodded nonchalantly towards where she and the rest of his pride rested.

"Now for those injuries of yours," Eve said, as she tore long strips from the hem of her skirt and secured them around Cleon's hindquarters. "There you go, have you better in no time."

Eve and Shai slumped down and nestled for warmth in Cleon's thick coat. All the excitement had proved too much for Shai's little body, and he closed his eyes and was asleep in seconds.

"Give us the lowdown on Leo," Eve asked.

"Leo was a blaze of vibrant colour, and sweet fragrances rose from the jungle bed. The sun never darkened. Then the Ashmen appeared, but nobody knew from where or how. Then their deadly reign began and they started to bore down deep into the ground; that's how the lion traps came about."

"Was that what we fell into?" Eve asked, as she suddenly remembered the strange words etched in the walls. "I can't remember what it said, but there was a strange verse all around us."

"The poem is just a myth! The Ashmen have no idea where the engravings originated. They are very superstitious and so put it down to the work of their Devil, Nupkana, the evil one." Cleon yawned. His eyelids heavy, he continued wearily. "It was the wax you fell into that drained your colour; it's sucked and transported through the tree roots in an unknown intricate network; its destination will become clear to you during the next sunrise."

"And the puncture marks? They didn't just appear, did they?"

"Oh, Eve, you have no idea. The majority of us have been caught by Ashmen one way or another; they cut a lock of hair from

215

our manes and that's all they need. We are given five ingredients to collect, the same ones you have been sent to find. If we don't obey, Ashman practises his sorcery, inane black magic rituals… We've all failed at the third hurdle; I wouldn't even attempt it, it's impossible, hence my body art." He looked down at his wounds. "So the skull and honey have never been pursued, until now that is… You've broken the cycle, and haven't stuck to the order. You've conquered the skull, so maybe the next ingredient is achievable after all. The fifth and final may as well be a wild goose chase. But you'll have your chance like all the others. Now close your eyes, Eve, your penultimate task awaits you."

"I couldn't disagree more with what Kendrick led us to believe. He made you all out to be vicious predators, killing machines… Doubt you'd even hurt a firefly," Eve said, as she smiled and glanced over at the comatose Goylin.

"We just want to be left alone, but the Ashmen have made that impossible! If Ashman's voodoo gains strength and enables him to fully control the sun and its colour, nothing will prosper, as without light all our lush plant life and vegetation will perish. This will have a knock-on effect on all of us… Then Leo as we know it will be no more, and Ashman will reign forever under the black sun. Nothing will be able to grow in the earth, and so they will feast only on the food created from the voodoo magic performed by Ashman, and there's nothing we can do to stop this."

Eve was lost for words as she looked at the forlorn white lion whom she now thought of as a friend.

"Night, Cleon," she said and gave him a peck on the cheek. She snuggled up to Shai and closed her eyes.

They were woken by a sudden warmth.

"Looks like our time's here again," Cleon said, and grabbed a few of the walnuts Deakin had left behind.

"Come on, you two, breakfast."

"You're looking better today, Cleon."

"Yeah, it's amazing what a good night's sleep can do for you." He gave an almighty yawn and stretched. "I s'pose you want a ride then?"

Eve and Shai climbed onto his back with ease, as it had become quite a regular occurrence. Shai had even got used to riding side-saddle.

"Best not forget this, eh?" Cleon snatched the lion's skull and swung it up for Shai to hold onto.

"Thanks for having us, Deakin!"

"Anytime!" the friendly lion shouted back as Cleon and his two passengers exited the safety of his home and headed back into the jungle's mysteries.

Carefully stepping over new saplings, they took the opportunity to bask in the sun's glory between thick knotted citrus trees, their fruit-bearing days a thing of the past. Then Cleon stopped at an unusual tree with overgrown branches, a complexity that stretched way above them.

"This is where you'll find your next ingredient," he said, looking up through the broad branches.

"What's that then?" Shai also looked up but on first glance saw nothing. He slipped down from Cleon's back and stepped away to get a better view. He noticed wisps of smoke between a labyrinth of tight-knit leaves.

"Cleon, the tree; it's on fire!"

"No, it's Ashman at work again. He uses open torches secured further up the tree, between which lies a hidden hive. His magic adds a soothing substance that keeps the bees calm. The Ashmen climb it frequently; honey's a big part of their staple diet. The clouds of smoke work as a temporary relaxant for the bees."

"In that case it's easy; we just climb up, remove some honeycomb, climb down and we're done..." Eve looked pleased. "Be a damn sight easier than getting that skull!"

Immense elongated roots clung together and embedded themselves deep into the earth. The odd bee loitered overhead as they returned to replenish the pollen stocks, their movements visibly impaired by the Ashman's voodoo.

"Can't get used to this insipid world you live in!" Eve said as she slipped off Cleon's back to join Shai. "White bees? Whatever next?"

"You going to join us this time?" Shai looked over to Cleon, but the nimble-footed cat decided he would rather sit this one out.

"This is your task to complete," he said and took up his favourite position, lay back and lapped up the heat of the day.

The boughs were easy to climb and Eve mounted the nearest branch.

"Give me a hand, Eve!" Shai said, standing on tiptoe. Then he noticed a thick braided rope that had fallen to the rear of the trunk. He anchored his small palms around it and scrambled up, bypassing Eve. She meticulously scaled the densely dressed branches and did her best to forget her fear of heights.

"That must be it, Eve!" Shai shouted down, as he parted the intricate leaves that disturbed their natural patterns.

The hive, a lattice of three-dimensional hexagonal-shaped tiles moulded into a dome-shaped residency, sat securely between two branches in the shape of a wishbone. On either side stood two smouldering bamboo torches that released a calming liquor, with a woven basket of bamboo leaves where the wick should have been. In Ashman's case, no wick was needed; an everlasting flame that emitted an intoxicating cocktail.

"Keep your eyes peeled, Eve; probably best if just one of us goes," Shai suggested as he held onto the rope and manoeuvred himself towards the hive.

The worker bees busied themselves as they filled the hexagonal cells with pollen. A few regurgitated stores of honey from their stomach, which they reshaped for the queen when she was ready to lay her new batch of eggs, adding strength to her colony. Shai was fascinated by the active insects and watched them intently.

Very educational for a firefly, he thought.

"Come on!" Eve shouted impatiently. "This isn't some kind of biology lesson!"

As Shai neared, his presence seemed to disturb the bees. They circled him inquisitively, but their relaxed state didn't allow them to take action. He reached into the mass of honeycomb cells and snapped away a large section.

"Think that'll do, Eve?" He dangled his specimen through the branches.

"Yeah, Shai, looks fine to me. Let's get back to Cleon. That's four down one to go, well done!"

Curious about their intruder, the bees swarmed, the tiny hairs on their legs stiff like the small bristles of a brush as they grazed his leathery skin. The hypnotic smoke that encapsulated the hive regressed and the friendly rendezvous lost its welcoming feel. Shai noticed the change of temperament in the bees as the enduring flames were doused by a dusky hand-made shadow. Ashman's safety net lifted as the bees' anger grew; a transition of colours, calm white to despicable black.

The regenerated bees swarmed around Shai, their wings vibrating as they picked up speed and rubbed their back legs together in defiance. They grouped at the entrance of the hive and prepared for their impending attack, their colour changing from a soft marshmallow white to the swarthy black of carnivorous hunting machines. Panic set in and Shai knew that he had to make a move, and quickly. One Goylin versus a few thousand bees – when he considered the odds he quickly realised they were stacked against him.

"Eve, quick, climb down, something's very wrong."

"What do you mean? What's wrong?" Eve tried to look up through the branches, but her view was distorted by a mass of grey leaves.

The enraged bees regrouped as their spear-like attack hit and missed Shai, who dodged between the misshapen branches, using the abundant foliage as a body shield. The few stings that penetrated his well thought-out defence hit him hard, their tiny hypodermic needles piercing the outer membrane of his thick hide. However, only surface deep, the poison was unable to seep through and invade his bloodstream.

Shai broke off a charred branch from above his head.

"Buzz off, you barbaric little weasels! Take that, and that!" He swung round and knocked many of the approaching critters unconscious, as yet unaware of an escapee in their midst.

Eve lost her footing and nearly fell from the tree in her blind panic. Meanwhile, Shai was getting tired and found it almost impossible to fend off the bees' constant onslaught.

Plan of action number two, he thought. The clever little Goylin scrunched himself into a ball inside his leather jacket and dangled one-handed from the rope like an oversized conker.

"Now try and get me!" he chuckled. *One up*, he thought to himself as he held a slice of broken-off honeycomb close to his chest. His sudden lack of movement threw the bees, who began to get bored, split into smaller groups and headed back towards the hive.

"Cleon! Cleon!" Eve screamed.

This immediately grabbed the bees' attention and Shai was left to dangle in peace. The thrashing leaves renewed great interest, and this time the queen was at the helm. Protective drones were at her side while the worker bees stayed back as flying reinforcement if needed. Eve launched herself out of the tree as the angry humming grew louder and louder.

"Help us, Cleon!"

Startled from his daydreaming, Cleon jumped up. Eve's movements appeared almost in slow motion. The extensive root channels crept up and pulled their elongated appendages through the earthen terrain. Like immense robust pythons they propelled themselves along by winding movements as they slithered towards their victim. Lifting their strong heads, they focused their hypnotic eyes and went in for the kill, coiling their muscular bodies around Eve's legs and dragging her to the floor. Little by little, their undulating motions encased her entire body and Eve was held fast.

"Cleon, HELP ME!" she groaned, disorientated and struggling to breathe.

The black mass in the shape of a spear assembled itself overhead, masking the sun's rays. Cleon bounded over to where Eve's vulnerable body lay in a state of shock. There was no time to think, the bees were on the move. He pounced, his silhouette momentarily hanging in midair before he hovered over her and then landed. He used his body as a protective rug, closed his eyes and hoped beyond hope that his camouflage would confuse the bees enough to make them give up the chase.

"Cleon, I can't breathe!" Eve whispered. She wriggled for breathing space, his body weight just too much for her small frame.

He rolled onto his side.

"The bees, the bees, where are they?" Eve asked. She saw the tail end of the pumpkin-sized queen as it signalled to a couple of workers, dilly-dallying and finally disappearing through the leaves that rustled in the breeze. Once again, all was quiet.

"That was a close one, eh Cleon?" She still looked like part of the root network, held tight against her will. The more she struggled, the firmer the root-like entities clasped her to them and started to pull her down into the ground.

"Break them, cut them, do anything, Cleon … I'm being buried alive!" Eve screamed hysterically, now at her wits' end.

Convulsed cries filtered up through the depths of the earth, the snide laughter mocking and enjoying the position in which she now found herself. The python-like death hug transformed into an array of Ashmen's bony arms, their callous deformed hands clenching together and their fingers interlocked. Drawn down with force, the undergrowth began to subside beneath her like volatile quicksand that wouldn't take no for an answer.

"CLEON, SHAI, GET ME OUT OF HERE!!!"

Shai's whereabouts were hidden, and Eve's neck was so tightly encased that she couldn't lift her head to locate Cleon either.

Shai had waited for the coast to clear and, feeling very pleased with himself, he now proudly descended with the honeycomb trophy lodged safely under his arm.

"I'm an agile little Goylin, Eve, definitely the right man for the job!" He suddenly noticed Cleon's lifeless body lying face down in the sun-dried grass. "EVE!"

His jaw dropped as he saw the earth open up before his eyes and Eve's body levitate above him in an hypnotic trance. Earth rose up around her petite figure. He caught a quick glimpse of a two-tone facial outline. *Must be a badger*, he thought, *digging out a sett for his family; but that still wouldn't explain why Eve was suspended in midair*. In a fear-fuelled frenzy, he careered towards the burrow and peered into the deep-set hollow, sunken like an open wound.

"Snap out of it!" he said as he grabbed hold of her shoulders. It was no animal!

"GET OFF! GET OFF!" Eve shouted, lashing out at the restraints that held her against her will.

Shai was sent flying as her fist made sudden impact with his enlarged head.

"Y'ouch…." He lay on the floor and nursed his bruised face.

Eve fought an invisible energy until the hidden organism that took her weight gave way like a trap door and it fell from beneath her. She plunged down and became entombed in the dark dank cavern. Woken from her nightmare in a blink of an eye, she sat bolt upright. Shai was a welcome face after what she'd been through.

"How did you do it? The roots, the hands…" Eve's rigid body began to relax, her eyes like shooting stars as they sparkled from obscurity.

"Ashman's hands?" Shai questioned as he pulled her out. "I could have sworn I saw his face decorated with white luminous tattoos. From a distance I thought it was a badger."

They sat together, their legs dangling down into the empty space that had so intimidated Eve only seconds earlier.

"No, they were holding me, everywhere, squeezing the life from my body. Surely you saw them, Shai…"

"I think your imagination must have run away with you." He looked around at the charred knotted roots. "See for yourself."

On second glance even she had to admit that what she was asking Shai to believe was rather farfetched. But farfetched or not, she knew what she had witnessed was real. Her jumbled thoughts stabilised and her mind refocused on Cleon. The white bag of bones lay motionless.

"Poor Cleon looks like he paid the price for helping me," she said, and tiptoed towards the unconscious lion. Black barbed stings protruded from his coat.

"Shai, look. There's so many stings that if I had a pen I could join them up like a dot-to-dot picture. Poor old thing must have gone into shock." She knelt beside him and tenderly brushed the thick mane from his eyes. "I think he's dead," she sobbed.

CHAPTER FIFTEEN

The Fifth Ingredient

Cleon's pitiful form lay crumpled and unassuming. Shai knelt, parted his tangled fur and rested his ear against the lion's chest, just in case he could find any signs of life.

"Let him be okay," Eve pleaded.

"Shush, quiet a minute. I can't be sure, but I swear I just heard a faint heartbeat." Shai listened again. "Yes, I've got something."

Although Cleon's breathing was shallow and laboured, their friend was still with them. Eve softly lifted the lids of his eyes to uncover a glazed stare and dilated pupils. Whether it was down to her actions or not, a suppressed whimper drifted out from between his lips and Cleon very gradually began to regain consciousness.

"Eve, you're okay," he groaned. The selfless lion didn't even stop to consider he was on the brink of death.

Tears of relief dripped off the end of Eve's nose like tiny pearls and then soaked away into Cleon's unkempt coat. "We need to get those stings out, Cleon. I'm sure you'll start to feel better then," she said.

The poison made him feel dizzy and listless, and he struggled to steady himself. Razor-edged needles stood proud; much larger than the average bee sting, they resembled porcupine quills. Poor Cleon felt more like a pincushion than a lion. The poisonous venom had penetrated into the deeper layers of his skin and started to destroy the surrounding tissue.

"I know one thing, Eve, Mesi's pincers would definitely have come in handy. Our own set of tweezers, eh?" Shai's cumbersome fingers struggled to extract the first of the many brutal invaders; their spiky tips didn't intend to give up without a fight.

"Thought you'd be in agony, Cleon," Eve said, quite surprised that he lay unperturbed with a relaxed expression on his face. "I wonder if perhaps these stings have got their own built-in anaesthetic…"

"I told you about Ashman's black magic relinquishing most of our senses, so you see I can't feel anything; first time in my life I've had something to thank him for."

Eve and Shai's hard work and determination soon had Cleon sting free. Still woozy from the bees' onslaught, he attempted to stand. Unsteady on his legs, he summoned the support of a nearby tree.

"Are you strong enough to walk?" Eve asked, her eyes filled with compassion.

"I think so," Cleon said as he stepped away from the security of the tree's crutch. "Yes, just about. But I'm afraid I won't be able to give piggyback rides for a while." He gave them both a rueful smile. "Come, while the sun's still on our side. There's one place I must still show you." He used all his reserves to continue.

Eve and Shai couldn't help but notice his drawn face and sluggish swagger. They only just remembered to retrieve the skull before he led them further into the brush. They soon passed all the familiar routes. The tight-knit trees opened out into immense fields of low-lying shrubs that hugged the ground's surface. Scorched by the sun's incandescent radiation and compressed by continual usage, it had become a downtrodden footpath.

"Take a long hard look, tell me what you see."

Eve and Shai squinted into the distance.

Shai rubbed his eyes. "I must be seeing things."

"Well that makes two of us!" Eve said, also thrown by what she saw. "It's an optical illusion, that's the only explanation!"

The drab everyday canvas had suddenly been given a burst of colour. A unique piece of land lay surrounded by an inky black lake, and held Leo's sought-after secret. A beautiful statuesque citrus tree with a difference stood proud, its decorative branches displaying a wealth of opulent fruits.

Eve's mouth watered. "I've never wanted fruit so badly!"

"That's because it's forbidden fruit," Cleon was quick to respond.

"Got the right name for the job, I suppose," she laughed.

"That's out of the question. A feat no one has ever conquered; the fruits are simply irretrievable."

Kendrick's words of warning came as a sudden flashback in Eve's mind.

A multitude of fruits inhabited its branches: golden lemons, tangerines and mandarins with an amber twist, spring green limes that played hide-and-seek between the variegated leaves, making way for the sweetest-looking ruby grapefruits Eve could ever have hoped to imagine hanging from the lower branches. Not forgetting the most important of all, the final ingredient … the kumquats, with their orange peel glow. The whole tree cried out temptation.

As they neared the lake, prides of lions sat in a uniform line while others waded neck deep in the inky substance, each heading for the island and the beautiful tree of many colours.

"What are they doing, Cleon?"

"What the Ashman has programmed them to do. I've never been one to follow rules, and I have the scars to prove it." He looked down at the puncture wounds that ravaged his legs and now made towards his heart.

"Since helping you, they have spread tenfold. This happens to all the defiant lions that don't adhere to the rules. I was given strict instructions to bring you here first, but hoped that after what you've been through you wouldn't even contemplate this one. We are all set the same challenge, a sick treasure hunt! We need the kumquats first to be allowed to move on to our second ingredient. I chose to forfeit my crossing to the tree, but that's when these puncture wounds began to appear," Cleon said as they neared the water's edge.

Eve looked down at her reflection. "But it's just water, what's the problem?"

"No, its appearance is there to deceive you … just watch and you'll see. That's enough for now." Cleon collapsed on the bank.

A constant influx of lions came and went. They brimmed with confidence on entering the lake, but all were deflated on return, unable to set a paw on the island.

Cleon rolled onto his side, his eyes resting on the citrus tree's beauty.

"So by now you've probably guessed how Leo's colour has been taken from us, fraudulently embezzled from our grasp. The roots of the trees are Ashman's key, he uses them as filtering devices; his voodoo rituals have enabled them to suck each drop of colour from our world and give it to that tiny island you see in front of you. With it he has compounded all our sense bar hearing, but how long that will remain I have no idea. This has all been a gradual process and has crept up on us over time."

"Our colour must have gone the same way then, sucked from our bodies when we were chased into the lions' trap."

"For the second time, Eve, I wasn't chasing you; I was just curious."

"Well, if you had some unknown predator chasing you, wouldn't you run?"

"Come on, you've seen enough; let's get out of this place," Cleon said, but the venomous stings had affected him more than he liked to admit and his limbs felt stiff, almost paralysed, and he was unable to straighten them enough even to stand.

"I'm not going anywhere without you. Can't see any harm in giving it a go; I'll be the first Goylin to ever have a crack at it anyway," Shai said.

Eve glanced down. Cleon did look a sorry sight, what with his open wounds and swollen and inflamed skin from the stings. He was unrecognisable as the beautiful and proud cat to whom they had first been introduced by Kendrick.

"No, Shai, you mustn't even try; it's a trap."

"My minds made up, I'll give it one go. 'Bout time I faced my fear, don't you think, Eve? Then I'm with you, Cleon, we're out of here."

Cleon could see there was no convincing him otherwise; if he was honest with himself he didn't have the strength or fight left in him to argue anyhow.

Shai put the skull into Cleon's front paws for safekeeping.

"Guard this with your life," he joked.

Eve threw him a look as if to say that was a bad choice of words. Apprehensively, though he tried not to show it, he stepped into the water, which was of a thicker consistency than he had expected. Eve watched as he waded in and intermingled with the lions. On approach, the water seemed slightly shallower and she watched a bedraggled Shai clad in leather coat fight against the undercurrent. But Shai and the lions all got to the same point and were stopped by what appeared to be an automatic reaction. A vacant expression masked Shai's face as he trudged his way back to Eve and Cleon.

"You were so close! What stopped you?"

A perplexed Shai walked back onto dry land. "I don't know, Eve, I just couldn't move. Next thing I knew I was on my way back." His skin glistened.

"Think we'll have that off you, Shai," Eve said as she rubbed his arms vigorously, but whatever the liquid was it was going nowhere and clung to him like a second skin.

"Good try, Shai, just not good enough."

Shai was unresponsive and quite vague. When he eventually did strike up a conversation, his words were laboured and repetitive.

"I did try, Eve … I did try…" and so he continued.

"I told you it was a trap. All the returning lions had the same vacant look. It was impossible to miss, yet neither of you noticed, did you? Of course you didn't. It's so easy to look and not see. This is something you'll soon pick up on in Antares." Cleon struggled to stay awake. "I feel so cold, Eve." He shivered.

"That's strange! It's a sense that doesn't exist here any more." Even Eve's senses had slowly begun to fade. She lay down next to him so he could share her body heat. Then he closed his eyes and drifted off into a deep sleep.

Eve thought this must be her chance. "Keep a close eye on him, Shai, don't go wandering off. He seems to have taken a turn for the worse."

She ruched up her dress and entered the lake. An oily scum floated on its surface as she pushed her way forward, and it felt more like syrup than water. The ripe fruit seemed to call her. As she reached the island, the lions next to her once again turned and headed back to shore, as if shocked by an invisible force field that seemed to suck away their fighting spirit and leave their morale at an all-time low. However, Eve felt no effects as she reached the island's outer perimeter. She looked up and noticed the dark veil as it encroached upon the sun's light once more; a mass exodus as the lions charged back to shore. Unfazed, Eve stepped out onto the lush green haven and watched as the last few lackadaisical lions tried to leave the lake, but they seemed to be rooted to the spot. The liquid had coagulated, and from where Eve stood it now looked more like thick mud. Suddenly, all the pieces of the jigsaw fitted together perfectly. She glanced down at her arms as a familiar substance with a dull sheen began to harden against her skin. She peeled it off with her nails and small particles flaked away. It was just as she thought … the whole lake was a vat of wax. She watched as the immobilised lions set like onyx candles shone from the shore like spotlights as others appeared from every direction. Complete prides stood in reverence, but Eve, oblivious to her outstanding achievement, didn't realise it was her they were in awe of. Either the colours on the island were more spectacular than she was used to or it was just that her eyes had grown accustomed to her black and white world. The rapid demise of the sun usually sent the lions into hiding, so why on this occasion they didn't retreat was beyond her.

Without hesitation she walked to the tree and carefully pulled off a handful of kumquats. Her mouth watered as the sweet essence of citrus discharged and encompassed her like a large wall that kept its bouquet of colour from escaping to the outside world. Shocked and taken aback, she watched as a spectrum of every known colour exploded skywards. Like a multifaceted rainbow it fell around her and resembled tiny shards of crystallised confetti, mushrooming from the island like a huge tidal wave. A sudden wind raged towards the waiting lions and yet Eve stood calmly, at peace with herself and protected inside the eye of the storm.

Yet in a split second everything was as it had been; was it all in Eve's mind? Had she lost her grip on reality? She gazed down to admire the kumquats, and then without warning their glorious tangerine glow began to melt away to leave a sepia-like textureless fruit in its place. The perfumed air disappeared and Eve felt like she was cocooned in an odourless vacuum. The dark shadow that had haunted the sun with its voodoo mask ruptured into an orb-like ball of white gold and its luminous beams lifted Leo to a totally different dimension.

Unnerved by the strange goings-on, Eve pocketed the kumquats as she careered into the liquefied waxen lake and propelled herself across. As she neared its bank, the exuberant lions came to greet her. All except one, the one that mattered the most to her – Cleon.

"You're our saviour, the god we've been waiting for to overthrow Ashman's reign," Deakin said, stepping out of the crowd and kneeling before her. "The first time I met you I felt that change was in the air and I was right; you've turned out to be our salvation."

Every lion from every pride bowed their head to the celestial being who stood in their midst.

"Look, it's a miracle!" Shai squealed as he peered skywards.

The continuous grey cloud that had hung over them, drab and heavy, had woken into a delicate powder blue. The insignificant grasses were transformed into an underlay of green pastels that merged into the fuller plants and shrubbery.

Eve walked over to Cleon's lifeless body, crouched down and cradled his head in her hands.

"Come on, Cleon. Look, everything's going to be alright now." It seemed to Eve as if he used his last ounce of strength to open his tired eyes just enough for him to see the subtle colour change and breathe in the scent of the jungle's ambience one last time.

He lifted his paw and gently stroked her cheek. "I never thought I'd see the day. Thank you, Eve, you've set us free." A brief smile of contentment lit up his face.

Before she realised what was happening, Eve felt his crumpled body give way and fall limply to the floor. Her feelings at that moment were bittersweet, and she grieved for the courageous lion that had instilled values in her that she would carry with her for the rest of her life. But she rejoiced in the fact that he'd lived long enough to see her play the leading role in Leo's rebirth. She sobbed inconsolably, her salty tears dripping onto Cleon's face so that it almost looked as if he was crying too.

"Come on, Eve, there's nothing more we can do," Shai said, trying his best to comfort her as he rested his hand on her shoulder. "Ashman can't hurt him any more."

"No, I'm not leaving him here alone."

"Don't worry, he won't be alone. I'll take him back to my pride, where we'll give him a proper lion's burial," Deakin said. He called over to two of his family members. "It's time; I'm afraid you must let him go."

Solemnity surrounded Eve and Shai as Cleon was draped over a muscular white lion's back. She couldn't help noticing as he was lifted that Ashman had succeeded in every way; the final puncture wound had pierced Cleon's heart.

You can run but you can't hide, Ashman, Eve thought to herself, *and I will have my day!*

At a loss of what to say or do, she sprawled out on the floor and stared up into space. She could hear the content grunts and cries of the large cats as they played and cavorted in the Mediterranean heat.

"Is there room for two?"

Her gaze switched to Deakin's friendly face.

"Make that three," Shai piped up as he sat between them.

Deakin cleared his throat. "That force field's been an enigma to us for as long as I can remember."

Eve sat up and glanced at the island, the enriched tree with all its previous wealth rubbed away into oblivion; a black and white portrait. Oh, how the tables had turned on Ashman and his trickery. Yin-yang had now turned full circle and come back to haunt him.

"The Ashmen got the shock of their lives, and the change was so sudden that many couldn't reach the tunnels. But I haven't the first idea where they've hidden themselves; they were there one minute, then in the next breath gone."

Eve and Shai only half listened to Deakin as they fumbled through the ingredients.

"Think that's your lot," Shai said as he reeled off the items. "Crushed marigolds … check…" he said as he passed them to Eve to deposit in the skull.

"Six rather hot chilli peppers," (now a vivid red), "check."

"One rather melted honeycomb. Plus a couple of dead bees." It stuck to his hands like glue and he had to prise it off and let it drop into the skull. "Well that's the honey then … check. What are we missing?"

"Think you're looking for these," Eve said, and presented him with four rather black deflated kumquats.

"Check."

"I'll give you check, mate," she forced a smile. "That's one for Cleon." She laughed. She so longed for him to return and be part of the joke.

"S'pose it's time I filled in the missing pieces. You brought us out of the darkness, so I'll do the same for you, in a manner of speaking." Deakin paused in thought. "Our ancestors were a very different breed to what we are today. There was only one pride, ruled by two brothers, Leo and Asher. They were as different as brothers could be; Leo was kind and compassionate while Asher was vindictive with a ruthless streak and wanted complete domination. Leo was wishy-washy in comparison, and Asher found this flaw advantageous. He spent large amounts of time away from his pride, during which he invented the very first lion trap and constructed the underground tunnel network the Ashmen now inhabit. Myth has it that Asher underwent an evil transformation, and as Leo's popularity grew so did Asher's resentment and jealousy. It is said that when the rivalry got too great for him to bear, he tricked his brother, sending him on a wild goose chase. The cleverly camouflaged trap made way for its first victim. Some say this is where Leo wrote his final epitaph, but its meaning has never been deciphered. But it replicates itself with each new trap built, like some kind of message or warning. We'll never know, like we'll never know what happened to Leo and Asher, who disappeared without a trace. The pride was divided, and fights broke out between the dominant males. Anarchy reigned, and the constant bloodshed wiped out much of our ancestral history. A new age was born, and with it the rising of Ashman. This species appeared through the darkness and it has been that way ever since, until now that is."

"So you all split into separate prides, and Leo was divided between you and the Ashman tribe?" Eve was fascinated by Deakin's history lesson. "With all the information I've been given so far I've come up with a three-way tie. Kendrick's version of the story is very different to yours. In his world you lions were the predators and you were doing everything possible to hunt the Ashmen to extinction. Apparently, one member of your pride brought the black sun upon us by his dabbling in the art of black magic."

"Do me a favour!" Deakin laughed.

"Well Cleon put the blame on Ashman himself as the instigator. I've got two stories, one of fiction and one of fact; I really haven't a clue which box to tick."

"Don't mean to interrupt you pair," Shai piped up, "but I also occasionally have some useful information to share. I think you should take a look at the island, you may have a pleasant surprise."

Eve thought Shai was just vying for attention, but gazed over quickly to placate him. "Well there's no great shakes from where I'm sitting. Exactly the same as last time I looked." Unimpressed by what she saw, Eve refocused on Deakin and picked up the conversation from where they had left off.

"NO, EVE! You may have looked, but you haven't seen." Shai stood and walked towards the lake.

Eve's gaze followed him. The waxen waters had now dissolved into a free-flowing liquid, and the sun's immense heat had released the unwilling captors as they waded from the open waters onto the green lush domain. For once Ashman had lost, as the eradication of the black sun meant these lions were no longer easy pickings for the tribe. The relieved large cats lay back on the bank and tenderly performed a family grooming session.

"Deakin, what's wrong with them?" Eve asked, as she noticed the odd behaviour and expressionless glaze in the eyes of each returning lion, immediately taking her back to the strange demeanour Shai had shown on his return.

"The build-up of wax has taken their reasoning as well as their colour, with a little more being absorbed each time they cross. The wax is a liquidated executioner, a death trap that awaits them."

Eve had an awful picture sketched in her mind of those poor lions ensnared in a congealed sarcophagus, as they died slowly in a sadistic game in which the Ashmen thrived.

"Cleon never crossed the river; he was no sheep and had his own mind," she said. "Cleon didn't formally introduce us. My name's Eve, and the odd-looking fellow, Goylin stroke firefly, is Shai."

"Nice to formally meet you then," Deakin said, handing her his paw. "To be honest, Eve, they don't gain either way. The lions that fall into the traps are never the same. Ashmen cut long strands from their manes, and like you and Shai they are given ingredients to collect for the Ashman ritual. Hence the crossing of the lake, as you've now both witnessed and been a part of yourselves. The strong-minded ones end up with those inhumane puncture marks, and once these appear I'm afraid to say they are living on borrowed time."

"So it's a no win situation. They're damned if they do and damned if they don't!"

"There are very few prides like mine, and we live in hiding. Only one of our pride is allowed to leave our safe haven at any one time. So far it's worked and we've managed to outsmart the savages through our growing knowledge."

"I'm not standing here for my health!" a paranoid Shai said, feeling as if he'd been left out of the loop for far too long. "Just look at the island, will you?"

His abrupt tone shocked Eve.

"Shai, I've looked once!"

"Well look again … closer this time!"

A blurred silhouette materialised in front of Eve's eyes, and she blinked and tried to refocus. What she saw opened up their horizons in a big way, although there was just the small complication of Daz. It stood in all its splendour, a white freestanding gate that blended in perfectly with its black and white surroundings. It must have lost itself somewhere when the island was masked by a kaleidoscope of varied colours.

"The gate, the gate, Cleon was right! There is a gate! We just weren't able to see what was right in front of our eyes!" She threw her arms around Shai, then Deakin, totally overcome by the fact that they'd found a way out. *Maybe now we're a step closer to home,* she thought, but then she thought again.

"That's strange, Shai," she said.

"Yes I know, the gate! Who'd have thought?"

"It's not that that's worrying me…" With an alarmed look on her face she continued. "You see, my last and only memory of home is the fair… with Oli, Ebony and Daz, and that's as far as it goes. So who actually is Eve? Who am I, Shai?"

"With everything you've experienced I'm not surprised you can't remember home. You're forgetting you're in a completely different dimension, a different planet for that matter. This is Antares; your unreality is now your reality." Shai's reasoning lightened the mood, and Eve's attention returned to the gate and then to Daz.

"Give you two guesses where we're going next," she said.

Funnily enough it took Shai only one guess. "Knowing our luck, when we go back he'll probably have been made an honorary member of their tribe." Shai could only begin to imagine.

CHAPTER SIXTEEN

Finding Daz

"I don't remember how to get back to Daz. Those tunnels are well hidden, and with the return of colour it'll be even more confusing." Eve sighed. "Just our luck!"

"Well you could always go through the gate without your friend," Deakin suggested.

"Although he's more trouble than he's worth, he means a lot to me."

"I think you mean us!" Shai felt he had built up a very special friendship with Daz also.

"In that case, maybe I can be of some assistance. Us cats have our own inbuilt atlas." Deakin laughed. "What also has a slight bearing on the tribe's habitat is the lush lavender fields, which only complement one small portion of Leo's extensive jungle, and my returning sense will get us there in no time."

"Daz has been left to his own devices for long enough. Time is of the essence." Eve bent down. "Best not go forgetting our entry ticket." She cradled the skull in her arms, quite expecting the great white lion to crouch down and offer them a ride, but that was a gesture only Cleon welcomed. The three ambled side by side through the vegetation's beautiful array of colours, like a new spring had dawned.

"I'll never take colour for granted again," Deakin said, admiring the source of his newfound allure.

Lions of all sizes wandered around contently in their prides. It seemed like Sunday visitation time as they mingled and played happy families. The white bland coats they had become accustomed to were now a rich golden yellow, and they were once again masters of their own domain and destiny. Ashman was now only a figment of their imagination, a blot on their landscape.

Newborn life burst its way through the undergrowth as Deakin led them through the laurel's glossy disguise. The purple lavender fields unleashed their perfumed vapours, which they all savoured, and the grey earthen shaft which had been so precisely covered was now an unprotected open mouth.

"You're on your own from here on, and if I were you I wouldn't spend any longer there than absolutely necessary. That's the Ashman's bed; not yours to lie in."

"Deakin, you are a handsome specimen," Eve admired his black and tan overcoat.

He looked down at his plush fur with its deepening burnt-gold tinge.

"Well you've improved beyond recognition too," Deakin said, as he admired the pink blush to her skin and the long golden locks that rested so beautifully on her shoulders. "And as for you, Shai … don't really know where to begin."

"Handsome would do for starters," Shai laughed.

"It's been a pleasure meeting you, Eve." Deakin bowed his head. "The star sign of Leo will be forever in your debt."

"Come on then, Shai," she said, and they walked down the open tunnel. Eve looked back over her shoulder until Deakin's friendly face disappeared from sight. The tunnels weren't hard to navigate through, even without Kendrick's guidance, and the sporadic candles led them straight back to the underground village.

A black and white undercoat still painted Ashman's surroundings.

"I don't understand! I thought colour had returned," Shai said, as he watched the Ashmen below run around like unorganised ants.

"Look, the traitors! They've returned," a voice rose out of nowhere.

The Ashmen stopped dead, their menacing eyes fixated on Eve and Shai, who turned to run but too late. Like roguish black panthers on the prowl, they crept up and surrounded them. The darkening bodies huddled together, no gaps or glimpse of light, like an interconnecting bracelet locked in animosity and resentment. A broken link, a tribal separation, Ashman stood before them in full tribal dress. Waxen tattoos brandished his high cheekbones and a black shock of bristle-like hair spiked around his angular face, resembling their very own black sun.

"NUPKANA, I believe? You've interrupted my reign, now I intend to get my retribution!"

"Hang on! How can we be punished?" Eve slid the skull along the floor towards Ashman. "Every ingredient you've asked for we've brought you and more! See for yourself!"

"I don't need to look! Your sickening colour says it all, and the iridescent sun! You're the Devil's spawn, Nupkana."

"I feel so sorry for you and your tribe, Ashman! You only see in black and white, missing all the important little grey areas which make for a balanced existence."

"Quiet, stop wittering, you undesirable! Which one of you cast a foot on my island and plucked the irretrievable fruit?"

Eve stepped forward. "I believe the one you're seeking is me!"

The chanting began and rose to a deafening crescendo.

"NUPKANA, NUPKANA, NUPKANA!!!" they chanted, creating an overpowering atmosphere as they stabbed their spears high into the air and stomped their feet in time.

"Take her away; confine her to the ritual chambers," Ashman shouted, his glance shifting briefly to Shai. "As for the half breed, the mutant, I'm sure we can accommodate it somewhere! Any associate of that," he pointed angrily at Eve, "is in league with the Devil."

What Eve and Shai had both failed to miss was Daz, who stood sheepishly and inconspicuously amongst the tribal gathering. His allegiance to either one hung in the balance as he watched his friends be restrained and carried away.

Eve's wrists burned from the rough hands and the tight grip as two Ashmen escorted her up through yet more unearthly tunnels. Dimly lit, she tripped up on more than one occasion. Many inscriptions were etched in the walls, but she was unable to make them out. An illegible haze appeared as she was whisked up the incline of tunnels, and a strong smell of incense and lavender oils fermented in the cool air. Melodic drumming grew ever nearer as an evasive white light shone down and lit their way ahead, encapsulating Eve as she stood in a two-dimensional waxen symbol, a circular form that housed a five-pointed star.

"This is the Pentacle of Asher! You may find this rather more difficult to fight your way out of! Ashman prepares himself as we speak." With that, the tribesmen left her alone.

Imprisoned by an invisible wall, she had no choice but to stand and wait. Disturbed by a muffled whisper within earshot, she heard a familiar voice.

"Kendrick, is that you?"

"Yes, we haven't much time. I thought I told you to leave, to go and not look back… It's too late for your silly little friend, he's Ashman's new right-hand man. He's the traitor not you, but your allegiance to Daz has led you straight into Ashman's trap."

"But I did what I was asked to, I got every ingredient."

"There's no such ritual, it was just a trap to keep you wandering aimlessly back and forth to the island… How do you think we capture the lions? They're transported here, and you're about to witness what happens next… I'll do my best to help you, but I give you no promises."

"Why are you telling me this? You're an Ashman, what possible reason could you have for helping me?"

"Let's just say I'm new round here. Like Cleon, I have managed to keep a mind of my own. Slightly different to Daz who's reeling in the art of black magic… Ashman has even presented him with his own spear. Trust no one but me; if any one can get you out of here, I can. If I do, don't look back, just head for the gate … Daz or no Daz." He disappeared back into the shadows.

A peephole had been dug out above them, a pocket that held the sunlight, a small niche where colour was allowed to thrive in Ashman's territory. Large moveable storage units were placed in rows along the wall furthest from where Eve stood and inscribed lettering in foreign tongues hung like leeches to the wall's outer skin. As they shuffled nearer, the sound of feet broke the silence. The entire community of Ashmen swarmed into the concealed chamber. Five tribal elders stepped forward, positioned their spears in the air, and without any prompting swung their arms forward in unison and dispelled their weapons at great speed.

Unable to avoid the onslaught, Eve dropped to the floor and hid her face. Like radio-controlled missiles they landed in perfect proximity, each embedding itself in the edge of the waxen circle on the tips of the five points of the regular star pentagram, Asher's pentacle.

"Nupkana! Scared of a few spears?" Ashman's voice taunted Eve.

She returned to her feet, dead central like a compass point.

"Does the Devil not know which way round one should stand?" he added.

"Do I look like the Devil? WELL DO I?"

"A wolf in sheep's clothing! You deceive well with your disguise. But this symbol you stand in not as a god but as a Devil. Turn yourself and invert the pentacle, evil one, so we can commence."

There were none of the usual chants from the Ashmen tribe, and instead a dimmed melodious hum was heard as the entranced Ashmen began to perform some kind of meditation ritual, as if under Ashman's spell. The sound pulsated in Eve's head as it reached an unbearable intensity. Ashman swung his snake-like hips and cavorted in a rehearsed sequence. Eve watched dizzily as he drew out his spear and blew rhythmical rushes of air from between his lips, charcoal vapours that soared up and then floated down to rest on the pentacle's silhouette. Black flames surged around her, a noxious chemical cocktail as smoke and fire intermingled. Eve was now only semi-conscious. Ashman's body was untouched by the flames as he entered the pentacle's force field, and he grabbed a handful of her shoulder-length locks.

"These are for safekeeping," he smirked, a few solitary hairs wrapped around his fingers. "Is Nupkana ailing or is it just my mind playing tricks on me?"

The tribe was in uproar as he stepped from the pentacle with his prize.

"I'll play with your senses like you've played with Leo's! It's ironic really, the star sign you are so eloquently imprisoned in. You see, I had the ingredients the whole time. The five interconnecting cross-sections of the star are the five senses, which slowly but surely you're on your way to losing. The outer rim of the circle contains the four elements, while the head of the star signifies the spirit of the damned. I'm going to banish Nupkana from Leo forever, and return the black sun to the sky and the lions to their black and white existence. Leo is *my* dynasty; I have ruled and intend to rule again. When your evil devilry is banished, my 'Eden' will return in all its splendour. I'll put you down to a blip, a circuitry interruption in Leo's fine workings… Not for much longer, though. Before I totally obliterate you, I offer you an uplifting education … or should I say some light entertainment."

"This is Asher's pentacle not yours, surely he must have a say in this!" Eve shouted. "What you don't own you can't control! You're nothing but Asher's puppet, a parasite that's sucked the colour and with it the life from Leo. With the last remaining breath in my body I'll make sure you rot in the darkened hell you've created!" Her depleted body collapsed on the floor.

It took four of the stronger Ashmen to push the storage unit and place it directly under the sun's golden rays shining down from an open crevice. Eve watched as a large mottled brown lion was mechanically marched towards Ashman and noticed his expressionless eyes; there appeared to be no fight left in him.

"Now for my party piece, Nupkana!" said Ashman sarcastically as he glanced at Eve.

The tribe stood in two long lines facing one another, and Ashman walked between them with a black glazed urn that he held tightly to his chest. He removed the lid and each tribesman dipped in his hand and pulled out what looked like potpourri. As the lion manoeuvred himself between the standing natives, they blew the ashen flakes into the air, which drifted like confetti until finally coming to rest on his fur.

Eve immediately recognised these flakes as the crushed marigolds that Cleon had handed her previously and explained were one of the main ingredients.

"This is Asher's signature ritual, after which might follow an introduction between you and he."

Ashman stepped up to the contained unit and momentarily played around with some awkward combination lock. The door swung open and revealed an empty polished casket. The Ashmen's mood now floated on a natural high, their frenzied state growing. The meditational humming switched to the repetitive chorus of Asher's name. Ashman's head rolled backwards and forwards, his eyes resembling buffed onyx gemstones, each facet of which penetrated deep into the lion's subconscious.

"Join us," he beckoned, motioning for the lion to enter the open casket.

Trance-like, the lion obeyed.

Horrified, Eve peeked out between the flames as the heavy door sealed the lion's fate; very little oxygen lay between him and the afterlife.

"You call me Nupkana?!" she hissed at Ashman. "You murderer. You are the Devil incarnate!"

"You speak only of yourself; I am the one and only god, the power. My rituals have the properties of resurrection. I breathe life into the lions and they are reborn again in my image. You have the nerve to contest my authority, and for that I think it time you paid Cleon a visit."

"How dare you speak badly of the dead! He was great, everything you're not!" Eve screamed. "He was more of a man than you'll ever be!"

Ashman cackled. "You don't know how close to the truth you are. Daz, bring me the replica of Nupkana."

Daz, who was as non compos mentis as the lions, pushed his way through the chanting tribesmen and handed Ashman a waxen effigy in three-dimensional form.

"Hair of the Devil!" Ashman said as he held up Eve's missing strands of hair and wrapped them around the wax figure. He then removed an elongated pin from his braided hair and thrust it into the hand-made voodoo doll.

Eve writhed around in pain, an overwhelming sensation burning through the skin of her right palm, its intensity fluctuating like a wave. Her immediate reaction was to rub at the site of the intense pain, and as she did so her fingers sank into a moist laceration. Shocked, she looked down to her injured hand and her blood ran cold as she saw the same puncture marks she'd seen appear on Cleon. True fear welled up in Eve and butterflies somersaulted in her stomach; she knew Ashman had neared the winning post. It was only a matter of time. She had no idea where Shai was, and as for Daz, his allegiance was clearly pointed towards Ashman.

The black storage unit, an obvious heat conductor, depicted a crimson blush and the whole apparatus glowed. The chamber fell into a deathly silence as Ashman reset the combination lock and opened the door slowly. An already shaken Eve became even more disturbed by what she witnessed next. The lion was now a reinvented being, a changeling. Eve rubbed her eyes, not quite believing what she saw. As an Ashman draped in lion skin emerged and knelt in front of the tribe, Eve's eyes checked out the casket.

There must be some plausible explanation, she thought, as she saw what was now just an empty shell.

"You are an honorary member of our tribe," Ashman said, and presented the newly changed native with a lion tooth pendant and placed it around his neck. "You are one of us now, brother."

Ashman prowled nearer to the pentacle that imprisoned Eve.

"The cat's finally been let out of the bag, so to speak, well almost. You see, the lions aren't the sharpest animals in the jungle, and they're so easy to entice. Once they fall into my Ashman-made traps they fall right into my hands. A lock of hair from their flowing manes and I have all I need – ultimate control over the majority of lion-like robots, brainwashed and entranced by my black magic. Steered by the sunrise they wade through my waxen lake for unattainable fruits. What they fail to realise is that when the black sun shows its face and the air cools, stragglers set like candles. My tribesmen sit and wait till the wax solidifies and seeps through their body's periphery, which in turn invades their blood vessels which expand with their newfound life force. These moulds before you are enormous melting pots, an enhancement of the lion's form. Soon we will grow in number. My Achilles heel up to now, however … females and the procreation of my tribe. When I have this art mastered, true Ashmen will rise and multiply. Then it will be my time! At this rate, Leo's star sign will soon be extinct and the dawning of Asher will rise, and with it the black sun."

"You're telling me you were all lions once?" Eve gasped.

242

"That's about the sum of it, and before I forget I have a long overdue introduction for you… Our god, our patron…" With that Ashman stepped between the black flames into the pentacle and stood before Eve. His head exploded into an inflated swarthy black cloud of smoke. It was an eerie transformation, a menacing lion's head attached to an Ashman's body. His voice reverberated around Eve's head and his onyx eyes were one on one.

"I got the better of my brother Leo once, and Devil or not I will dispel you, Nupkana; and if your quick mind hasn't yet figured it out … my real name's Asher, my pseudonym is Ashman."

This was all too much for Eve. Aries and Cancer had been a challenge, but this time she was way out of her depth.

"Maybe that no good mutant of yours will make a more productive Ashman." He signalled to a member of the tribe, and a monotonous humming resumed around the chamber.

Eve was more than a little surprised when Kendrick approached Ashman, with Shai tightly restrained.

"I THOUGHT YOU WERE OUR FRIEND!!!" an exasperated Eve shouted.

Kendrick's gaze dropped to the floor; he hadn't the courage to make eye contact. He handed Shai over to Ashman and stepped back to rejoin the tribe.

"Eve, help me…" Shai looked so tiny and vulnerable against the gangly Ashmen who towered over him. "Flames have never held you back before. Please, Eve," he whimpered.

But try as she might, the force field's hold would not release her.

Ashman pointed to the empty mould. "Be my guest."

Shai had nowhere to go and the terrified Goylin looked back at Eve, his eyes crying out for help, and then the door closed once more.

Bleary-eyed, Eve's vision struggled to penetrate the smoky veneer that rose around her. She sobbed for her lost friends, but then something or rather someone caught her eye. She blinked back the tears, but there was no mistake. Stood in the midst of the chanting tribe was Daz, standing shoulder to shoulder with Kendrick. With her heart in her mouth, her emotions surged from the deep grief she felt for Shai almost to hatred for Daz and Kendrick's betrayal, a hatred that bubbled up inside her and fused all her nerve endings. She seethed with anger.

Suddenly, an apparition manifested itself from the sooty vapour, its outer form somewhat recognisable to Eve, but she couldn't place from where. Unfazed, however, and devoid of any normal feeling, the crispness of its facial features suddenly brought it all back. The deadpan eyes and wrinkled complexion were enough for the rest to fall into place.

But how, and why? she thought to herself.

The tribal dirge faded into the background. Eve's persona was like an acted part as she played her own outer-body experience, the gypsy her leading lady. The odorous stench crept throughout the pentacle, her bony fingers fumbling for a while in a deep pocket attached to the side seam of her blue silken gown. She then revealed a pack of playing cards, quickly manoeuvred them into place and gave them a quick shuffle before removing six at random and placing them carefully in Eve's hand.

"The death cards would be apt," Eve said, staring up at the wizened face and remembering what seemed like a lifetime ago, when she had handed her and her friends the four cards in the gypsy caravan at the start of their interchanging rollercoaster ride. "Maybe death is a kindness you now offer me."

The mute gypsy's expression changed, but this was one card Eve couldn't read. With the gypsy's sudden disappearance the flames came alive, their black demeanour now an overactive flush of ruby shards that spat like tongues at the unsuspecting tribesmen. With it an immense heat radiated its presence around the chamber, and facial expressions, panic and shock were all in slow motion.

Kendrick's actions were well hidden in the commotion; he knew Ashman's black magic was contained somewhere on Daz's being. His attention was drawn to a waxen amulet that hung from Daz's neck and had replaced the lion's tooth. The white magic must have worn thin before all Daz's senses had been returned to him, and Ashman had used his black magic for keeps. Now Daz's mentor, he had no option but to follow in Ashman's footsteps.

Daz jerked back as Kendrick flicked the clasp between his

fingers; it fell to the floor and dispersed a black powder that freed Daz.

"Alright, me duck, fancy a dance?"

Daz was back.

"No time to explain, just follow me." Kendrick grabbed Daz by the hand and hurried towards the mould.

"How dare you practise your sorcery here? This is my sanctuary; be gone, Satan!" Ashman shouted. His attention focused on Eve and the burning flames that risked his entire empire. "You're far too dangerous a risk for me to keep alive!" Ashman brandished his spear and headed to the pentacle, but the pure intensity of the heat forced him back.

Yet Eve stood in the middle unharmed. Out of the corner of her eye she noticed Kendrick and Daz close behind. Baffled by the lock's combination, Kendrick played with it for what seemed like an age before it finally came loose and fell to the floor. They pulled the heavy door open between them and an overpowering heat wave was emitted from what resembled a greenhouse.

"What's me leather jacket doin' in there, duck?" Daz asked as he bent down and reached inside to reclaim his prized possession.

But Kendrick had more important things on his mind than Daz's leather jacket.

The tribe were now frantic, their waxen exteriors beginning to malfunction and liquefy as the wax secretion ran from their bodies like teardrops. Becoming a frail and unbalanced tribe as they attempted to escape, many were caught up in the mass evacuation while some left it too late and their Ashman existence perished, and all that lay in their place were waxen pyramid structures. They'd created their own waxwork model village.

"Burn in hell, Nupkana, go back to where you belong," Ashman's voice thundered around the chamber as he cowered away from the growing heat.

The glistening inferno released Eve's incarcerated body and she walked triumphantly through the flames.

"Be gone, Satan!" Ashman shouted as he turned to run.

Eve's eyes glowed red, and fiery bullets shot towards his defenceless body. Deep imprints gouged randomly into his waxen physique, and his anatomy now resembled a slice of Swiss cheese. The walls began to buckle and all the inscriptive texts etched into them merged into a gloopy river. Ashman paddled in his own made glue.

Eve was relieved to finally be reunited with Daz and a weakened Kendrick.

"My body can't take this furnace much longer," Kendrick said, as he glanced down at the wax running down his frail body and dripping around his feet. "But if I manage to make my way above ground, one promise I will do my best to keep is to be your chaperone." He looked from Eve to Daz, an honourable truth reflected in his eyes. "If the forces above look favourably on me, I will ensure both of you safe passage to the island and through the gate."

Ashman scrambled across hordes of his evaporated tribesmen towards an undefined melting pot that awaited them all. Luminous etchings that appeared to be the work of an invisible entity were on the wall's surface like a poetic scroll, with bold italics blossoming a bouquet of words that adorned the chamber walls. Ashman's face was the very picture of terror, his black skin faded to sepia in an instant.

The morning dew starts to fall
On a nowhere journey
Down a nowhere wall
Like an endless mist
There's no way through
You're a nowhere man
There's no place for you
You travel down that one-way street
There's no one there for you to meet
You look to the sky
But the sun sinks low
ASHER'S a nowhere man
With no place to go

It wasn't only the whereabouts that had transpired but also the dark meaning that lay behind them. An eerie laughter generated itself and clung to the smoke-filled chamber, and a projectile swelling ballooned out from the melted waxen interior. The head of a grand lion morphed as its facial silhouette burst through the preordained verse.

"Leo my brother? It can't be!" Ashman exclaimed aghast, daunted by the supernatural being. "You took the last breath from my lips, my cries in vain as my lungs filled and burned with wax. You drowned everything, Asher … except my soul, the immortality of which your actions induced. These walls have allowed me the senses you destroyed. I've seen, felt and breathed your actions for far too long, and now, my long lost sibling, I've come back to reclaim you."

The brotherly reunion distracted Ashman and the flames offered an undulated smokescreen behind which Eve, Daz and Kendrick were able to pass, effectively like a cloaked exit.

Eve took one last look at the melted waxen tomb.

"Come closer, Asher, don't be afraid," Leo whispered.

These were the last muffled words Eve heard before she passed from chamber to tunnel.

Chants rose before them from the fleeing natives in a last attempt to save their dwindling mortality. The ground was now a heated waxen river that flowed to the outside world, its syrupy consistency swelling around their waists.

"Now you've learnt the Ashman curse for yourselves, you're a nowhere man with no place to go," Kendrick said. He threw a solemn look from Eve to Daz. "As for that promise I made you, I'm afraid it's one I won't be able to keep." His hand reached out for Eve, but on impact his palm trickled between her fingers. She watched as his height depreciated and his waxen frame was sucked down to meet his fellow tribesmen, his body and the river melding into one. There was no time to stop as the whole waxen empire caved in around them.

"Hurry, Eve, or we'll end up like Kendrick."

But the harder they tried to run, the more the thick molasses-like substance pulled them back. Every step was a struggle, yet they fought on, the gate their only goal.

"Look, Daz, light! We're going to be okay."

They thrashed and fought against the treacherous incline; it was a case of two steps forward three steps back as they sank deeper into the waxen stream that ran down from the walls and continually deepened. They finally pulled their aching limbs above ground and their shattered bodies collapsed as they rolled onto their backs and tried to regain their breath.

"Well, Daz, I think you've got some explaining to do! How could you possibly befriend Ashman? Because of you, we've lost Shai."

Daz's face dropped. "No, I can't explain what I don't understand myself. It's like I knew the actions I took were wrong, but I just couldn't stop myself." He paused. "Like a clockwork toy I was bein' controlled. I wouldn't hurt Shai for the world." He snivelled.

Eve knew how much Shai meant to him, and although she wouldn't admit it she felt quite sorry for Daz, who now sat with his face on the floor. She looked around as a cold shiver ran down her spine.

"I've been here before," she said, an ominous look taking over her face. "Cleon brought both me and Shai here to collect a lion's skull…" The melodious ticking and tapping in the distance brought it all flooding back. "So this is how Ashman carried out his voodoo on Aquert … the lions' sacred ground."

"You've lost me, ducky," Daz said.

"Well that isn't hard, is it? You were playing happy families with Ashman at the time," she said sarcastically. "So it was this tunnel that led him straight here… He even had the power to control the dead." Eve was astounded by Ashman's complete monopoly over the star sign Leo. "Think we best make a move, Daz … those bugs are anything but friendly."

The ground started to tremble and Eve knew the unwanted little visitors drew ever closer. The colour that had burst through the undergrowth confused her perception, making everything look so very different and adding a completely new dimension to the jungle's bustling foliage. She stood, looked up through the immense trees and for the first time felt at a complete loss at what to do next. That and the loss of Shai was too much, and she fell to her knees and sobbed uncontrollably.

"'Ere y'are, me duck…" Daz reached into his pocket, groped

around and pulled out a very crumpled handkerchief. "Can't be that bad."

Eve blew her nose. "Thanks, Daz." Something sticky stuck to the side of her face. "Eww, you could have given me a clean hankie! Not one with a massive bogey attached to it!" Eve shuddered. "That's disgusting."

Daz looked, and looked again. "Well, that's one blumin' good-looking bogey!" He chuckled.

"Get it off my face, you idiot!"

"Be me pleasure." He pulled the offending object off Eve's cheek and held it in the palm of his hand. "Nah, ducky, think you'll be pleasantly surprised! Look!"

"I'm sure Ashman's voodoo has done something to your head!" she said as she turned away.

"Eve, stop messing with me! You never take me seriously…"

"What do you expect?!" she grunted.

"For one, the hankie wasn't dirty, and secondly, that thing you called a bogey … IT'S SHAI, he's a blumin' firefly again!!"

Eve couldn't believe it, but sure enough, a small waxen cocoon with Shai inside lay in Daz's palm.

"Don't just stand there looking at him, get him out!"

Daz peeled the waxen skin from around Shai's lifeless little body.

"The heat in the moulding chamber must have counteracted with the Goylin potion… He's automatically been turned back to his true form, thank heavens! He would have made one ugly looking Ashman anyway," Eve chuckled to herself.

Daz started to rub Shai's rigid body. "Looks as dead as a dodo to me."

"More rubbing less talking… Give him here, let me have a go!" Eve cupped him in the palms of her hands and blew warm air from between her lips. "I think he's going to be okay," she said as she felt a slight movement. "Come on, Shai, put us out of our misery." She rubbed him again and tried to encourage his circulation.

He stretched his little legs as if he had woken from a very long sleep and managed to open one eye, obviously weakened from his horrific ordeal.

"Lucky he has changed back to a firefly, would 'ave bin a lot more tricky to carry a Goylin around, and he certainly wouldn't 'ave fitted in me pocket."

"Well that's the best place for Shai at the moment; he needs to get his strength back."

It was a toss-up between the pocket in Eve's dress and Daz's jacket, but on reflection Eve had to agree that Daz's was much cosier for the little firefly's rehabilitation. She popped him inside and he nestled down comfortably.

"Hopefully that's him safe and sound," Eve sighed. "Well, Daz, think its 'bout time for our departure." She looked down and saw something poking out the small pocket of her skirt , and then she remembered. She pulled out the six cards the gypsy had passed her in the pentacle. "'Ere, Daz, can you look after these for me?"

"Okay, me duck. Where d'ya get 'em from?" Daz asked, intrigued.

"Just keep them safe will you, no time for explanations now."

Daz didn't need to be told twice and dropped them in the opposite pocket to Shai.

"That's about it then, think it's time we found the gate."

CHAPTER SEVENTEEN

Goodbye Leo

"This lake's illusive! I'm sure we're walking around in circles!" Eve had almost lost the will to go on.

"Psst… Looking at you pair, a guide wouldn't go amiss."

"DEAKIN!! You have no idea how happy I am to see you," Eve shouted, and grabbed both sides of his mane and placed a big kiss on his wet nose.

Daz, on the other hand, jumped straight into the middle of a laurel bush. Eve and Deakin rolled around, their sides aching with laughter.

"Come out, scaredy-cat!"

Daz cautiously parted the leaves to reveal one eye.

"Trust me, Daz, he's my friend; he'll take us to the island and the gate."

"You're our saviour … any lion would be honoured to assist you. You've released us from our chains," Deakin said.

Daz pushed his way out of the bush's clutches and looked over at Deakin, baffled. "What chains, Eve? He don't look tied up from where I'm standin'."

"Metaphorically speaking! Trust you, Daz," Eve grinned. His unorthodox character was a trait that she couldn't help but warm to.

They ambled along together as Eve and Deakin filled in the missing pieces for Daz. Their sepia world was now a magnitude of colour and the lions roamed freely. Total relaxation existed as prides played together, completely at ease with one another and with no bitter undertone to mar their now perfect existence. Pride by pride, they assembled a cortège of lions and escorted Daz and Eve on their way, and in no time at all the happy gathering approached the lake.

"Daz, look … there. It's waiting for us." Eve pointed towards the tree, its uninviting fruit hanging down listlessly.

"I thought we were lookin' for the gate, ducky."

"Look closer… It's there, staring us right in the face."

Its architectural blueprint was overshadowed by the tree's foliage, a black and white mosaic. Daz struggled to detect its outline.

"Don't strain your eyes too much, as long as you've got the key!"

"Yup thanks, duck, just one of the many novelties I've collected along the way."

"Well, Deakin, looks like the time's come for us to say our goodbyes." Eve bowed in acknowledgement to the numerous prides as they gathered to pay their respects.

Deakin held out his paw. "Put it there, Daz."

Daz obliged. "Thanks, me friend."

"As for you, Eve, you'll go down in Leo's history." Deakin paused. "By the way, before you go, what happened to that ugly companion of yours?"

"Let's just say he's sleeping it off somewhere." With a last farewell glance, Eve dipped her feet into the waxen lake. "Well, Daz, looks like this is it."

Hand in hand, they waded deeper into the lake's obscure veil.

"One way or another, we always come good, eh?" Daz said.

"Yes, don't we just." Eve grinned. She turned with a last wave for Deakin when an unusual occurrence caught her attention. Effervescent bubbles frothed and headed in their direction.

"Daz, look… That's odd, I thought only fish swam in water."

"Well, ducky, there's a first time for everything. Looking at the size of those bubbles, it's a blumin' great shoal or something!"

Eve didn't intend to hang around to find out. Daz, however, a little more inquisitive, couldn't resist a second, third, fourth and fifth look.

"Come on, slow coach, we're nearly there!" Eve pulled herself out of the gelatine-like liquid and scrambled up the island's grassy bank.

Daz wasn't far behind, and they both sat between the black blades of grass to dry off.

"I now know what it must feel like to be a snake," Daz sniggered, as he rubbed his arms and watched the dry pieces of wax flake off.

"Whatever happens from now on, we must work as a team … whatever secrets the gate may hold for us." Eve nuzzled up and rested her head on Daz's shoulder.

They sat there in silence and reflected momentarily on their life-changing adventures, wondering where Oli and Ebony's gate had taken them! Eve looked up into Daz's eyes and he met her gaze; for a split second it wasn't just the wax that melted. Like a natural instinct, there was something between them that neither had felt before. He leant his face towards hers…

Eve was suddenly paralysed with shock.

"YOU'VE DONE YOUR WORST! NOW YOU MUST EXIT FROM LEO, NUPKANA!" With no time for Eve to catch her breath, Ashman's tacky fingers tightened around her blonde tresses. "BE GONE, SATAN!" He charged towards the tree and launched her limp body like a ragdoll through the pearly white gate.

Daz jumped to his feet. "You didn't have to go that far! We were leaving together."

Ashman was stronger than his fellow tribesmen, but the sun's intolerable heat was like a molten explosion and Daz noticed droplets of wax beginning to run down Ashman's face.

"No, Daz, you're going nowhere! You see, I need help to reinvent my black magic. We can do great things, you and I; restore Leo's black and white existence, right the wrongs Nupkana's bestowed upon us. I can't do it alone; you now carry the title of my brother."

"You 'ad a brother! You could have ruled together as lions; you 'ad it all, but it still wasn't enough, was it Asher? You're doomed, and I'm not hangin' around to be the sinkin' ship that goes down with you! My allegiance is with Eve!" Daz edged towards the gate.

"In that case, your allegiance is with the Devil!" Ashman shouted, but what he hadn't noticed were the scores of lions wading towards the island, full of anger as they hungered for revenge.

The spherical bubbles accelerated with a certain buoyancy as a surging tidal wave took over and fronted the lions who swarmed the shore. Leo exploded, his white waxen coat shining like polished ivory.

"Well, Asher, you may have eluded me in the chamber, but I can assure you, my brother … it's the last time you'll ever get one over on me or my prides."

Daz wanted out, but he also wanted to see Leo get his revenge. He ran between the lions, knowing there was safety in numbers and that they meant him no harm. A partially melted Asher now stood alone.

"You killed me once, now I've got a score to settle." Leo's waxen image glided through the air and resembled a large white swan; he melded like an airtight vacuum over Asher's dwindling body.

Daz and the lions watched as the blackness of Asher and the defining white of Leo initially intermingled in a swirling circular form and then just as quickly redefined itself as half of each colour. Now there were two semicircles, one black and one white, the return of yin-yang lying under the tree where it was preordained to do so, where this all began.

An unnerving sound could be heard as wood snapped and splintered.

"Look!" Daz pointed towards the tree.

The roots' arm-like structures forced their way up through the ground and slithered like the snakes of Medusa, encapsulating the waxen-like pendant and sucking it down deep into the island's core. The whole vicinity shook as the ground dislocated and opened up like an unhinged jaw that exhumed the entire tree and re-adjoined itself, as if nothing had ever been there. Now, good and evil, Leo and Asher, were one symbol but two opposites … lost forever, and with it came the rebirth of the star sign Leo.

The lions cheered and utter euphoria took over as they turned and waded back to land. All except Deakin and his pride, that is.

"Well, Daz," he said, "we needed you, and you rescued us in every possible way. But Eve needs you now and you must go to her."

Daz smiled at the lion. "Thanks for your help, we'd never have found the island if it weren't for you."

"We'd never have seen the return of colour if you and Eve hadn't paid us a visit."

Daz took one last glance at the mainland's new beautifully painted complexion, turned and left through the gate. He reached for the key, and with one turn locked the gate and left Leo and all of its complexity behind him.

But where was Eve? Why hadn't she waited for him? He looked around, but she was nowhere to be seen. Feeling very alone all of a sudden, he retrieved Shai from his pocket.

"Keep that Ashman away from me!" Shai screamed in panic, but did look a little more like his old self.

"Relax, ducky, Ashman's a shadow of your past, and so is the star sign Leo. But as for our future ... who knows? And as for Eve ... who knows where she is?" *From one calamity to another, we'd sworn to stay together, so here we go again*, he thought. He thrust the key back in his pocket for safekeeping and pulled out the six cards Eve had passed him earlier. He turned them over one at a time: the first revealed the fool, the second the wheel of fortune, the third the pentacle, but the last three were a total blank.

"I don't understand," Daz said as he flicked between them over and over again, trying to find some logical meaning behind them.

Shai flew and rested on his shoulder, taking a quick peek himself. "From where I'm sitting it looks pretty straightforward to me. Think back ... the first card, 'The Fool', represents you, the jester in Aries. The 'Wheel of Fortune' is the Wheel of Life we travelled on in Cancer, and the 'Pentacle' is the walls that imprisoned Eve in Leo..."

Daz was suddenly taken back in time to the gypsy caravan. Was it only a matter of time before one of them came face-to-face with the death card? Or could Eve already have met with her fate? These were questions Daz couldn't answer, he'd just have to wait and see...